MW01631374

# BEHIND THE WALLS

Miriam Cohen

# BEHIND THE WALLS

The Story of a Young Girl's
Spiritual and Physical Survival
during the War Years

FELDHEIM PUBLISHERS
JERUSALEM NEW YORK

Originally published in Hebrew as *Me'achorei HaChomos* (Feldheim Publishers, 2002)

Translated into English by Miriam Samsonowitz

First published 2006



ISBN 1-58330-879-2



FELDHEIM PUBLISHERS
POB 43163 / Jerusalem, Israel

208 Airport Executive Park
Nanuet, NY 10954

www.feldheim.com

*Printed in Israel*

10 9 8 7 6 5 4 3

*A yahrtzheit candle in memory of my family members*

*who were murdered in the Holocaust:*

*My dear parents,*

*R' Shimon Dovid and Sarah Zucker*

*My beloved brother,*

*Meir Zucker*

*My husband's parents,*

*R' Yosef and Chana Kaufman*

*May Hashem avenge their blood.*

ב"ה

To Mrs. Chanah Kaufman,

I read your story with bated breath, and every member of my family read it after me.

The travails of life have generated many incredible stories in which young men and women displayed astonishing spiritual heroism. How did their souls prevail while their bodies struggled to survive? How did their intellect remain staunch to dictate the content of their lives? How did they set their body's physical needs according to their soul?

To read the story and see for oneself the results of this struggle, allows one to conclude unequivocally that evil was vanquished. The influence of the holy martyrs, those true Jewish heroes, who were praying above together with their messengers below, is what prevailed. The double victory over the Nazi Satan who sought to destroy, and the Christian vipers who sought to apostatize, found powerful expression in your book.

With your generous permission, I would like to use your story in my lectures in order to fulfill "Remember what Amalek did to you" and "Remember what Hashem did for Miriam."

Sincerely,

(Rabbi) Mordechai Dovid Neugroschel

ב"ה

לכב' הגב' חנה ק. תחי'

קראתי את ספורך בנשימה עצורה, ואחרי קראוהו כל בני ביתי.
רבים הם הספורים הבאים ממבוך החיים שמעבר להרי החושך, שם התגלו צעירים וצעירות במלוא גבהם הרוחני. כיצד שרדה אצלם הנשמה תוך כדי מאבקי ההשרדות של הגוף, כיצד הזכרון לא הכזיב והכתיב את קצב החיים ואת הצרכים האמתיים של הגוף בהתאם לצרכי הנפש.
לקרוא את הספור, ולהכיר חלק מתוצאות המאבק הנ"ל, ניתן לומר בפה מלא כי אכן נוצח השטן וכי יד קדושי עליון אבירי הכח גבורי ישראל, הן אלה שהתפללו מלמעלה והן שליחיהם כאן למטה, היתה על העליונה. הניצחון הכפול, הן על השטן הנאצי שרצה להשמיד והן על ראש הפתנים הנוצרי שרצה לשמד, בא לידי ביטוי בספורך בעצמה רבה.
נוטל אני לעצמי את הרשות, ברשותכם האדיבה כמובן, להשתמש בספוריכם בהרצאותי, על מנת לקיים "זכור את אשר עשה לך עמלק" וגם "זכור את אשר עשה ה' למרים..."

בברכה

מרדכי דוד נויגרשל

# Foreword

THIS DIARY OF A young child who survived the trauma of the Holocaust years was written so that coming generations would know of the suffering and the hell we experienced.

I thank the Creator of the universe, Who gave me the emotional strength to withstand the most horrific situations — placing my faith and trust in Him, and for leaving me among the living.

I am ever grateful that I was privileged, together with my husband, to establish generations of children and grandchildren who are going in the way of Hashem.

I want to express my gratitude to:

R' Mordechai Shikrika (who is called "Grandfather" in this book) who was Providence's messenger to rescue us.

R' Zelig and Mrs. Rosa Bamberger from Belgium, who rescued and raised me after the Holocaust.

Mrs. Miriam Cohen, who initially suggested that I write my story and who brought the project to fruition.

And the most beloved last, my husband, who has supported me and stood at my side for over fifty years. May we merit to receive much *nachas* from our children until 120!

Chanah Kaufman

# Contents

# 1
# Two Letters

The trees flew past us rapidly. I turned my head to the left and looked at one of the trees, following its rapid movement until it disappeared. Just as quickly, a new tree appeared on the right... I knew which was right and which was left because Maman had taught me. But little Meir still didn't know the difference between them yet, and it didn't matter to him. He was sitting next to me and we were both looking out the window of the moving train. He wasn't exactly sitting; he was really jumping up and down, banging on the closed window! Papa had closed it because Meir had been sticking his head out, even though Maman had warned him it was dangerous. He just kept forgetting, and finally, Papa had closed it. Meir would be safe now, but the tinted windows clouded the beautiful scenery.

Even with the closed windows, Meir was excited about everything he saw. "Look at this, Chanah'le! Look at the cows! They're drinking water from the canal! Look! The cows are eating grass. Look! There's a little dog standing next to those big cows and it's not even afraid of them. Look, look!" He pulled on my dress.

"Enough already! Let go of my nice blue dress." I carefully straightened the pleats, checked my buttons to see they were still buttoned properly, and adjusted my big sailor's collar. Meir was also wearing a sailor suit: dark blue knickers and a white shirt with a large blue collar. Both of our outfits also sported stylish gold buttons with a small anchor design on each one. Maman had stayed up late the night before, sewing us these lovely outfits in honor of our trip.

How wonderful to be traveling on a train! Low bushes dotted with pink flowers grew along the length of the train tracks, and tall, majestic trees were interspersed among them. The train sped along and this scenic view traveled with us. Vast green plains stretched out for miles, it seemed, beyond the shrubs and trees.

It had all started the week before, when Papa had returned home in high spirits. “Hello everyone!” he practically sang, and with a sweeping motion, he lifted Meir up in the air. When my tall father lifted Meir up that way, he would almost reach the ceiling! Then, with Meir still in his arms, he hugged me tightly, and all three of us tumbled onto the large brown sofa. The elegant pillows Maman had embroidered bounced up and down with us.

“I see you have good news,” Maman left the kitchen and gave Papa a questioning look.

Papa’s eyes danced. “You’re right!” he replied, grinning broadly.

Maman sank into the cozy armchair — the one we called “Grandfather’s chair.” Something out of the ordinary had happened, and she was curious! Cupping her chin in her hands, she looked straight at Papa. “*Nu*, tell us already!” Maman said. “Don’t keep me in suspense for so long!”

But Papa, his eyes still twinkling, refused. “I want you to try to guess. I’ll give you a hint — we received something that will make you happy."

Maman straightened up. "A letter?" she said immediately.

"Exactly! How did you guess?" Papa shook his head back and forth in feigned amazement, and pulled a rustling paper out of his pocket. I clapped my hands excitedly and began jumping on the sofa. "A letter!" I cheered. "A letter from Bubby and Zeidy in Poland!"

Papa stroked my hair gently. "Not just one, Chanah'le! Two letters! One from Bubby and Zeidy, and one from Avrum and Leah." Uncle Avrum, Papa's brother, was married to Aunt Leah — Maman's sister. Their names were mentioned in our home frequently, together with the story behind their wedding. After Papa and Maman left Poland to seek their fortune in Belgium, both sets of parents remained in Poland. They missed their children so much and longed to see them once again. But Belgium was miles away and transportation was costly. They decided to unite their families again — Uncle Avrum and Aunt Leah'le married soon after. Once a new Zucker family was formed, both Papa's and Maman's parents reported in their letters that they didn't feel so lonely.

Papa read the letters out loud — first the one from Bubby and Zeidy, and then the letter from Avrum and Leah'le. The news they contained brought tears to Maman's eyes. "Avrum and Leah'le are moving to Eretz Yisrael — how I wish we could see them again and bid them farewell!" she lamented. "I want to go to Poland, to see your parents and mine, and to say good-bye to Avrum and Leah'le. Oh, how I miss them! Our parents don't even know our precious children — whom they prayed for so fervently! Were it not for their *tefillos*, we would still be waiting for them until today — our two miracle children! It's only in the merit of our righteous parents' prayers that we merited to receive these two treasures."

Meir shook my hand behind Papa's back. I looked at him and saw that his big, dark eyes — which seemed to have grown even bigger now — were focused on Maman. I looked at Papa, and saw tears in his eyes too. He also missed his family.

I hugged him and whispered, "Papa! Please say yes! Since Meir was born, you keep promising that we'll travel to Poland and finally meet our family."

Papa and Maman frequently told us about the double miracle of how Meir and I were born. They unequivocally believed that it was in the merit of our grandparents' endless supplications, and in the merit of the many blessings our grandparents had received from *tzaddikim* on our parents' behalf. Our grandparents had traveled from one *tzaddik* to the next, entreating them to bless our parents with children. The story always ended with Papa and Maman expressing the hope that we would soon travel to Poland so our grandparents would finally see us. "To see that it was worth it," as Maman used to say.

On Shabbos, when Papa told us stories from the *parashah* about our illustrious forefathers who weren't blessed with children for many years because Hashem wanted to hear their prayers, I thought about my parents. I thought about my grandparents — whom I only knew from pictures. I knew that they had moved heaven and earth so that Papa and Maman would receive the blessing of children, and Hashem had listened to their prayers. Maybe my grandparents were *tzaddikim* like Avraham Avinu, Sarah Imenu,

Yitzchak Avinu and Rivkah Imenu?

In my eyes, my grandparents were holy people, human angels, so to speak. I pictured my grandmothers reciting chapter after chapter of *Tehillim* with tears streaming from their eyes, and my grandfathers adorned in their *talleisim* and *tefillin* from morning until evening.

Meir jumped into Maman's arms, hugged her and said, "Let's go, so they can see us!" Maman smiled at him, but her voice was sad. "Our parents have aged so much — it's even an effort for them to write to us," she told Papa.

All the laughter and joy that had entered our home with Papa suddenly dissipated. Papa tried to stay positive. "Don't worry so much, Sarah," he said. "Let's think about it; let's try to find a way. Maybe we really will manage to make the trip to Poland..."

The shimmering bolt of deep blue material spread out on the table caught my eye immediately. The fabric was simply magnificent! Maman's sewing jobs were mainly alterations — this fabric must be for us! "Maman, is this for me?" I asked. "Are you sewing me a new dress?"

"Yes, my Chanah'le," Maman stroked my cheek affectionately. "A new dress for you and a matching outfit for Meir. We'll be visiting Uncle Yankel and his family soon, and the two of you must look like a prince and princess!"

Papa laughed. "They're a prince and princess already, Sarah, even without fancy clothing."

"Of course they are," agreed Maman. "You and I know it, but I want it to be obvious to everyone who sees them..."

"If I'm a princess and you're my mother — then you're a queen," I reached the logical conclusion. Maman smiled and hugged me tightly. "Yes, Chanah'le, you turned me into a queen. You and Meir made me and Papa into a king and a queen, and our home into a palace."

"But that's only how it seems," Papa quickly added his reservation. "Hashem is our true King. He is the King of all kings."

"He is the King in Heaven and you are the king in the house," I said, but Papa repeated gently, but firmly, "No, my Chanah'le. Hashem is the King in the Heavens and on earth. His Glory fills the world and He exists in every place."

And now we were on our way to Uncle Yankel, dressed like a prince and princess, reclining on red upholstered chairs in the long, speeding train. Papa and Maman had decided to travel first to Uncle Yankel — who lived with his family in nearby Mellis — and to plan a joint trip to Poland.

# 2
# The Decision

The steady clickety-clack of the train's wheels on the tracks seemed to be singing my personal song: "We're traveling to Uncle Yankel, traveling to Uncle Yankel... and soon we'll travel to Poland, too! To Poland, too!" Papa and Maman, sitting on the bench facing me, were chuckling quietly. Could it be that they were laughing at me because I kept straightening out my new clothes and Meir's?

Just thinking about our new clothing made me swell with happiness. "Oh, Maman, the outfits are so beautiful!" I exclaimed.

"The children who are wearing them are beautiful," Maman answered with a glowing smile. "The clothes just add a little more color to your precious faces."

The conductor passed through our car and checked the tickets. He promised that we would reach Mellis in exactly half an hour. "You have to eat now," Maman told us when she heard that. But how could we eat when we were so excited? Meir and I tried to listen to Maman. We sat down in the comfortable seats and held our sandwiches. But we didn't sit for long! The view from the windows was more enticing. We stood glued to the glass panes, admiring the picturesque villages. Children stood next to the small houses and waved at the passing train — at us! We were finally traveling! The train kept singing, "Traveling to Uncle Yankel! Traveling to Uncle Yankel!"

Slowly the fields and country meadows disappeared and signs of city life took their place. We now saw towering apartment buildings and crowded houses instead of the quaint village cottages and their wide courtyards. With a grinding halt, the train pulled into the station. We had arrived! Papa and Maman carefully pulled down the suitcases from the overhead compartments. Maman gave us our coats to put on, and even though it wasn't cold outside, we didn't protest. A feeling of anticipation welled up inside of us. We had arrived at Mellis!

Uncle Yankel and Aunt Esti were waiting for us at the platform with Rivkah'le, their youngest daughter. I looked at Rivkah'le in amazement. Was this the "little Rivkah'le" that Maman and Papa always spoke about? But she was not a little girl — she was a real young lady. In the commotion of the reunion, and amid the tears of excitement, Rivkah'le picked me up and hugged me warmly.

"Come, the wagon is waiting," my uncle pressed us. The adults lifted us and the suitcases up, and then joined us in the wagon. Meir was a little uncomfortable around all the unfamiliar faces, but I was delighted to be next to Rivkah'le and my confidence soared.

Our uncle and aunt's children and grandchildren were waiting in their house. The oldest grandchild was Meir's age, and the younger ones were all adorable babies. All of them doted on me and handsome Meir, but I especially took to the cute babies — they were so sweet! I loved Rivkah'le very much too; she took me with her wherever she went, played with me and told me stories.

It was a week of laughter, fun and pampering. During the week, a decision was made: Uncle Yankel, Aunt Esti and Rivkah'le would travel together with us to Poland, *b'ezras Hashem*. "I want to take Rivkah'le," Aunt Esti said. "Maybe we'll find a *shidduch* for her in Poland. It's so hard to find a proper *shidduch* in Belgium."

What's a *shidduch*? I wondered. And why can't you find one here in Belgium? I didn't really need an answer, though — the main thing was that Rivkah'le would be traveling with us to Poland!

The trip was planned for next year, around Sukkos time. My parents and uncle and aunt had already saved up part of the money for the trip, and from now on, we would try to save every penny. Meir and I decided, between ourselves, not to ask Papa and Maman to buy us anything. We would be happy with whatever they'd give us. As long as there would be money to cover the trip, that would be enough for us! Papa said he would take a loan to complete the sum, but Maman was against it. "A loan has to be repaid at the end," she reminded him. "It's better to save as much as possible and not need to take a loan."

Meir and I decided to apply ourselves to our studies diligently, so we wouldn't be embarrassed when we would meet our cousins in Poland. We would show them that even in Belgium we know how to be good Jews! Since we were both good students, it wasn't hard to keep this promise. In addition to our studies in school, Maman sat with me every day. She taught me how to *daven* and told me stories from the *parashah*. Meir also learned much more than before.

We did everything with such joy. Happiness permeated our home, climaxing toward evening, when Papa returned home from work. He came home later than usual, because he had taken on a second job to pay for our trip. He would also bring home sewing jobs for Maman for the same reason. At the end of the day, he was very tired, but he still found the strength to sit with us on the brown sofa. Meir and I sat on either side of him, and Maman sat opposite us in the old, sturdy armchair. That's how we spent every evening — our small and united family.

***Chanah's parents***

# 3
# Getting Ready

When Papa sang, the house filled with joy. Meir and I tried to sing together with him. Maman, who spent every spare minute sewing buttons and hems on leather coats, would also hum along. She appreciated the opportunity she had to supplement the family's income. Each time she finished a mending job, she said in satisfaction, "One more step toward the trip!"

I imagined a large highway leaving Belgium in the direction of Poland. Papa, Maman, Meir and I would be marching along the highway, putting down one coat and taking one step, putting down another coat, and taking another step. At that rate, it would be years before we would arrive in Poland! Then I would remind myself how lucky we were — we wouldn't have to go by foot! With the money that Papa and Maman were making, we would buy tickets for the train. Meir and I tried to be good children and not to interrupt Maman when she was sewing. When she sent us to sleep, we went immediately — all we asked for was "one more song..."

"Just one song always brings just another, and then just another..." Maman said. "*Nu*, good. Get into bed, and Papa will sing just one song."

"Maman, I'll fix the beds myself," I volunteered. "And I will also help Meir with his buttons and shoelaces. You can keep sewing."

Meir and I went into the second room, where I took off the twin bedspreads that Maman had sewed for us before Pesach. Meir helped me pull out the blankets from the box under the bed. It was a good thing that it was summer, because we could never take out the heavy winter blankets by ourselves. "Fast," I urged Meir, "Come, let's get into bed so Papa will sing us the song about Eretz Yisrael."

But Meir wasn't as fast as me. He couldn't unbutton his buttons, even though I had tried to teach him many times. He claimed that his fingers were too fat, but it wasn't true. His fingers were much more delicate than mine. In fact, maybe they were even too thin. I never let him touch his shoelaces because he always made knots. Maman told me not to get upset at him — he would learn next year. She would patiently tie and untie his shoelaces for him. I didn't have Maman's patience, though. When I was Meir's age, I didn't need any help. So why couldn't he also manage by himself?

But I was a girl. Apparently, boys are slower in these kinds of things. That's how it was with embroidery too. I already knew how to embroider, and Maman kept teaching me new techniques and helping me advance. She said that she wouldn't teach Meir how to embroider because he was a boy. Boys can't do what girls do. Sometimes, when I'd get impatient with him because he wasn't as dexterous as I was, Maman would remind me that not only was he younger than me, but he was also a boy... How lucky I was to be a girl!

When both of us were finally under the covers, I called out, "Papa, we're in our beds! Can you come and sing us a song?"

Papa came in and sat down on my bed. He took my hand in one of his and held Meir's hand in his other. All three of us sang together in Yiddish:

| | |
|---|---|
| *Oif dem veg shtait a baum* | On the path stands a tree |
| *Shtait erein geboigen* | Bent over from age |
| *Fort a Yid* | A Jew is traveling |
| *Noch Eretz Yisrael* | to Eretz Yisrael |
| *Mit farvinte oigen* | With teary eyes |
| *Gutt, Gutt, tayer Gutt* | Hashem, dear Hashem, |
| *Lummir daven minchah* | We will *daven Minchah* |
| *Ven Yidden velen foren* | And when Jews travel |
| *Noch Eretz Yisrael* | to Eretz Yisrael |
| *Grois vet zein di simchah.* | The happiness will be great. |

That's it! The song was over. Papa kissed us on our foreheads and left the room. I started thinking about Uncle Avrum and Aunt Leah — and their plans to move to Eretz Yisrael, the land of dreams. How does one travel to the land of dreams? When we get up in the morning, we are in the same bed that we went to sleep in. I know; I've tried it! Poland is a land of dreams just for me and Meir — Papa and Maman had actually been there. But Eretz Yisrael must truly be a land of dreams. After all, no one was ever there!

Sometimes I travel to Poland in my dreams and visit all my relatives, but when I wake up, I am always in my bed, in my room here in Belgium. Maman would tell me that I really did visit Poland — I just came back home when it was time to wake up. But she laughed when she said that. I still can't figure out if she was laughing at me or if she was laughing because she's happy, as she says. Since we decided to travel to Poland, the house is full of happiness and laughter. Maman laughs all the time, and so do we. We had always sung together, but now we sing even more and laugh more. Papa said that even the walls are laughing! I wonder where the sound comes out of?

I felt myself drifting off. I patted the wall alongside my bed, trying to find its laughing mouth...

Our days revolved around the anticipated trip — we were all so excited! A dream would soon be a reality. The letters flew back and forth between our house in Belgium and the families "back home" in Poland. Every letter raised our spirits even higher. Uncle Avrum and Aunt Leah'le, who had planned to leave for Eretz Yisrael already, pushed off their trip until after Sukkos, so they would be with us when we arrived. Uncle Yankel and Aunt Esti also exchanged letters with us and even paid us quick visits.

One day Uncle Yankel arrived in our city. He spent the day in various government offices, trying to receive numerous documents his family needed for the trip. He didn't manage to arrange everything in one day, so he stayed with us overnight. That night we went to sleep late. Papa, Maman, and Uncle Yankel were so busy reminiscing that they forgot all about us. Meir was sitting on the sofa between Papa and Uncle Yankel and fell asleep there, his head leaning on Uncle Yankel's shoulder. Maman didn't notice, and I didn't say a thing. I knew that as soon as the adults would realize that Meir had fallen asleep, they would send me straight to bed. I wanted to stay in the living room — I didn't want to miss any stories of Papa's childhood.

Papa and Uncle Yankel reminded each other of the time they had jumped into a river with their clothes on. Bubby had hit them with a wooden ladle! They described how they had once jumped up on their house's slanted roof and then couldn't get down. In the end, a neighbor brought a tall ladder and helped them down. I looked at them, amazed. My big Papa, my distinguished Papa, was once a mischievous child? It was hard to believe.

The stories continued. Papa and Uncle Yankel chuckled as they reminded each other of the time they stood under the window of the *chazan*'s house, pestering him while he practiced. I could imagine that; anything that had to do with music attracted Papa. But other stories were simply unbelievable: Could it really have happened, for example, that my serious Uncle Yankel had chopped off his sister's braid?

# 4
# Important Guests

Uncle Yankel, Aunt Esti and Rivkah'le were coming for Shabbos! Meir and I could not sit still for a second once we heard the wonderful news. I had a thousand questions, and Meir had even more. "When are they coming? Today or tomorrow? How will they get here? What time will they arrive? Who is coming with them? What, only Rivkah'le? What about the other children and grandchildren? What about the adorable babies? What special things are you preparing for them? Will they like your food? Which song will we sing?" With every passing second, I had another question.

Meir was a little worried, though. "Maman, will I have to tell the *parashah*? What happens if I make a mistake? Will they think I'm not smart? Maman, what if I spill my food? Will they laugh at me?"

Maman was getting annoyed. "Enough! How can I cook and prepare the house for our guests with all these questions? Go visit Irena. It's been a whole day since you saw her, Chanah'le. Go see how she's managing without you..."

"Will Irena and her parents eat with us on Shabbos?" I asked.

"Yes, they're also invited. And Aunt Silka is cooking part of the food."

"But Maman, they're not even related to Uncle Yankel

and Aunt Esti," I pointed out.

"You're right, Chanah'le, but Aunt Silka is a distant relative of mine. Not only that, we've been good friends since we were young girls in Poland. Since she lives here in Belgium, we've become even closer, so that we're even closer than sisters," Maman explained.

"How is it possible to be closer than brothers and sisters?" I didn't understand.

"Go take Meir with you to Irena, and ask her all your questions." Maman closed the discussion without resolving my doubts.

I took Meir's hand, and we walked together to Irena's house. I held his hand very tightly. "Meir," I told him, "maybe we fight sometimes, but you are the closest one to me in the world after Papa and Maman, because you're my brother! No friend will ever be closer to me than you." Maman's comments were very confusing. I knew, though, that if I would ask her to explain them to me again, I would probably get the well-known answer, "When you grow up, you'll understand." I hated that answer! It seemed to me that the adults use it when they don't know how to explain something. When they do explain something to me — I understand it very well!

When we came back from Irena's, the house had been transformed. It looked as if it was a holiday. Maman had finally finished her cooking, baking and cleaning — and we were not allowed to move. We couldn't even sit on the sofa, because Maman had changed the regular pillows with the special pillows that I loved. My favorite pillow was the pink one with birds embroidered on it. Maman had embroidered beautiful birds standing on a green, leafy branch. The design looked so real that I almost expected the birds to start chirping any second. Meir said that the pillow with the flowers was the prettiest, and Irena thought that the one with a river and a bridge and trees was the nicest pillow. Instead of arguing, I suggested that when Rivkah'le would come, we would ask her opinion.

Maman was an expert embroiderer. Whenever she had spare time, she would embroider. Even now, between all her extra sewing jobs, she found the time for it. She embroidered two gorgeous tablecloths for our grandparents. I couldn't wait for out trip to Poland — we would bring them along as a gift.

We scanned the festive room, exclaiming over the new additions. The Shabbos table had suddenly grown! I didn't know that it could be extended. Irena and I set the table. We covered it with a sparkling white tablecloth and set out napkins, colorful flowers, and a new, embroidered challah cover — Maman's artwork.

The room suddenly looked like a palace. Now only the guests were missing! When would they finally come?

"They're coming! They're coming!" Meir's excited voice burst out from his lookout on the porch. The rest of us rushed to join him. Our tall Papa, who had gone to the train station to meet our guests, was approaching the house with a large suitcase in his hand and a big smile on his face! And there was Uncle Yankel and Aunt Esti, and Rivkah'le! We flew down the stairs and were enveloped with hugs and kisses. Aunt Esti was very impressed with Irena. She had met us just two months ago when we had visited them, but she hadn't seen Irena in a long time.

"How big you've grown! You're a young lady already! I

can't lift you up anymore," laughed Aunt Esti.

"Aunt Esti, you're not Irena's aunt, so how do you know her?" I asked. Aunt Esti laughed again. "I'm closer to her than a real aunt."

Aunt Esti also said that one can be closer to a person than a relative! Again I was perplexed, but I didn't ask her why. In any case, I wouldn't get an answer, just, "When you grow up, you'll understand."

We happily raced up the steps, with our guests following behind. Maman was waiting for us by the door and invited everyone into the living room. Irena and I sat on both sides of Rivkah'le, and Meir positioned himself on Uncle Yankel's knees. Everyone began talking at once, which I found very funny. How can we hear anything, if everyone is speaking at once?

On Shabbos night, Papa and Uncle Yankel sang together, harmonizing beautifully. I didn't know that my uncle's voice was also as nice as Papa's. When the two brothers sang *zemiros* together, it sounded like a concert. They continued singing long after the candles burnt out. Even Meir stayed up and sang with them. Uncle Yankel, impressed with Meir's clear voice, declared, "That is a Zucker voice. When Meir gets a little older, you should really send him for training in the *shul*'s choir."

In honor of their visit, we all went to *shul* the next morning, even though it was a long walk. Everyone promised that they would help Meir and Irena; I was big already and didn't need help. The adults didn't carry anything, but we children each took along a bag of food and candies — provision for the long way. We went happily and enthusiastically, and arrived without any difficulty. On the way home, though, we felt how long the walk really was.

The wonderful Shabbos passed quickly. After *havdalah*, we danced in a circle and sang the *zemiros* for *Motza'ei Shabbos*. "*A gutte voch* — a good week, *a gutte voch. HaMavdil bein Kodesh l'chol, chatoseinu Hu yimchol.... Eliyahu HaNavi, Eliyahu HaTishbi, Eliyahu HaGiladi, b'miheirah yavo eileinu im Mashiach ben David.*"

That was the last time we had a Shabbos with complete happiness. It was the last Shabbos that we were all together. My last memory of Aunt Esti and Rivkah'le is from the memory of this Shabbos: a joyous memory of happiness, song and dancing.

***Chanah and Meir, half a year before the war.***

# 5
# "War Is a Terrible Thing"

Something happened. Something bad. Papa had stopped singing, and Maman's eyes were full of sorrow. We weren't going to make our long-awaited trip to Poland after all!

"But, Maman, why?" I asked worriedly, refusing to believe. The disappointment was too deep. After all the plans, all the extra work, all our excited anticipation — how could they just cancel the trip? Won't we ever get to see our grandparents and uncles and aunts? No! It can't be!

"Because war broke out," Maman said, wiping away her tears.

"War? What is war? I want to travel to Poland!" I protested. "So what if there's war?"

"Chanah'le, you don't understand. War is a terrible thing," Maman explained, her voice full of grief.

Slowly I began to understand that war is a terrible thing. At first, the disappointment of the cancelled trip was unbearable, but soon my thoughts were occupied with other things — all the frightening changes that were suddenly taking place in my life.

Our large radio was one of the first things to change. Until now, we had only heard music and concerts — which we all loved — coming out of it. Now it began to emit shouting voices, particularly the shouts of a certain man with a screeching voice. I didn't understand what he was saying, but Maman always cried when she heard him. In class, too, they spoke about the war all the time. The girls didn't know exactly what it meant, but they knew it was a bad and dangerous thing. There was bombing, houses were destroyed, people died.

Something strange happened in my class. We, the Jewish girls in the class — who were about a third of the class — were suddenly isolated. I had been sitting next to Janet — we were good friends. She would let me copy all the notes and classwork I missed because I didn't come to school on Shabbos. Janet was always happy to explain everything to me, but now she changed her seat. She moved next to Maria and wouldn't speak to me! Chanah Spieler, who had sat next to Christine until now, came to sit next to me. Now we were two "Chanahs" together. All the Jewish girls now sat in one row.

Well, that was fine! Chanah lived in my neighborhood, and we would be able to prepare homework together. We could also go to the community's Sunday school together. How I wished it would become a day school so we wouldn't have to learn with those gentile girls...

I loved the community's Sunday school. Unlike my regular school, it was far from our house. Papa would take me there and Maman would bring me back. The classes were difficult, but we were happy to learn "our" subjects: prayers, Jewish laws, *alef-beis*, and the main thing — the *heiliger Torah*.

The letters from Poland stopped. Papa and Maman were very worried. Maman wouldn't let me walk to Irena's house by myself. Her mother — Aunt Silka — also accompanied her when she came to our house, which was only three blocks away from theirs. When they came, Aunt Silka and Maman disappeared into the kitchen. They whispered together and sighed endlessly. Fear was our shadow, stalking us all the time. We, the children, didn't know of what and of whom we had to be afraid, but we didn't dare ask the adults. Our questions upset them, and they wouldn't have answered us anyway.

Irena and I would sit together on the brown sofa often and I would read her stories. One day, our mothers were in the kitchen, as usual, and we were sitting on the sofa. Suddenly, Papa came home. Why did he come home so early? Irena and I looked at each other in confusion, but no one offered any information. Immediately after him UncleYossel — Irena's father — appeared at the door. All the adults gathered around the radio, listening to shouts. The shouting was loud and scary, and we began crying. The book forgotten, Irena and I clung to each other. Meir scrambled up on the sofa next to us. Fear hovered over the house; we could almost touch it with our hands.

Another day, Uncle Yankel showed up. Again everyone listened to the shouting radio. Again Maman cried. She was upset with Uncle Yankel. "You shouldn't leave the women alone at a time like this," she told him.

"But it's safer here," Uncle Yankel said. "I came to look for an apartment so I can bring my family here."

Papa didn't agree. "It's frightening everywhere. I don't think Brussels is safer than Mellis. Everyone is better off staying in his own house."

I couldn't understand that. UncleYankel and Aunt Esti wanted to move to Brussels — and Papa said they shouldn't, that they should stay in Mellis! Papa was always sad that his brother lived so far away, and now that Uncle Yankel was considering living near us, Papa was trying to dissuade him... How can one understand adults?

Maman didn't let us play in the yard behind our building. Even after I had finished my homework, and although it was still light outside, she still wouldn't let me go. "But there are lots of children there," I begged her.

"They're all non-Jewish," she replied.

"There are always non-Jewish children downstairs! Maman, you know that I don't play with them — even though they are our neighbors. I only play with Irena and Meir."

"Jewish children don't go outside. They can play nicely at home," Maman said stubbornly.

"But you always let us play downstairs!"

"True, until now I let. But now everything has changed, because of Hitler."

Hitler. I had heard that name — he was the evil man who shouted on the radio. But what did that have to do with us, the children? Why couldn't we play downstairs because of Hitler? We had to run around and let out our energy! In the house, only quiet games were permitted — we weren't allowed to run around inside! But all my questions and begging didn't help. Maman would not be swayed.

I stood next to the window of my parents' room. I could see the yard behind the house and the neighbors' children playing hide-and-seek. A stone fence encircled the yard, and the older children were walking along it, competing with each other to see who could reach the end without falling. I noticed that there really weren't so many children downstairs, and that the children who were there stayed in the yard the entire time. They didn't go into the street. I saw their mothers peeking out of the windows very often, checking that everything was fine. The gentiles were also afraid! Maybe Maman had a good reason for worrying?

# 6
# The List

"Goodbye, Meir! I hope you have a nice day with your teachers, and I hope they have a nice day with you!" I blithely took leave of my little brother that morning as usual, next to his school. He answered me the same way. Maman would say goodbye to us in this manner every morning, as we left the house. It made us burst out laughing every time. Afterwards, we would repeat the same words to each other when we parted at Meir's school. With a smile, I continued alone to my school.

The impressive school building was big and tall. It was shaped like a U, with the bottom of the U facing the street. There was a large courtyard in the middle of the building, between the two sides. We would play there during recess, and, during the summer days, the students would line up there for roll-call every morning. The students stood in orderly pairs, and one of the teachers read a passage from a book. Afterwards, we all sang Belgium's national anthem and saluted the flag. Then we entered our classrooms. In the winter, the roll-call was held in the school's large lobby.

The building was surrounded by a high fence, and to enter, one had to pass through a gate. A guard — named Phillip — stood near the entrance. When I arrived every morning, I always politely wished him good morning. Today, Phillip was not standing at the side as he usually did; he stood in front of the gate, blocking the entrance. "You can't come in," he said tonelessly.

I stared at him, stunned. "What? Why can't I come in?"

"You're on the list. You can't come in!" Phillip repeated, raising his voice a decibel.

I didn't understand. "Which list?"

"The list of Jewish girls. You can't come in. Go home!"

My palms became clammy. "Mr. Phillip, what are you talking about? Why are you frightening me? I don't understand."

"What don't you understand?" Phillip became irritated. "You can't come in! Go home! I have to argue with every single one of you."

"Why should I go home? This is my school and I learn here," I said stubbornly. "As if you don't know who I am."

"If I know you or I don't, what difference does it make? I told you to go home!"

"But I didn't come late and I wasn't punished. I'm a good pupil — I was *never* punished! Why are you angry at me?" Tears welled up in my eyes.

"I'm not angry at you, but this is not your school anymore. Get out of here fast, before you really see me angry!"

I turned around and ran home, crying hysterically. I ran as fast as I could the whole way home. Fear propelled me forward, chased after me, and finally threw me, bawling, into Maman's arms.

"Maman! They didn't let me... they wouldn't let me in! Maman, I didn't do anything, I wasn't even late. I came on time, I promise!" I tried to tell her what had happened, but I was sobbing so heavily that I couldn't talk clearly.

"Who didn't let you come in? Where? What happened?" Maman hugged me, strokinging my hair and drying my tears. "Calm down, Chanah'le, and tell me everything."

I took a few deep breaths and tried again. "The gatekeeper Phillip stood in front of the gate and said that all Jewish girls can't come in. He said I'm on the list. He said I have to go home quickly."

I clung to Maman, feeling slightly better in her warm embrace, but still sobbing and very confused. Maman whispered to herself, "What? Already? So quickly?" I lifted my head questioningly and I saw that Maman's eyes were full of tears.

"Maman, what happened? Why didn't he let me go in?" I asked.

Without a word, Maman took me to the porch and pointed to the street corner. "Do you see that soldier there, Chanah'le? He is a German. The Germans invaded Belgium last night. Because of them, Phillip didn't let you past the school's gate."

I stood on the porch and looked at the soldier. He looked like a normal person — a normal person in a soldier's uniform. What was it to him that I go to school? Why was I forbidden to attend school because of him?

The soldier marched from one street corner to the next, crossed the street, and disappeared from my view. Why did he come here? What do the Germans want from Belgium? Germany is a very big country. I saw it often on the large map that hung in the school lobby. So why do they want to defeat Belgium? Their country isn't big enough for them?

I leaned on the railing, looking down at our street. We lived on a wide street. The cobblestone street was straight and smooth. The nearby streets were much narrower, and they were bumpy and uneven. When one ran on them, one could easily fall and get hurt. The houses on our street were pretty and well-kept. There were curtains in almost every window, and window boxes full of bright geraniums were a common sight. But...Oh no! I stopped admiring my beautiful neighborhood with a start. There was my brother Meir! He also was returning home. He wasn't running, like I did; he was dragging his feet slowly, his head lowered.

Why was he coming home? He didn't attend a non-Jewish school. He studies only with Jewish children. Did the Germans also cancel their lessons?

The soldier returned to the corner opposite our house. He didn't even look at Meir, and Meir didn't look at him. Meir still didn't know that the soldier was at fault, that because of this soldier, Jewish children were being sent home instead of benefiting from a day of learning.

Suddenly all my fear, bitterness, and anger erupted. "Soldier! Go away! Go back to Germany! Get away from here!" I shouted in rage. "We don't want you here! What are you looking for here? Who invited you? Get out of our country!"

Maman heard me shouting and rushed to the porch. She was visibly frightened. "Chanah'le, what are you doing? Don't shout! It's forbidden! Come in the house immediately. Chanah'le," she tried to explain, "From today on, our lives will be different. You may not raise your voice anymore. You can't draw any attention to yourself, because we are Jews."

I didn't understand what Maman was saying, but I couldn't miss her pale face and the terrible look in her eyes. That was enough. I promised to be a good, quiet girl.

Meir entered our apartment crying, and Maman tried to calm him down. “Don’t worry, Meir,” she said. “From now on, you won’t go to school. It’s not that bad. You’ll stay home with me, and maybe I will teach you.”

Meir looked at me with red eyes. “You too?” he asked.

I nodded my head and whispered, “Yes, me too.”

# 7
# War Comes Closer

"Get up, Chanah'le. Get up fast!" Maman's voice was anxious. I pulled myself out of my bed, rubbing my eyes, trying to quickly shake off my sleep. Maman also woke up Meir, and she and Papa quickly bundled us up in coats on top of our pajamas. "Come quickly!"

We ran to the cellar. Outside we heard loud thunder, and a terrible screeching siren — the alarm. I covered my ears with my hands. Then I heard it — an explosion! The building rocked back and forth. They were bombing us! We clung to each other. All the residents in the building huddled together agitatedly, hoping to find safety in numbers, but our family remained at the side, isolated in the corner of the cellar. We were the only Jews in our entire building.

We heard the all-clear siren in the morning. We returned home, utterly exhausted, and immediately fell into our beds. At noon, Maman sent me to the grocery store to buy bread.

Groups of people were milling about outside, talking excitedly. As I turned the corner, arriving at the nearby street, I stopped in shock. The beautiful plaza had been completely destroyed! The lovely statue of a king riding a horse had been smashed — pieces of marble were scattered around. Only several flowers remained, from the beautiful flower garden, a remembrance to the blooming scene that had existed just the night before. As I continued on, I saw that several stately, tall trees had been uprooted along the avenue. Their large branches covered the sidewalk, among piles of debris and dust. There were also countless glass fragments sparkling on the sidewalk — compliments of the shattered windows. People stood and simply stared at the destruction, stunned and disheartened.

I returned home agitated, and Maman said, "*Nu*, at least it's only that. Only the statue was destroyed, and only the trees and flowers. Thank God no house fell on its residents."

Our happiness was premature. The bombings continued for a long time, and many houses were destroyed, burying their residents beneath them. Night after night, the nightmare continued: the terrible screeching siren that broke through the silent darkness, the frenzied running to the cellar, fearful explosions, and in the morning — the all-clear siren. During the day, everyone was tired and tense. Papa had to go to work that way, tired and worried, but he was grateful that his place of work was important and hadn't been closed down. Many other places of work had been closed, leaving the employees without a livelihood. The rest of our family tried to sleep a little, at least until noon. Then I would get up and leave to go shopping, afraid each time anew of what I would see. The city was slowly being destroyed. Every day I returned with less food and more stories, dreadful, horrific stories.

We stopped singing, laughing and playing. We were frightened, the adults just as much as the children.

Meir and I sat almost every day on the sofa. Sometimes I would read him a story, but we spent most of the time talking quietly, clinging to each other. Aunt Silka and Irena came to our house every day. They were afraid to be alone. Irena sat with Meir and me on the sofa and joined in our whispering. I don't know why, but we were afraid to speak out loud. Maman and Aunt Silka also held their conversations in whispers.

Papa came home from work early because of the curfews — the edict which didn't permit us be outside our homes after a certain hour in the evenings. Uncle Yossel would come to pick up Aunt Silka and Irena. When he came, they would go with him immediately, so they could reach their home before the curfew.

Our entire life was now determined by regulations and edicts. Every day the Germans posted new regulations, printed in both French and Flemish. Everyone had to fulfill the regulations — whoever didn't was punished. "I didn't know" was not an excuse. So every day we went to the billboard and read the new regulations.

In the first week of the invasion, refugees came to Irena's home, and to a few other Jewish homes. We lived in a non-Jewish area, so refugees didn't come to us. The Markowitz family came to Irena's house. They had two daughters — one was a teenager and the other one was my age. Mr. Markowitz's brother and his wife moved in with one of Irena's neighbors — the Roth family, and Mrs. Markowitz's two teenaged sisters stayed with the Blums. Aunt Silka brought down another two mattresses from the attic, put them in Irena's room, and that became the refugees' temporary home. I went to visit Irena and see them, but everyone was sleeping.

Irena told me that they lived in Liége, only forty kilometers away from Germany. On the day of the invasion, their entire extended family fled to the train station. There were thousands of people at the station. Everyone wanted to flee. It didn't matter where, they just wanted to get out of Liége.

The Markowitzes managed to board a train, but this was just the beginning of their ordeal: fighter jets that suddenly appeared above dropped their bombs on the moving trains. The passengers jumped out of the windows and fled into the fields, and lay there quaking under the trees. After the bombing subsided, everyone returned to the train, and it continued on. After several hours, the train was bombed again, and again the passengers jumped out the windows and fled into the fields. Their oldest daughter, Breta, began shrieking from fear and couldn't stop. Her mother was very angry at her, "There are families here with little children and even babies. They're holding strong — why can't you control yourself?!"

But Breta kept shrieking. She couldn't calm down — until her mother slapped her on the face. Then she fell silent. The younger daughter, Mary, who told Irena all this, said that she never saw her mother so angry! She certainly had never slapped her older daughter, Breta! This is what war does to people.

The Markowitzes decided not to return to the train. They took their suitcases and began to walk on foot through the muddy fields. When night descended, they searched for a place to lodge and found a cellar full of water. Utterly exhausted, they fell asleep despite the water. When they reached Brussels, after another two days of walking and sleeping in the fields, they were dirty, hungry and exhausted. After they ate and bathed, they lay down to sleep, and slept for almost an entire day. In the meantime, Aunt Silka washed all their clothing.

After several days of rest, food and sleep, the refugees went to the train station again to continue their flight. They urged Uncle Yossel and Aunt Silka to flee with them, but Uncle Yossel refused. He told them he doesn't believe one can escape from his fate. "And even if we run away — where will we go? The Germans have taken over the whole continent!"

Uncle Yossel and Papa argued often on this topic. Papa arranged papers for us so we could escape to France, and he suggested that Uncle Yossel do the same. But Uncle Yossel absolutely refused. He wouldn't listen to the Markowitzes' pleadings either.

Aunt Silka, who had become very close to the family, accompanied them to the train station. When she returned she was terrified, and said, "You have no idea what's happening at the train station. It's full of people. Half of Brussels is there, and crowds of people from the villages all around. The noise is terrible! There is no place to even stand in a train — not to mention sitting or lying down! People have been waiting there for days on end!"

The Markowitzes were afraid to enter a traincar crowded with people. They were afraid they wouldn't remain together and there wouldn't be enough air to breathe. In the end, they managed to board a freight train. They stood near the traincar door with some other people so it would appear that the traincar was full, and no one else could fit in. This way, they were able to guarantee themselves a place to sit on the floor during the trip, and enough air for everyone, so they wouldn't suffocate. They promised to let us know if they arrived safely. Maybe by then, Uncle Yossel would change his mind, and he would agree to join them with his family.

# 8
# "They"

Papa bought yellow patches in the shape of a Star of David, and Maman sewed them on our clothes. Aunt Silka also sewed these patches on her family's clothing. Why? I didn't like them. But I already had learned that it was no use to ask. No one would give me an answer. Either they didn't know, or they were too afraid to answer.

Fear. Fear lurked everywhere. We were frightened by everything, of every movement, of the sound of a wafting leaf. We trembled at every rustle of the wind or flapping of a bird's wing. We lived in constant fear. I didn't even know what I was afraid of.

We must hide! From what? Maman prepared a small hiding place for me inside the clothes closet. Our closet was large and wide. There was a pole for hanging clothing, and underneath that, there were two big shelves. Maman removed one of the shelves, broke it into two pieces along its length and placed only one half back. She filled that half with neatly folded towels. When someone opened the closet, he saw clothing hanging and underneath them, two shelves full of towels. One couldn't see that the towels were only in front. I climbed into the closet and lay down in the back, in place of the second half of the shelf. Since I was so thin, the hanging clothing did not get messed. Maman would arrange and straighten them and the towels so that I was completely hidden. The closet door's lock was slightly broken. Since it was impossible to close the door totally, I had enough air.

"You see, Maman?" I laughed. "What luck that I'm so thin! And you were always worried about me!"

I slept in this hideout every night. Papa, Maman and Meir's hideouts were in the attic. At first, they had arranged Meir's hideout inside the linen chest, but Aunt Silka said that was one of the first places they search. Hearing that, Papa and Maman decided that Meir would hide in the attic with them. Each family had a room in the attic. It was easy for us to go up there, because we lived on the top floor, but we first had to go into the stairwell to climb up into our room in the attic.

The attic was a storage room — we kept charcoal and blocks of wood for heating there, and things that we didn't need, like clothes that were already too small on us, also were stored in the attic. The attic was also our laundry room. We strung our laundry ropes up there, and so did all the neighbors. They would go up to the attic to do their laundry, and from time to time, to take charcoal and blocks of wood. Papa, Maman and Meir had to be very careful not to meet up with neighbors when they went up to the attic at night and came down in the morning. To our good fortune, there were two creaky steps that warned us when someone was coming up. Papa, Maman and Meir learned to skip over those steps.

Meir's hideout was in an old crate of clothes. Maman padded it with blankets, and after Meir lay down in the crate, she covered him with old clothes. No one could see that a child was hiding among those items. She herself hid in a woodpile. Papa arranged the wood so that from the back, there was a big enough hole for Maman to lie down in, while from the front, it seemed that the whole area was filled with wood. For himself, Papa prepared a wide, tall shelf, very close to the tiles of the roof, which appeared to be part of the structure.

We went to sleep in our secret hideouts every evening, and lay there the whole night long. We weren't allowed to get up and walk around. In the morning we woke up full of aches and pains from the awkward positions we had been sleeping in, and from the hard boards we had lain on. We were exhausted — we could not sleep properly under such conditions. Maman warned us again and again, "Don't cry in the hideout. Don't cough. Don't even breathe out loud!"

Maybe, maybe, if *they* come, they will think that the apartment is empty, and they'll leave.

*They*. This was the source of the terrible fear that pursued us non-stop, day and night. "They" strutted arrogantly up and down the street, and their high black boots pounded cruelly on the pavement and in our hearts. "They" hung up new edicts on the billboards. "They" entered houses. We were like frightened rats. At the first sound of steps — or at times, we just imagined the sounds — each one of us rushed to his hideout immediately.

Our gentile neighbors cut off all ties with us, ties that had never been especially close. They were afraid to talk with us, even to exchange a "Good morning." During the bombings — which already were subsiding — we were isolated in the joint cellar. "It's of no matter," Maman said. "Why should we mind if the neighbors don't speak to us, or treat us as if we were flies? Their greetings were superficial and false before the war too. Let's be thankful that they're not expelling us, that they let us in the cellar. Oh, but most importantly — I hope they don't inform on us. I hope they don't tell the Nazis that Jews live here."

That's what Maman said. But "they" knew exactly where we were living. They didn't need our neighbors' help! They had precise lists and addresses of all the Jews in Brussels.

The Jews living around us slowly began to disappear! Uncle Yossel and Aunt Silka were always up-to-date, and told us who else had disappeared. Papa stopped going to work. After hearing about people — even whole families — who had disappeared, Maman didn't let us leave the house at all, even to go to *shul.* Papa *davened* at home and taught Meir how to *daven* with him. Papa sat with his large Gemara and learned during the day. "All my life I wanted to sit and learn, and look, the Germans came and gave me the chance," he said with a smile. But there was no happiness in his voice, and his eyes were full of sorrow.

Papa spent time learning with Meir, and Meir felt very important. "I need to learn Torah with Papa, I have no time for your and Irena's chatter," he would tell me pompously. But the minute Papa finished teaching him, and went to study by himself or with Uncle Yossel, Meir would head straight to the sofa and join us. The brown sofa had become our fortress; we played on it, read on it, sat on it and spoke. It wasn't as if we had no other place to play. Our bedroom was spacious — as rooms went then. It had a small round table with three upholstered chairs. There were two beds — Meir's and mine — a large night table, and a toy chest. Nevertheless, we spent most of our time on the sofa in the living room. Papa and Uncle Yossel sat at the dining room table and studied, and Maman sat on one large armchair with

Aunt Silka next to her on the other. We all felt the need to be together, in one room.

Maman found it very difficult to leave the house. “I can’t bear to look at all the gentiles,” she said. “Their looks cut me like knives.” So I began to do the shopping. I was already big enough; I was ten years old. Maman would tell me exactly what to buy, and the owner of our neighborhood grocery knew me well and treated me very nicely, even though he knew I was a Jew. Even so, the trips to the grocery were sorely different than before the war. There was always a line of people waiting, and the grocery shelves were not well-stocked. The grocer tried to give me what I asked for, and when an item was missing, he would give me something else in its place, together with a kind word. *Baruch Hashem*, I never returned home empty-handed. We always had food.

# 9
# Farewell to the Brown Sofa

We began to get used to this new, strange way of life. Soon Maman recovered, and was able to leave the house. At first, she only went out for a few minutes, just to see the changes that had been caused by the bombings. Afterwards, her outings became longer and Maman went back to doing the shopping herself.

Strange things began to happen at home, though. Pesach was months away, but Papa began taking down the Pesach dishes! Maman wrapped them in small packages, and whenever she left the house, she took one small package with her and returned without it. Meir said that Maman was selling the fancy dishes. He figured that since Papa wasn't working, they had to sell things from the house so we would have money.

"What will we do on Pesach?" I worried.

"By then, the war will be over, and Maman will buy new dishes," Meir concluded confidently. How smart my younger brother was!

Soon the Pesach dishes were all sold, and my parents began to package more of our household items. The contents of our large linen closet were duly packed — the linens and the lovely tablecloths that Maman had embroidered. Papa also took down the curtains. Without a word, Maman washed and ironed them and packed them neatly in a package. She took that package, too, with her when she left on her outings. The house was emptying out! Two strange people arrived one afternoon and took our dining room table and chairs. They also took the small round table with its upholstered chairs from the children's room. After Maman begged them repeatedly, they also took both armchairs.

Maman moved the kitchen table and chairs into the dining room, but in a short time, a young gentile came and took them too. Our "chairs" were now the empty toy chest and several other crates that Papa took down from the attic.

The neighbors from downstairs came and took the radio — which I hated so much lately. They also took the pots and dishes, and all the kitchenware — both nice and plain. We had only one bent pot left and several chipped dishes. These neighbors told us that their son would come the next day for the brown sofa.

"What, Maman? The brown sofa too?!" I asked in trepidation. "So where will we sit?" When they took all the houseware, I wasn't so upset, but the brown sofa! It was our fortress, the place where we spent most of our day! "What will we do now?" I repeated.

"I'll lay an old blanket on the floor for you," Maman suggested. "That can be your new sofa!" An old blanket! How could she compare an old, torn blanket to our expensive sofa? But I didn't dare ask Maman that question. Besides, she cried every time she returned home without the package that she took, or when gentiles came to take things from the house. She would hug me and Meir, the tears rolling down her cheeks, and Papa wouldn't even try to calm her down. At times like these, Papa just sat on his crate, a Gemara on his knees, and looked — not at the pages of his *sefer* — at us. He gazed at us intently, without uttering a sound. It seemed to me that he wasn't even learning; he was simply sitting and staring. He barely ate anything — he drank cups and cups of coffee substitute. When Maman begged him to eat, he would absentmindedly put some food in his mouth.

We, the children, stayed on the old blanket and whispered together. We didn't dare ask, or try to figure out why everything was disappearing and our parents were so sad. Irena told us that she asked Aunt Silka why our mother sold all our possessions. Aunt Silka didn't want to answer. When Irena kept nudging her, she said, "That's the way it is, that's what has to be done, and that's all. Don't ask questions. It's wartime, and that's how it is during wartime."

"So why are only they selling their things, and we're not?" Irena persisted. Instead of answering, Aunt Silka hugged Irena and said, "We won't separate! We'll stay together in good and bad."

Irena and I tried to decipher the meaning of this declaration, but we were stumped. My family was also together, so what did Aunt Silka mean? And anyway, what did the war have to do with selling all our things? Was it really because of money, as Meir claimed? I didn't think so. Why would we need so much money to buy food? How did Aunt Silka buy food without selling all the contents of her house?

These questions disturbed me. I couldn't put Aunt Silka's incomprehensible words out of my mind. They engulfed me with an unexplainable dread.

# 10
# "You Must Go"

"I have the entire sum!" Maman told Papa cheerily, as if telling him good news. But then she immediately erupted in wracking sobs, her whole body shaking. Instead of calming her down, Papa wept together with her. Meir and I clung to each other on the blanket, bewildered and scared. Maman's sobbing was nothing new. Even before the war she would cry — when she told us a sad story, when she received a letter from Poland, or when she lit the Shabbos candles. But Papa's weeping frightened us. Our big, strong Papa was crying! I had never seen him cry, and now he was sobbing heavily. I was terrified.

Papa got up from the crate he was sitting on and approached us. He hugged me tightly and said in a trembling voice, "Chanah, my Chanah'le, you will live! You will remember us. You will be the continuation of our family! My Chanah'le, you are a Jewish girl. Never, ever, forget that you are a Jew."

"Papa, what are you talking about? What do you mean? Papa, I don't understand what you're saying."

Papa, still holding me close, looked at me with tear-filled eyes, eyes that once twinkled with constant laughter and joy. "Chanah'le, my Chanah'le," he whispered, his voice cracking. He was quiet for a few seconds — long, drawn-out seconds. Then he inhaled deeply and spoke again. This time his voice was determined and strong. "I'm telling you, I'm commanding you, I'm pleading with you: You will live! You must live!"

I realized something else was changing. The force in Papa's voice made that very clear. But what? And why specifically would I live through this war? And of course I know I'm a Jewish girl! Still bewildered, I looked at Maman, hoping for an explanation.

"Maman, will you tell me what Papa means? Please, Maman," I pleaded. Maman didn't say a word. She bit her lips and remained silent. Her terrifying sobs had already stopped, but her tears continued to flow silently down her cheeks.

Above Maman's head was a lighter square on the wall, where a picture had hung just days before. It, too, had been sold along with all of our belongings. Suddenly, that square appeared to be shining with a light that wasn't there before. A light from another world. I closed my eyes tightly so I wouldn't see that frightening light. When I opened them, Papa was looking straight at me. He continued to bid me, pleadingly, "Chanah'le, you will live! Remember us. You will be our continuity. My Chanah'le, you are a Jew. You are a *bas Yisrael*. You must never forget this, no matter where you are."

Maybe Meir knows what's going on here? I thought. It seemed to me that everyone understood what was happening besides me. Meir was only seven, but he was wise beyond his years and at times knew how to explain things that I didn't understand.

"Meir, what does Papa want from me?" I whispered. But

this time he had no explanation to offer me. He just said, "Chanah'le, I'm scared. I'm so afraid. Hold me tight, don't let anyone take me. Watch over me! You're my big sister."

"Don't be afraid, Meir. I'll watch you. I promise."

Maman made an effort to change the heavy mood. "Today we are sleeping in our beds!" she announced, trying to sound cheerful. Lately, we had been sleeping in our hiding places, but the beds were still in our house. The doorman of our building had already bought them, but he was only supposed to take them the next day. Meir clapped his hands and called out, "Sleeping in a bed! Sleeping in a bed!" But his cheers were hollow, without real joy.

I lay alert in my bed that night, unable to fall asleep. Numerous questions preyed on my mind, questions that had no answers. Why had Papa spoken like that to me? Why weren't we sleeping in our hiding places? Has the danger already passed? It certainly didn't seem like it had. Something strange was happening here. Suddenly, I felt Maman's hand stroking my face, and I felt the soft touch of her lips on my forehead. I pretended to be sleeping. I wanted Maman to come back and pat me again and give me another kiss.

She didn't pat Meir's face or kiss him, only me. Why? What happened? I couldn't understand why Maman was still awake. It must have been past midnight! Suddenly, Papa was next to me too. He also patted my face lovingly, and then I felt tears falling on my face — my parents' tears. Why? I knew they also loved Meir dearly. So why were they only crying next to my bed? Was something terrible about to happen to me, just to me?

They're not telling me anything, they're not explaining a thing. Why aren't they telling me what's happening? Papa and Maman always explain everything to us, they share things with us. But this time, there has not been one word of explanation. Only hugs and sobs and Papa's mysterious words.

What did Papa mean when he said that I would live? We'll all live, *b'ezras Hashem*. Does Papa think that... *chas v'shalom*... enough! I'm not going to think about it. But what about Meir? Why didn't Papa tell him also, "You will live"? Why only me?

Papa and Maman had already left the room, but I still couldn't fall asleep. I tossed and turned in my "real bed;" I hadn't slept in a bed in a long time, but I was too troubled to enjoy the comfort. All of our linens had already been sold. Maman had covered our beds with a piece of old material that she used to cover crates in the attic. "Meir, Meir," I whispered. He didn't answer. Apparently, he had fallen asleep quickly on the comfortable bed. And now I wanted him to be up... I tried to speak to him, to let out some of my anxiety. How could he sleep at such a tense time? My hands were cold, my feet were numb, my heart was pounding. Why wasn't the pounding of my heart waking Meir up?

I was afraid to move. "Meir, Meir," I whispered a little more loudly. Again, Meir didn't respond. I wanted to climb on his bed and shake him, but I simply couldn't get out of bed. I was frozen in place.

I must have fallen asleep, because I awoke suddenly. Maman was hugging me tightly and whispering in my ear, "Wake up, Chanah'le, wake up quietly."

"But Maman, it's still dark," I protested.

"Shhh ...don't wake up Meir. Get up quietly and come to the other room."

I crawled out of my bed, throwing a quick glance at Meir's bed. He lay quietly and didn't move. Was he in a deep sleep, or maybe just pretending? I restrained myself and didn't approach him. I went straight to the living room, where Maman was waiting for me. "Come, put on all the clothes I prepared for you here. We're going," she whispered.

"We're going, Maman? Where? In the middle of the night? But there's a curfew! And what about Meir?"

Maman gently placed her finger on my lips. I knew that meant I should keep quiet. I began to dress. How many outfits did Maman lay out here? "Should I wear all these clothes?" I asked in surprise. "All of them, one on top of the other?"

Maman nodded, and without a word, I put on all the clothes. It was a little difficult, but I didn't ask any more questions.

"*Nu, nu,* faster. Time is passing, my precious child," Maman whispered, helping me put on yet another layer. "Take this," she gave me a small package. "There is a blanket here, and the pillow that you love." She took my hand in her hand and brought me to the door. There was Papa, standing in the entrance. He placed his hands on my head and blessed me, as if it was Shabbos night after Kiddush. Then he bent down and hugged me, and I felt his wet face. Suddenly I began to understand, and a dreadful fear overcame me. "I don't want to go! I want to be with you! We all have to stay together!"

But Papa put me down and gently steered me out the front door. I held on to him with all my might. "I don't want to leave! I'm only going with you!"

"Chanah'le, you must go. You have to live," Papa whispered to me, his voice trembling. Maman pulled my hand. "Come, come already." As we went down the stairs, I felt my feet moving forward, but my heart remained behind with Papa. He stood in the doorway and wept. Only now did I understand what Papa told me in the evening. His words were words of farewell.

We left out courtyard and went into the street. Darkness. Total darkness — aside from the twinkling stars. I lifted my eyes to the stars above. "Hashem in Heaven, do You let children be separated from their parents?" I asked soundlessly. Countless stars sparkled before my eyes. I never knew there could be so many stars in the skies of Brussels like the millions of stars in Spa — a resort area we used to travel to for our yearly vacation.

We hugged the buildings as we walked, scuffing our toes on the sidewalk stones to feel our way in the dark. Oh, how I hoped no soldier would pass by now! It was prohibited to be outside during curfew hours. I felt the icy wind whipping through my many layers of clothing. It was cold, biting cold. The air was frigid, but we continued on our way without stopping. Interesting — I always thought I knew our street very well. I thought I could walk down it confidently — even with my eyes closed. And now, in the darkness of night, I realized that this was not true. I don't even know where I am, and I must feel with my feet and be careful not to fall. "Maman, Maman," I pulled on her arm. But Maman hushed me, "Quiet, Chanah'le, don't speak in the street."

We turned another corner. Some of the cobblestone on this street were straight, and others were broken. Now we had to be twice as careful! Are we going to Irena's house, I wondered. The cobblestones on our street were also old and crooked. No, we can't be going to Irena — when we left the house, we turned left, not right. Now we turned into another street. Maman patted the walls of the building next to us until she found a door. The door wasn't locked. Maman opened it quietly, and we entered the stairwell. I followed Maman up the stairs and then she knocked softly, three times, on the apartment door. The door opened immediately and we walked in.

A dim light shone in the house. Mrs. Salsky was waiting for us here — the non-Jewish lady who used to launder our clothes every week. She looked at us worriedly. "Did anyone see you coming here? Did anyone see you on the street?"

"The street was completely deserted," Maman reassured her. "No one is walking around during these hours. Even the guards weren't out on such a cold night."

Mrs. Salsky looked at me and shook her head. Then she turned to Maman and said, "*Nu*, what do you have for her?"

With a trembling hand, Maman took out a small bag from her coat pocket. I recognized the bag immediately — that pouch contained all the money Maman and Papa had saved up for our trip to Poland. Maman had also kept the money she had received from selling all of our household goods in that bag. Maman placed the bag in Mrs. Salsky's hands and whispered, "After the war, you will receive double this amount. My father will send the money from abroad. The main thing is that you carefully watch over my child!"

Where would Maman receive double this amount from after the war? How could my grandfather send money? From conversations I overheard in the house, I knew that my grandparents didn't have money. And here, in this bag, were all of Papa and Maman's possessions. I hoped they didn't put everything in the bag; I hoped they saved something to buy food with. But I didn't say anything. I didn't dare utter a word. Then Maman looked at me, and I mustered my courage. I whispered to her in Yiddish, "But Maman, you said that we would buy tickets with this money and escape to France!"

Maman wrapped me in a warm embrace. "No, my child. France was also conquered. We have nowhere to go."

Mrs. Salsky grasped my hand and we went down, together with Maman, to her cellar. In her neighborhood, every family had their own private cellar, not a large communal cellar as we had in our building.

I pulled my hand away from Mrs. Salsky's and clutched Maman with both my hands. "Maman, don't leave me!"

Maman spoke calmly. "Be a good, quiet girl, Chanah'le. It's forbidden for the neighbors to know that you're here. You may not make any noise. During the day, you will be here alone, and every night Mrs. Salsky will come down to you. She will bring you food and drinks, and she will empty the pail. Believe me, Chanah'le, it's for your good! Mrs. Salsky will watch you until the end of the war. After the war, Papa and I will come and take you home. Until then, we won't be able to meet. I cannot come and visit you here — it might endanger you and me."

"Maman!" I sobbed. "Maman! Don't leave me alone!"

But Maman only hugged me and said, "There is no other choice, Chanah'le, it's better this way. It's safer."

"But why only me? Why did you only bring me here? What about Meir? Why can't both of us stay together?"

Maman's eyes grew dark and serious when she answered, “No, Chanah’le, it’s impossible. Meir had a *bris milah*. Enough, Chanah’le, be a good, quiet girl. Wait for us here patiently. We will come! When the war is over, we will come back for you.”

Another hug and another kiss, one last hug, and that was it. I was alone. Alone. No one was with me.

# 11 Alone

I sat on the chair and cried. For a long time I sat and cried, until my body felt like stone. The tiny stump of candle that Mrs. Salsky had left in the cellar was about to go out. I began to peel off the many layers of clothing I was wearing, hoping to undress while I still had light. Afterwards, I lay down in bed. The bed was small, and the blanket was thin. What luck that Maman packed me another blanket. It wasn't a feather quilt — that Maman had already sold — but I figured that two blankets together would keep me warm. I hugged my beloved pillow and cried until the stump of the candle burned out. It was pitch black in the cellar, and cold, oh so cold. I was very cold even under both my blankets. I got out of bed and felt around for the chair, where all my clothes were. I put them on again and crawled back under the covers. Now I wasn't cold anymore, and I fell asleep while crying.

When I woke up, it was still dark. I was scared. Why is it so dark here? I held up my hand in front of my eyes, and I could barely see it. I sat up in bed, willing my eyes to see through the darkness, but to no avail. A strange weakness overcame me. Despite doing nothing, I felt drained. I lay down again, and fell asleep right away.

Again I awoke to darkness. What time was it now? Day?

Night? Evening? It seemed an eternity since Maman had left me alone, all alone.

I sat up and carefully placed my feet on the ground — first my right foot, then my left. I stretched out my arms, trying to feel my way around. My hand bumped into the chair. I patted the chair and found a plate with cooked vegetables, and bread next to the plate. I kept feeling my way around and discovered a spoon and a cup. There was also a pitcher with water inside. Mrs. Salsky must have come down here while I slept. Too bad she didn't wake me up! I had no desire to eat, but I would have been happy to see her. It would have relieved some of the terrible loneliness which I felt. I lay down again in bed, but this time I couldn't fall asleep. I was alone here, alone. There, in the house, all of them were together. What did Meir think when he woke up in the morning and didn't find me in the house? I didn't even say good-bye to him! And I had promised him that I wouldn't leave him, that I would watch over him. How can I watch over him when I'm here in the dark, and he's not with me? Maman had given Mrs. Salsky so much money. Couldn't she watch over Meir too in exchange for all this money? We could be here together; there's enough room in this little bed for both of us. Why should Mrs. Salsky care if I'm here alone or both of us are together? We would manage with one portion of food for both of us. What does a *bris milah* have to do with anything? All boys have a *bris*. Anyway, it's not as if he had a *bris* today, or just recently — he had a *bris* when he was born, when he was a tiny baby. Why couldn't he come here because of his *bris*?

"Meir, where are you now? Are you angry at me because I didn't stay home to watch over you? What are you thinking about me?" I asked in the silence.

Suddenly I heard steps above my head. Someone is coming! I pulled my blanket over my head, frightened. But the steps grew distant and disappeared. I pulled the blanket off my head and sat up. It wasn't pitch black anymore; I could see the outlines of the various objects in the room. I got up and began to explore. My bed was in one corner, and a chair was next to it. In the other corner was the pail that Maman had mentioned. And that was it. I was back at my bed again — the room was not large. The doorway was directly opposite my bed. I felt the walls. They were rough and unfinished. Apparently, they hadn't even covered the cement with plaster. The floor was also made of jagged cement. This was new to me. Any floor I had ever seen before — whether in a private home or a public place — was always made of wood or covered with a carpet to reduce the cold in the winter.

Again steps! I tried to hunch myself up tightly, so I would take up less room and they wouldn't sense I was there. Again and again I heard steps above me. I was sorely troubled — worried that someone was coming for me — until I realized that the cellar was exactly under the lobby of the building. All the footsteps were simply regular people coming and leaving. Maybe the steps that I heard now were Mrs. Salsky's? No, they continued on into the street. I figured out which side the street was on according to the types of noises I heard. Soon afterwards, I heard running steps — a child was passing over me. I had nothing to do besides listening to footsteps.

Evening arrived, I decided, when the small amount of light that was in the cellar vanished. The truth is, it was not light, it was only a little less darkness. And now that also had disappeared and was gone. Night must be drawing near, and soon Mrs. Salsky will come. I better eat all the food immediately, I thought, before she arrives, so she won't be angry.

I had finished everything and Mrs. Salsky still hadn't come. What's taking her so long? She promised to bring me food every night and sit with me. Why didn't she come? What's she waiting for? Will she really come?

I sat hunched over in the darkness, waiting. Even if I had a watch, I wouldn't be able to see what time it was. Even if I had books, I wouldn't be able to read them. Maybe it's better that I don't have anything. Maybe I should dream about a story? A story about traveling on vacation, about all the lovely things from home and wonderful times together with my family. I just did not want to think about what happened at home yesterday!

I tried not to think about Papa, Maman and Meir. Not about our house, not about school, not about Irena. But I couldn't. It was impossible to fight my thoughts. I thought about all of them, heartbroken that I was not together with them.

Finally I heard the clinking of a key turning in the keyhole. Very quietly, the door swung open. Mrs. Salsky entered the cellar and lit a candle. Light! Light! The light spread a soft glow over the small room, and Mrs. Salsky noticed my fresh tears. "Don't cry, Anna," she said gently. "Don't cry. You'll yet see that the war will finish, and your mother will come to take you home. Don't cry."

Mrs. Salsky held a wicker basket in her hand. She took out food from the basket and then placed the empty dishes inside. Thank goodness, I had finished everything... Afterwards she took the pail and went out. She returned a minute later with an empty pail and sat next to me in bed. "I'm happy that you ate well," she said. "Come now, and eat what I brought you."

"Don't be upset, Mrs. Salsky, but right now I can't eat. Leave the food with me, and I'll eat it later when I'm alone."

"Fine, you can eat whenever you want to. But look, I made hot soup. Don't wait until it gets cold. It's not a good idea to eat cold soup. I haven't cooked such a rich soup in a long time; it's so hard to find food now. In your merit, I was able to get excellent food, and I cooked a healthy, thick soup like I used to do before the war." She looked very satisfied, but I wasn't as enthusiastic as she was. I was sure she was able to buy the expensive food with the money that Maman gave her!

Suddenly Mrs. Salsky noticed that I was wearing all my clothes together. "Don't do that," she told me. "When these clothes will wear out, I won't be able to buy you other clothes. Everyone knows I don't have a daughter, and if I buy girl's clothing, they'll be suspicious. Take them off. It's enough if you wear one dress with a sweater. Take your shoes off, too, so no one will hear you. I'll bring you some thick socks that I knitted. It is best for you to lie in bed during the day — you must keep absolutely quiet! At night, you can move around a little, but be careful, so no one will realize you're here. Only use the pail at night so no one will hear you." Mrs. Salsky finished giving me all these instructions and nodded absentmindedly. Then she got ready to leave. She stretched out her hand and picked up the candle.

"No, Mrs. Salsky, please! Don't take the candle! Don't leave me alone again in the dark!"

"I can't leave the candle with you, Anna. What's gotten

into you? It's very dangerous! I'll bring a candle with me tomorrow. You'll have light when I'm here, but as for the rest of the time, you'll just have to get used to the dark. I left a tiny stump of candle yesterday because I knew it would burn out right away and wouldn't endanger the whole house." She blew out the candle, took it and the basket, patted my head and went out, closing the door very quietly and locking it with a key. I couldn't even hear her receding steps. Apparently, she walked on tiptoes so no one would hear her.

I didn't take my clothes off despite Mrs. Salsky's warnings. I had no desire to eat. I lay in bed and stared at the dark.

After some time, I got up and ate the soup. It was still a little warm, and I understood that only a short time had passed since Mrs. Salsky's visit. I didn't want her to get angry, so I took off layer after layer of clothing. I folded them as neatly as I could and laid them on the floor. Then I returned to bed and slept deeply for the rest of that night.

In the morning, I awoke to the sound of loud footsteps overhead. It took me some time to remember where I was. I ate some of the food and decided to leave the rest for later. It's not a good idea to eat everything at once. I walked to the door, and from the door to the bed. I took the dishes off the chair and put them under the bed. I sat on the chair. Then I got up to walk around again. I sat down again. This is how I spent the day — there was no other way to pass the time! I walked around and sat down again and again, but night still hadn't fallen. I didn't hear steps above, the room wasn't yet steeped in total darkness. I lay down and got up, walked around, and sat down. I ate the rest of the food, chewing each bite slowly, trying to "use" time, but Mrs. Salsky still didn't come. I was afraid of the dark, and was waiting desperately for her visit.

Slowly the room became darker, and the footsteps above became less frequent. Night finally arrived, and I knew Mrs. Salsky would come!

Sure enough, she soon arrived, a candle in her hand. She lit the candle and I breathed a sigh of relief. How I longed for light! I dreamed about it constantly during the long hours of the day.

Mrs. Salsky brought me a pair of thick, knitted socks, and I happily put them on. She also brought a large, thick sweater. "You can wear this old sweater; it's big and very warm. You won't be cold with it at all. It's really cold today and outside the snow keeps coming down." Mrs. Salsky chatted about the weather and tried to make some small talk. She told me about the neighbors in the building, and about her outings to find food but she didn't mention a word about my parents. "I don't know anything about them, and I can't even go to check on them. It's better not to have contact between me and your parents as long as you're with me," she said.

She was happy that I had finished all the food. I told her that I ate a little bit throughout the day, just to help the time pass. She nodded, and didn't say a word. She switched the empty dishes with full ones, and with that, her short visit was over. She stood up, picked up the candle, and left.

# 12
# Footsteps in the Dark

Dark. It's dark the entire day. I have some room to move around, to take a few steps, but everything is dark. There's no light outside and no light inside, from the moment Mrs. Salsky leaves with her candle. Why did she absolutely refuse to leave the candle? Why is it dangerous? I wouldn't be able to fall asleep as long as the candle lit up the dark. I would watch over the candle as if it were my most precious possession!

I slowly learned to differentiate between the various footsteps. I tried to imagine to whom the footsteps belonged. I could tell that there were several children in the building — they belonged to the running jumps and stamping feet. There was one old man who walked with a cane. I would hear it thumping above my head. Or maybe it belonged to an old lady? Some neighbors walked slowly, dragging their feet, and others walked quickly. Some had a heavy tread, and others, brisk and light. I had nothing to do in the cellar; I couldn't see a thing. The only pastime I had was listening to footsteps and trying to guess whose they were. During her nightly visits, Mrs. Salsky would tell me all kinds of things about the neighbors, and I tried to match the stories to the footsteps. I also invented all kinds of stories about them — just to pass the time.

Early every morning, I heard the gatekeeper opening the main entrance. I recognized his steps right away. I heard the creaking of his key in the gate, and the swishing of his broom. Next, I heard the hurried footsteps of people rushing to work. A little later, it was the school children; I identified their footsteps easily. Still later, I heard calm, measured footsteps — of people who were not in a rush. Maybe they were going shopping, or going to visit relatives or friends. In the next stage, I heard the children coming home, and afterwards, the adults returning from work.

When the footsteps stopped, I knew that it was evening already and that curfew hour had arrived. The gatekeeper locked the gate with a creaking key, and went home. And then, after more time, which seemed like eternity, Mrs. Salsky would come. She would bring me food, drink, and clean, freshly-washed clothing. But most importantly, she always brought along a candle. She lit it, and spent some time with me. We spoke in whispers. I held her hand and whispered in her ear, "It's cold here, and dark... when will Maman come? When will this cursed war finally end?"

Mrs. Salsky tried to encourage me. "Don't worry. Maman will come. The war will end; wars always end. Maman will come as soon as she can. It's impossible for her to come now, but it's easier for her since she doesn't have to worry about you. She has enough to worry about with your young brother."

"Maybe bring him here," I pleaded. "He is small and quiet; he doesn't make noise and doesn't take up much space. I'll be much calmer if I'm with him. You won't have to work harder — we'll sleep together in one bed, and the food you bring will be enough for both of us. You'll see, I'll eat only half, and I'll leave the other half for Meir. Please, Mrs. Salsky! Please! I'm so miserable being here alone!"

But Mrs. Salsky wouldn't agree. Every night I pleaded with her, begged her, but she wouldn't budge, and firmly refused. Sometimes I changed my tactics. "Mrs. Salsky, take me home with you. I'll help you in the house, I'll do everything. I know how to work hard. Nothing is too hard for me. It's so dark here."

But she always refused. "I can't take you. I live alone and everyone knows it. I don't have children, and never had. If they see me suddenly with a girl — they'll kill both of us."

Every night, the same scene repeated itself. She left me there in the cellar, left me behind in the dark, with all my frightening thoughts and terrifying dreams, with time that refused to pass. I tried to recall all the lovely stories I used to read in my past life, my childhood which ended so brutally. I loved to read, and I was one of those girls who was constantly taking out new books and returning others to the library. I always read my books aloud to Meir and Irena. I still remembered many stories, and I kept retelling them to myself. I also tried to *daven* whatever I remembered. I was especially particular to say *berachos* before and after food, as Papa and Maman had taught me. I would walk around a little in that tiny room, sit down for a short while on the chair. I spent most of my time lying in bed.

The days passed slowly. Alone there in the dark, I felt like a prisoner. I had read many stories about people who sat in jail, but never, in my wildest dreams, did I imagine that I would be locked up like that. I hadn't even been accused of a crime which I didn't commit! There was no reason for my imprisonment — I just had to sit, without knowing why, in this prison. My circumstances may have made for a thrilling plot in a suspense novel, but in real life there was no thrill at all.

How I wish I could run away! I thought. It's better to be with Papa and Maman, no matter what happens to them. Everything is better than being here alone in the dark. Why did they want me to be here, and not with them? I promised Meir I would watch over him. How can I watch over him here? Maybe they also brought him to another lady's cellar? Maybe Maman didn't give Mrs. Salsky all the money? After all, I didn't see exactly how much there was and how much she got. I only recognized the bag, but maybe Maman divided the money and put half of it in another bag, for Meir? Why didn't they keep us together? How come Papa only spoke so seriously to me — and bid me to live and remain a Jew? Why did he direct his farewell words only to me? Maybe he said the same thing afterwards to Meir?

These questions, questions without answers, tormented me without stop. I kept asking myself the same questions over and over. I had nothing else to do. I promised Maman I would wait for her here — that's why I didn't entertain thoughts of escape. I knew that I wouldn't plan to steal the key from Mrs. Salsky! I didn't even want to think those thoughts. I had promised Maman I would wait for her here. Maman always taught us that promises must be kept.

I hate this darkness, I hate it and am afraid of it. Papa, Maman, Meir, I miss you so much! Meir, what are you doing now? Are you reading books to yourself? You always wanted me to read to you, even though you're already big and can read well yourself. You said it's more interesting when I read to you. Are you in a hiding place? How do you pass the days and nights? I'm happy you're not in the dark. I wish you could be here, next to me, but at the same time I'm happy that you're not in this terrible darkness. I was always the brave one, and you were easily frightened. Now I'm lying here scared. Scared of the dark. Scared of the cold. Scared of footsteps.

I spent a lot of time *davening* — whichever *tefillos* I remembered. I didn't know so many, so I kept repeating the same *tefillos*. And so, while I lay in bed and thought about my family, my home and school, I tried to occupy myself. I thought about our relatives and friends. I realized that Aunt Silka surely knew about the plans to give me to Mrs. Salsky. That's why she had told Irena that their family would always stay together.

After this never-ending tidal wave of thoughts, one crashing down on top of the other, came the tears. Hot, copious tears rolled down my cheeks and pitiful sobs racked my thin body. I simply couldn't — and I didn't even want to — stop my sobbing.

# 13
# Hovering Figures

Dizziness. Everything around me was turning: the chair, my food, the entire room. Even my bed was swirling around. I couldn't stop the dizziness, my loud wheezing or the chattering of my teeth. I knew the gatekeeper might hear me, but I was unable to make even the slightest effort to stop.

So what. I don't care anymore. What difference does it make? From minute to minute I'm feeling worse and worse. What could be worse than this?

I see Papa and Maman circling the room — in the air. And there is Meir! What are they doing in my room? Why are they going in circles? How could they hang in the air without falling? Maybe they're not really here and I'm just dreaming? But I can see them clearly. Maybe this is a sign that I'm going to die? Maybe this is how dying people feel?

Maman is talking to me; I'm trying to concentrate on her words. She is dressed in her light blue Shabbos dress and has a white kerchief on her head, the one she always wears when she lights candles. Is it Shabbos today? I can't understand what Maman's saying. And now she is coming close, hovering over me: "Chanah'le, *daven.* Please, Chanah'le, *daven.*"

I try *daven*ing all the prayers that I know, but I am getting confused. First I say *Shema Yisrael.* Is it morning now, or evening? What's the difference? I also say, *Modeh Ani*, and everything else I remember from *Shacharis*. Then I say *HaMapil chevlei sheinah* and even *ha-motzi*. I say all the *tefillos* and *berachos* I can remember. "Hashem, I'm confused. Please take whichever of my prayers was the right one!" Maybe I shouldn't be speaking to Hashem this way?

My head aches. I want to vomit, but can't. Oh, how can I *daven*? I didn't wash my hands! I must sit up and wash my hands. But it's impossible. I can't lift my head; I can't even open my eyes.

Once, in the Jewish school, they told me a story about a sinful Jew. Before his death he had regret for his bad ways. He prayed to Hashem and said *Viduy* — and he was completely forgiven! Forgiven. Forgiven... The *rav* said that he was forgiven. Heaven erased all his sins, as if he hadn't sinned at all. What is *Viduy*? How is *Viduy* said? I don't want to die without saying *Viduy*. I want all of my sins erased!

Oh, yes, I remember. You have to repent too. I have to ask forgiveness. From whom? I'm alone here...

My confusing thoughts came and went, repeating themselves again and again. *Viduy*... Forgiven... Suddenly I saw Papa again. He was hovering in the air in the room and telling me something. "What, Papa? What?"

I heard Papa's voice clearly. It sounded like he was shouting. "Chanah'le, you shall live! You must live! I command you: You will live!"

Suddenly I felt a hand on my forehead. It was Mrs. Salsky. "Anna! Anna!" She sat on my bed and stroked me. "Anna, do you hear me? Anna, do you see me?"

I gripped her hand, "Yes, Mrs. Salsky, I hear and see you.

But I feel terrible. I am in pain. Everything hurts."

"You're burning with fever. You're very sick. I don't know what to do. I'm afraid." Then Mrs. Salsky said, "Wait a minute. I'll come back immediately."

She went out quickly, not bothering to walk on her tiptoes as she always did. The sound of the door clicking shut sounded like a frightful noise. Mrs. Salsky came back shortly afterwards, holding several rags and a pitcher full of water. She wet the rags and spread them across my forehead. Then she lifted up my head and dripped water in my mouth. "What else can I do?" she muttered to herself.

After a while, she removed the rags from my forehead. The rags had become hot from my fever. She dipped them in the pitcher again, squeezed them out, and spread them on my forehead once more. "What else can I do? How else can I help?" she muttered to herself. She apparently didn't expect an answer from me.

I think Mrs. Salsky sat next to me the entire night. I slept a troubled sleep, alternately dropping off and waking up in, and each time I woke up, I heard her and felt her presence. But I didn't see her because I couldn't open my eyes.

"Anna, it's already morning. I must go." There was an urgency in Mrs. Salsky's voice. "Now you have to put the wet rags on your forehead yourself — to help the fever go down. Every so often wet them again, squeeze them and place them on your forehead. You also must drink several drops of water each time, just as I dripped several drops in your mouth."

I nodded my head in acceptance. Yes. Morning had come and she had to go. During the day, she could not stay with me in the cellar, even if I was sick.

"Anna, put one of these wet rags on your forehead. I want

to see if you can."

The rag was heavy and I could barely lift it. I dipped it into the water and placed it on my forehead without squeezing it out. "That's fine," Mrs. Salsky said. "Continue. I must leave here fast, before the neighbors start walking around." She dripped a little more water in my mouth, patted me gently and left the cellar.

I fell into a troubled sleep. Every so often I woke up, remembered where I was and changed the dry rags for "fresh" wet ones. My head hurt me terribly, and it was difficult to breathe. I knew I was wheezing loudly, and I knew I shouldn't. I had to keep absolute quiet! But how?

I fell asleep again. I woke up and heard Papa. Papa was speaking to me, crying and pleading, "My Chanah'le, you must live! Chanah'le, you will live... you will live... you will live..."

I remembered I had to drink. I had to lift my head to drink, and that was simply impossible! I tried, but my head was so heavy. Just thinking about lifting it made the ache greater. Then I had an idea. I took a wet rag, put it into my mouth and sucked the water. I made an effort to always keep one rag in my mouth and one on my forehead. It was very hard. I felt exhausted.

From afar, I heard Papa's voice, "My Chanah'le! You must live."

I'll live, Papa. Just don't cry, please! I'll live, I promise. I can't hear you cry, it breaks my heart...

When I felt Mrs. Salsky's presence, I knew night had finally arrived. It was a relief to have her there. She stroked me, took the rag out of my mouth and dripped water — real water — straight in my mouth. Oh, how delicious that water was — cool droplets of water, not warm water sucked from an old rag.

Mrs. Salsky was worried and frightened. “I can’t bring a doctor here. What will I do if you die?”

“No, I won’t die, I’ll live. I must live,” I explained to her. It seemed to me that she didn’t hear me, but I didn’t have strength to speak any louder. I drifted out of consciousness again. When I woke up, Mrs. Salsky was gone. Apparently, morning had arrived again. With great effort, I managed to place the rags on my forehead and in my mouth.

Maybe this is my punishment because I didn’t watch Meir as I promised? I should be with Meir, watching over him. I’m his big sister! So how come I’m here and he’s not? Where are you, Meir?

# 14
# Recovery

The next time I woke up I was alone. My head was no longer so heavy, and I managed to lift myself up a little without feeling dizzy or wanting to vomit. I saw a cup of water on the chair and realized how thirsty I was. I stretched out my hand toward the cup, but my hand shook and I couldn't grasp the cup. I finally did manage to lift the cup to my lips and drink. Some of the water spilled, but I drank the rest.

I placed the cup back on the chair and lay down again. It took a great effort, but I felt wonderful: I already managed to drink by myself! My breathing was also easier, and didn't hurt, even though I was still wheezing noisily.

"Hello," I whispered when Mrs. Salsky entered the room. She ran to me excitedly, and bent over my bed. "Anna, Anna! You're talking? Do you feel better?"

"Yes, Mrs. Salsky. I feel better," I replied. She hugged and kissed me, thrilled. "Oh! What luck! I was so afraid. The God of the Jews watched over you! What luck!" she repeated again and again.

Once she calmed down, she helped me sit down on the chair, removed the linens, and took my clothes. She said, "I'll be right back. I'm bringing you clean laundry and water to wash you. And I'll bring you hot soup. That is the best remedy — it will help you get your strength back. You're still not healthy."

I dozed off on the chair while Mrs. Salsky was gone. When she returned, I woke up. She spoon-fed me the hot soup, but to her great distress, I couldn't swallow more than two spoonfuls. "Try to eat a little more, Anna," she cajoled me. "You haven't put a thing in your mouth besides water for over a month! And even before this illness, you were already thin and emaciated!"

But I couldn't manage to eat anything else. "I'm afraid that if I eat anything else, I'll throw up. Thanks, Mrs. Salsky, you brought me back to life! Maybe later I'll manage to eat some more."

Mrs. Salsky washed me, slowly and carefully, while I sat on the chair. I felt refreshed and it was relatively easy to breathe. But I couldn't move by myself. Mrs. Salsky put me in bed. What a wonderful feeling it was to lie down in a clean bed with clean sheets, just after I washed up and felt refreshed, without feeling dizzy, cold or shaking.

The next few days I slept throughout the day until Mrs. Salsky arrived. With great patience, she fed me soup every night. After several nights, I managed to eat a tablespoon of mashed potatoes, and Mrs. Salsky clapped her hands in joy: "Anna, you're getting healthy!" I felt myself getting stronger, and knew that the day would soon come when I could take the five steps to the pail without having to lean on the wall. My legs still shook, but I knew I was recovering.

I understood from Mrs. Salsky that I had been sick for over a month. For most of that time, I had slept and had been hallucinating in my sleep. I spoke Yiddish, and she was very afraid that someone would hear me. But, as Mrs. Salsky had said, the God of the Jews watched over me. No one heard me, and in the end I recovered.

"You know, Mrs. Salsky," I told her one night, "if I could go outside and sit in the sun, I would recover completely and would stop coughing! It's hard to recover in the dark."

"You're right, but it's impossible. You cannot go out! You shouldn't even think of such an idea. Besides that, now there is no sun outside — only snow and frost, which might make you sick again."

"I don't care. Even if there is snow outside, there's still daylight. I so desperately want to see real light, not just the little candle that you light. I want to go outside," I begged her, "even for just one minute!"

"No, Anna, it's too dangerous!" Mrs. Salsky was insistent. "The war still isn't over, and the end of both of us might be bitter if anyone finds out you're hiding here."

I tried to eat all the food that Mrs. Salsky brought me. She brought me a lot so I would recover quickly: hot cereal, soup, and cooked vegetables. She told me how difficult it was to obtain food. There wasn't always food for sale, and when there was, it wasn't always edible. Even on the black market, it was difficult to obtain food — and it cost a fortune! Despite all the difficulties, she continued making efforts to obtain food — she told me how important it was that I recover completely, and that I get rid of my terrible cough. She was convinced that I had recovered only in the merit of her prayers. What would she have done if I had died, G-d forbid? Mrs. Salsky was very afraid of that happening, so she had gone to church daily. She also asked the priest to pray for me — she told him that her neighbor's daughter was ill.

"You didn't have to worry, Mrs. Salsky. I wouldn't have

died — my father wouldn't let me," I said. "He was here in the room the whole time and demanded that I remain alive. And besides that, when Maman comes after the war, I have to be healthy."

I was still very weak. I frequently suffered coughing spells. The slightest activity wore me out, and sometimes I felt dizzy and my breathing was heavy — but not as loud as before. Mrs. Salsky said that I had come down with a particularly nasty case of pneumonia, and since I couldn't see a doctor, the only medication I could take was water on my forehead and drops of water in my mouth. I had no doubt that the only reason I lived through my illness was in the merit of Papa, who hovered over me and encouraged me. I walked around the small room, and each day I felt better and better. But my dress hung on me like a sack! I wondered what Maman would say about that when she would come to bring me home. Then I told myself that actually, when Maman comes — after the war —I'll be able to go outside. To the air, to the sun! Then I would recover completely, I would stop coughing and I would gain weight. I desperately missed the sun and fresh air — with them I would recover much more quickly. But as much as I longed for sunlight and air, I missed Papa's tight hugs and Maman's loving kisses even more. It was difficult to think about them without crying.

Every night, Mrs. Salsky would tell me about my illness and her fears. "What would I have done if you would have died here?" she would repeat over and over. "It's a miracle that you recovered. It's not possible that such a thin, weak child could recover from such a serious illness with only the help of wet rags and nothing else."

I was getting fed up of hearing this, but Mrs. Salsky

couldn't calm down from the great miracle that had happened to me, and kept repeating herself every night. Each time, I would answer that the God of the Jews did a miracle for me, because I am a Jew.

"Miracles don't happen for all the Jews," she told me once. "What's happening now to the Jews shows that they certainly need miracles, and no miracles are happening..."

"What's happening to them? What do you mean?" I became terrified.

"Nothing, nothing," she quickly retracted her frightening words. "Some bad people are spreading rumors. They're talking as if something bad is happening to the Jews. But I didn't see anything. People like to say all kinds of things."

"But what about my parents? Where do they live? Are they at home? Do they have food to eat? Please, Mrs. Salsky, go find out what happened to them. You can go to our house — they'll think you came to do laundry."

All my begging and weeping didn't help. "I'm not stepping foot on your street," Mrs. Salsky said determinedly.

The boredom which I had felt before I became sick returned and plagued me. Again I listened to the sounds of footsteps throughout the day, again I waited for Mrs. Salsky to come at night with a candle and food. So passed those long, monotonous days, days with no changes. Suddenly one day, however, a drastic change occurred and turned my life upside down.

# 15
# "Where Are You Taking Me?"

"Anna, eat quickly and put these clothes on." Mrs. Salsky dropped a bundle of clothing on my chair. There was something strange in her voice that night when she came down to visit me. She sounded excited – and also anxious. What was the sudden urgency? I ate and got dressed, and then Mrs. Salsky brought me a pair of shoes. Shoes! I hadn't worn shoes since my arrival in the cellar. I walked around in socks so no one would hear my footsteps. And suddenly – shoes! I wiggled my feet up and down, enjoying the feeling of wearing shoes!

"Quick, Anna, come," Mrs. Salsky urged me.

"Come? What do you mean? Am I going outside? Where are we going?" I asked with a pounding heart. "Where are you taking me?"

"Come, we're leaving here," she stated without explaining.

"But where?" Suddenly, a terrible fear overwhelmed me. "But... my Maman! When Maman comes back she won't find me! She said I have to wait for her here!"

"Don't worry! If she comes, I'll tell her where you are. I'll bring her to you."

We left the cellar on our tiptoes. Mrs. Salsky slowly opened the creaking gate. I thought only the gatekeeper had a key to this gate, but she also had one. She held my hand and began to walk rapidly in the dark night. I couldn't keep up with her. I had been in my small dungeon for more than a year. During that time, I was only able to walk a few steps at a time. And even those steps I took slowly. What was there to hurry for? To the contrary, I preferred taking each step as slowly as possible, to fill the never-ending time with something.

"Please, stop a second," I pleaded, panting. "Let me breathe the fresh air. Let me enjoy being outside."

"No, no, come quickly! Quick!" Mrs. Salsky pulled me along. "They shouldn't catch us!"

"When will we return? Can I go outside during the day too — when there's light?" I asked hopefully.

"You're not coming back with me, Anna. You're going to a good place, a place with light, a place where you'll get good food and also a doctor if you'll need one."

"I'm not coming back? Where are you taking me? What will my parents say? Maman said I have to stay with you!"

"Don't worry. When your parents come back, they'll find you in the new place. I know the address, and besides that, I also told a Jewish underground organization where I'm taking you. If you stay with me, you might die if you get sick again. I can't bring you to a doctor. It's better for you to be in a different place, where they'll take care of you whenever you need it. You mustn't continue looking like this — you're almost twelve years old and you look like an eight year old."

I walked alongside her, trying to hurry as fast as I could. Various emotions churned inside me. On one hand, I was thrilled to leave my dungeon and breathe fresh air. Maybe I would also see sunlight. On the other hand, I was afraid.

Where could she be taking me? Why wouldn't she tell me where?"

Finally we stopped. I breathed in relief. We were at the train station, facing a strange woman who was sitting on a bench. Mrs. Salsky began speaking to her in Flemish. I didn't understand a word. Then Mrs. Salsky turned to me. "Now you'll be traveling with this woman."

"No!" Terror filled me, surpassing all other emotions. "I don't want to! I want you! I want to stay with you! Don't leave me! Take me with you!"

"Absolutely not!" Mrs. Salsky answered me resolutely. "I'm not willing to watch you anymore. You might die. You must travel with this woman!" Then she added in a gentler voice, "You'll see, Anna, you'll be with girls your age. It will be much better there than with me." She warned me not to speak to the strange woman or tell her about my stay in the cellar. Then she turned around and left. She simply disappeared from my life.

I sat on the bench, shaking, trying to suppress my sobs. When the train arrived, we boarded silently. The woman didn't speak to me. We were silent throughout the trip. I eagerly looked out the window. The night was beginning to turn to day. Dawn broke, painting the heavens in pink. The air became lighter and more clear, and the sun shone in full glory. Light! Real light! I was so thirsty for light and air, for scenic views, for the green of plants and the brown of earth. I couldn't get enough of the view, and of the abundance that suddenly appeared before me.

Suddenly, I was on another train, another trip, so long ago. Meir was jumping next to me, dressed in his handsome blue sailor suit, banging on the closed window. "Chanah'le, look, Chanah'le. Cows! Cows are eating all the grass!"

But I quickly blocked that scene out of my memory. I didn't want to remember! I just wanted to see the passing scenery and absorb the light.

We descended from the train in Leuvan, an unfamiliar city I had never visited. The woman held my hand tightly, and I obediently went with her. From afar, I saw a large building surrounded by a very tall, formidable stone wall. Maybe this was a fortress? The top of the wall was lined with glass shards to keep thieves out.

When we came closer to the building, I saw an enormous cross on the gate. Two smaller crosses, one on each side, surrounded the large cross. There were more crosses on the wall. It was a convent! The strange woman was bringing me to a convent — to a Christian place! I tried to pull my hand out of hers and run away, but she held onto me with all her strength. I balked, but she was stronger than me and forcefully pulled me after her toward the gate. There was an iron door knocker on the gate — shaped like a small fist.

Then I understood why Mrs. Salsky hadn't told me where she was sending me. She knew I would try to run away. The woman held me firmly with one hand, and raised the door knocker with her other hand.

# 16 Seeing Black

A small window in the gate opened abruptly and the gatekeeper poked his head out in the open. "Where to?" he asked, looking us over.

"To Sister Lucie. She's expecting us," the woman replied.

The gatekeeper swung open the gate. My companion held me with both her hands and literally dragged me inside. With a harsh clang, the gate closed and locked behind me. I was trapped inside. I raised my eyes and saw a nun dressed in black approaching us. I was very frightened. Once, when I was small, I had been hospitalized in a mission hospital where nuns worked. Maman stayed at my side the entire time. She didn't leave me for a second, because I was afraid of those nuns and their long, black clothes. Now, I was being entrusted to nuns, and Maman wasn't with me to protect me!

"No, no! I don't want to come here!" I shouted. But the woman and the nun paid no attention to my protests. They brought me to a large, high room full of light. My companion spoke to the nun for several minutes. I heard her saying that my parents and brother had disappeared and that's why they sent me here. Then, she left. The nun led me to a chair and patted me. "It will be good for you here," she promised me gently. "You will have friends. It's a good place here. Everyone — every girl who comes here — is afraid on the first day, but slowly they all get used to it. Calm down. Don't cry."

She gave me a tissue to dry my eyes and brought me a cup of water. She waited patiently until I finished drinking. "I'm Sister Lucie, the head nun," she introduced herself to me. "I'm the only one who knows who you are and what your real name is. But from the moment you leave this room, no one may know that you are a Jew. If your secret is revealed, they will kill you — and me too. We'll tell everyone that you're a Protestant and that's why you don't know our Catholic prayers. Now listen to me: from today on, your name is Arlette Vanderlas. Remember that. Arlette Vanderlas."

She told me which town I came from, when I was born, and where. She told me the names of my parents, and basically created a new life for me — completely different from my real life. She commanded me to review those details again and again, until I could say them in my sleep. She warned me that I must never make a mistake, so the secret of my true identity would never be revealed.

"In the meantime, while you still don't know all the details well, don't answer any of the questions that the girls ask you. Pretend that you're shy or confused. The most important thing is not to make a mistake! And always remember how lucky you are that you were accepted to our convent, the Couvent Misericorde. We are saving you from death outside, from the hands of the Germans, and you will always have to thank us for that. As soon as you get used to life in the convent, and learn our prayers, you'll thank us even more — because this is the gratitude we expect from you."

Sister Lucie finished speaking and picked up an ornamental ceramic bell from her table. She rang it a few times, and immediately, there was a soft knock on the door. Another nun entered the room. Apparently, the bell's ring was heard in the room next door. I assumed that only the bell was heard there, and not people's normal speech, otherwise, how could Sister Lucie talk about the terrible secret which shouldn't be revealed at all costs?

The new nun was young, tall, and pretty. She didn't seem to be as warm and friendly as Sister Lucie. "Sister Marta, please take Arlette, get her dressed and show her around," Sister Lucie instructed her. "She is a new pupil, and she needs to be shown everything."

Now I was sorry to leave Sister Lucie. Her gentle demeanor and pleasant speech had soothed my troubled heart. She had acted lovingly toward me — comforting me when I was frightened — and I felt similar feelings toward her. Impulsively, I went over to her and kissed her on her cheek. Sister Marta clucked her tongue and shook her head. I understood that I had done something wrong, but I didn't know what.

"Arlette, you may not kiss the head nun that way," Sister Marta explained. "You have to curtsy before her and kiss her hand."

Sister Lucie smiled. "Arlette will yet learn how to behave among us. She must be taught; she can't be expected to know it by herself." Still smiling, she accompanied us to the door. When we descended the steps, I turned around and looked at her. She was still standing in the entrance, smiling at me. I smiled back and went with Sister Marta to a new life, drawing confidence from the knowledge that I had one friend, at least, here in this Christian convent.

Sister Marta took me to a large hall — full of shelves. In

one corner sat a nun next to a sewing machine. She rose and approached us, and Sister Marta introduced me to her. "This is Arlette, a new pupil. Please fit her with clothes."

The nun pulled out a measuring tape and began to measure me from all sides. "How old are you, Arlette?"

"I'm eleven."

"Eleven?!" the nun was astonished. "How can that be? You look like an eight year old! When were you born?" I was happy that they hadn't changed my birthday; otherwise, I wouldn't have been able to answer.

The nun drew near to one of the shelves and took down clothes. "Measure these clothes against you," she said. I put them against myself, and she looked me over. In the end she decided the clothes fit me.

"You'll wear these clothes here from now on," she commanded me. Right then and there, I undressed and put on the new clothing while the nun supervised. First, I put on some warm, comfortable underwear. On top of that went a white, sleeveless full slip and above that a long, black dress. There was a large pocket in the slip, but you had to lift up your dress to reach it. It was strange. The nun gave me black, thick tights, and shiny black shoes. "You have to make sure that your shoes are always shined," she warned me, "and take care of your clothes so they'll always be clean and orderly." She chose some other clothes for me and wrapped them in a package. "These are your other clothes," she explained. "This is your nightgown, and this is your holiday dress." Everything was black.

My own clothes, which Mrs. Salsky had packed for me, were taken away with the clothes I had been wearing when I came. Here, there were no personal clothes. Everyone wore the same thing, and everything was black. The building was full of light, light which I had been longing for so much — but everything else was black.

They changed my name, they changed my parents, religion and clothes. Everything looked black. Maybe this black would help me remember the details of my new life, I thought, and help me also remember what I must not mention — but must not forget.

I left the storage room with Sister Marta, lost in reflection. Here I must remain, behind the tall wall. I have to be in this place, and live like a Christian. I have to pretend I'm a goy to save myself, so I can live, because Papa commanded me to live. But Papa also commanded me never to forget that I'm a Jew. So what should I do? I have no one to ask, no one to give me advice. I must live! I don't have anywhere else to be. Sister Lucie explained that I can't run away because I wouldn't be able to survive outside the convent's wall.

Sister Marta opened a door and we entered a classroom. All the girls stood up in honor of the nun, and the teacher — who wasn't wearing black — approached us. Sister Marta introduced me to all the girls of the class. "This is the new pupil. Her name is Arlette Vanderlas. Accept her properly and treat her as you should. She is one of you." Afterwards, in a whisper, she told the teacher that I was very frightened, and instructed her not to ask me questions.

I looked at the girls. They were arranged in three rows in the classroom. There were four tables in each row, and two girls sat at every table. I saw several empty places, but the thing that struck me the most was the color black. Everyone wore black dresses like mine.

They sat me next to a girl dressed in black. They told me

her name, but I didn't catch it. I was shaking as I sat down. Tears filled my eyes, but I tried not to cry. What was I doing here? I had come from total isolation and heavy darkness to an airy room full of light and girls my age — and I wanted to run away! I would have been happy to return to that terrible darkness, to the cellar — anywhere, just not here.

The girl sitting next to me whispered something, but I wasn't able to listen. I was too involved in my confusing thoughts. What a terrible dilemma I faced! Should I live here as a Christian, or remain a Jew and die? What should I do? Could I live here like a *goy* until the end of the war — and then when Maman would come to take me back I would live like a Jew again? Was it possible? Would Maman want to take me back if I was living like a Christian in a convent?

# 17
# I Don't Want to Die

The teacher's voice droned on in the background, but I didn't hear a thing. Everything around me was black and inside I felt a black, cold dread. Frightening thoughts preyed on my mind. Maybe it is better to die than to live as a Christian? Maybe I should run away, and if they kill me, at least I'll die a Jew? Papa commanded me to live, but he also begged me not to forget that I'm a Jewish girl! So what should I do? I don't want to die. I don't want to die.

When the bell had rung, all the girls got up. Only I remained sitting. The teacher, Mademoiselle Vermeul, approached me. "What's your name?" she asked congenially. I almost said Anna, but I caught myself. I bit my tongue in fright, and finally recovered enough to whisper, "Arlette."

I wondered if the teacher knew of my true identity. The nun had whispered something to her, and I heard only part of what she said. I scrutinized the teacher's face, trying to read her expression. But her expression didn't seem to be out of the ordinary.

"Girls, don't bother Arlette with questions now," Mademoiselle Vermeul said. "Leave her alone until she gets used to the place. It doesn't look like she feels so good."

That was the truth. I didn't feel good. I was scared and confused. But the teacher's request didn't help. As soon as she left the classroom, all the girls jumped on me, forming a threatening black circle around me. They were all taller than me. A volley of questions fell on me from all sides: “What’s your name? Where are you from? Who are your parents? Why did they bring you here? What happened to you? What’s going on outside? How is the war going?”

So many questions! Tears blurred my vision and the group of girls turned into one large mass. The only thing I saw was the black of their clothes. Apparently, I had become very pale. One of the girls must have called the teacher, because suddenly she was next to me, shooing the girls away.

“Tomorrow, tomorrow you can ask her everything,” she admonished them. “Today she needs to rest. She came from far away, and she’s very tired. Leave her alone, don’t you see what you did to her?”

Good Mademoiselle Vermeul helped me out of my chair, and led me out of the classroom. She took me to a corner of another large room. The women there were dressed in colorful clothes. I assumed they were teachers. She gave me a cup of tea, and told me, “Drink!” I didn’t want to drink, but I didn’t dare refuse. It was simpler to drink a little than to explain that I was choking on a lump in my throat. I forced myself to swallow, and the hot drink slowly swished down my throat.

I heard the bell again. Mademoiselle Vermeul had left me in the corner with my drink while she chatted with her friends. When the bell rang, she returned to me. She took the cup from my hand and placed it on the table. We returned together to the class, and she reminded me where I sat. The girls stood up in her honor and she asked them again, “Please, leave Arlette alone today. You can ask her questions tomorrow.”

The girls left me alone, in the meantime. Until tomorrow — and what would happen tomorrow? How would I remember the right answers? How could I avoid saying the wrong things? I must make signs that will help me remember my new name — Arlette Vanderlas. What kind of name is that? I don't know anyone called Arlette. None of my friends — Jewish or non-Jewish — were called Arlette. I have never, ever heard that name!

I remember all of them, all of my friends from school. Not one of them was Arlette. Neither were any of the children in our building, nor any of my friends from the Jewish school — the girls my age, the older ones, or the younger ones. I remember all of them. Where are they now, my Jewish friends? What's happening to them? They're probably hiding in closets and in dark cellars. Maybe there are a few who reached a convent, like me? Maybe some are even here, in this convent? And what happened to those who couldn't hide? And what about Meir? No! I must even stop thinking of his name! I have to remember other names now. Alyssa and Pavel are my parents. How can I remember that? And my last name: Vanderlas. A typical gentile name. Vanderlas. If I forget these names, they'll kill me. And Papa — my real Papa — commanded me to live.

Papa, my dear Papa, where are you? Did it ever occur to you that I would end up in such a situation? That to live, I would have to deny being a Jewish girl? This is who I am, the most important thing I am!

I'm now an only child: Arlette, the daughter of Alyssa and Pavel Vanderlas. I'm happy that they didn't give me brothers and sisters, so I won't have to remember more names and details. Meir, my dear brother, my only brother! I have to forget you, to forget that I have such a precious, beautiful brother like you.

At least I still "live" in Brussels. My new address isn't much different than my real one: just a few houses from our house. That's because we live in a mixed neighborhood, and not in a Jewish neighborhood.

The ring of the bell broke into my reverie and my efforts to review the details of my new life: my name, and the names of my parents, the name of the school where I learned. I must not get confused or speak hesitantly, I thought. I must not hesitate for even a second when I'm asked about my life before I came to the convent.

The school day was over and Mademoiselle Vermeul went home. A nun entered the class. This was Sister Danielle, the nun responsible for our class. "Are you the new girl?" she turned to me. "What's your name?"

"Arlette Vanderlas," I replied, satisfied that I had supplied the right answer immediately. Sister Danielle pointed at my package of black clothes that was on the shelf and instructed me to take them. Everyone stood up, and I did too. We formed pairs and marched in a straight line to the dining room.

We were walking down a wide corridor lined with doors on both sides. I peeked into some of the open doors and discovered other classrooms. Another class of girls, led by a nun, walked in front of us. They, like us, were also arranged in pairs. The corridor led to a wide, tall lobby. Round windows looked down upon us, and opposite us — a wide entrance with a rounded top. This was the entrance to the dining room.

We entered the enormous, magnificent room. Light

flooded the room, pouring in through the many windows. Elaborate stained-glass designs decorated the tops of the windows. Many tables were arranged in rows and colorful tablecloths bedecked each one. Amid all that color though, I saw lots of dominant black — all the girls seated at the tables were dressed in morbid black. A nun sat at the head of each table. Several tables were empty.

Sister Danielle held my hand the entire time. The girls in my class sat around two tables, and an unfamiliar nun sat at the head of one of them. Then I had an awkward moment. Sister Danielle didn't sit down. Still holding my hand, she stepped onto a small, raised platform in the center of the hall. In the silence that reigned, her voice rang out clearly. "Girls, this is Arlette, your new friend. Please receive her nicely!"

The girls clapped their hands and turned to look at me. Hundreds of eyes gazed at me, and I felt myself blushing. I lowered my head in embarrassment, but Sister Danielle put her hand under my chin and whispered, "Lift your head; there is no reason to be embarrassed. It's better to let the girls see you now, instead of every one coming to see you separately."

In the meantime, more classes had arrived, and soon all the tables filled up. Sister Danielle sat me next to her, at the head of the table, and then the ceremony began. Everyone bent their head, held their hands together and prayed. I noticed that the girls were peeking at me, even though their heads were lowered. They were praying, but they kept sneaking glances at me. I put my hands together and moved my lips. Everyone prayed aloud, and I didn't know what they were saying. They would tolerate that I was only moving my lips — it was only my first day. They would assume that I was still embarrassed to make my voice heard. But what about tomorrow and the next day? I have to learn everything quickly, so as not to be different! I looked worriedly at Sister Danielle, and she nodded her head, as if to say, "Don't worry. Everything will be alright." I calmed down.

When the prayer ended, the sign was given to begin eating. I was starved — I had only drunk a cup of tea in Sister Lucie's room that morning, and afterwards, just a few gulps of tea that Mademoiselle Vermeul had offered me. Every girl had a plate in front of her and a few slices of bread. A soup tureen stood in the center of the table, and Sister Danielle served us all. The only thing that broke the silence around us was the clatter of spoons hitting bowls. It appeared that one must not talk during the meal.

The soup and slices of bread were quickly gone. I ate my entire portion and was still hungry. From the whispering around me, I understood that other girls were hungry too, but Sister Danielle silenced them with a harsh look. Again, at a signal, everyone rose and left the dining room in orderly pairs. Every class left separately, accompanied by the nun responsible for it.

A new, unfamiliar nun approached me, and motioned to me to come with her.

# 18 Large Crosses

We approached the steps. I caught my breath! I had never seen such enormous steps or staircase before! The stairwell was as wide as a ballroom, and as tall as all four floors of the convent. It seemed to me that if we would put our entire apartment building in this stairwell, we would still have enough room for another building. The polished wooden floor shone. A decorative brass fixture topped the entire length of the wooden railing. The brass glittered and shone like gold. Magnificent chandeliers hung everywhere. Artwork and pictures hung on the walls. What size, what breadth! Everything shone and glittered and sparkled. I stood immobile at the bottom of the staircase and looked around me in astonishment.

The nun accompanying me apparently understood how I felt and didn't rush me along. She stood and waited patiently. "Nice, isn't it?" she asked with a smile.

"Yes," I replied. "I never saw such a beautiful place! It's like the palaces described in stories! How can someone live in such a beautiful place? Who polishes and shines all this?"

The nun smiled again. "You'll get used to living among all this luxury, and soon you won't even notice it!" I didn't believe her. Would I get used to it and not notice it? How is that possible? I was afraid to step down or touch anything, lest I ruin the shine.

"Come, Arlette, your bedroom is on the second floor. Let's go." She offered me her hand again and we ascended the stairs. On the second floor, we turned into a wide corridor, as sunny as the corridor below. Here too there were doors on both sides of the corridor. All the doors were closed, and a small copper plaque with writing on it hung on each door. The nun opened the fourth door. "Here is your group's bedroom."

The room was large and high, with narrow, long windows on the tops of the walls. The windows began at approximately a distance of five feet from the floor. I couldn't even reach the windowsill... Many beds were made, and a small closet stood next to each bed. The room was pleasant enough, but then, unintentionally, something caught my eye. A large cross hung above every bed!

"Here is your bed, Arlette, and this is your closet," the nun's voice was cheerful. "Come, put your clothes here."

I didn't react. I remained frozen in place, repulsed by the cross. The nun approached me and took the bundle of clothes from my hand. She opened it and began to straighten out the wrinkled clothes and fold them nicely. I didn't help her. I stood there like stone, my eyes bearing revulsion and fear for the large cross over my bed. How would I be able to sleep under it?

I began to cry, and the nun patted my head and waited quietly. After I had calmed down a little, she gently asked me to arrange the clothes in the closet. With shaking hands I did as commanded, tears still streaming down my face.

"Don't worry, Arlette. You'll get used to things here quickly. The girls in your room are good girls, and with time, you'll become good friends with them," the nun said. She must have thought that I was alarmed by the number of girls I'd be sharing a room with. She didn't imagine that that was the only thing that made me happy; I would never be alone in the dark again! It didn't occur to her that my tears were prompted by the large, threatening cross.

"Come, now we'll leave. During the day, you are not allowed in this room — it's a bedroom, only to be used at night."

We left the large, cold, unwelcoming room and turned into another corridor, also long, but not as wide as the previous one. This corridor also had doors on every side. We entered one of the doors and came to the homework room.

"How will I know where each room is? How will I remember?" I asked worriedly. "How can I not become confused between all the halls, rooms and corridors? How do you always know which is the right door to open?"

"With time you'll get used to it and see that it's not complicated," the nun tried to assure me." It's only frightening in the beginning, but afterwards you'll learn to manage."

I didn't believe her. "How can I? Everything here is big and huge!"

"You're right," the nun agreed. "Everything here is big and huge. This is a huge convent — spread over very large grounds. Now you see only this building, but we have several other buildings as big as this one, and some small houses, yards and gardens and many other things. I am not familiar with the entire convent either, and I've been here for five years. But you'll get to know the building where you live pretty well. There's nothing to worry about."

The homework room had many tables. Four girls sat at

each table writing busily. The room was, of course, big and high. Narrow, long windows began at the height of the ceiling in a normal room. Bright light streamed into the room from the windows — cozy, bright daylight. The walls were painted with a very light sky blue color, and the floor was made of polished wood. All the wooden tables also shone with a dazzling shine. Everything here was enormous, tall and shiny. People seemed to be swallowed up in this expanse. I felt myself tiny, and everyone else in the room looked tiny, like elves in a land of giants.

There was a desk and a high-backed chair in the center of the room. Sister Danielle sat there. She could see all the girls from her seat. Sister Danielle was a tall woman, but even she appeared dwarfed. Everyone seemed tranquil and calm — the size of the place only bothered me. It seemed normal to them.

Sister Danielle approached us, thanked the nun that accompanied me, and took me to an empty place which would be my seat from now on. I sat down and she brought me a book, notebook and pencil from a large closet that stood in a corner. She gave me some writing exercises to test my scholastic abilities. All the girls stopped their writing to stare at me, but as soon as Sister Danielle returned to her place, they stuck their heads back in their notebooks.

Preparing the homework was easy. I quickly finished my writing exercises, and then received math problems, which were also easy. It seemed that my long stay in the dark hadn't affected my intelligence.

When everyone finished writing, Sister Danielle collected all the notebooks and sat at her table checking everyone's work . We remained sitting with folded hands until she had finished. Every so often she would call over one of the girls to comment on her work. The girls whispered among themselves, but without making a sound — just moving their lips.

After a while, Sister Danielle called my name. "I see that you solved the math problems correctly, and your writing skills are excellent as well. Continue on," she said in a stiff voice without a smile, as if she had chided me for my level of knowledge, instead of the opposite.

The signal was given and all of us rose in an orderly fashion, formed pairs and left the room. We were always in order, always in pairs, always according to a signal. We could not even sit before a signal was sounded. We entered another room — very much like the room we had left, but this one had more closets. This was the sewing room. In this room, only two girls sat at each table, so there would be room for their sewing materials.

The girl sitting at my table smiled warmly at me. "My name is Janet," she said. "My bed is next to your bed." I looked at her but didn't answer her.

"I know how you are feeling," Janet said. "I came here just two months ago. I was the same way during the first few days; I didn't want to speak, I was scared of everything, from this huge place. I wanted to run back home. But you'll get used to it, you'll see."

She thinks she understands, but she's a Christian. What does she understand! I'm a Jew who has to get used to living here among gentiles.

# 19
# A Little Girl in a Big Convent

I looked around the room. The girls were busy with various crafts: sewing, knitting and embroidering. I began daydreaming about the large tablecloth that Maman had embroidered in honor of Shabbos. She had also fashioned special embroidered cloths for the buffet, the radio, and even the windowsills for Shabbos, and other ones for the weekday. Our brown sofa also had embroidered pillows. Maman was an expert embroiderer and her work was magnificent. Where were her exquisite tablecloths and intricately designed pillows now? She had packed all of her creations in a bag and sold them, and she had given the money to Mrs. Salsky. In exchange, Mrs. Salsky was supposed to watch over me in the cellar of her house. But Mrs. Salsky brought me here to the convent. After the war, when Maman will come to take me, she won't find me. Even if Mrs. Salsky tells her where I am, she won't know that my name was changed to Arlette Vanderlas. How will she find me?

Tears ran down my cheeks and I didn't know if I was crying from longing or hunger. Maybe both of them together. And exactly then, as if it had come on invitation, they brought us food: a piece of bread spread with jam and a cup of water. The food revived me. It's interesting — in Mrs. Salsky's cellar I had eaten very little and wasn't hungry. But in the convent, I wanted to eat all the time. Maybe the air and the light whetted my appetite.

The sewing class ended. We all sat quietly, our hands folded, while the monitors collected our work and put them in each girl's private cubby hole. We arranged ourselves in pairs and went to the yard. A large yard, full of light, air and space. I wanted to run, to spread my hands to the heavens, to jump and exult! But I sat on a stone at the side. All the girls ran and played, and I sat alone on the stone, letting the sun's warming rays wash over me, filling my body with the light it so craved.

When it was time to go inside, we again formed a straight line of pairs, and marched to the dining hall. We all sat down silently, placed our hands together, lowered our heads and prayed. I did as the others did, but I didn't say anything. I felt the nun's eyes fixed on me. Did she realize that I merely moved my lips? The other girls had already finished their prayers and were now waiting patiently with folded hands in total silence for the signal that would let them begin eating. But the signal wasn't given. I thought it might have been my fault that everyone was kept waiting. Maybe they had seen that I didn't really pray. I was very hungry. The bowl of porridge and the slice of bread beckoned to me from the table. I well knew which blessing I must recite before eating — the *berachah* of *ha-motzi*. But how could I say Hashem's Name in the convent, opposite all these Christian symbols? One may only say non-Jewish prayers in the convent. If I didn't learn to pray like them, they wouldn't let me eat. Was it because of me that they wouldn't let the other girls eat?

Suddenly the signal was given, without an apology or explanation about the long wait. Each girl took her spoon in her right hand and her slice of bread in her left, and began eating. No one said anything to me about saying the prayer, and I also ate like everyone else. Tomorrow, tomorrow I'll learn to pray like them, I promised myself, and then they won't hold back food from the others because of me.

When we finished eating, we remained seated without uttering a word. I looked at the other girls — they seemed content, not upset at all. Maybe they have to sit and wait here for every single thing, and it wasn't my fault? Finally, a signal was given — the nun who sat on the raised platform at the front of the hall clapped her hands. I thought that we would all leave the dining room, but something else happened: the girls stretched out their hands to each other, and began singing a very pretty song. I wasn't familiar with the song, but the cheerful, uplifting tune raised my spirits. My acute feelings of fear and anxiety completely melted away. The girls sang happily, swaying back and forth, with their arms linked. Could it be that here, too, among the girls dressed in black, there were songs and happiness?

We did everything in rows and pairs. We didn't go anywhere alone — the only time we didn't need a partner was in the yard, where it was permitted to run wild alone. Now we left the dining room for the bedroom in a straight row. In any case, that's what I thought — but the nun who led us thought differently. In her opinion, the row wasn't straight enough, and she began to shout. I trembled with fear, and Sybil, the girl standing next to me, held my hand to calm me down. I would have to get used to this too.

In the bedroom, each girl went straight to her bed, took out her nightgown and headed to the nearby bathroom. I remained standing in the middle of the room, until Janet approached me, took my hand and brought me to my bed. "Here, this is your bed. Take your nightgown and come with me," she said. I followed her and did exactly what I was told. I wasn't able to think for myself.

In the bathroom, girls were in various stages of washing up and getting dressed. The nun stood next to a white basin of water, and a row of girls were lined up near her. They even stood in rows as they waited to wash. Janet pulled me into line, in front of her. When my turn came, the nun unbraided my long braids and told me in an icy voice, "Your hair will soon be cut. You can't stay here with such long hair. We have no way to take care of it."

After she washed us, we put on our nightgowns and went back to the cold bedroom. I wanted to climb into bed and warm up under the blanket, but not yet; we couldn't go into our beds. First we had to pray. Every girl bent down on her knees, put her hands together and prayed out loud.

I bent down on my knees like everyone else, but I began to cry. I asked Hashem to forgive me for this bowing down, for this gentile way of praying, and for looking at the cross opposite me. Then I recited *Kerias Shema* by heart. "'*HaMalach ha-go'el osi mi-kol ra* — The angel who redeemed me...' Don't look at what's going on around me, redeem me from all evil! Please Hashem, watch over me in this place of impurity! Watch over Papa, Maman and Meir!"

The nun walked around the room, passing by each girl and checking how each one was praying. When she approached me, she saw I was crying, and patted me on the head.

Who needs your patting? Get out of here! I thought in my heart. But she remained next to me and continued to pat me without saying a word. I thanked her silently that she did only that. If she insisted on standing next to me, at least she didn't ask me to pray out loud — because I was praying to the Creator of the world, and not to that accursed cross!

After what seemed like eternity, the nun left me. She gave the signal and everyone rose. We were finally allowed to get into bed! The nun pulled up a chair and sat down. Apparently, she stayed here in the room until the girls fell asleep.

I pulled the blanket over my head and let the tears flow freely. Papa dear, look what I have above my head — a cross! It's so large and threatening. Papa, I'm in captivity among gentiles. Papa, Maman, where are you? Why did the non-Jewish woman who brought me here tell Sister Lucie that my parents and brother disappeared? You didn't disappear! You're only hiding in the attic!

Papa, how will I live here among these nuns? They want me to bow down and pray this nonsense. Papa, what should I do?

It was very cold. I shuddered, and my teeth clacked together noisily. If the nun would hear my chattering, she would immediately come to pat me. I didn't want her next to me, so I tried — unsuccessfully — to stop my chattering. I stuck a piece of the blanket into my mouth, between my teeth, hoping to stop the noise. I couldn't leave my bed and get dressed — the nun would see me. My feet were like two blocks of ice; I really wanted to put on socks. I curled up and began to rub my feet together in an effort to warm them. But who cares about that anyway? What really matters is the cross. In this convent, I'll have to live like a gentile until the end of the war, and who knows when it will be over?

Oh, Papa, Maman, come already! Take me away from here! I wanted to stay with you, to be with the family... Why aren't you coming to save me?

The pillow under my head was drenched with tears. It wasn't my pillow. My beloved pillow had stayed with Mrs. Salsky. How I wished I had it, a reminder from my home! I lifted my head and saw a small light shining near the door. I was happy they left a light on all night. I noticed that the nun's chair was empty. She had probably thought everyone was sleeping, so she left the room. I no longer had to worry that someone would hear my teeth chattering. I turned the pillow over to the other side that wasn't wet, and I closed my eyes tightly. But it didn't help. The tears continued to flow.

Suddenly Papa was standing next to me, his entire body trembling, stretching out a hand and saying, "Chanah'le, do everything you can to live. The main thing is to remain alive! After the war, you will live among Jews again. You must live!"

It wasn't a dream. I wasn't sleeping. I knew that Papa wasn't here, even though I could see him clearly and I heard every word that he told me. "Papa, how are you able to appear before me?" I whispered. "Where are you now? Papa, look, I have a cross over my head! I'm captive in the hands of gentiles!"

In the morning, my eyes were red and puffy and my head hurt. My rasping cough had become worse during the night I had spent in bitter weeping. No one mentioned anything about it, however. Apparently, they were used to girls crying at night.

We got dressed and went to the church — a very large place with high ceilings. The church's floor was made of large, smooth stones, and the high windows were of stained glass. We bent down on our knees and prayed a very long prayer. When the prayers were finally over, we formed straight rows and went to the dining room. I wasn't hungry at all, but I was afraid not to eat. I forced the food down my throat — I didn't even know what I ate.

Again, we formed a straight row in pairs and proceeded to the classroom. I felt I was in a kind of dream, as if only part of me was there. My main self was somewhere else, far, far away. I sat down in the same place where I had sat the day before. Several girls tried to speak to me, but I didn't hear what they said. I was seeing things as if through a transparent screen — I saw their lips moving, but I heard nothing. I felt like I was in a bubble, as if only I was real, and everything around me was just a figment of my imagination.

The teacher entered and the girls rose respectfully. The girl who sat next to me saw that I wasn't moving, and she pulled me up. When everyone sat down, she pushed me down as if I was a rag doll.

The teacher, Mademoiselle Vermeul, saw my state and approached me. She patted me, put her hand under my chin, and lifted my face up. "How are you doing, Arlette? Did you sleep at night?"

Her gentle, warm voice penetrated the transparent screen around me, and I heard her words. "No, I didn't sleep," I replied, and burst into bitter sobbing. "I don't want to be here. I don't feel good. I'm cold. I'm sad. I feel awful here!"

Mademoiselle Vermeul hugged me and tried to comfort me. "You will yet see, Arlette, that you'll slowly get used to it. It's not that terrible here. It will take time, maybe a lot of time, but eventually you'll get used to this place and like it. You may even like it a lot!" She spoke warmly, and I could see that she really cared about me. I felt better, and stopped crying.

But I didn't participate in the class; I didn't listen at all. I had no desire to study there. I didn't want to take any part in the life of the convent. Even during recess I sat on the side and didn't play. My sewing and needlework, the craft I had once excelled in and enjoyed so much, remained as it was; my hands did not touch it.

Where everyone went, I also went. When everyone sat, I sat. But I didn't participate in any activity. I was only active in the dining room: in general, I was hungry and ate everything. This is how I passed the days. The nights were much harder. Though I was exhausted, I was plagued with sleeplessness. Every night I lay awake, consumed by longing and fear, fear of this place, fear of the cross over my head. Afterwards, during the day, I was tired and irritable. If any of the girls spoke to me, I would burst out in tears — regardless of what she had said.

The girls tried to become friendly with me, but I rejected their overtures. Maman's warnings echoed in my memory: "Don't play with non-Jewish friends; don't become close to them! It's enough that according to the law you have to attend school with them." Maman didn't approve of my non-Jewish friends. She was happy when Breta left me at the outset of the war, and I became friendly with Chanah, a Jewish girl. It's better to keep as much of a distance as possible from non-Jews, she had said.

In the convent, though, I was surrounded by non-Jewish girls. They wanted to be my friend, and I didn't want them. I was also afraid that if I would chat with them, I might, *chas v'shalom*, get confused and say something which didn't fit with "my" past, or accidentally mention something from my real past. I must live in deceit, to tell lies. A mistake might cost me my life, and also Sister Lucie's life — the head nun who had taken me in despite knowing my origin. She pitied me and offered to help me — and she doesn't deserve death because of it, as she had told me on the first day in the convent.

I reminded myself frequently of Sister Lucie's words. The convent was my protection from death. I knew I shouldn't run away, I knew I had to stay there. I didn't have a choice. I had to adapt to my surroundings, to be like everyone, even though it was hard. I had to adjust even though there were things that bothered me a lot, like the cross above my head.

The cross frightened me terribly. I was constantly afraid it would fall on me. I was afraid to lie down under it. When I did fall asleep, the cross tormented me in my dreams. I would envision it falling off the wall, its long bar poking me. Then I would wake up in a cold sweat, shuddering. I had some respite during the day, when I was far away from that cross. Even though I was surrounded by other crosses, I wasn't so worried. Every convent is full of them. I compared them to worms infesting a house — worms crawling on the walls, on the furniture, and even embroidered on the curtains. I would imagine them crawling toward me, wriggling their legs at me. I knew that it wasn't really happening, but I still felt an intense repugnance for them. I would try stopping my imagination — my visions only made life much harder. But I couldn't. I was captive to those images which I had spun myself.

# 20 Sunday

Sunday in the convent was different than the other days of the week. On Sunday, we wore different clothes — our holiday clothes, which were also black, of course. But our Sunday dresses had a large, hand-knitted white collar. We also wore black hats —held in place by two hat pins. We wore the hat in church. The nuns wore a black hat with a large white covering hanging down in the front. The entire week, we looked like black spiders from head to toe. On Sunday, with our white collars, we looked like dressed-up spiders...

We went to pray in the convent's large church. There were two entrances to the church — one facing the street, for the many people from the area who came to pray, and another from the direction of the convent. All the convent girls, nuns, and convent workers entered through that one.

On that first Sunday I began thinking about escape. If one day I decide to run away, I thought, I'll run away from here, from the church, through the entrance that faces the street. I knew that at that moment, it was impossible, but I still harbored thoughts that maybe, one day, I'd escape. The church was packed. We stood in a group, separate from the other worshipers. I was sure no one would immediately notice if I'd run away. I figured they would only realize I was gone at the end of the prayers, when the girls would form rows to go to the dining room.

Throughout the entire prayer session, which took a long time, I thought about my "escape." We were in the church for hours, and most of the time we were down on our knees with our hands pressed together. I lifted my head slightly and scrutinized the people. I was hoping to find a kind face, someone who appeared sufficiently reliable that I could plan my escape with him. Which of these people might help me? I wondered. And how could I speak with one of them without the nuns noticing it? And from where would I get normal clothes? If I'd leave here in the convent's clothes, anyone who sees me would send me right back here.

And so I made my plans, one more fanciful than the other, and of course, none of which could be put into action. I knew that, but despite that, I continued planning and dreaming of escape.

My knees were red and painful from the daily kneeling in the small church where we prayed during the week — only the girls and the nuns together with the priest — and kneeling every evening next to my bed. The small church had a rough, wooden floor, and it pricked my knees. The large church, where we prayed on Sundays, had a very cold, marble floor. I tried folding my long dress under my aching knees, to provide some degree of padding, but it didn't help much. Just when I felt I couldn't bear it any longer, the signal was finally given to rise.

The boys of the church choir stood behind the priest, and sang in perfect unison, accompanied by a huge musical instrument. I had never seen an instrument like that and had never heard such melodious sounds. The songs and music calmed me down. I sat on the bench listening to the music and felt tranquil.

When the choir finished singing, everyone approached the priest. He stood next to a large square booth called the "altar" and placed a small wafer right into each person's mouth. I didn't approach him. Everyone thought I was a Protestant, and didn't want to take the wafer which was only for Catholics. If they only knew who I was...

When everything finally finished, we walked in orderly rows to the dining room. The tables were set festively, with nice tablecloths and individual napkins. There were even flowers on each table. I gazed at the girls seated around the tables, bedecked in their holiday dresses with the white collars. The spotless white collars contrasting with the stark black dresses also added to the festive atmosphere. Although I didn't want to admit it, the scene was very pretty. The meal was also special. We received thick soup, meat, vegetables, and an unidentifiable compote which was delicious. I devoured everything with relish — innocently enjoying the non-kosher food. I didn't know what kind of meat it was; I didn't even think about where it came from. I was happy that at least once a week they gave us good food in abundance, and not the measly portions like the other days.

There were no regular classes on Sunday. After lunch, several classes gathered together in a large, pleasant room. The room was bright, warm and comfortable. Here the priest stood in the front of the room and told us stories with a religious theme. I didn't listen. I sidled up close to the electric heaters, enjoying their warmth. Let the priest speak about whatever he wants, I thought. What do I care? All that mattered to me was that I wasn't hungry or cold, and I had light and air. How I wished I could have brought Meir here!

But there were only girls in the convent, no boys.

After the priest's stories, we went on a trip. My heart skipped a beat — I was so excited. A trip! I was sure that we would go outside, beyond the imposing convent walls. But that didn't happen. We simply visited one of the many wings on the convent grounds. There were so many wings in the convent, that even if we would have taken a trip every day, it would have taken us a few months to visit them all.

We entered a huge hall full of antique furniture. Beautiful artwork lined the walls, and tiles were arranged in interesting patterns on the floor. An old, toothless priest acted as our tourguide and told us about the various paintings, pieces of furniture, and even the history behind the tile designs. It was hard to understand him, but the hall and its contents were beautiful and interesting even without explanations.

When we returned from our walk, we were led to the music room. I recognized several musical instruments, including the large musical instrument which I had seen that morning in church. They called it an organ. The music teacher did not live in the convent — she was from "outside." Mademoiselle Shriver was an elderly, cheerful woman, who had an ever-present smile on her lips and dimples on both cheeks. Mademoiselle Shriver taught us new songs, and was very happy when we picked them up quickly and sang on tune. When she heard me sing, she clapped her hands with delight. "You sing beautifully! I'll put you in the choir — we're missing a voice just like yours. How wonderful!"

I loved to sing. In our house, we always sang together. But in a choir? I never had an opportunity like this. At home, Papa and Maman had spoken about the possibility of Meir joining the *shul* choir. And here, they had a choir for girls!

Yes, in the frightening and terrible convent they had one good thing, a marvelous thing! I had been invited to sing in a choir! For me, this was a ray of light in my dark sorrow. The other girls noticed my happiness, and told Mademoiselle Shriver that this was the first time since I came to the convent that they saw me smiling. Until that point, they had only seen me crying and crying.

"With the help of music, one can penetrate all hearts, and make all the sorrowful happy," the teacher said, and smiled her charming smile.

Every good thing eventually comes to an end, and so did the music lesson. We continued on to the homework room, where we received bread and jam — as we did every day. Afterwards, we went out to play in the yard for the short time that remained before bedtime. So that was Sunday: long prayers, a good meal, an outing, a music lesson, and free play in the yard.

But once every four weeks, there was a change in the routine. Every fourth Sunday was a visiting day.

# 21
# Visiting Day

Visiting day on Sunday! The girls were very excited from the moment they woke up. Every girl was on her best behavior, so she wouldn't lose the privilege of a visit or so that nothing bad would be reported to the guests. They smoothed their dresses down, combed their short hair again and again, and tried to shine their Sunday shoes even more so the brass buckle would shine like real gold. Everyone waited impatiently for guests. Most of the girls had close relatives — parents, brothers and sisters came to visit. A few girls also had grandparents who visited them. The girls who didn't have close family members at least had aunts or other relatives who visited them. Only for me no one would come.

Who would come visit me? Mrs. Salsky? That strange woman who brought me here? Besides them, who even knew where I was?

When visiting time arrived, I went into the Sunday room — the visiting room — with all the other girls. It had been cleaned and polished well for the occasion, and decorated with embroidered tablecloths and flowers from the large garden. Suddenly, Sister Louise approached me. She grasped my hand and took me out of the room. "Come with me," she said, as if I had a choice. I followed her up the stairs, climbing step after step — until we reached the top floor. We entered a medium-sized room. It was freezing cold.

"You'll remain here until all the visitors leave, and then I'll come to take you."

"Here? Alone? What will I do alone?"

"Find something to do. Here, there are books in this closet with nice stories about the early Christians and the life of Jesus. Read them and you'll enjoy them." Sister Louise left and locked the door behind her.

Intense fear washed over me. I banged on the door with clenched fists, and Sister Louise returned and opened it again. "Why did you lock me in here alone?" I sobbed. "I'm afraid! Please don't lock me in!"

"I have no choice, Arlette. It's visiting day. Everyone has visitors except for you. We can't have people noticing that, and therefore you must stay here, locked in."

"No! No! I'm scared!" I gripped her hand tightly. "Please don't lock the door," I pleaded.

"Don't be afraid; nothing will happen to you. I must lock it," she tried to free my hand from hers, but I wouldn't let go. "Then at least don't go," I asked her. "Stay here with me."

"I'm sorry, Arlette," Sister Louise began to lose her patience. "I have work to do, and you are holding me back. You must stay here alone until I come to take you."

"Then, please, at least don't lock the door! No one knows I'm here. I won't go out — I'll sit in the corner on this chair and won't move!" I promised emotionally. And to show her how nicely I could sit, I let go of her hand and sat down on the chair in the corner. Sister Louise quickly took advantage of the oppurtunity. In a split second, she slid outside and locked the door, and called out, "Don't be scared!"

But I *was* scared. My whole body quivered with fear. I stayed on the chair, gripping the back. I tried to think of something else to take my mind off the fact that I was again locked alone in a small room. My thought turned instantly to what was constantly on my mind: My family. Today is visiting day. Why didn't Papa and Maman come to visit me? They couldn't. They're afraid to leave the house. They're even afraid to go to the store, so how could they come here? Do they even know that I'm here? Maybe Mrs. Salsky told them. So who is going to the store to buy food? How are they living? Are they still hiding in the attic? Are Maman and Meir still covering themselves with charcoal and pieces of wood to hide? Maybe they found a different hideout for themselves?

Suddenly I heard a child's voice downstairs in the yard. Maybe it's Meir? I thought. My heart pounded wildly. Maybe Mrs. Salsky did tell them, and they found a way to visit me? So why didn't they call me, and take me out of here? My parents are looking for Anna; they don't know that I'm called Arlette here. How I wish I could look outside the window! But all the windows in the convent are very high. I can't reach them.

I dragged the table from its place and pushed it firmly against the wall with the window. Then I put a chair on it and climbed up. I still couldn't reach the window. I went down again and took out all the books that were in the closet. Sister Louise had told me that I could use all the books. I piled them up on the table and gingerly placed the chair on top of them. Then I climbed up again. This time I was able to see into the yard. The yard was full of people dressed in coats and hats. A child was shouting. He was wearing a dark blue coat and a fur hat. But it wasn't Meir. It didn't even look like him. Just a small gentile boy.

Disappointed, I continued looking down at everyone else's visitors. Suddenly, I heard footsteps in the corridor. I hurried down from my lookout, took the chair off the table and returned all the books to the closet. Then I pushed the table back to its place. It was suddenly heavy and made a lot of noise. I fervently hoped that no one would hear the noise. I arranged everything quickly and sat down primly on the chair, my hands folded and my heart pounding, waiting for the door to open and one of the nuns to scream at me. But nothing happened. No one came. I was alone, alone in the locked room.

I stood up and walked to the door. I jiggled the handle vigorously, again and again, but to no avail. The door was locked. I went back to my chair and sat down. But fear slithered back like a snake, its venomous fangs piercing my heart. Again, I found myself next to the door, knocking on it with all my might and shouting, "Open up, open the door!" A cold sweat covered me. I kept pounding on the door and screaming hysterically. My hand was sore from all the banging, and my throat hoarse from all the screams. I was sure they had forgotten me here in that dark room. I would have to stay there forever. I didn't know how much time had already passed... who would remember that a little girl was waiting, all alone, in a room on the top floor? They couldn't hear my screams or my banging. The convent walls were very thick and the heavy wooden doors were as strong as iron. It was impossible to hear me below.

Night had fallen. There were gas lamps on the walls, as there were in all the other rooms, but there weren't any matches. I searched desperately in every place possible. No matches. It was impossible to light the gas lamps. The darkness became thicker, and the room became black and threatening. I sat on the floor, exhausted, leaning my head against the door. Fear suffocated me, and I was completely wet from cold sweat. I was freezing cold. My teeth chattered loudly. That was the only sound I heard. I'll yet die here from the fear, I thought. The Germans won't kill me. The nuns who wanted to save me — they'll be the cause of my death.

When Sister Louise came to open the door, I was completely frozen, blue from cold, hoarse from shouting. My knuckles were bloody from knocking so vigorously and for so long.

"Arlette! What happened? I only closed you in for the two hours of the visit. Why do you take everything so hard?"

I couldn't answer her. I wasn't even able to stand up. She had to pick me up and carry me in her hands. I couldn't straighten my legs or hold up my head, which had fallen limply on her shoulder. Sister Louise took me down the stairs and brought me to the bedroom — next to the heater. Slowly, she undressed me, rubbed my frozen body, and dressed me in my nightgown. She had brought another nightgown from the storage room, a large sweater and two pairs of warm woolen socks. She dressed me up in all those layers, while I sat, immobile, where she had put me down. I wasn't able to move, speak or even cry.

Sister Louise lay me down in bed and covered me with several blankets. She stayed next to me the whole night, alternately rubbing my hands and feet. That night I came down with fever, and in the morning, they transferred me to the infirmary.

# 22
# The Wonderful Infirmary

Stretched out on a large, comfortable bed, I looked at my new surroundings. The infirmary was in a medium-sized room. There were only six beds there, and next to each bed was a small night table. A nun sat on a high-backed chair next to a larger table near the door. She stayed there throughout the day, reading, knitting, embroidering or sewing. At the side, between two windows, was a white porcelain sink with a shelf over it. On the shelf stood a large, white pitcher and next to it, a small pitcher and a white, embroidered towel.

Only one bed was occupied — the girl lying on it seemed to be sleeping. The other beds were empty and covered with woolen bedcoverings. My bed was large and wide. The pillow was also big, and the blanket was much thicker than my regular blanket. The room had two windows, and, although it was morning, the gas lamp above each bed was lit. Apparently, without the extra light the room would be dim. I liked what I saw in the room — the warm blankets and comfortable beds, the cozy lamps and cheery sunlight. But something seemed strange — something was missing. What was it? I wondered. What was in the bedroom that was not in the infirmary? In a flash, I realized what it was: there were no crosses above the beds! I was sitting in a convent bed and above my head there was only a burning lamp, no cross! My heart felt tremendous relief. I could sleep tranquilly there.

The nun got up from her chair and approached me. It was old Sister Zizu, who was responsible for the infirmary. She took my temperature and stroked me gently. Afterwards, she went to the second patient, who had woken up in the meantime, and took her temperature. "Wait here for me, Arlette and Henrietta," she said. "I'm going out for a minute. I'll be right back."

She returned with two cups of warm, sweet milk. I took a small sip — and didn't want the milk to finish. It was the most delicious drink I had ever drunk in the convent. "It tastes good, doesn't it?" Sister Zizu asked. "I put honey in the drink so you'll get healthy faster." She gave us pieces of sugar to suck on, and patted us again. Afterwards, she sat in the middle of the room, knitting, and told us stories. I didn't understand all the stories. They were more for Henrietta's age. She was one of the older girls who had been living in the convent for several years.

When the doctor appeared, he went straight to the sink. He poured some white liquid into the small pitcher and washed his hands with it. The white liquid had an acrid smell. Sister Zizu told me that it was a special disinfectant to destroy germs.

"Oh, so, this is Arlette the scaredy-cat," the doctor said, coming toward me. "They left her alone and she became sick, is that so? Come, let's get rid of your fears once and for all!"

I was frightened. What was he going to do to me? But his voice was friendly and he was smiling. He pulled a small, wrapped-up square out of his pocket. "Open your mouth," he commanded me. I was sure he was giving me some medicine, but it was something incredibly delicious and sweet. Chocolate! I was astonished! I looked at the doctor and he winked at me and smiled. Yes, it was chocolate — a candy from a different world. A treat from before the war.

The doctor checked me, left instructions with Sister Zizu, and washed his hands again before going to check Henrietta. He also gave her a candy, but when he turned away from her bed, his eyes had lost their twinkle. He had a serious, even sorrowful, look in his eyes. He washed his hands a third time, said good-bye and left.

Sister Zizu emptied the water in the sink, filled both of the pitchers with water and changed the towel. I calmly watched her. I liked the infirmary. A room without crosses, and with delicious, good food: Milk with honey and even chocolate! What else could one ask for? I wouldn't mind being sick for a long time.

When Sister Zizu gave me permission to leave my bed for a few minutes, I approached Henrietta's bed. She was pretty and very pale. Her face was the same color as my white pillow case. Even her golden hair seemed white. Her hand, which lay on the blanket, was thin and almost transparent. She smiled at me, but didn't let me come near. "Don't get any closer, Arlette. I have a serious illness and I don't want you to catch it from me, God forbid."

"But how can you have a serious illness? You're so pretty, your eyes are clear and blue like the pond near my house. I want to sit near you."

"No, you may not," Henrietta shook her head in refusal. She only let me stand at the edge of her bed. Sister Zizu was worried about the state of her health. She called Sister Lucie, the head nun, who came immediately. Sister Lucie sat down next to Henrietta, and they spoke quietly for a long time. I couldn't hear what they were saying.

Afterwards, Sister Lucie came to visit me. Her eyes were red and swollen. "You're crying?" I asked in fear, and she replied, "It's so difficult for me to see my angelic girls like this. Henrietta is an angel." I didn't understand what she meant, but I was too embarrassed to ask anything else.

Sister Lucie usually didn't have time — she was very busy. But here, in the infirmary, she had time and patience. "Arlette, I understand that you were very frightened," she said. "I know that you were locked in a dark room for several months. If I had known that Sister Louise would leave you in the room without light, I wouldn't have allowed it. We're trying very hard to help you. I want you to know: the small lamps that are lit in the bedrooms every night are lit only since you came to us. Before that, we didn't leave a light on at night. The nuns don't know it's because of you; I instructed them to leave a light on in every bedroom so no one would be suspicious. They must not know what you went through. They might become suspicious of your real origins." Sister Lucie looked at me with sincere worry. "I know that you cry a lot at night. You're always alone, you aren't friends with anyone, you don't participate in the lessons and you don't play. Please, Arlette, try to move forward and free yourself from this state. You're intelligent enough to understand that this is for your good. When your parents return after the war, I want them to find a healthy and happy girl. Look at you now — you are so emaciated and sad. Your parents won't be happy to see you that way. You must try to be like everyone else!"

Two days later Henrietta was taken to the hospital. She

didn't return to our room. Sometime later, after I had recovered, I tried to find out how she was doing. I asked Sister Danielle, and she told me that now Henrietta was a real angel, an angel in heaven. I understood that she was no longer among the living. Sister Danielle explained that Henrietta had been sick with tuberculosis. When she came to the convent years ago, after her mother's death, the illness had already been consuming her body. Sister Danielle told me that Henrietta's mother had also died of tuberculosis. Then I understood Sister Lucie's words when she had compared Henrietta to an angel. I remembered her gentle appearance as she lay in her bed in the infirmary — white and transparent, just like an angel.

I was in the infirmary for an entire week. The doctor came every day and gave me a chocolate and a merry wink. But on the day they took Henrietta to the hospital, I saw that his eyes were red, like those of all the nuns who had come to bid her farewell.

Sister Lucie also came to visit me every day. She sat at my bedside and spoke to me, encouraging me to change, urging me to behave as I should. "When you act withdrawn, you are only hurting yourself, Arlette. When you cry endlessly, you're the one who's suffering. You have to act mature and stop being different. You must try to get along with everyone, even if you don't like everything here. Even if there are things that frighten you, you're not a baby anymore."

Mademoiselle Vermeul also visited me every day after class. Instead of going home, she sat next to me and taught me privately what she had taught in class so I wouldn't fall behind in my studies. She wasn't worried about getting sick from me; she sat on my bed and hugged and kissed me, almost like a mother. It was so wonderful in the infirmary! I felt wanted and loved. On the day when the doctor announced I was healthy, and could be discharged from the infirmary, I was very sad. I wanted to continue being pampered. But the time had come to be like everyone else.

# 23
# Breta

The girls received me very nicely. They were happy that I had recovered, and I was also happy to be with them again. Not only had I recovered from my illness, but I had freed myself of the fears that had gripped me. Now, more than ever before, I allowed myself to belong. To be one of them.

While I was gone, a new girl, Breta, had arrived. I looked at her: a dark-complexioned child with large, dark eyes, full of sadness. Jewish eyes, so Jewish. I didn't ask her anything, I did not mention a word about her background or mine. But I immediately became friendly with her, and as a result, I managed to find friends among the other girls too. Until now had I felt alone. Different, out of place. I felt I didn't belong there among all those gentile girls. Now that Breta had arrived, it was easier for me to acclimate, because I wasn't the only Jewish girl there. Breta was with me. I sat next to her in class and in the sewing room. We became friends without speaking even one word about the past. It was better that way: better not to touch what was forbidden, not to jog cruel memories. I knew in my heart that Breta was a Jew, and she certainly knew that I was too, but we didn't speak about it.

I didn't know if Breta realized that because of her, I was finally able to integrate with the others. I did everything to help her acclimate to life in the convent, and this helped me as well. Breta didn't know of the difficulties I had before she arrived. I enjoyed being with her, and we only related to our present without touching on our past or future. I was afraid to speak about the past. And for some undefined reason, which I couldn't comprehend, I was even more afraid to talk about the future, about what would happen when the war would be over.

The barrier that surrounded me cracked open. Slowly, I began to participate in the various activities. The first thing I did was embroidery. Surrounded by other girls in the sewing room, I finally picked up my piece of fabric and the colored embroidery threads. I fingered the fabric, smoothed it down gently, and remembered Maman's motions when she had embroidered. Maybe I'll learn to embroider like Maman, I suddenly thought. Won't she be proud of me when she returns! With this encouraging thought, I began to embroider.

I began to show some interest in my studies too. Most of the lessons, however, revolved around their Catholic religion, and I had no intention of learning about that! Theirs was a religion of lies, of terror, a religion that perpetrated pogroms against my people — should I learn such a thing?! The girls in my class studied diligently — they had to memorize long sections of various Christian writings. I closed my heart during the lessons on religion so the impurity wouldn't infiltrate.

But I began to listen to the other lessons. A priest would teach the lessons on religion, but Mademoiselle Vermeul taught the general studies. She was happy to see me participating, and greatly encouraged me. The classes were on a rather low level, and didn't require any effort on my part. I participated, studied, and even enjoyed it.

In Mrs. Salsky's dark cellar, I had reviewed everything I had learned in school. I replayed all my classes in my mind, repeating the material over and over again, even though I couldn't learn anything new. In that formidable darkness, I longed for my studies. But those longings paled next to my fierce longings for Papa, Maman and Meir, and my deep desire for light and air. Without light and fresh air, it is very difficult to live. Down in the cellar, I realized that it was possible, but very hard. Without studies, one can certainly live. But once I began studying again, I felt how much I had missed learning.

Every afternoon, we did our homework under Sister Danielle's supervision. We had to sit and write everything down properly. Sister Danielle was very particular about our behavior while we did our homework. We had to raise our hands and receive her permission to speak or to leave our seats, just like in class. After the homework session, there was an hour of handiwork. I was progressing very well in embroidery, and I let myself enjoy it — I enjoyed the actual embroidery, but I also liked the class because I knew Maman would be happy to see my work at the end of the war.

I also got used to the rules in the dining room. I learned to mumble the right words before eating like everyone else. Inwardly, in my heart, I said the blessing of *ha-motzi*. The portions were small but fixed; we weren't full, but we also weren't hungry. The food was sufficient to keep us alive, but not enough to enjoy it. Lying in bed at night, I decided that this was for the best. I was eating gentiles' food, non-kosher food. I had to eat enough to stay alive, as Papa commanded me. But to enjoy non-kosher food? Wasn't that forbidden?

In general, at night, there were a number of things I did not permit myself to do. I didn't know if these things were permissible or not, but my night resolutions were only to help me never forget, even for one second, that I'm a Jew. They were a reminder that I was in this "jail" only so I would stay alive. Throughout the day, I functioned like everyone, joining in all the activities, playing with Breta and other girls, and occasionally even laughing and enjoying myself. In the beginning, I was worried about that — how could I laugh? But I got used to that too, and allowed myself the liberty of laughter. However, that was only during the day. Once night fell, my repressed longings surfaced. I soaked my pillow with tears every night.

One frigid winter day, when the high snow covered everything with a white blanket, we bundled up warmly and went outside. The clear, brisk air was nonetheless freezing cold. We wrapped our scarves around our faces and stood quietly, spellbound, gazing at the white beauty that reigned outside. The snow was like velvet. It made everything look soft. Even the high wall suddenly appeared friendly, soft and rounded, its sharp pieces of glass hidden by the snowfall. The imposing black gate had also turned white under the mantle of snow, and no longer seemed so threatening.

After a short while, the girls began to run playfully and whoop in excitement. Someone began rolling balls for a snowman, and we all joined in excitedly. With great enthusiasm we rolled snowballs, watching them grow larger and larger with each push. Soon we had formed a snowman's body. Once I had also built a snowman — together with Meir and Irena.

It had been snowing heavily then, just like now: white,

clean, pretty snowflakes. We went downstairs, happy and excited, and packed the snow together to form a snowman. It wasn't particularly big, but in our eyes, it was perfect. Maman and Aunt Silka stood on the porch above and looked down at us, amazed at our pretty creation. We waved to them, laughing happily. And just at that moment, a snowball came flying from the other side of the yard, where the gentile children had built their own snowman — and struck our snowman, knocking off his head. We heard them breaking out in laughter at our upset. Tears of rage blinded my eyes. I wanted to take revenge on those nasty children. They had built an enormous snowman — they were a large group of children — and I wanted to destroy it. Before the war had started, we had built our own snowman and the gentile children had made their own, but they had never bothered us. More than that, we had even helped each other. But that time, once the war had started, they no longer wanted to help us or even to look at us. That was fine. But to destroy our snowman? Why? What did we do to them?

A crowd of laughing children — from our building and the nearby buildings — stood there defiantly, mocking us out loud. "I'm going to destroy theirs," I had said in determination. "I'll show them! So many big children against three little children... They think they're smart? I'll teach them a lesson!" I tried to shake myself loose from Meir and Irena who were holding me back, and if Maman hadn't rushed down to the yard, I don't want to think about how this would have finished. Maman grabbed my hands and shouted to Meir and Irena to immediately go up to the house. She forcefully dragged me up the stairs. I argued with her, "I don't want to go up! I'll show them! I'll knock their snowman down!"

But Maman was firm, and I had no choice. As I dragged my feet up the stairs, I heard the hooting of the gentile children below.

Now, I stood in the middle of the convent's yard, exactly where everyone had to pass to build the snowman. The girls bumped into me and pushed me, shouting, "Why are you standing there? Why are you making trouble? Why aren't you helping us build the snowman?" I was lost in my memories, and I let them push me aside. They continued to play and have fun, and I stood alone at the side. Then Breta came over and asked me quietly, "Are you thinking of a different snow? Of a different time?"

I nodded. She didn't ask me anything else, and I didn't say a word. We held each other's hands and stood together quietly until it was time to go inside. I was no longer alone. I had a friend who understood me.

# 24
# "I'm Eating This?!"

One Sunday, in the middle of our weekly excursion on the convent's grounds, I heard strange sounds coming from the direction of a long shack. A tall fence surrounded the shack and I wondered what was inside. We had come to a simple courtyard, plain and not tended, tiled with large, uneven stones. All the other yards in the convent which we had visited in the past were pretty and well-kept. This one was the exception. We heard the noises from far, and when we entered the yard, the noise became ear-splitting. The girls ran happily to the fenced-in shack, and I ran with everyone, curious to know what the noise was all about.

We stood next to the fence and peeked inside. There were fat, pink animals with short legs and big mouths gobbling incessantly, squealing and grunting loudly. The noise was deafening, and the smell — sickening. It was a pigsty. The girls threw pieces of dry bread to the pigs, and the greedy animals pushed each other in their rush to devour the food. I stared, shocked.

"Suzanne," I turned to the girl next to me, "Is this new? The convent has pigs?"

"Of course! Arlette, didn't you know? The pork we eat every Sunday is from these pigs. Where did you think the meat came from? All of our food is produced here, in the convent!"

Suzanne said proudly, and turned back to watch the squealing animals.

I felt sick. I ran to the side, hid myself behind a wide bush, and vomited until I had nothing else to vomit. I still felt terribly nauseous. I looked around and saw a dripping faucet. I walked toward it shakily and washed my mouth out again and again. I was upset at myself: Why hadn't I thought of this? I had eaten pork — the worst thing that I could have eaten. And in my innocence, I was happy to get meat... Why hadn't I thought about this possibility? The *goyim* raised pork everywhere, even in their homes. I had heard that pigs are the easiest and cheapest animal to raise. I berated myself again — why hadn't I thought about what I was putting in my mouth? I knew that the food wasn't kosher, but I had to eat in order to stay alive. But pork? The sensation of nausea washed over me again. I couldn't believe that the whole time I was in the convent, I had been enjoying and even looking forward to Sunday — the day we received meat. Although I had never seen pork before, and there was no way I could have identified it, I still felt horrible. For every despicable and abominable thing, Maman used to say, "*Chazir treif* — It's *treif* like pork." I had been raised with this attitude, this sensation of disgust toward these creatures, from the day I was born. And in the convent, I had eaten their meat with pleasure...

I withdrew into myself in the shadow of the bush, anxious to leave the pigs' courtyard. I didn't look in the direction of the pigsty, but the terrible noises deafened my ears and the stench was impossible to ignore. The other girls were in no rush. They enjoyed feeding the pigs and watching them; this was their Sunday recreation.

Suddenly I knew why that day, of all days, I had found out the secret of where the meat came from. That morning, when we went to church, Sister Danielle had asked me where my hat was. For an entire week, I had been scared to tell her the truth — that I had lost the hat the Sunday before. All my friends had helped me search for it, but in vain. I could have lost it in the bakery we visited that week.

Sister Danielle was very angry. As she liked to do, she slapped my hands with her cross until they turned blue. "You can't enter church without a hat! You are irresponsible! Why didn't you tell me earlier? I would have sent someone to the bakery to search, or I would have made sure you had another hat. What will I do now? How can you enter the church? You always make problems! Why can't you be like the others? Did any other girl ever lose a hat? How come these things always happen only to you?"

I remembered very well that Louise had also lost her hat — but she wasn't beaten and she had received a new hat. But I didn't dare say a word. I only cried. My hands ached terribly, and Sister Danielle continued shouting, "Stand here outside the church door until we leave."

I couldn't believe my good fortune! It was a good thing my hands hurt so much and I kept crying; otherwise Sister Danielle would have noticed my sudden happiness. She thought she had given me a severe punishment, but I was thrilled — I wouldn't have to enter that hateful church!

It was clear to me that because I hadn't kneeled before the cross and joined their prayers, I had found out about the pork we ate every Sunday. From today on, I decided resolutely, I won't eat pork anymore. I'll figure out a way to get rid of the meat on my plate without anyone realizing it.

Papa, don't worry, I remember that I'm a Jewish girl! I ate the meat because I didn't know what it was. From now on, I'll be more careful. I promise you, Papa.

When the girls finally formed lines to leave the yard, I took my place in line as if nothing had happened. No one noticed that I had vomited or that I was feeling weak. Only Breta squeezed my hand and looked at me sadly. I was afraid to talk to her about what we had seen and about the decision I had made. She had also seen the source of the meat. She could decide for herself what to do — she did not have to tell me. It was hard enough for me to keep my own secrets; I didn't want to carry other secrets. I squeezed her hand back, and we continued going with the others.

The cold winter air became more intense and penetrated our bones. All of us developed cold sores on our fingers and toes, even though we wore woolen socks and gloves. We stuffed our shoes with paper, but it didn't keep out the cold. Instead, it just made our shoes narrower, causing us to limp. We stopped going outside. We clung to each other as much as we could, and gathered around the oven. Every room had a charcoal oven or a fireplace with blocks of wood. But since the rooms were large and the ceilings very high, the ovens couldn't heat them properly.

Visiting day arrived one Sunday, accompanied by a blizzard and extraordinary cold. There weren't many visitors; only visitors who lived near the convent dared to venture out in this weather. Most of the girls remained in the room above. Maybe it wasn't nice of me, but I was happy. Finally, I wasn't the only one without visitors! How I wished that in another month, on the next visitors' day, there would be another blizzard. If the weather would be pleasant, Breta and I would be the only ones without visitors. Again we would be different than the others. Again we would remain alone — although not completely — since that Sunday when I had fallen ill, a nun always stayed with us in the isolation room during visiting hours.

That Sunday, almost everyone was in the room, happily playing together. But I hated that room! It's a bad room, I thought. A room for lonely girls whom no one comes to visit — girls who are miserable, girls who must not be visited. Do Papa and Maman know where I am? Did Mrs. Salsky tell them? Papa, did you ever imagine that your Chanah'le would be in a convent, that your Chanah'le would be among goyim, would sleep under a cross? Papa, I go to the church everyday and I bend on my knees every night, while I hear your words ringing in my ears: "Chanah'le, *nisht oif diknee'en* — Don't sit on your knees!" When I'm on my knees, I say "*Shema Yisrael*" and all the *tefillos* that I remember. I ask that "the angel who redeemed me, should save me from all evil and bless me" — even though I'm here, in this place of impurity. I ask the angel not to pay attention to the non-Jewish way I'm forced to pray. Can the good, pure angels enter the convent to bless me and watch over me? One may not daven while kneeling, I know, but this is the only time I can *daven*. If they see my lips moving at any other time, they'll be suspicious of me. I must pray what I still remember, so I won't forget anything. The *tefillos* help me remember that I'm a Jew.

The meat also helps me remember. Since I found out where it came from, I don't eat it. I take advantage of a second when everyone is busy eating and no one is looking at me to quickly hide my piece of meat in the pocket of my slip. After the meal, I wrap it in paper and throw it in the garbage.

Until now, no one caught on, but I'm always worried that maybe one of the nuns will discover the meat in the garbage and try to figure out who threw it out. After all, it's impossible to ignore such contempt for "good" food! Now, during wartime, it's difficult to obtain food. People outside are dying from hunger, as Mademoiselle Vermeul had told us — and I'm throwing meat out... I would happily give my portion to one of the non-Jewish girls, but if I do such a thing, they'll suspect that I'm a Jew. Everyone knows that Jews don't eat pork. Besides the meat, I eat everything. I have no choice, after all, I can't fast all the time! But I won't put that disgusting thing in my mouth. Even if I wanted to eat it, I couldn't. Just the very thought of it makes me feel nauseous.

Papa, you commanded me to live, so I'm eating to stay alive. But I haven't forgotten — not even for one day! — that I'm a Jewish girl. This impure meat helps me remember that. When I throw it out, I'm doing something for the Torah, for *HaKadosh Baruch Hu.*

Everyone played together, and I sat alone at the side, thinking all those thoughts. The nun in charge of us noticed me and rebuked me, "Again you're alone, Arlette? Go play with everyone!"

Actually, she was right. Why did I suddenly start thinking these things today? The anguish I felt at night wasn't enough? I knew I shouldn't be sad during the day also. I looked at the nun, frightened, and she hurried to soften her voice. "Oh, Arlette, please don't start crying now, I beg you! Go play with the girls, be a little happy. Don't be sad all the time."

I tried to follow her instructions. I had to be like everyone — life demanded it.

# 25
# A Big Surprise

With the snow slowly melting in the sun's rays, something also thawed inside me. The cold wasn't as biting as before, and we finally ventured away from the oven. We played all kinds of games — not just sitting games that we had played before without moving away from the warm oven. I participated in all the games, ran and played with everyone, and romped through the large convent rooms. We "captured" one wing for ourselves, and decided that it was ours. The nuns, surprisingly, didn't refuse us. They let us run and play everywhere, and they didn't even scream at us when we raised our voices. Apparently, something had thawed in them too, and they loosened their strict reins of discipline.

Maybe the change for the better occurred because of the new girls who joined the convent. Almost every day saw new girls of all ages arriving at the convent doors. I was sure that at least some of them were Jews, but of course I didn't say a word about it. All the girls told us that they had suffered terribly from the cold, so their parents decided to bring them to the convent, where they would have a roof, heating and food. It might be that the staff decided that the new girls would adapt more easily if the daily regime was less strict, but we all gained from it. For me, especially, it made a big difference. The pampering I had been given because of my illness, Breta's joining our group, followed by the more relaxed atmosphere — all of those things helped free me from my withdrawal and helped me integrate socially with the other girls. The new girls looked up to me — they viewed me as one of the old-timers who could help them adapt. I no longer felt different and alone.

It was only at bedtime that I still had some difficulty. I still cried under the cross every night, but for a short time only — I was very tired and fell asleep quickly. I woke up happily every morning, looking forward to beginning a new day.

One night, when I bent down on my knees for the bedtime prayers, I covered my eyes and hastily whispered *Shema Yisrael* as I always did. Afterwards I stole a look around me to see if anyone had noticed. To my dismay, I saw that Lucienne — one of the new girls — was staring at me. I simply stopped breathing — I was paralyzed with fear. What should I do now? I asked myself. Suddenly I saw Lousianne beginning to cry. Tears streamed down her cheeks, and she lifted her right hand and covered her eyes, her lips moving. She was whispering *Shema Yisrael* too.

I breathed deeply in relief. Lousianne was also a Jew! She was also reciting our eternal declaration of faith. Even while being forced to bend on her knees like the gentiles, she also bravely announced, "...Hashem, our God, Hashem is One!"

I hurried to look somewhere else. Don't worry, Lucienne, I whispered to her in my heart. I won't breathe a word of what I saw. You have nothing to worry about, but I'm happy that I know. How wonderful that you saw me, and were encouraged to follow my example!

That night I didn't cry when I lay down to go to sleep. I stared straight at that menacing cross and said to it in my heart, "I'm not afraid of you anymore! I'm not here alone. The convent is full of Jewish girls, and in the end, all of us will leave. You won't succeed in making us Christians, because Someone is watching over us."

We were in the middle of choir practice when one of the younger girls entered the music room and told me to go immediately to Sister Lucie's room. I was very frightened. A summons to the head nun's room was considered the very worst punishment; it had never happened to me before. What did I do wrong? What happened? I must have become very pale, because one of the choir girls ran to bring me a drink of water and forced me to drink. My feet trembled and felt like lead. All the girls in the choir looked at me in alarm. A tense silence settled over the room. What did I do? I wondered. Maybe it's because of the hats which I had begun to lose on a regular basis? The Sunday before, I had lost my third hat. Sister Danielle was furious. She had slapped me harshly next to the church door — in front of everyone. After prayers, she had beaten me with her large cross necklace. The pain was terrible, but I didn't regret it, because one couldn't enter the large church without a hat. To the contrary, I was sorry that we didn't have to wear a hat in the small church where we prayed during the rest of the week. But I knew I had gone too far and was putting myself in danger. I decided to stop losing my hats, and had promised Sister Danielle that from then on I would be more careful. Sister Danielle had said that she forgave me, and afterwards she treated me normally. But with the summons to the head nun's room, I figured that Sister Danielle hadn't believed my promises, and had informed on me.

I slowly went up the stairs, my heart pounding. This time I expected a serious punishment, not just the usual blows. I knew the situation must be grave. I tried hard not to cry, telling myself that it would be foolish to begin crying even before I was given a punishment. Deeply worried, I knocked on the door and opened it.

Opposite me stood an old man wearing large sunglasses with thick lenses and holding a blind man's cane in his hand. He was familiar, but I couldn't figure out where I knew him from. While I was still staring at him, I heard an emotional cry, "Chanah'le!" and a very familiar, beloved figure jumped into my arms.

"Irena!" I said in amazement. "My Irena!" We stood hugging and crying, and the old blind man, who was Irena's grandfather, also cried. Even Sister Lucie wiped away a tear.

"Irena, where are my father and mother? And what's with Meir? Where are your parents? Since when is your grandfather blind? What is happening in Brussels, Irena? What's happening to the Jews?" I bombarded her with a volley of questions, but Irena didn't answer. She only hugged me tighter and cried harder.

Sister Lucie brought us cups of water. Irena, still sobbing, refused to lift her head from my shoulder. It was only after much cajoling that she agreed to lift her head up and drink a little. After she drank, she tried to calm down and speak clearly. She whispered to me, "You don't have parents anymore, Chanah'le. I also don't. They took them."

"What do you mean, they took them? I don't understand

what you mean. Where did they take them? And Meir, what about Meir?"

"They took everyone, Meir too. I don't know where."

They took them. Who took them? When? Why?

Irena tried to continue speaking, but instead she cried harder and I didn't understand a word. I turned to Sister Lucie. She had tears in her eyes and was patting us lovingly. "Sister Lucie, please tell me what happened," I pleaded with her.

But Sister Lucie shook her head and didn't explain a thing. With her quiet, authoritative voice she said, "You can remain here in my room until Irena explains everything to you. Only don't forget: From here, you will leave as two Christian girls!" She sat down next to us, continuing to pat our hands. I looked up at Irena's grandfather, who was sitting on a chair at the side. I wanted to sit next to him, but Irena held me tightly and wouldn't let me move. "Irena's grandfather, where are my father and mother? Where is my brother? Where did they take them?" I asked.

He got up from his seat and approached us. He took off his large glasses and wiped his eyes. Afterwards, he turned to his granddaughter. "Come, Irena," he said gently. He washed her hands and led her easily to the sofa in the corner. I looked at him in amazement, and suddenly I understood. "You're not really blind, right?"

"Right. I'm only disguised as a blind person. I live in the public old age home where I worked for many years, with good people who know I am a Jew. They suggested that I disguise myself as a blind man. When *they* see an old, blind, hapless man, they don't bother him, and don't check if he's a Jew or a non-Jew."

Irena and her grandfather spoke in hushed tones on the sofa while I waited anxiously to hear more details about the world outside. Finally, Irena calmed down. Perched on the edge of the sofa, she dried her tears and began telling us her terrible story.

# 26
# "Where Has Everyone Gone?"

Irena left one morning to buy bread. Shopping had become an increasingly difficult chore from day to day. The day before, her father had returned home empty-handed, beaten and bruised. Irena's parents had sent her out that morning — hoping that a small child would fare better. After a long wait, Irena finally returned — with bread. To her surprise, she found the apartment door open, and the place was empty. She searched through all the rooms, but no one was in the house. The few belongings they still had — which they hadn't yet sold for food — were strewn on the floor, broken and torn. The beds were turned over, and even the large, wooden closet was lying on the floor. Irena called out loud for her parents and even shouted, but the only response she heard was a dim echo. In desperation, she ran to the neighbors — all of their neighbors were Jews — but every apartment was a repeat of her own home: Possessions lying broken on the floor, and not one living person in the house. Irena walked through one empty apartment after another, crying hysterically. What happened? Where is everyone? Where did they suddenly disappear to? She ran to our house, hoping to find shelter with my parents, but there, too, the door was wide open and the house empty. Irena ran back to her house, but nothing had changed there. In that entire apartment building, there was no living soul besides her.

Suddenly she understood everything. *They* took them. She knew. Her parents had spoken about it frequently, quietly, in whispers. They took — which means: they murdered.

Irena's father, Uncle Yossel, had said so. "I don't believe they're taking the Jews to a different land, to a new place to live, as the Nazis say. If that were the goal, it wouldn't be carried out with such cruelty. They're planning to kill, destroy and utterly eliminate us."

The cold dread that had numbed Irena's mind and body suddenly changed to a fierce resolve — to flee! The Nazis certainly know about her existence. They'll return and take her too! They'll kill her! She must leave immediately! Irena left the building and cautiously looked around. The street was deserted. Not one person was outside — neither Jew nor non-Jew. She ran across the street to the garage that faced their building. Irena's father was on friendly terms with the mechanic who owned the garage, and several times, the mechanic had brought them bread and other necessities. He had also helped them out by selling some of their belongings — as a gentile, he received much more money for those items than they, Jews, would have received. He would help her now, Irena knew. He must help her! She didn't know any other gentiles besides him.

She ran into the garage crying hysterically, and the gentile approached her in consternation. "What happened? What happened to you, Weissman's daughter? Why are you crying so hard?" Irena told him everything that had happened since the morning. The mechanic did not waste any time. He immediately brought her into an inner room and showed her how to hide, in case German soldiers would come to the garage. They did frequent his shop — to fix their army vehicles — which is why the garage was prospering despite the war. Afterwards, he brought her a drink, sat next to her and began to talk.

"Slowly, the Jews are all disappearing," he sighed. "I don't know where they are taking them, but it doesn't smell good. There are all kinds of terrible rumors."

Irena told him her father's opinion, but he shook his head. "No, one mustn't exaggerate. It's not possible that they just go and kill men, women and children! It doesn't make sense that they're killing everyone. Why are they guilty because they were born Jews? That's not a reason to kill them. Everyone has the right to live. It's true that the Jews are disappearing and the Germans are acting cruelly, but to murder them? No, it can't be. And now, what shall we do with you?"

"My grandfather lives in a nursing home on the other side of Brussels," Irena said. "But I can't go there by myself. I don't know the way, and I'm very scared."

"Don't worry. I'll take you," the mechanic assured her.

And as soon as evening came, the two of them got into his car and he drove her to the nursing home. Her grandfather was very shaken, and he brought her into his room. In the morning, he tried to find out what had happened to her parents, but he was warned to stop his inquiries immediately, lest someone suspect that he's a Jew and take him too.

Irena remained in the nursing home for several days. She stayed in her grandfather's bed and cried the entire time. Grandfather came and went, bringing her food and arranging everything for her. She wouldn't move out of his bed. She was consumed with guilt: why had she left the house precisely at that time? Why wasn't she together with her parents? Why were they taken, and she left behind?

"You're not guilty, my Irena," her grandfather tried to explain again and again. "We don't determine our fate; that's what our Father in Heaven wanted. He wanted me to have at least you, the only remnant of our family. The one and only, you are all that I have now in the world."

Grandfather forced her to get up and walk around, to eat and drink. If Hashem decided that she would remain alive, she had to take care of herself. All the elderly people tried to help. One gave her grandfather a folding cot for Irena, another volunteered a blanket, and a third gave candies. But Irena couldn't remain in the nursing home. It wasn't an appropriate place for a young girl. Grandfather began to search for a suitable place for her. All of his friends in the nursing home helped him out. Even though they were gentiles, they desperately wanted to save Irena. One of them suggested turning to the underground — those courageous people had undertaken to hide Jewish children, among other things. Grandfather contacted them and first asked them to find out where Irena's parents had been taken, and where her aunt and uncle — my parents — were. But they firmly told Irena's grandfather that they could not help him in those matters.

"We have no time to focus on matters which in any event we can't do anything about," they had said. When Grandfather told them that Irena had survived alone and was with him, they suggested putting her in a convent. They explained that there were several convents that were hiding Jewish children, and they allowed him to look over their list. Irena's grandfather discovered my name on the list and the whereabouts of "my" convent. When he came back to the nursing home and told Irena about his discovery, she agreed to come with him to my convent.

"If Chanah'le is really there, I agree to stay with her. But if we go there and Chanah'le's not there, I'm coming back with you to the nursing home," she said said. Grandfather willingly agreed to her condition, since he was sure I was there. With that, Irena concluded her story.

Irena and I were sitting side-by-side on Sister Lucie's sofa. The room was still — aside from our sobs and sniffs. I still hadn't completely digested the harrowing facts. Where was my family?

Irena looked at me intently. "You know," she told me, "your parents never agreed to say where you had disappeared to. I didn't stop asking about you, but they never told me that you were in a convent."

"My parents didn't bring me here!" I said. "They hid me with a gentile, with Mrs. Salsky, who used to wash our laundry. They gave her everything we owned so she would watch over me, and she brought me here. She said that she would tell whoever has to know that I'm here in the convent. I didn't believe her, but now I see that she did it." I was silent for a moment, thinking about Mrs. Salsky, seeing her again standing opposite me, ignoring my pleadings and leaving me at the train station with the strange woman. "She promised to bring Maman here when the war is over and she comes searching for me," I added.

"Chanah'le, listen to me." Suddenly Irena's voice was no longer the voice of a small child. "Your mother will not come to take you after the war. There's no one to search for you."

"You're talking nonsense!" I said angrily. "You said yourself that they took them somewhere. After the war, they'll return from that place and come to bring me home!" I raised my voice and shouted again and again, “My mother will come!”

Irena and her grandfather looked at me with bottomless sadness, and didn’t say a word. “They’ll come back from that place!” I continued stubbornly. But deep in my heart I knew I was fooling myself.

Papa and Maman and Meir were in a place from where one doesn’t return.

# 27
# "They'll Yet Return!"

The door opened and Sister Lucie walked in. I hadn't even noticed that she had left the room; I was completely engrossed in Irena's terrible story. Sister Lucie approached us and took us to the small bathroom near her room. "You have to wash your faces well so no one will see you cried," she instructed us. "Afterwards, say good-bye to your grandfather and go to class."

Irena's grandfather waited for us in the hallway. He hugged Irena and promised to come visit us on the next visiting day. He would visit both of us; from that day on, he became the grandfather of both of us, since he had told Sister Lucie that we were cousins. Irena and I were to give this explanation to anyone who would ask.

I had already turned to go downstairs, but Irena couldn't part from her grandfather. She clung to him tightly, refusing to say good-bye. Only after much pleading did she agree to leave him and accompany me. We went downstairs together, and on the way I reminded her that my name was now Arlette. "It will be bad for both of us if you call me Chanah'le!" I warned her. "You must remember that I'm Arlette!"

"Yes, Sister Lucie also told me that if I call you by your real name, your life will be in danger. Don't worry, I won't endanger you! I'll remember your new name very well." Irena squeezed my hand warmly. We were very lucky that her name didn't have to be changed. Both Jews and gentiles alike were called "Irena," so she was saved the worry of remembering a new name.

"What story will you tell the other girls when they ask about your life?" I asked.

Irena smiled. "I lived all my life with my grandfather, but now he is very old and also blind, and can't take care of me anymore. That's why he brought me here." It was a simple, and even partially true, story. Irena didn't have to review and remember all kinds of details and names of strange people like me. They had taken into consideration that she was younger than me, and might get confused. She didn't even have to change her mother's name — Silka — since it was a name which the gentiles used too.

We met all the girls in the sewing room, and I introduced them to Irena. "This is Irena, my cousin. She used to live with our grandfather, but he is old and blind and poor, and can't take care of her anymore," I said out loud, so everyone would hear and no one would ask unnecessary questions.

According to Sister Lucie's instructions, Irena was permitted to sleep in my bedroom, even though she was younger and belonged to a different age-group. In school, we were in different classes, but that was the only time we were separated. Irena was allowed to eat with my age-group and prepare homework with us, and at night, she slept in the bed next to mine. When our room became quiet, she would creep into my bed. We would hug each other, and Irena would tell me about events that had taken place in Brussels since Maman had brought me to Mrs. Salsky. She described the lack of food, the absolute darkness that prevailed at night, and primarily — the mysterious disappearance of Jews.

Everything was forbidden for the Jews. They weren't permitted to visit Brussels's scenic parks, or travel on the trolley or the trains or even walk on the sidewalk. They were only permitted to walk on the street, between the cars and horse-drawn wagons. Jews were forbidden to enter any public place — even the synagogues. There was no way they could disguise themselves; the prominent yellow star on their arms could be seen from afar.

The Jews organized a myriad of unusual hiding places, and they lived in constant fear — of the Germans and the Belgians. The Germans' wickedness and cruelty was beyond the perception of a normal person, but many Belgians were anti-Semites and the Jews were afraid of them too.

The worst problem was food. The situation in Brussels was terrible. There were separate lines for each food item, and people stood on each line for hours. No matter how early they came, the Jews were always pushed to the end of the line, and sometimes the food ran out before the end of the line. Villagers who lived near the city put themselves into danger to bring food to sell. People sold all their property for food, and they only received a little food in exchange for many possessions. Theft was rampant. People stole just to survive. The unimaginable human suffering turned quiet and honest people into thieves and robbers.

Of course, the Jews were blamed for everything. Because of them, the war had broken out; because of them, the Germans had invaded Belgium; the food scarcity was their fault, as was the black market and the astronomical price of each loaf of bread; they're all thieves; Jews were responsible for

Belgium's misery.

These statements were scrawled on walls of buildings and were broadcast on the radio. Before long, the Belgian non-Jews began to connive against the Jews, unwittingly helping the German enemy. The war had devastated Jewish families — of all of Belgium's citizens, they had suffered the most — but the gentiles didn't want to believe that. They preferred having someone to blame for all their suffering.

If a gentile thief was caught, the police would reprimand him and put him in prison for a few days. That was the extent of his punishment. But if they merely *suspected* that a Jew had planned to steal something, they killed him immediately and threw his body into the street. All the Jews, from the most distinguished down, suffered hunger. They scoured garbage cans, and whoever found a rotten vegetable or a piece of moldy bread considered himself fortunate. Irena had no idea how my parents, who no longer had anything to sell, had managed. During that period, Irena's family no longer visited my house. Every family stayed inside their own home, afraid to venture outside unnecessarily.

After Irena cried herself asleep, I lay awake a long time, picturing Meir crying, begging Maman for a piece of bread, but she had nothing to give him. And it was all my fault! It was all because of me, because Maman had given all the money to Mrs. Salsky to hide me. I tormented myself with these thoughts. I imagined my parents' and brother's suffering at that moment — confronting terrible, oppressive hunger, and I disregarded what Irena had told me in Sister Lucie's room. I didn't want to believe that they could no longer feel hunger, that they had been permanently taken from this painful world.

Every time Irena would hint to me that our parents would not return, I silenced her immediately. I also wouldn't allow her to say that we were orphans. "We're not orphans, Irena! You'll see, after the war, our parents will come back. They just "took" them. They didn't kill them! Even the mechanic told you that!"

"You're a fool! You're acting like a baby!" Irena responded vehemently. "I'm younger than you but I'm more mature. You have to open your eyes and see reality."

I didn't listen to her. I knew that I absolutely shouldn't think like her. If I would begin to believe it, then why should I live? Why was I taking care of myself? If *chas v'shalom* it was true and I no longer had a Papa and Maman or a little brother, why should I suffer so much here? I would have preferred to be together with my family, and share their fate. Under no circumstances was I able to live with this knowledge, so I fiercely denied it. "They'll yet return," I would tell Irena confidently. "I know. I feel in my heart that they're alive. You'll see. After the war they'll come and take us."

But Irena was angry with my immaturity, and told me more and more terrible things. Night after night I heard harrowing stories from Irena, while she tried to restrain her weeping so she wouldn't wake the other girls up. Before Irena came to the convent, I had managed to stop my nightly crying attacks. Now the situation had regressed.

Even when we were alone, just the two of us, Irena was particular to call me "Arlette" so she wouldn't make a mistake on other occasions. That really bothered me. I wanted her to call me "Chanah'le." I wanted to return and be myself at least in those seconds. But I didn't dare ask her that. I knew she was right, even though she was younger.

Irena had arrived at the convent in a state of starvation. Meal time was holy to her; she didn't lift her eyes from the plate until it was time to leave the dining room. I shared a little of my food with her at every meal. The other girls had pity on her and would slip her some of their portions, too. Even this little bit was difficult for us to give up, for we weren't receiving lavish portions. But our friends saw how Irena devoured her portion and they couldn't ignore the hunger in her eyes. They outdid themselves by giving her from their own portion, and they felt like heroes. Irena didn't even notice that it was a sacrifice on their parts. In her enthusiasm to eat, she took whatever they offered her, and swallowed it without leaving over a crumb.

When I pointed this out to her, she responded, "Arlette, you don't know what it means to be hungry. You don't understand it at all; you don't know what hunger does to people. Do you remember Mr. Moshe Weiss, who lived on the street parallel to your street?"

I remembered him. He was a tall, strict man. "He became an informer," Irena said. "He walked around with the Nazis and showed them where Jews were hiding. For every Jew that he exposed, the Nazis gave him some flour and brown sugar, and sometimes a piece of black soap. That's what a Jew was worth: a little flour and a little brown sugar. With these items, Mr. Weiss kept his many children alive. My father explained to me that this is what hunger does to a person. He told me that that's why we *daven*. Even if we don't know what the words mean, the *tefillah* helps us be good and not fall to such despicable behavior. This man, Moshe Weiss, didn't *daven*. He told my father that it's easier for him to hear the curses of Jews than the cries of his children. But my father told him that these curses will pursue him all his life and will never give him rest."

My poor Irena! It was her fate to see and hear such terrible things!

# 28
# Louise and Alfonse

For most of the hours during the day, I stayed next to Irena. I felt a need to touch her, not only to look at her — to prove to myself that she really was here with me. It was a wonderful feeling.

But the nights... the nights had become miserable since her arrival. Every night Irena remembered more terrible stories that had happened to families we knew. And each such story brought with it another sleepless night of weeping.

"Arlette, do you remember the Markowitzes, the refugees who arrived from Liège?" Irena asked me one night. "They managed to enter France, to a small town called Marmande, where they were accepted as refugees. No one knew they were Jews; they treated them nicely and took care of them. They sent us a note with Pierre Levine, urging us to join them. Pierre was prepared to take us with him when he fled there, but my parents absolutely refused. They were afraid. If only they would have agreed to go — maybe they would still be alive! My mother was scared to make the dangerous journey, to travel in Pierre's ancient truck. He already had a few passengers for the trip, but there would have been enough room for us, too, he said. He even promised to give us a very good deal. He told my parents that he knew the winding roads and paths like the back of his hand and that he knew how to bypass the patrols next to the border without getting caught. Papa tried to convince Maman, but she was afraid. If she would have been braver, all of us could be living in France now. We would have come to that small town where Markowitz is. Breta, the older daughter, wrote Papa exactly where Marmande is. But Maman didn't want to go. She said that if something bad is decreed against us, it would happen to us no matter where we would run, for no man can escape Hashem. Papa was unable to convince her, and now my whole life I'll be haunted by the thought that if it weren't for her opposition, Papa and Maman would be living there now."

Irena burst out in terrible sobs, and I tried to comfort her. "Maybe your mother was right," I said. "You can't be sure that you would have reached Marmande in peace. And at least you're alive, and you came to save me from life in the convent, which was becoming unbearable." That was the truth. I was crying more at night since Irena joined me, but her arrival had given me a new lease on life.

"Arlette, do you remember that dwarf couple — Louise and Alfonse?" Irena began one night. I remembered them well. They were good people, and despite their impairment, they were always cheerful and happy. Both of them played violins and made others happy.

"The Germans took them. They said they wanted to check them in Germany, to figure out what causes people to become dwarfs. Their neighbor, Paula Briver, told Maman how they savagely dragged them to the car. When Alfonse asked permission to bring along their violins, a young soldier ran to bring them — and then he took the violins and smashed them on Louise and Alfonse's heads. Afterwards he forcefully grabbed Louise by her hair and threw her inside the car, and lifted Alfonse and threw him in after her. Why, Arlette? Why are they so cruel to people? Those dwarfs weren't even Jews... What did they gain by smashing the violins on their heads? Mrs. Briver told us that Louise and Alfonse's screams echoed through the street, and the Germans just watched the spectacle, laughing hysterically. How can one laugh at seeing the pain of others?"

Irena, my poor unfortunate Irena! I didn't know what to tell her. Was there anyone in the world that could answer such questions? Such questions never had, don't have and never will have answers. Never.

The repeated nightly crying brought back my pesky cough. One day at recess, Mademoiselle Vermeul took me to her room and had a heart-to-heart talk with me. "Arlette, you already finished with this. You already overcame those crying spells. You may not restart them! A person must always try to go forward."

"But Irena told me that my parents disappeared, and no one knows where they are! Maybe they're not even alive, because they had nothing to eat!"

"They probably moved to one of the villages where it's easier to find work and food than in the large cities," my teacher tried to calm me. I didn't reply. I couldn't tell her that the Nazis took them — I didn't know if she was aware of my true origin or not. Mademoiselle Vermeul noticed that I didn't answer, and she began to speak about the period after the war. She told me how good it would be when everyone would be free. She said she'd be delighted to meet my parents, when they would come to retrieve me from the convent. She reassured me that once again everyone would have plenty of food. Everything that was destroyed would be built anew, and Belgium would again become a tranquil kingdom where it is good to live. After that soothing introduction, she admonished me and told me that I was doing an injustice to Irena. Instead of encouraging her and watching over her, I was pulling her into my depression. That's why, like me, she was crying for hours every night.

Her words made an impression on me. I promised Mademoiselle Vermeul that from then on I would take care of Irena as I should. She was just a young child, after all, and I had to make sure that she found her place in the convent and acted like all the other girls.

I really tried, but I wasn't particularly successful. I tried to curb my emotional turmoil every evening and not broach the subject of the Jews' persecution but I couldn't. I always ended up persuading Irena to tell me more stories, which brought both of us to tears.

One day, Irena stopped cooperating with me. "I have nothing else to tell you," she said. "I already told you everything! Why should I keep repeating the same things again and again? If we keep crying every night, we'll make ourselves sick. We have to be strong."

Apparently, after the nuns saw that speaking with me didn't help, they had also spoken with Irena. Irena's determination helped me a lot. Together, we pushed the past behind us and the terrible stories stopped. Now we began to look forward to the future.

# 29
# I Also Have a Guest!

When visiting day arrived on Sunday, I finally had a visitor too! Irena's grandfather had come to visit both of us. We ran together to the visiting room, and I almost danced from excitement. There was Grandfather, sitting regally at the table, wearing his black glasses. He looked like a distinguished elder! We ran to him and he welcomed us with open joy. He was happy to see both of us, and didn't differentiate between us. Everyone who saw him was sure that he was both my grandfather and Irena's. After the initial greetings, Grandfather pulled two bags out of his pocket and gave us each one. He had brought bags of candies! Who knows how much effort he had to put forth to get them for us... Candies were a very rare commodity during wartime.

"Chanah'le, you must watch Irena," Grandfather told me. "You have to make sure that she is eating everything they give her, is applying herself to her studies and obeying instructions. You are responsible for her, and I am relying on you."

I bombarded him with questions about what was going on outside. He told us that more of Brussels was being destroyed, and the unfortunate citizens were starving. There was no food to be had. Belgium's economy had been devastated, the stores had been plundered, and most of the factories had closed down. I was not especially interested in the stores and factories; I wanted to know what was happening with my fellow Jews. Grandfather told me that all the Jews had disappeared. All Belgian Jews had been transported to Mellis, but Mellis is an extremely small town. How did the Germans manage to fit so many people there? The gentiles were saying terrible things, but Grandfather didn't pay any attention to their words. "I don't believe them," he declared. "It's not possible for the Nazis to kill all of them. You're not talking about a few dozen people, or even numbers in the hundreds. You're speaking about thousands upon thousands — men, women, children, and the elderly. It just doesn't make sense. They say that the Nazis rounded up Jews from every country and are methodically sending them to a specific location. It's not only happening in Belgium. If so, you're talking about millions! It's impossible to murder so many people! Nevertheless, the situation clearly isn't good, and you have to carefully guard the secret that you're Jews. Better to be safe."

"And how are you doing?" Irena asked worriedly. He just shouldn't disappear just like her parents did! But Grandfather calmed her down. "The old age home I'm living in is safe. The Germans don't even dream that I'm a Jew, and the elderly people there are my friends and detest the Nazis who destroyed Belgium. They certainly don't want to give me into their hands. The important thing, girls, is that you should be careful. We will outlive them!"

"And then, when we outlive them — will our parents return?" I asked eagerly.

"I don't know, Chanah'le. How can I know? I have no idea what happened to them, and I don't want to lie to you. I have a terrible fear in my heart. But we have a great God in heaven, Who sees and knows all. I pray to Him when no one is watching me. Only He can save us."

Grandfather got up to go. I accompanied him until the gate, watching him feel his way with his stick just like a real blind person. We kept straight faces as we helped guide him out of the building. "Grandfather, here, go down these steps. Okay, this is the last step. Now turn right." He coordinated his steps according to our instructions.

"How are you able to put on such a good act?" I whispered to him. He smiled and explained to me that he shuts his eyes so his act would be perfect, because it's a question of life and death. Afterwards he reminded me again that I was responsible for Irena. "Only the fact that I have her, and also you, gives me the strength to continue," he said. I promised him to watch his granddaughter carefully.

My new responsibility, taking care of Irena, gave new purpose to my life. I made sure that her clothes were orderly, that she did her homework properly, and that she played nicely with everyone. I particularly made sure she participated in all of our activities. I was hesitant, however, to tell her anything about the meat we were served. I was afraid to take responsibility for this; after all, she had arrived here totally starved. In the months before she came to the convent, she and her parents had lived on bread and tea alone. I was worried that she might get sick, *chas v'shalom*, if she wouldn't eat meat. In the end, I decided that I would ask Grandfather about it on the next visiting day. I would tell him which meat they served us and the decision would be his.

My new responsibility reinforced my decision not to pressure Irena to tell me stories from the past. I didn't want to depress her. I resolved only to speak about encounters and episodes from our daily life — in the convent! We would put the fearful events of the past aside, and we would only discuss pleasant memories.

"Arlette, do you remember your brown sofa?" Irena asked me one day, when we went out with the girls to play in the yard. "I loved it so much, even though it was old and worn-out."

"Of course I remember it!" I answered with a smile. "It was the center of our lives. We relaxed and played on it, we quarreled and sang on it, and when we wanted to just chat, we did that on the brown sofa too."

"You know, after your parents sold it, I didn't want to come to your house anymore. I was angry at them. I didn't know then that the sofa had been sold to save you. Oh, Arlette, do you remember how the three of us used to sit on the sofa and sing? We would always sing, do you remember?"

"How could I forget? In our house, song had always been part of our lives, just like food and sleep."

"Let's sing something now, just the two of us," Irena asked with longing in her voice. I agreed readily, and we settled ourselves on a bench at the side of the yard. The girls were engrossed in their games some distance away, so we were not worried that anyone would hear our hushed singing. We sang one of our favorite songs:

*Oifen pripitashtak* In the hearth
*Brent a fire'l* Burns a small fire

| | |
|---|---|
| *Un ein shtub is heiz* | It is warm in the house |
| *zitz der rebe* | The rebbe is sitting |
| *mit di kleine kinderlach* | With the little children |
| *Un lernt "alef beis."* | Teaching them "*alef beis*." |

We sat closely together, singing quietly. Suddenly, Diana passed by and snapped at us, "What are you singing? Stop it immediately! You're not allowed to sing that way here! Come play like everyone else!"

"What's the matter, Diana?" I was surprised. "We're not bothering you. We're just singing quietly and not bothering anyone. We can sing if we want! Why are you upset?"

Diana drew closer to us, and said with barely disguised anger, "You're not singing for no reason. I heard it! Don't you dare sing that song here!" She glared at us and then moved off. I looked after her, astonished. Diana had arrived at the convent some time after me, and had adjusted easily. She knew all the prayers by heart, and she excelled in her theological studies and was considered a strict Catholic. I would never have imagined that she was a Jew. But if she was so shaken by the song, that meant she must have known it well. Fear paralyzed me, and Irena ran after Diana to promise her that she wouldn't sing songs like that one anymore; she would only sing songs that we learned in the convent's choir.

"You'll be in big trouble if you sing songs that are not acceptable in the convent!" Diana warned us again. Irena returned to the bench and we sat on it close to each other, thinking about this surprising discovery. Who would have imagined that Diana was a Jew? Happy-go-lucky Diana always kept a distance from me, and I thought it was because she liked to laugh and be happy, while I was generally sad. I wonder who that woman is who comes to visit her on every visiting day? She has a face like a gentile, and Diana calls her Auntie. She can't possibly have a non-Jewish aunt. Enough! Better not to ask questions or think too much about it.

# 30
# The Punishment

Time passed and Irena began to get used to life in the convent. After a while, the nuns informed her that she would have to do her homework and craftwork together with the girls in her class — not with the girls in my group. She made new friends, and each of us spent our days with girls our own ages. At night, they still let us stay together, more because of me than because of Irena. Our beds were next to each other, and we used to whisper together until they reprimanded us. It was a change for the good: instead of asking us to stop crying, they asked us to stop talking.

After everyone fell asleep, Irena crept into my bed. We spoke in hushed whispers about our Jewish identity. Together, we reviewed all the prayers we could remember. I told her what I remembered about the *Yomim Tovim*. Although I could not remember the specific dates of each of the holidays, I still remembered some stories and songs connected to the various holidays. Papa had told me some of the stories, and some I had heard in the community school. Irena didn't remember very much, but after I told her a story, she would remember. We tried to hang on to every scrap of memory that we could, afraid we would forget the little that we knew.

During recess one day, I saw Irena running toward me.

"What happened?" I asked her. "Didn't we decide that during recess, each of us would play with the girls in her class?"

Irena disregarded my question. She grabbed my hand firmly, and said, "Arlette, I have to go to the bathroom — now!"

I was frightened. I didn't know what to do. One wasn't allowed to go to the bathroom whenever she wanted. There were fixed times for everything in the convent, even trips to the bathroom. Each class went in a row, walking in pairs. "I must!" Irena cried hysterically. I was in a quandary. On one hand, I was responsible for her — I had promised her grandfather that I would take care of her. On the other hand, I didn't dare break the convent's strict rules.

The bathrooms were on the second floor. A large gate separated the floors, and it was securely locked when the second floor was off-limits. We walked toward the gate anyway — with the slight hope that we would find it open — but it was of course locked. Our only option was to climb over it. After a hurried glance over my shoulder, I gave the word. "Let's hurry!" I told Irena, and that's what we did. We scurried up one side, and slid down the other, and then dashed upstairs to the bathrooms. When we climbed over the gate again to return to our classes, one of the nuns passed by and caught us. She shouted at us very loudly and hit us hard, all the while promising that "they" wouldn't let such a terrible thing pass quietly. For such a scandal we would be punished.

I sat in class trembling with fear. What terrible punishment would they give us now? I thought. Had we really done such an awful thing? Was it so impossible to understand that sometimes one has to go to the bathroom outside of the fixed times? What will they do to us? I was so distraught that I could not concentrate on the lesson, and my teacher, Mademoiselle Vermeul, noticed it. Had it been another nun, I would have received another punishment. But Mademoiselle Vermeul just patted me on the head kindly and asked me what had happened, for she was used to seeing me attentive and learning well.

I was afraid to tell her the truth. I didn't want her to get angry at me too. Mademoiselle Vermeul was always so good to me; She loved me and accepted me. But my need to share my fears with someone else won over my initial reticence, and I decided to trust her. I whispered in her ear what had happened, so the other girls wouldn't hear. She listened to my story and said nothing; instead, she continued to stroke me and squeeze my hand firmly. I knew that she couldn't do a thing against the convent's regulations.

At recess, when my classmates all went outside, I remained in the classroom. I had no desire to play. Mademoiselle Vermeul approached me again and said, "Arlette, you must be stronger. Don't let yourself fall apart from every occurrence." She hugged and kissed me, knowing that I needed her warmth and that it would give me courage.

Finally evening approached. I had been saturated with fear the entire day — I quaked at the sight of every passing nun in the corridor. It was Sister Danielle who came to mete out our punishment. She gave each of us a notebook, and commanded us to fill the entire book with the words "One may not climb." Irena sat down and began writing immediately, but I burst into tears.

"It's not fair, it's not just! The gate was locked, so what could we do? It's not my fault." I sat and cried, while Irena sat and wrote. Everyone else had already gone to sleep, but we had to finish our writing first. Irena urged me to hurry. "Stop crying and start writing," she said. But my delicate sense of justice refused to accept the verdict. While Irena filled her notebook with words, I filled mine with tear stains. When Irena finished writing, she tried to convince me to go to sleep, but I was afraid. I sent her to the bedroom and I remained alone next to the table. I wrote a little, but I was utterly exhausted. I fell asleep at the table, my head slumped on the notebook.

In the morning, Sister Danielle took the notebooks from us without a word. I waited, frightened, for the moment they would come to punish me with a more severe punishment. But no nun came. They didn't say anything to me. It was strange. I couldn't understand how it could be that in the strict convent they would close their eyes to a punishment which hadn't been carried out. I was sure I would receive my due "reward" soon. Awaiting a punishment can be far worse than the punishment itself, and that day, too, I was very nervous. "Mademoiselle Vermeul," I turned to my teacher, "what will they do to me? I barely did the punishment..."

"Arlette, Arlette, when will you be like the others? When will you learn to stop worrying? You must free yourself from your fears — you must stop creating problems for yourself. Go play and enjoy yourself! Have fun like the other girls; stop being afraid of everything. Relax, and calm down." Mademoiselle Vermeul looked at me pitifully. She was the only one who truly liked me here, and I needed love so much! How I thirsted for her hugs, just as a plant thirsts for water. Sometimes during our recesses, she would take me to her room and show me pictures and tell me about her parents and her married sister who lived in France. The correspondence with her sister had stopped at the German invasion, and she didn't know what was happening to her. She told me about the place where she lived, and told me many other stories, chatting with me about whatever she thought would interest me. She lavished attention on me; I might not have held up in the convent without her warm, caring concern.

The nuns didn't like the girls. They were aloof and cold, and treated us harshly. There was a pronounced distance between us and them, and we were expected to honor them greatly. Every nun, even the youngest, was allowed to punish us as she saw fit, and punish us they did!

Only Sister Lucie was different. Sister Lucie loved us and we loved her. But she stayed in her office all day, taking care of the myriad duties involved in running the convent. As the head nun, she was responsible for the girls' wing, and couldn't spend time with us privately, aside from on rare occasions. She was like a winter sun whose light was too far to warm us up.

The other nuns punished us for every small misdemeanor. Blows were routine, and I had almost stopped paying attention when I heard cries because they were so common. I was quiet and disciplined, so the nuns had little reason to punish me, but there were mischievous girls who were often naughty. They weren't frightened of blows and punishment, like I was.

My fears made me try to behave as they desired, but I also had the feeling that the nuns were afraid to start up with me. They didn't like my frequent crying spells — which lasted a long time — and were afraid I would become sick because of them, as had already happened once. The nun who had ignored my pleadings, and had locked me in that hateful room on visiting day, had been punished. Since then, all of the nuns were careful not to start up with me. They said that Sister Lucie afforded me special treatment. I wasn't sure that was true, but I was happy they weren't as quick to hit me as they were with other girls.

The nuns were strict with all the girls, but they treated the Jewish girls much worse. Although all the Jewish girls tried to hide their identity as well as possible, it was not hard to guess who the Jewish girls were. The nuns made them suffer much more because of their identity. During our biweekly delousing sessions, their offensive behavior was particularly noticeable. They would wash our hair twice a week and comb it with a fine-tooth comb to get the lice out. In the beginning, in my naivete, I thought that the nuns pulled everyone's hair without mercy. After all, getting rid of the lice was a highly unpleasant task. We were a large group of girls living in close proximity to each other — we even bathed in the same water — so of course we kept infesting each other. The nuns hated the job of cleaning our hair, and we felt it in our flesh. But we weren't treated equally. Irena was the one who pointed it out to me. "Take a good look, Arlette! Look — whose hair do they pull out, and whose hair do they comb gently?" I started paying attention and noticed that she was right. The Jewish girls were treated far more cruelly.

The delousing procedure was horrible. After shampooing our hair — we all had very short hair — they pushed our heads into a pail of ammonia. The strong, acrid smell of ammonia made us choke and gag. Maybe it helped choke the lice also, but it was a nightmare for us. We coughed and wheezed a long time after, trying to inhale the oxygen that our lungs needed. The nun always plunged my head deep inside the pail, and pinned it down for a long time, despite my efforts to push her away. After that treatment, I would need several hours for my breathing to return to normal, and to be able to stop wheezing and coughing. My eyes remained red and teary for a day or two, and my entire head hurt from the vicious combing. After my talk with Irena, I realized that only girls who were suspected of being Jews were treated this way. When the nuns were treating a non-Jewish girl, they would immerse the girl's head in the awful ammonia for a short time, and that was it.

After the treatment, we were free of lice for at least a week. We lived in constant fear of the moment when we would catch it again, and the treatments would resume. We tried to pick the lice out of each other's heads, but we were never able to beat them. We kept suffering the hated treatment. We thought nothing could be worse than it — until impetigo started making its rounds.

Impetigo is a contagious disease, which appears as stubborn pussy sores — primarily on one's head, face and hands. The sores stung and were very painful. Just touching the sores caused a wave of excruciating pain, but no one showed us the slightest consideration — neither the lice, who continued to infest us despite our sores and pus — nor the nuns, who continued with their vigorous combing and vicious hair-pulling, which caused us unbearable pain. Our heads had large patches of baldness around each sore for a very long time. Our appearance was terrible, but the pain we suffered was even worse. We begged the nuns to shave our heads so we wouldn't have to be combed, but they refused, saying that we would look like monsters.

The nuns' behavior toward the Jewish girls was incomprehensible. On one hand, they agreed to shelter us in the convent, to watch us, to take care of us and to give us food — even though it put them in certain danger. On the other hand, they abused us and discriminated against us. I thought a lot about this paradox and came to the conclusion that the administration — that is, Sister Lucie — wanted to save us, but the nuns who had to take care of us didn't like Jews.

At first, I didn't particularly suffer from the nuns, because I was timid and disciplined. But the situation began to change once Irena joined the convent. Irena had a strong mischievous streak and she would come up with all kinds of unusual ideas. Even though I was the older one, I submissively joined in all her pranks, well-aware that I would pay the price afterwards, because I was afraid I would lose her. I was afraid that if I would refuse to go along, she would carry them out alone — or, even worse, with other girls. I was afraid that new friends would take my place in her heart. Her grandfather had appointed me to be responsible for her, but in fact, I emotionally needed her more than she needed me.

Every day Irena thought of a new prank, and every prank carried a punishment in its wake. The punishments did not fit the seriousness of her misdeed; for every deviation, no matter how small, we could expect a bitter and cruel punishment. For entire days, Irena and I sat in the stifling, windowless cellar, and by the dim light of a kerosene lamp, peeled enormous quantities of potatoes for all the residents of the huge convent. Everyone had long forgotten that I was afraid of dark cellars.

When the nun came down to the cellar, she screamed at us because of our paltry output. I tried to peel faster, but we had to peel thin, nice peels, something we could do only if we peeled slowly. If the peels were too thick, we were forced to eat them instead of lunch. The nun couldn't care less that the knife we had been given wasn't suitable for peeling, and that my hand kept getting cut. She didn't want to listen either when I argued that many people worked in the convent for their living, and peeling potatoes was their job. "It's your punishment," she said in a coldhearted voice, "and you have to do it."

Peeling was considered a relatively easy punishment, because at least it was useful. We took comfort in the fact that people were enjoying our efforts. Although we had scars on our hands, we felt less bitterness in our hearts than we did with the useless punishments. For example, one punishment involved standing in a corner, facing the wall and raising both hands to the ceiling for hours. When we were finally allowed to lower our hands, they were numb, and they hurt for several days. The pain was so intense that I wasn't able to fall asleep at night. Another common punishment involved bending down on one's knees while lifting both hands, which added paralyzing pain to the legs. The rough wooden floors cut into our knees, and we were helpless to do anything to alleviate our pain. It was impossible to stand straight afterwards. Every step was painful, and we were left with scars on our knees from those cuts.

The nuns were harsh and rigid, without a drop of gentleness. Maybe that's why they chose to become nuns. A gentle and loving woman would probably prefer to become a mother. The administration treated the nuns harshly too, and made many demands of them. The nuns had no vacation. Day in and day out, they worked ceaselessly, or were bent over in prayer — for hours at a time. They were required to be quiet and demure, and weren't allowed to draw attention to themselves. They took out all their anger and frustration on us — the girls. For every petty prank we did, or were suspected of doing, we were severely punished. At any given moment, there were always girls bent over, standing with their hands raised or doing something else as a punishment.

Once I complained to Sister Lucie that I had been punished for something I hadn't done. "Is that so?" she said. "Well, maybe you weren't at fault for that particular thing, but you probably acted improperly on other occasions, and deserve to be punished. It's good to be punished — it helps us humble our rebelliousness and overcome our bad character." I couldn't believe that this answer had come from the kindly Sister Lucie. I always tried to be so good and disciplined, and to behave in class! I did join in Irena's pranks, I admitted to myself, but how could a girl improve when the nuns watch her every movement, scheming to ensnare her in their trap? Every day they came up with new demands and new regulations so they could give us more punishments.

# 31 Seeking Our Souls

We were in the middle of a lesson when the classroom door suddenly opened and Sister Cecile entered. Sister Cecile was a new, young nun, who was very different from the older nuns. She was cheerful and smiled a lot, and two dimples adorned her face when she laughed. Her job was to assist the convent's administrators, so we girls didn't have direct contact with her. But every time she passed by, she smiled a warm, genuine smile. We liked her.

Sister Cecile called out the names of several girls, mine among them. "You have to go to the doctor," she said. "Come with me." We were surprised — we weren't sick — but we followed her docilely, as we had been trained to do. Sister Cecile urged us to hurry and made us run to the steps. "Quickly, go downstairs to the crypt," she instructed us, and she immediately turned to another class to call out other girls. We warily made our way down the stairs to the mysterious crypt — the "holiest" place in the convent, an underground cellar which served nuns as a place for introspection. We found several girls from other classes there already, and other girls came after us.

The crypt was a secret place, out of bounds for the girls. It was a large, dark room, with almost no lighting. Only two kerosene lamps in the center of the room were lit, and they only lit up a small area. We crowded together in that small space and stared at each other. Each of us realized immediately that only the girls suspected of being Jews had been called to this frightening place, and we became very scared. Where is Irena? I worried. Maybe they are hiding all the Jews because of something menacing? She should be here too! Just then she arrived with other girls from her class, and I breathed in relief.

Sister Lucie arrived in the crypt and asked us to be quiet. "Don't make a sound, because the Germans are in the convent," she warned us. "They are searching if there are any girls in our convent who do not belong here. Someone may have informed on us." She didn't mention the word "Jews" but we understood what she meant.

Sister Lucie rushed out as soon as she had finished speaking. She had to be in her room in case the Germans wanted to speak with her, since she was the one responsible for the girls. They wouldn't come to the crypt; it was a place for introspection and prayer only for the old nuns' use. No one entered it for any other reason. Under normal circumstances, the girls were forbidden to even come near it. We stood there looking around, without uttering a sound. There were two circles of light around the two kerosene lamps, and the rest of the place was dark, full of mysterious, frightening shadows.

After what seemed like eternity, they took us out and strictly warned us not to speak about what had happened. After several days the story repeated itself: the same girls were called again to "see the doctor." Again we ran to the crypt, and like the previous time, I held Irena's hand until the danger had passed.

The searches became more frequent, and with them, the atmosphere in the convent grew more and more tense. It was impossible to continue using the excuse of "going to the doctor"; we clearly weren't sick. The Jewish girls were always on edge. Even when we played outside in the yard, we tried to stay close to the door, so we could run to the crypt as soon as the signal would be given.

We were invited for a special meeting with the priest who taught us the Catholic view of Christianity. "These searches will apparently continue," he told us. "Maybe they will become more frequent. It's impossible to continue this way. What will happen if one of your friends will say something naively and the Germans will discover your tracks? If they catch you, all of us will be in danger. You are a big problem, a problem which has only one solution: you must convert to Christianity. There is no choice. Either you convert to Christianity, or we'll send you away from the convent. It's impossible to endanger everyone for you."

We left the meeting confused. We didn't speak about the topic among ourselves. We didn't know what to do. The next day the priest called us in again, and he repeated his words. "You must convert to Christianity. This is your last chance for life. There is no other choice for you."

That night, I lay in bed, wide awake, and thought about his words. I believed him. I thought that if I converted to Christianity, the Nazis wouldn't view me as a Jew.

But I am a Jew! I'm a Jewish girl. If I don't convert to Christianity, they will send me away from the convent. I won't be protected, and outside — I will be targeted. They'll kill me just like they killed all the Jews. Why? Why should they kill me? What did I do to them? Why does it bother them that I'm a Jew? And if I suddenly become a Christian, why will it stop bothering them? I don't understand this!

What should I do? How should I behave? I don't know how to decide for myself, and I have to decide for Irena, too — I'm responsible for her. This responsibility, which until now strengthened me and gave me a purpose to live, suddenly was too much for me. Irena would certainly follow what I would do; how could I make such a fateful decision alone?

"Chanah'le, don't forget that you're a Jew." That's what my father had begged me. But it's been a while since I've been Chanah'le. Now I'm Arlette. I see my father, crying and telling me again and again, "Don't forget us! Be our continuation! Don't forget that you're a Jew! Follow in our family's ways!"

When I woke up in the morning after a night of sleeplessness and crying, I looked at all the other girls who had been called together with me to the priest. Every girl had red, puffy eyes. They had probably all fallen asleep crying.

For several days all was quiet. We weren't called to the priest. No searches took place. Those were very difficult days, however, full of tension. At night, I longed for morning and in the morning, time didn't move. On Friday, we were brought to the priest's room once again. "You must decide," he said, "and the faster the better." They were forcing us to convert to Christianity, but they asked us to make the decision — as if we had asked for it!

I stopped eating, studying, working and playing. Mademoiselle Vermeul tried to encourage me. "Arlette, why are you sad? You have to let go of your worries and learn to participate. You cannot spend your life this way."

I didn't tell her about my new dilemma. She wouldn't understand. As a Christian, she would certainly want me to convert. I responded to her concern with more weeping, and she became angry. "Look at yourself! You're no longer just thin; you're a walking skeleton!"

But I simply couldn't eat. I sat in the dining room and tried, but I wasn't able to swallow. The food was stuck in my throat. The girls who sat near me happily finished off what I had left on my plate, and that's why the nuns didn't notice that I almost hadn't eaten a thing. During playtime, I sat at the side, while the following words echoed in my mind without stop: "Converting to Christianity is agreeing to *shmad*." During our hour of needlework, I sat immobile, holding the weaving in one hand and the needle in the other. I couldn't even function during choir practice — which I loved so much. I stood silently in my place. I was afraid that if I opened my mouth, sobs would burst out of my throat, instead of songs. The good Mademoiselle Shriver tried to cajole me to sing, but how could I sing in my sorrow?

I remembered a sad, mournful song that Papa used to sing sometimes: "*Al Naharos Bavel.*" One evening, Papa sat on the floor and explained this song to Meir and me. The Jews had a house, he told us, the most beautiful house in the world, called the Beis HaMikdash. The non-Jews destroyed it and took the Jews from Eretz Yisrael into exile. Since then, the Jewish nation has been suffering. When the gentiles took the Jews from Eretz Yisrael, they commanded them to play on their musical instruments and sing the songs they used to sing in the Beis HaMikdash. The Jews hung their harps on the trees and cut their thumbs off, so they wouldn't be able to play such holy music for the wicked gentiles.

I didn't know how to play any instruments, and I didn't have a harp either. I had always loved singing and dreamed of singing in a choir, but now, with the threat of Christianity looming over my head, how could I sing?

Oh, my Maman! If you could see me now, what would you say? You always told me that a Jew has to be proud, that there is nothing better in the world than being a Jew. That *HaKadosh Baruch Hu* accompanies each Jew always, and that gentiles afflict the Jews because they are jealous. They also want to gain the hidden light — that's what you said. Maman dear, now there isn't any light here. Everything is black and dark. The nights as well as the days. The gentiles aren't jealous of us now, they only hate us. They claim that we killed their messiah, and because of that, we have to suffer. They're so dumb! If he truly had been the messiah, how could anyone have killed him? And it happened so many years ago. How can they punish us for what happened almost two thousand years ago?! They're dumb, bad and cruel, these gentiles! I don't want to belong to them or be like them! Maman, I need a miracle. Can't you do anything for your Chanah'le?

The searches did not stop. We did not get used to the frightened dashes to the crypt, however. The fear was constant, almost tangible. Maybe all the searches began because of the new girls that came to the convent almost every day. Some of them were very young, toddlers and even babies, something new for the convent. We organized new sleeping rooms for them, and more nuns came from other convents in the area to help take care of them. I imagined they were all Jews, at least certainly the babies. Who would send a baby to a convent unless her life was in danger? Their parents surely feared for their fate, and knew that here they would be protected.

The priest kept pressuring us. “You must undergo communion just like all the girls in the convent. You must convert to Christianity.” Communion was a ceremony of eating “holy bread.” The priest would stand near the altar and place a small piece of bread in each girl’s mouth. “You can’t perform communion for someone who isn’t a Catholic. If you don’t convert to Christianity, we can’t keep you here. The Germans aren’t fools; it’s impossible to tell them that half the girls in a Catholic convent are Protestant.”

We had to decide. What should we do? How could I take such responsibility for Irena? Irena was unconcerned about the whole issue. She said she would do whatever I’d tell her to do. Things were simpler for her. She was young and was used to others worrying about her and deciding for her. But I was at my wit’s end.

Papa — what would Papa say? His last request of me had been to always remember that I’m a Jewish girl. I wanted to approach the other Jewish girls my age, hear their opinions and discuss the matter together. I wanted their advice on how we should respond. But I didn’t dare approach them. I couldn’t explain to myself why — after all, they were probably having a hard time trying to decide themselves. It was as if an inner mental block prevented us from talking it over together.

One night, when I was laying in bed and crying, Sister Danielle sat down next to my bed. “Why are you crying, Arlette? Why do you make so many problems for us and for yourself? What is it that we are asking of you anyhow? It will be better for you too if you convert to Christianity! Nowadays it is so difficult to be a Jew. Jews are persecuted and killed. It is bad to be a Jew, and we are seeking your good. Right now, you are endangering everyone. The cursed Germans may murder all of us because of you. Would you really want that, would you really want us to be murdered because of you? Please, Arlette, think about us too, not just about yourself. We are doing everything for you. We have given you a place to live, clothes to wear, and bread to eat. What is so bad about us that you're afraid to become one of us? What is so good about your Judaism, that you're willing to have us all murdered? Stop crying now, and think seriously about what I said."

That was all I needed to hear. Because of us, the Germans would kill everyone — all the nuns, all the people in the convent, all the people who saved us from death! Although they were by no means kind to us — treating us harshly on every occasion, and punishing us with extra severity for minor offenses — nevertheless, they were saving us from death. Because of them, we were still alive. The convent gave us refuge, food, clothes, studies, and medical treatment.

"And in exchange, they want our souls."

Where had I heard these words, powerful words which suddenly echoed resoundingly in my memory? "They're saving our bodies, and in exchange, they want our souls." Once, in the peaceful life that once was, I read Meir and Irena a story about the wicked Chmielnitzki, who had promised the Jews that whoever would convert to Christianity would not be killed. Everyone chose to die rather than convert. But at that time, everyone was together — the children looked to their parents for guidance, and their parents turned to the *rabbanim* who ultimately told everyone what to do. And I —

I was alone, only with Irena. There was no one to guide us, to tell us what was the right thing to do.

Papa had declared that I would live. Did he mean also in the case where I would have to convert to live? Will Hashem punish us for converting to Christianity, even though we were forced? Oh, Master of the world, how should I decide? What should I do? I'm not a hero. I don't want to die. I want to live.

Master of the world, I'm afraid. Maybe I no longer have a father, mother and brother. Maybe in the end no one will come to take me home. When Irena's grandfather comes to visit, he always promises that after the war, he'll take both of us out of the convent to live with him. But will he want us if we convert to Christianity? Maybe he'll tell us then, "You're gentiles, Christians! I'll have nothing more to do with you!"

No, he wouldn't say that! He wants only our welfare. But maybe they won't let him take us. Is it possible to become a Jew again after one converts to Christianity? Maybe it's not. Maybe the people in the convent will say that we belong to them. Maybe I'll be forced to remain a Christian... Oh, I can't decide alone. I must consult with Grandfather. But the priests and nuns are pressuring me so — how can I push off my decision until the next visiting day?

I lay there, tossing and turning in bed, with the thoughts tumbling one after the other in my mind, not letting me fall asleep. In the middle of these troubling thoughts, a forgotten picture surfaced, a picture which, until now, I had successfully kept hidden on the back burner of my memory.

# 32
# Tormenting Thoughts

Evening had descended, and there was no bread in the house. The stores were already closed, so my parents sent me to Irena's house to borrow a little bread for supper. On the way, I suddenly heard blood-curdling shouts, and was very frightened. I slipped into the yard of a house, and closed the gate securely behind me. I peeked between the bars of the fence and watched a harrowing scene. Nazi soldiers were chasing Jewish families out of the apartment building across the street. They whipped the Jews mercilessly, and chased them into two large trucks parked at the side of the road. The Jews ran to the trucks under the volley of cruel blows and harsh shouts, carrying babies and small children in their arms, crying and begging. The Germans ignored their pleadings. They kept whipping them and shouting, "*Raus*! *Raus*! *Shneller*! *Shneller*!" They threw the children into the trucks and forced the adults to run faster and faster. The Jews filled the trucks; their fearful cries were heartrending. In my hiding place behind the fence I tried to make myself as small as possible. I was trembling from fear. Maybe they would catch me in another second, and throw me into the truck also!

It was only long after the truck had left and quiet had returned to the street, that I finally dared to leave my hiding place and run to Irena's home. I shook from my weeping. Aunt Silka hugged me, washed my face and asked, "What happened, Chanah'le? What happened?" I could barely speak; I was crying so heavily. I finally managed to tell her of the terrifying scene I had witnessed. She hugged me again and said, "Hashem should watch you, and have mercy on us!" Once I calmed down somewhat, she accompanied me part of the way home — until after I had passed that terrible place. I continued running on the rest of the way by myself, while she stood there and watched me from afar. I kept turning my head, checking that Aunt Silka was still standing there and watching me.

When I returned home, I didn't say anything. I didn't want to upset Maman. She was angry at me, "What took you so long? Why did you let me worry so long?" I shrugged and didn't answer. I preferred to remain silent, even though Maman was angry at me and thought I had just stayed longer to play with Irena — anything just so she wouldn't cry.

And now, I am lying down on my bed in the large convent, fear paralyzing me. If I don't agree to convert to Christianity, would they also throw me and Irena into a truck? What happened to those people inside the truck? Where did they take them? Did they truly murder them? There were children and babies there!

My friend Becky's grandmother was also in the truck. She was a sweet old lady who always had taffies in her pocket and she always gave me an extra one to give to Meir. Sometimes, when she met me in the street, she asked me to go shopping for her. She, like Maman, didn't know French well and spoke only Yiddish. When I went shopping for her in the store, I saved her from having to "break her teeth" on a foreign language. She would go slowly, supported by a cane. On that terrible day, I saw her trying to run without her stick. Apparently the Nazis had taken it from her. She was holding onto another woman, and a German soldier was beating her shoulders and shouting, "Shnell! Shnell!" Why did he beat her? Couldn't he see that she was old, and couldn't go any faster? Where did they take her? How would she be able to manage there without her cane? Maybe they killed her also, and she no longer needs a cane...

But what did this sweet old lady do to them? Why would they want to kill her? What did all those little Jewish children do to them? What did Meir do to them? And perhaps, perhaps, despite all, they didn't kill them? Perhaps, despite all, they only took them to some far-off place? It can't be that they killed everyone. It's true that they are bad and cruel, but, after all, they're also human. Once, Mademoiselle Vermeul explained to us that animals only seek prey when they are hungry. An animal who is full doesn't attack another animal. If even animals don't kill without reason, how could humans murder the elderly and children without reason, people who are non-combatants? Soldiers against soldiers — that's the law of war, which is bad enough. Civilians may die in shellings, but soldiers don't target them intentionally.

I don't know what to think. Irena had told me that the Nazis were killing all the Jews. She wasn't simply trying to frighten me. The nuns also had said that if the Germans would discover Jewish girls in the convent, they would kill them.

I felt as if there were two different girls inside me: a

Chanah'le who believed in the German's cruelty, who knew that they murdered her family, and knew she's an orphan. But next to her was a different Chanah'le, who knew that people are spreading ridiculous rumors, and that such incomprehensible evil couldn't really exist.

Those two Chanah'les fought between themselves constantly. When the first prevailed, I was sunk in hopeless despair, but when the second prevailed — I calmed down and knew that after the war I would meet my parents and my brother, and therefore I had to do everything to remain alive. From Irena's story, I understood that the underground kept a record of where I was. Just as Irena's grandfather had found me, so would Maman find me.

Were they also so cruel to my family? Did they also throw them into the truck? Did they also shout such blood-curdling shouts at them? *Ribbono Shel Olam*, where did they take them?

And if I convert to Christianity now, and after the war, Papa and Maman and Meir come looking for me, would they want me back? Maybe they wouldn't want to see me if they would find out that I converted. Maybe they wouldn't even look at me? "You're no longer our daughter," I could hear their voices saying in my dreams. "You did *shmad* and you're a gentile child."

These thoughts tormented me every night and I barely slept. I was exhausted and tense during the day. I ate very little and didn't listen in class. Mademoiselle Vermeul's words went in one ear and out the other.

One day I was called alone to the doctor. This time it was really to see the doctor. He checked me and asked what was bothering me. "Why are you so pale? Why has your heavy coughing returned?"

I didn't know what to tell him. I didn't suffer any physical pain. Could I tell him that my soul was hurting, my Jewish soul? He wouldn't understand.

The doctor weighed me and shook his finger at me. "Arlette, you are very underweight. Something is bothering you, and you don't want to talk about it." I didn't answer him, and he told Sister Lucie that I was underweight and anemic, and that's why I didn't have strength to study and play. Anemia was the reason for my weakness, paleness, and fatigue. He instructed her to give me wholesome food and to free me of all my chores.

"The convent doesn't have special food to give Arlette. We barely have a minimum of food for everyone," Sister Danielle said. She and Sister Lucie breathed in relief. "The main thing is that she doesn't have tuberculosis as we feared." They sent me happily back to class, never imagining that my shaky emotions were the true reason for my poor state. After the check-up, the nuns began to pay attention to how I was eating, and they forced me to eat everything on my plate. I choked down the food, and suffered from stomachaches afterwards.

Finally, visiting day arrived! A heavy stone rolled off my heart when Irena's grandfather arrived. He'll help me decide. He'll tell me what to do, I thought with relief.

Grandfather saw immediately that something wasn't right. "What happened, Chanah'le? Did someone hurt you?"

I inhaled deeply and then let the terrible words out of my mouth. "Grandfather, they want me, and all the Jewish girls here, to convert to Christianity. If we refuse, they will send us out of the convent, because the Germans suspect there are

Jewish girls here."

Even though Grandfather wore dark glasses, I could sense that he was looking at me with love and pity. "Foolish girl! For that you were suffering so much? Do what they tell you, and that's all!"

"How can you say that?" I was shocked. "You're telling me to betray my people, the holy Torah, the promise I made to my father?! How can you tell me to convert to Christianity, as if it's nothing?"

"It's not a real conversion. All they'll do is throw some water over you. You think they can turn you into a Christian, and take away your Jewish identity? Nonsense. It's just a little water, a ceremony and nothing else."

It was hard for me to accept his words. The months of crying under the menacing cross had ingrained my intense aversion to the convent and its religion. And especially after that past month, when my crying bouts lasted practically the entire night while I deliberated about my future, I was very uneasy about regarding the matter of conversion so nonchalantly.

"But I promised Papa that I'll never forget that I'm a Jew!"

Grandfather smiled at me kindly. "And you really won't forget that you're a Jew! You'll remain a Jew forever. The gentiles think that they can turn you into a Christian by sprinkling some water on you, but you were born to a Jewish mother and you will always remain a kosher Jew. This conversion to Christianity is just a show. Now they're coercing you to cooperate with them, but after the war, I'll take you out of this convent and you'll fully return to practicing Judaism. Now it's a question of saving your life. When they sprinkle their water on you, think in your heart that it's all fake, that you're only agreeing to it outwardly — just to save your life. Don't worry. *HaKadosh Baruch Hu* knows your true intentions."

So all the awful worry which I had suffered for weeks had been in vain. I could calm down now, and simply put on a show. I was an expert at that already — from the moment I had entered the convent I had been putting on an act.

Grandfather sat down with Irena and me on either side of him, and told us about the Spanish Jews, the Marranos, who were forced to act like Christians outwardly and even went to church on Sunday. But privately, in the cellars of their homes, they kept the *mitzvos*. Many of them openly returned to Judaism as soon as it was possible to leave Spain.

That night I did not cry. After an unbearable month, my doubts had been resolved. I fell asleep easily. I had a wonderful dream that night — a dream that confirmed Grandfather's words. In my dream I saw Papa, sitting on the brown sofa with Meir on his lap, and singing, "*Oy, vi gut un vi fein, iz a Yiddele tzu zein* — Oh, how good and pleasant it is to be a Jew."

"Papa," I promised him, "I will remain a Jew! It's only an act, like the Marranos from Spain. In my heart I will remain a Jew. When the war ends, Irena's grandfather will help me to return to *Yiddishkeit* and find you."

Papa smiled and nodded. Meir also smiled at me, and both of them began to sing.

| | |
|---|---|
| *Golus, golus, vi grois bist du* | Exile, exile, how long are you |
| *Shechinah, Shechinah,* | *Shechinah, Shechinah,* |
| *Vi vait bist du* | How distant are You |

| | |
|---|---|
| *Ven di golus* | When the exile |
| *Vet zein kertzer* | Will be shorter |
| *Vet di Shechinah zein netter.* | The *Shechinah* will be closer. |

I clapped my hands delightfully. Papa never sang when he was angry. Now I knew that he wasn't angry at me! He still loved me!

"Chanah'le, you will live," Papa told me when he finished singing. "You must live; you must continue the family line."

When I woke up, I remembered every detail of the dream, and a tremendous tranquility filled my heart. I knew that everything would be alright. Papa had commanded me to live, even if I would have to act as if I was converting. Papa was certainly hinting to me that my difficulties would soon pass. The exile was already short, and the *Shechinah*, the Divine Presence, was close. The war would be over soon, and then I would once again be a Jewish girl openly.*

* This story is based on a young girl's memories, and under no circumstances should one conclude from it what is permitted or forbidden in this complex issue.

# 33 Communion

In the afternoon, the Jewish girls were once again called together to the priest's room. Before he could start his persuasive tactics I stood up and said, "Irena and I are ready to convert to Christianity." The other girls immediately followed suit, and they declared their willingness to convert, as well. We hadn't spoken among ourselves on the topic, but everyone knew that our grandfather had visited the day before, and they realized that we must have discussed the matter with him.

That evening, at supper, Sister Lucie stood on the platform in the center of the dining room and announced jubilantly, "All the Protestant girls are prepared to accept the Catholic religion upon themselves!" Cheerful clapping filled the dining room. Every girl received a spoon of jelly in honor of the event. Happiness pervaded the usually solemn atmosphere — the nuns were happy that we finally agreed to convert, and the girls were happy with their spoonful of jelly. Although we, the Jewish girls, also put on a cheerful façade, inside our hearts, we were deeply distressed.

Before our conversion could take place, we had a lot of studying to do. We were expected to learn a comprehensive amount about the practices of the Christian religion. The priest added more theology classes to our schedules, and I played my part of the eager convert-to-be, listening and participating. The priest claimed that we had to review all the material that we had covered already, since we had been poor students and hadn't cooperated.

There were many preparations for the baptismal ceremony, and everyone in the convent joined in. The church was cleaned thoroughly, festive decorations were prepared, and beautiful tablecloths were spread on the tables. Everyone waited in anticipation for the great day. The excitement was tangible. Only we, the Jewish girls, who had prompted this great commotion, hoped that this day would never arrive.

But it did arrive. It began with the baptismal ceremony, which was held on a Friday. A large entourage of singing nuns and girls escorted us to the church. We lined up in front of the priest, who presided over the ceremony. He merrily sprinkled a few drops of "holy water" on us. It's all nonsense, I kept saying to myself. I believe only in Hashem. I'm a Jew, I was born to a Jewish mother, and I'll always remain a Jew.

I felt like I was in a dream. My body was there — but my heart was far away. I made sure that the tears pent up in my eyes didn't flow out, so they wouldn't notice I was just putting on an act to save my life. I'm a Jew, and I'll remain a Jew! I didn't change my religion, it's just a show. This is just simple water, and it's all nonsense. Even when I said the Christian prayers, I silently repeated to myself: This is nonsense.

On Sunday, the great ceremony was held — our first communion. All the girls who had converted on Friday gathered in one room. There we received new white dresses, which we put on instead of our dismal, black ones. We each wore a wreath of flowers on our heads and held a bouquet of flowers. We marched to the decorated church. Every girl was accompanied by someone else — who was called her "godmother." My godmother was Mademoiselle Vermeul, and from then on, she was considered to be responsible for me. She had always loved me very much, and after my communion, she urged me to come live with her and be her adopted daughter. I also loved her, and it was difficult to refuse her. But she wanted only me, without Irena, which gave me the strength to resist her appealing offer. "I must stay with Irena and watch over her," I explained to Mademoiselle Vermeul.

After the communion ceremony, we went to the dining room. The room had undergone its own transformation. It was decorated festively and the fancy food bespoke the importance of the occasion. Even during the Christian holidays, the meals had never been so special. We, the "converts," sat in our seats of honor on a raised platform. We spent the entire day dressed in our white dresses and wearing our flowers, and the other girls fussed over us.

That long day also came to its end. Finally, I was alone in my bed. I lifted my eyes to the cross above my head and whispered, "You don't frighten me anymore; you can't annoy me any longer! I know the secret code that will protect me from you. All I have to say is: It's false! It's just a show; everything is nonsense." I closed my eyes and thought about Maman and Papa. If they had seen me today, what would they have said about their Chanah'le? I wondered.

I began to sing to myself, very quietly, allowing my pent-up emotions to surface. My tears fell freely as I sang:

| | |
|---|---|
| *Oy, vi gut un vi fein,* | How good and pleasant it is |
| *Iz a Yiddele tzu zein.* | To be a Jew. |
| *Vile a Yiddele tzu zein* | Because to be a Jew |

| | |
|---|---|
| *Iz doch gut, un voyel, un fein.* | Is good, and enjoyable, and pleasant. |

The following day everything returned to its routine. I was a good girl, I stopped losing hats, I joined all the prayers, and I began to eat meat again. I listened and participated in the priest's theology classes. I didn't want to upset the nuns or the priest. Irena's grandfather had promised that Hashem would forgive me. *Im yirtzeh Hashem*, the war will be over soon, and everything will change. I wondered, though, how long that would take. Sometimes it seemed to me that the war would never end!

After several weeks, another communion ceremony was held for the younger girls — Irena was in that group. I was her "godmother" and I received a special dress in honor of the event. The same festivities were repeated, the white dresses and flower wreaths. Irena looked beautiful! The white dress suited her. With her black hair and dark eyes, Irena looked completely black in our regular black dress. Bedecked in a snow-white dress with a wreath of flowers on her head, she almost looked like a shining princess — and she would have, were it not for the painful circumstances.

***On the day of Irena's communion. Chanah as her "godmother."***

The church was full of

guests. I overheard one visitor say to the other, "It's so good to have a little joy in this terrible period." It seemed that all the guests shared the same sentiments. I heard that same comment repeated many times during the celebration. I suddenly understood that besides the terrible suffering which I, my family members and all the Jews were experiencing, this war had caused a certain amount of suffering even to the gentiles. They saw in this ceremony, which caused us such anguish, a festive occasion which helped them temporarily forget their sufferings.

Irena and I knew the communion was meaningless — we were just putting on a show. The other girls, however, carried it out in all seriousness.

At the communion, the priest gave each girl a new name. Mine was Anna Marie, and Irena's — Mary Anas. I didn't always remember my new name, but I didn't feel pressured. All the other girls who had "converted" also had trouble remembering their new names. Even the nuns would occasionally call us by our former names.

I hoped that once the communion was behind me, my fears about abandoning my religion would dissipate, and I would enjoy restful nights. But my troublesome thoughts still came back to haunt me. I simply couldn't rid myself of them. On the next visiting day, Grandfather noticed the dark circles under my eyes. He understood immediately that my nightmares and guilt feelings still plagued me and was quick to reassure me that what I had done was absolutely meaningless. He explained again and again that I hadn't become a Christian. I was comforted and convinced after that visit. Grandfather had effectively driven away my nightmares, and I finally became a normal girl, like everyone else.

# 34
# Will They Amputate?

The influx of new girls didn't stop. Another sleeping hall opened up, and more tables were added in the dining hall. Nurseries were also opened for the babies that arrived. I was certain that those babies were Jewish babies, Jewish girls just like me. But, unlike me, they didn't know it. They were too young to remember their previous lives. If their parents wouldn't return, they would be raised like gentiles in every way. Most of the new girls were young, Irena's age and younger. Girls my age didn't come. Would these girls ever remember their parents and their people? I added another prayer to the prayers I recited every night in bed. I began to pray for them. "Please, Hashem," I would beg wholeheartedly, "please return the parents of these little children after the war. Help them to be raised like Jews."

Our poverty and misery became worse. There was no extra food or clothing to go around, even though many more girls had joined us. The veterans among the girls were upset with the arrival of the newer ones. Because of them, we had to crowd together, and because of them, everyone had less food. And since the new girls were small, they didn't take part in the heavy cleaning work we had to do. Most of the work in the convent was done by us girls. My group was almost the oldest group — there was only one group above us

— and we were loaded with work.

My job was to scrape the church's rough, wooden floor. I had to bend down on my hands and knees to accomplish this job. Breta polished all the bronze candlesticks, and Annette rubbed the benches with soapy water that was as cold as ice, but Suzanne's and my work — scraping the floor — was the hardest job. In general, we didn't complain about the work. It was simply part of the routine here.

One day, however, my knee hurt me very much. When I couldn't bear the pain anymore, I stood up and bent over at the waist to clean the floor. But working this way wasn't as efficient as bending down on one's knees. Sister Danielle, who was supervising us and the girls who were cleaning the windows, yelled at me. "That's not the way to clean! Your work is worthless!"

I knew that if I would tell her about the pain in my knee, she would think that I was just looking for excuses to evade work. In the end, I would get more blows for complaining. Suzanne gave me a questioning look, wondering what was really the problem. I pointed to my aching knee and she whispered, "I'll help you. I'll do more than my share." At that moment, I felt better.

Suzanne worked feverishly and when Sister Danielle turned to the windows further away, Breta and Annette also joined in my work. The floor was shining when Sister Danielle returned, and she pursed her lips in satisfaction. "With you, nothing works without shouting," she said.

The following day, when I kneeled down for prayers, fierce pains shot through my knee. I tried leaning on one knee and holding the painful one in the air, but I quickly lost my balance. I wanted to put my hand under my knee and cushion it somewhat, but Sister Maria didn't take her eyes off our group for a minute. Sister Maria used every opportunity to make life miserable for me. She hadn't stopped abusing the Jewish girls even after our conversion ceremony. I tried to hold myself straight and pray nicely so she wouldn't scold or mock me, as she often did. I was afraid of her stabbing, hurtful tongue.

The pain became worse. I folded my dress under my knee, but it didn't help. I barely was able to hold myself back from groaning. I prayed that I would be able to control myself and wouldn't burst into tears. Finally the prayers ended and we sat on the bench to hear the priest's sermon. I lifted the hem of my dress and drew in my breath. My knee was red and swollen.

When we left the church, Sister Maria began shouting at me, "Why are you limping? Why were you writhing like a snake the whole time instead of praying nicely? You think I didn't see? Walk properly now! Walk like a person and don't complain!"

I tried to walk straight, but the pain was too acute. Sister Maria incited the girls to mock me and imitate my limp. Throughout the day I was in agony, and everyone laughed at me, thinking I was putting on a show. I cried the entire night from the pain and frustration. Of all the nuns, it was Sister Maria who was appointed over us that night. Usually they took turns, and the nun who supervised us during the day didn't stay with us at night. But this time, no other nun arrived to relieve Sister Maria. I stuck my head deep in my pillow so she wouldn't hear my sobbing. However, my sobs were loud, and the quiet night offered no protecting noises to muffle my crying. Sister Maria heard my sobbing and hurried to berate me. She wasn't even willing to look at my leg, which was swelling at a frightening speed.

In the morning, I barely managed to crawl out of bed and inch my way to the washroom. When the girls saw my bizarre gait, they immediately began to poke fun at me, perhaps to find favor in Sister Maria's eyes. But when they saw my leg, which had become completely swollen overnight and was now red down to the foot, they were frightened and kept quiet. Breta, who was a true friend, slipped away to the office despite the possibility of receiving a punishment, and told Sister Lucie.

Sister Lucie loved all of us, and treated us wonderfully. Even though she was very busy, she occasionally made time to visit us, speak with us and tell us stories. She listened to all our gripes, and always reminded us, "If you have a problem, don't hesitate to come to my room and tell me. My door is always open for you." When Breta told her about my leg, she came immediately. She inspected my knee and was shocked. "Why didn't you speak up? Why did you wait until now?"

I told her the whole truth. I usually didn't tell her about how the nuns treated us; experience had taught me that every time we informed on a nun we paid a high price for it. But Sister Maria had gone too far this time. If she would only have been willing to peek at my leg once, she would have seen right away that I hadn't been crying the whole night just to annoy her. "Every time Sister Maria watches over us, bad things happen," I told Sister Lucie. "Maybe it would be better if she would watch over something else besides girls."

Sister Lucie didn't reply, of course. She brought me to the infirmary, gave me a cup of milk, and immediately called the doctor. The doctor checked my knee and said that a foreign object — like a splinter — must have penetrated my knee and had caused a severe infection. He was astonished that it had been neglected. "Why did you wait until the leg reached a state where it has to be amputated?"

To be amputated? Trepidation seized me. *Ribbono Shel Olam*! Could this be happening? Will they really cut off my leg? Will I be a cripple my whole life?

"I'll try to operate," the doctor told Sister Lucie. "I hope I can save the leg. It's probably better for me to operate on her here — it's clean and orderly, and you have more equipment here than the hospital does. Everything is in subnormal conditions there because of the war."

He gave me some anesthesia, and when I woke up, I found myself in bed with my leg completely bandaged, resting atop a pile of pillows. The pain was terrible, and I felt it not only in my leg, but all over my body. Then nuns gave me continuous medication — tranquilizers, medications to reduce the swelling and medications against infection. So many medications — but despite them, I writhed in pain. I didn't want any visitors, I didn't want anyone to speak to me at all. I slept most of the time, but when I was awake, I suffered terribly.

The pain became more tolerable after just a few days. The pains intensified several times in the day, particularly when the doctor changed the bandages. I was still forbidden to get up from bed, and I received special food. Now, when I felt a little better, my friends came to visit me. They were jealous when they saw how I was laying in bed with the nuns serving me and bringing me good food. I didn't have to work or even learn. It really would have been pleasant, were it not for the intense pain and the fear of amputation. That distressed me even more than the terrible pain.

Slowly the swelling subsided. The nuns placed hot and cold compresses alternately on my knee, and although it hurt, I didn't complain. I was willing to suffer any treatment as long as they wouldn't amputate my leg. After two weeks, when the redness had gone down, they told me to walk around a little — they even let me leave the infirmary. Another week passed, and they let me go down the stairs and out to the yard to breathe some fresh air.

Autumn was swiftly approaching. Strong winds blew and a slight chill had crept into the air. I looked around the yard in wonder — the majestic beauty of the changing leaves had transformed our garden. The green grass, red, orange, yellow and brown leaves, and a multitude of flowers in a burst of color decorated the yard. A wonderful smell of flowers and nectar wafted through the air.

But best of all – I was walking on my own two feet! The bandaged leg still hurt, but I had my leg. They didn't amputate it. I didn't become a cripple.

The clear, fragrant air and the bright colors of nature provided a welcome contrast to the completely white infirmary. I felt that I was getting stronger with each breath I took. I stood up, leaning against a tree for support, and looked at the blossoming garden around me. How good it is to be alive and healthy! Even the sight of the high wall topped with the glass shards couldn't dampen my joy. I didn't care that I was in a convent, in the grip of gentiles. I was filled with gratitude to Hashem that I was alive, healthy, and walking on my own two feet!

# 35
# Rosh Hashanah

Irena's grandfather came to visit. I was still in the infirmary, but they gave me permission to go down to him. I showed him my foot, still swathed in a large bandage and still very painful, and I told him about the miracle that had happened to me.

Grandfather was very shaken up. "Oh, Chanah'le, how fortunate we are that you're here in the convent!" he said. "Where else would they bring you a doctor, medications and nutritious food? People are dying from hunger now — there is nothing to eat."

"What about you, Grandfather? Do you have food to eat?" I asked in trepidation. Grandfather smiled his good-natured smile. "Don't worry, my dear child. I have enough. In the old age home, there is plenty of food to go around." I looked at the bag of candies he held, and Grandfather understood what I was thinking. He quickly calmed me down. "The senior citizens who live with me in the nursing home gave me these candies. I didn't deprive myself to bring them to you."

Then Grandfather lowered his voice. "Girls, next Tuesday is Rosh Hashanah. Don't forget it! Despite the loathsome water they threw on you, you are Jewish girls. Neither you nor I will be able to hear *tekias shofar*, and you won't remember the prayers. But remember that this day is the *Yom HaDin*, the day on which the entire world is standing in judgment before *HaKadosh Baruch Hu*. The Nazis and their helpers will receive their punishment from heaven. We can't get back at them, but our Father in Heaven will take care of them. They too will be punished for their wicked ways. As for you, try not to write or do craftwork during those two days. Don't forget!"

Rosh Hashanah. Yom Kippur. Maman would utter those words in a voice trembling with awe. "Grandfather, maybe you can take off your glasses for just a second?" I asked. I wanted to see his eyes when he spoke about Rosh Hashanah. Grandfather removed his thick glasses and looked at us with loving eyes. "A week later, on Thursday, it will be Yom Kippur," he said. "This is a great and awesome day. You must *daven* on these days. It doesn't matter if you don't remember the *tefillos* — *daven* in French, and ask Hashem for forgiveness. He hears every *tefillah*, in every language and in every place. He will hear you here too."

My bandage was removed and I joined the other girls. I only had to return to the infirmary once a week to be inspected by the doctor. He was very pleased with my recovery — but I had no peace of mind.

How I wished I could remember just one prayer! I remembered Maman's kerchief. She had a white, shiny kerchief, special for the *Yomim Nora'im*. That's what they called Rosh Hashanah and Yom Kippur: *Yomim Nora'im* — High Holidays. The stark beauty of Maman's white kerchief reflected and glistened on her face. Or maybe her face shone because of the holiness of the days?

I recalled Reb Dovid, the *ba'al toke'ah*. He had a long,

white beard, and he wore a spotless white *kittel*. His yarmulka was also white. He was completely enwrapped in a *tallis*; only his face and the shofar were visible. Every time I looked at him, he reminded me of Eliyahu HaNavi. Papa had told us that before Mashiach comes, Eliyahu HaNavi would come and blow a big shofar. Each time Papa said this, I thought of Reb Dovid and his shofar.

I remembered the white kerchief and Reb Dovid's shofar. I didn't remember the *tefillos*. I remembered our seats in the women's balcony and the *machzors* all the women held. But no matter what, I couldn't remember what was written inside.

Maman's kerchief had been sold with all the other household items. And Reb Dovid, who knows where he was? He was already old then. Maybe he was no longer alive. And what had happened to his shofar? I hoped with all my heart that the shofar wasn't lost. Maybe Eliyahu HaNavi would need it when he came to blow the shofar and announce that Mashiach had finally come.

On Tuesday, I sat in class and didn't write. Mademoiselle Vermeul put her hand on my forehead, afraid I was sick. "Anna Marie, do you feel all right?" she asked worriedly.

"No. My head hurts me, and also my stomach," I answered with fervor. I hoped that they would tell me to lie down in the infirmary, where I could devote myself to thinking about Rosh Hashanah without interruptions. But I didn't have a fever, and Sister Danielle said that the pains would pass if I would behave as I should.

It rained the entire day. When we were in the dining room, we suddenly heard rolling waves of thunder, coming one after another. They are blowing shofar in Heaven, I thought to myself. Here on earth, this terrible war is going on, and no one can blow the shofar, so the angels in Heaven are blowing it for us. I felt bad that I wasn't sitting next to Irena. I wanted to share my thoughts with her. I caught her eye, though, and made a round fist around my mouth, as if I was blowing shofar, and she nodded back. The thunder also reminded her of shofar blowing.

That day during sewing class, I stood near the window. Irena and I had decided that we wouldn't sit next to our work tables today, and the craftwork teacher decided to ignore us. We were usually diligent workers, so she decided it was senseless to punish us for misbehaving just once. I stood on my tip-toes and looked outside to the heavens. Irena came and stood next to me, trying to see the cloudy skies through the high window. She clung to me and whispered in excitement, "The Heavens are blowing shofar. The gentiles think this is plain thunder, but we know the truth."

A week later, on Wednesday night, everyone was preparing for bed, when I suddenly said out loud, "Now it's Yom Kippur night — *Kol Nidrei.*"

"What are you babbling about?" several gentile girls asked. "What did you say?"

I didn't answer them. I looked around me and saw understanding eyes fixed on me, as if an electric current had passed through the room. Breta looked at me, pale, and I nodded at her, as if to say, "Yes, you heard right."

Breta burst into tears, and I heard Simone inhale deeply. I hurried into my bed and covered my head. The arrow I had shot out had hit the mark. The nuns and gentile girls hadn't understood the strange words, but the Jewish girls had. I laid down in bed, completely covered, and tried as hard as I could to remember some prayers. Suddenly I felt a hand gently touching my shoulders. It was Jolette. "Do you remember the prayers?" she whispered.

"No. I don't. But our grandfather told us that we can pray in our own words and ask forgiveness. And we can promise that as soon as we can, we'll return to Judaism."

"I also forgot," Jolette whispered regretfully. "I only remember that in one prayer, you're supposed to beat your heart." She left, and I watched her as she made her way back to bed. I saw her stop next to Breta's bed and whisper something in her ear. Breta shook her head from side to side. She also didn't remember. None of us remembered the prayers.

I pounded on my heart under the blanket, as Jolette had said, and while crying, I pleaded, "Forgive me! Forgive me for converting, forgive me for kneeling down on my knees, forgive me for eating *treif* food, forgive me for wearing a cross. I am a Jew, a Jew! Please, Hashem, forgive me and all the Jewish girls who are here. Immediately after the war, when Irena's grandfather takes me out of this terrible place and I'll be able to live with Jews, I'll fulfill all the *mitzvos* and will keep all the laws."

I lifted myself up and examined each bed, one by one. All Jewish girls were still awake. Only the gentile girls were sleeping peacefully. "Please, Hashem," I whispered. "Even in this place of impurity, accept our prayers, the prayers of girls who are shackled by the wicked. They are trying to make us forget that we are Jews. But I just said 'Yom Kippur' and '*Kol Nidrei*,' and everyone came to life. We're all here against our will, and are forced to follow the convent's rules, but we haven't forgotten our origin. Please, let this war end before we forget!"

The girls tossed back and forth in their beds, peace of mind eluding them. Some girls buried their face in their pillows and cried. How I wished that I could remember just one prayer! I would say it out loud now. We all needed it. It's too bad I didn't ask Grandfather to teach me one prayer. I had an idea. "*Fargabong*," I whispered in the air. "*Fargabong* — forgive us. We have to ask *fargabong* from God, and He will forgive us."

The nun who watched over us that night approached me and scolded me quietly. "What is happening, Anna Marie? You are disturbing everyone. Lie quietly and go to sleep already!"

I lay down quietly, satisfied that I had managed to announce my whispered message. I didn't care that the nun had scolded me — at least I had gotten the message across to my friends.

In the morning, I sat in class with folded hands. I didn't bother anyone, but I also didn't participate. Mademoiselle Vermeul didn't notice this time, and the priest didn't pay attention either. I sat quietly and thought about Yom Kippur. But the problem began in the dining room. I wanted to fast, but the supervising nun was upset. "You didn't eat this morning either!" she shouted. "You must eat." I refused to open my mouth, and in the end, she went to call Sister Lucie. This time, Sister Lucie was angry, which was unusual for her. "You must eat, Anna Marie. The doctor said that if you don't eat, you will get sick again. I can't give you the more wholesome food that he requested, but the simple food that we do have here, you must eat — immediately!"

I ate it. We all ate. "After the war," I promised myself, "I will always fast on Yom Kippur."

# 36
# Two Thousand Years

Sukkos arrived a few days after Yom Kippur. I had fond, clear memories of the holiday. Papa would sing beautiful songs with us about Sukkos. Since we didn't have a *sukkah*, Papa, Meir and I would join Irena and Uncle Yossel and help them build their *sukkah* on their porch. It was a pleasant experience — we sang and had much fun as we worked. We also joined Irena's family for all the meals on Sukkos. It was the rainy season in Belgium at that time of year, and many meals were interrupted by a steady downpour of rain. I remember dashing inside and waiting in the house for the rain to stop. As soon as it did, we would run back to the *sukkah*. I will always remember Sukkos as a time of abundant happiness, contentment and laughter. Even when the rain would start before we finished eating, and we would hurry into the house and continue the meal there, our spirits weren't dampened.

Papa told us that in Eretz Yisrael, it is very unusual for rain to fall on Sukkos, and the people there eat all their holiday meals in a *sukkah*. In the beginning I had believed him, but once he told me that people also *sleep* in their *sukkahs* in Eretz Yisrael, I knew he was joking. How can one sleep in a *sukkah*? But Papa assured me that it was true. I finally accepted it — after all, in Eretz Yisrael, everything was possible. It was a heavenly land, where even the most incredible things could happen.

I remember Papa pointing at an exquisite "*Mizrach*" sign hanging in Irena's *sukkah*. "There, in Yerushalayim, in Eretz Yisrael, where the Beis HaMikdash stood — there, people, stay in a *sukkah* during the day and throughout the night."

I had looked at the "*Mizrach*" sign, confused. I didn't see Eretz Yisrael in it! I only saw a lovely picture which my Maman had embroidered during the long years she was waiting to become a mother. It was one of Maman's most intricate, breath-taking creations, and whoever entered the *sukkah* would immediately stop to look at and comment on its beauty. Maman would always laugh and say, "How much happier I am that I don't have time for such creations anymore!" I could never understand that — why would Maman be happy that she had no more time to embroider such nice things?

One Sukkos evening, before we left Irena's *sukkah*, I closely looked at the "*Mizrach*" wall-hanging. I thought about Papa's words about Yerushalayim. Maybe Papa meant that the direction of Yerushalayim was where the picture was, instead of Yerushalayim being in the picture itself? I decided that I would look for Yerushalayim and the Beis HaMikdash while we walked home, but I didn't know what I was looking for. I had never seen Yerushalayim; Eretz Yisrael was a magical, mystery land. Fog covered the sky, though, and I couldn't see anything. I kept tilting my head heavenward, hoping to catch a glimpse of something. Finally, the clouds parted, and I triumphantly pointed to the far-off stars and said, "Yes, there, there is Yerushalayim, in the stars."

That night, as we did every Sukkos evening, we continued singing the Yom Tov songs quietly as we walked home. There was one song which we especially loved, and I remembered it — word for word.

In my mind, the sukkah, the "*Mizrach*" wall-hanging, Yerushalayim in heaven, and that special song blended together into one.

I wanted to sing it again, to relive the light of Sukkos inside the convent's black walls.

It was during one of our recess breaks, and Irena and I had been strolling through the convent's halls. I turned to her and asked, "Irena, do you remember the *sukkah* song?"

"No," she said.

"How can that be? Everything that I remember about Sukkos involves this song."

"I don't remember the same things you do!" Irena said. "I have my own memories. But please, teach me the song. Maybe when I learn it, I'll remember it."

We ran up countless polished steps, until we reached the convent's highest floor. People barely ever ventured up so high, and we could sing without any fears of intruders. We settled down on one of those steps — and I began to sing:

| | |
|---:|---|
| *A sukkahleh, a kleine* | A small *sukkah'leh* |
| *Mit bretalach gemeina* | Made from small, thin boards |
| *Hub ich mir* | I have built myself |
| *a sukkahleh gemacht* | a *sukkah'leh* |
| *Badekt dem dach* | I've covered the roof |
| *Mit a bissele schach* | With a little bit of *schach* |
| *Zitz ich mir in sukkahleh* | And I sit in it |
| *Bei nacht.* | At night. |

| | |
|---|---|
| *A vint a kalten* | A cold wind |
| *Bluzt dorch di shpalten* | Is blowing through the cracks |
| *Un di lichtalach* | And many candles |
| *zei leshen fil* | It is extinguishing |
| *Es iz mir a chiddush* | It is surprising to me |
| *Vi ich mach mir kiddush* | That while I made *Kiddush* |
| *Un di lichtalach zei brennen* | The flames that still burn |
| *ganz shtill.* | do not flicker. |
| | |
| *Zei nisht kein na'ar* | Don't be a fool |
| *Un hub nisht kein tza'ar* | And don't agonize |
| *Zol dir di sukkah nisht zein bank* | Don't worry about the *sukkah* |
| *Es iz shoen ga'ar* | It is already almost |
| *Balt tzvei toizand yor* | Two thousand years old |
| *Un di sukkaleh shteit* | And the *sukkah'leh* stands |
| *Noch gantz lang.* | A long time. |

After Sukkos, Irena's grandfather came for a visit. He told us that he dreamed about the *Arba Minim* throughout the holiday, and everything he ate smelled like an *esrog*. I didn't know what he was talking about. I didn't remember the *esrog*. "You know, Grandfather," I said in reflection. "I think I remember my parents' house primarily through songs. I remember everything that was connected to a song, but all the other things are hazy."

"Yes, Chanah'le, I also remember your house as a house full of song. They were always singing there. With a voice like your father had, and your uncle too, what's the surprise? You know, Chanah'le, your grandfather was an exceptional *chazan*, and people came from all over to hear him. Your grandfather's *Rebbe* used to say about him that his prayers broke through to the Heavens and opened hearts."

Grandfather told us that this year we wouldn't have been able to eat in a *sukkah* even if we would have had one, because torrents of rain fell the entire holiday. The rain reminded me of Papa's stories about sunny Yerushalayim, where they eat all the holiday meals in a *sukkah*, and even sleep there.

"Grandfather, where is Yerushalayim?" I asked.

"Yerushalayim..." Grandfather's voice became dreamy. "After the war, we will all go to Yerushalayim. There, everyone will know that you are Jewish girls. There, everyone will see that you are faithful Jewish girls. There in Yerushalayim, after the war..."

I sighed. Those words were familiar: After the war. They've been telling us "after the war" for so long already! Will this war ever come to an end?

# 37
# Frigid Winter

One afternoon, we were playing in the playroom, but Irena wasn't there. *Where is she?* I asked myself worriedly. I went to look for her, and found her sitting on a bench next to the dining room, flushed and shivering.

"What happened, Irena? What did they do to you?"

"Nothing happened. I'm just tired, and my head hurts me."

"But why are you shaking? Are you cold?"

"No, why do you think I'm cold? I'm not cold at all. I'm hot."

I put my hand on her forehead. She was burning with fever. I was very scared. There was no one else around; it was just the two of us in the long corridor. "Irena, don't get up! Stay here, I'll be back in a minute!"

"Fine," Irena agreed. "Anyway, I don't have energy to stand. I guess I ran too hard, and now I have no strength to move."

I ran to the second wing and alerted the first nun I found. It was Sister Elisabeth. I let out a jumble of frightened words. She had to ask me several times to repeat myself, but in the end, she understood my confused, hysterical words, and went with me to Irena. When she felt Irena's forehead she was also shocked. She immediately brought Irena to the infirmary, and sent me to call Sister Lucie.

When I arrived at the infirmary with Sister Lucie, Irena was already dressed in a nightgown and lying in bed. Sister Elisabeth took her temperature, and the two nuns looked at the thermometer. They spoke together quietly and I couldn't hear what they were saying.

I sat near Irena's bed and held her hand. Sister Lucie brought her a cup of milk, as she did for every sick child. She also brought me a cup of milk. "But I'm not sick," I reminded her.

Sister Lucie smiled. "Just drink it anyway," she said. "You have to grow a little. You're so thin."

I loved milk. But I liked the feeling that Sister Lucie was thinking about me and pampering me, even more than the sweet taste of milk. I drank it happily.

Irena on the other hand, couldn't drink. Sister Lucie supported her head and patiently helped her drink. She cajoled her to take one sip and then another, and wouldn't desist until Irena had finished the whole cup. She left shortly afterwards, and I stayed next to Irena. Sister Elisabeth also remained with us and told us stories. She was so nice! All the girls in the convent loved her. Why couldn't all the nuns be as good as Sister Lucie and Sister Elisabeth? I thought. Then life would be so good...

The doctor arrived that evening. They sent me out of the infirmary. I stood behind the door, waiting. When the nun came out of the room with the doctor and saw I was standing behind the door, she began to admonish me. The doctor stopped her and patted my head fondly. "Who are you to the sick child?" he asked.

"She's my cousin," I explained.

"Don't worry. She's not feeling well, but she'll rest, take her medicine and will recover. As for you, go back to your friends, and eat supper and sleep well. Tomorrow after class, you can come visit your cousin again."

Irena had a fast recovery. When I had been sick, I had lain in bed for over two weeks, and even when I was discharged, I walked with a cane and continued taking medicine for almost a week, and remained very weak for a long time. But Irena returned to her group after only four days, completely healthy.

Winter reached its peak. The fierce cold was terrible, and thick snow fell without stop. There wasn't even one nice day when we could go outside to play. We were imprisoned in the cold convent, huddled together and hunched over from cold. It was always freezing.

Then nuns gave every girl another pair of socks and another pair of warm underwear to help keep us warm. But it was still bitter cold. We looked for pieces of paper to stuff our shoes. The girls said that this would warm us up, but I didn't feel any difference. My shoes fit me perfectly, and the extra paper pinched my toes. I preferred giving Irena the paper I found. In any case, with paper or without, our feet were cold and blue.

We didn't play anymore. On occasion, we would run through the long corridors to warm ourselves up. It was always dark in the convent. The light was very dim, and the dimness, together with the cold, made us listless. We had no desire to play. The nuns told us horror stories, and the girls also shared sad and frightening stories with each other. Even choir practice had stopped; Mademoiselle Shriver couldn't come in such inclement weather, and we didn't sing at all.

There was nothing cheerful in that somber place.

Our studies occupied our mornings, but every afternoon, while we sat bored in the playroom, time seemed to stop. We counted the minutes till evening and bedtime. Once we entered our beds, though, we had a hard time falling asleep. Bedtime had been pushed forward to save the convent hours of lighting and heating, and we weren't tired. We just tossed and turned from side to side, waiting for morning.

The cold intensified from day to day and it became freezing. Mademoiselle Vermeul was absent for several days due to the unbearable weather conditions. Afterwards, when she finally arrived, a terrible blizzard hit and she couldn't leave. She slept in the convent, and in the afternoons, she came to the playroom and organized activities.

Those few days with Mademoiselle Vermeul were bliss. We ran, jumped and warmed up. During those days, there was laughter and happiness in the convent. But when we asked Mademoiselle Vermeul to stay with us every day, and not just during the blizzard, she refused. We tried to enlist Sister Lucie's help, but she said that she couldn't force Mademoiselle Vermeul to remain against her will.

On visiting day, to our great surprise, Irena's grandfather appeared. We didn't expect he would come — the cold was so terrible, and he was an elderly man! But Grandfather didn't disappoint us. He arrived, even though it was dangerous for a man his age to go out in such cold. When we saw him, we were the happiest girls in the convent. We will never forget that wonderful kindness he did for us, coming to visit us despite the severe weather.

Grandfather told us about rumors that the Germans were losing in Russia. The powerful German army was beginning to crumble, and maybe, just maybe, the end of the war was approaching. I didn't believe it. I had heard about "after the war" so many times already, that it didn't seem to me it would ever come. Even if it was true that the Germans were suffering losses in Russia, Russia was a far away country. We were in Belgium, where the Germans were in undisputed control.

The kitchen shift was the hardest shift. Our kitchen was very large and the chefs cooked for everyone in the huge convent: priests, nuns, students, teachers and service people. We also cooked for all the small convents in the area. Delivery men arrived every day to pick up prepared food packages.

I was hungry. I was always hungry. When I was sent to the kitchen shift, I thought that this was my opportunity. If I'm working so hard here, at least let me get some benefit from it. When I thought no one was looking, I took a piece of bread and hid it in the pocket of my underdress. My friend who was working next to me did the same. But the supervising nun saw us and shouted, "You stole bread! Admit it immediately!"

"Yes, we each took a piece of bread. We're hungry..."

"Everyone is hungry! We don't have enough food. There's a frightening war happening now. How do you think we'll win this war if everyone steals bread? As a punishment, you have to go to confession."

I had never been sent to confession for a sin. I was terrified. The nun sent us back to our group, and I cried the whole way. My friend urged me to stop crying so we could eat the bread right away. After all the commotion the nun had made, she hadn't thought to search us for the stolen bread. I was distraught, however, that I could barely agree. We stood in a corner of the long corridor and quickly devoured the bread. My friend rubbed her stomach and said, "I don't care about going to confession as long as I'm full. Confession is so much easier than being hungry."

"Oh, what will we do?" I began to worry again. "When we go to confession, everyone will know that we sinned!"

My friend was unconcerned. "So what?" she said. "Everyone goes." But I wasn't comforted. That night I couldn't sleep. Thoughts of horrible punishments filled my troubled mind as I lay there in my bed. I tried to remember which punishments my friends had received when they went to confession, but I couldn't. The truth is, I had never been interested in knowing; I was so preoccupied with my own troubles that I had never involved myself in other girls' troubles. Now I was filled with a terrible fear of the unknown. I was too ashamed to ask anyone, so I just lay there imagining all kinds of punishments. My greatest fear was that I'd be expelled from the convent.

What will happen if they expel me? Where would I go? How would I live? What would Irena do? Where would I hide? Would I be able to live with Mrs. Salsky again? But I don't want to hide again in the dark. And besides that, she doesn't want me anymore. Maybe I could go to Irena's grandfather? But where does he live? I only know that his nursing home is somewhere in Brussels. Even if I manage to find his address and am able to reach him, I might be putting him in danger.

But maybe my sin isn't so bad and they won't expel me? I don't think they ever expelled someone. So then, what will they do to me?

These questions and many more whirled around in my mind, and I tossed and turned, unable to relax. To my luck, the deaf Sister Syril was watching us that night. She didn't hear anything and didn't admonish me.

After prayers the next morning, my friend and I remained in the church while the others prepared to leave. They understood immediately that we had to go to confession. Breta looked at me shocked, and asked, "What, you, Anna Marie?" I blushed in shame.

When my turn came, I entered the small cubicle. A thin curtain hung in the middle of the room, opposite the door, and a priest stood on the other side. I bent down before the curtain; my heart was pounding like a hammer.

"Yes, what did you do?" called a voice from behind the curtain. I couldn't see the speaker, nor could he see me. I began to cry.

"Why are you crying? What did you do?" the terrible voice asked.

"I stole a piece of bread."

"Is it permitted to steal?"

"I was very hungry. I was working in the kitchen, where there is a lot of bread, and my intense hunger made me forget myself."

"It is forbidden to steal. If you're hungry, you must ask, not steal."

Then the voice pronounced my punishment: to recite some prayer three times! That was all! This was the "horrible" punishment I had been so worried about, which had made me lose a full night's sleep!

I was never assigned to the kitchen shift again — the nuns were afraid I might continue stealing. I was very happy

***With the priest in the convent yard.***

***Years later in the same place: The nuns' clothing is gray and white, and they do not wear a head covering. Today a regional school occupies the convent building.***

about that. The work was very hard. I had to clean pots that were bigger than me, and the scrub brush was very heavy. And while I struggled to wash those cumbersome pots, I would always get sprayed with cold water. At the end of the day I would be completely wet. I was always afraid I would fall into the huge pots and not be able to get out.

That night in bed, I started crying again. When the nun approached me to see what had happened, I told her how I missed my parents. Even Irena's grandfather had no idea what had happened to them. I had stopped asking him, but I was so worried about them. Who knows where they are? Do they even have a piece of bread to eat, and shelter from the terrible cold?

The nun patted me and promised me she would pray for their safe return. This time, for a change, she wasn't upset with me and only tried to encourage me.

# 38
# Outside the Wall

I had already spent three years in the convent, and hadn't gone beyond its high walls even once. Every Sunday, when there wasn't a blizzard, we went on a walk. But all these walks were held on the convent's expansive grounds. We visited each place many times, but we didn't care! We enjoyed the trips very much, and were happy with every chance to go out.

I especially loved to visit the bakery. In the bakery's courtyard, there was one spot where the farmers would unload their sacks of milled flour. The pungent aroma of freshly milled flour filled the air. Inside the bakery, we would watch the bakers prepare the dough: we saw them kneading it and then cutting it into long strips, which turned into round loaves of tasty bread in the oven.

On each visit, a worker would take a large, hot loaf of bread, cut it up and offer us slices of fresh, warm bread straight from the oven. I never ate my piece right away. First, I would turn my piece from side to side, smelling it all the while and enjoying the bread's delicious aroma. We always returned satisfied from this trip, though I'm not sure whether it was because of the bread or the lovely smell.

Another one of our trips was to the chicken coop. It was interesting to watch the chickens scrabble in the yard, fighting out loud for every crumb. On the whole, the trips were wonderful, a welcome change from the convent's drab routine. The only place I didn't enjoy was the visit to the pigsty, even though there were girls who liked it a lot.

But aside from the weekly outings, there was another kind of trip — a most coveted one, too. Every so often, a few nuns would travel around the neighboring towns, peddling the beautiful embroidered items and other craftwork produced in the convent. Each time, a different girl would accompany the nuns on their travels —which took several weeks. Now my turn had finally come! That day I would venture outside the convent's walls.

In the handicrafts class we had been preparing tablecloths, doilies and napkins. We had embroidered them artfully, and finished them off with neat, precise hems. The nuns also embroidered and knit beautiful creations, and the finished products were to be sold outside the convent.

The night before, I was too excited to fall asleep. I was the first one out of bed in the morning and I hurried to dress. My clothes had been laundered and ironed more carefully than usual. I waited impatiently for my friends, and danced all the way to church, and from church to the dining room. After breakfast, I cheerfully wished all my friends farewell, particularly Irena. In the past week, I had given her innumerable instructions concerning how to behave while I was away. My repeated instructions were annoying her and she chided me in irritation, "It's impossible to speak with you about anything besides this trip."

Afterwards, I went to Sister Lucie's room, where Sister Elisabeth and Sister Alice were waiting with the luggage. Each one of us received two full suitcases of handiwork, and we carried knapsacks on our shoulders with our personal items.

Sister Elisabeth was the head of our "delegation," and she received many instructions from Sister Lucie. Sister Lucie had a personal warning for me, too, "Don't forget that you represent our convent. You must behave in a dignified manner."

In our honor, the gatekeeper unlocked the small gate that was set in the large gate. He swung the doors open, and we were off. We were outside the convent! The nuns began to walk briskly, but I protested, "One minute! Stop! Let me just get a breath of free air!"

The two nuns laughed good-naturedly and agreed to stop for a minute. I put the suitcases down and spread my arms out wide. I lifted my head, looked up to the heavens, and inhaled deeply. Free air! Without crosses, without icons! The heavens were gray, and the trampled snow was black and dirty. But in my eyes, there had never been such a beautiful day! I wanted to dance, but Sister Elisabeth wouldn't let. "Enough! We must hurry so we won't miss the train."

The train station was full of people. There was a small bookstore that also sold newspapers. We stood next to the folded newspapers and tried to learn something about the outside world, some news about the war...

When Sister Elisabeth approached the cashier to buy tickets, the crowd of people parted respectfully and let her go to the front of the line. The train arrived with a thundering blast. When we drew near to it to climb up, once again, people moved aside in reverence. That's how it was throughout our journey. There was an advantage to our black uniforms. People treated us respectfully, didn't push us, and rose to give us seats.

The train traveled slowly, and it was late afternoon by the time we reached our destination. Sister Elisabeth knew the place, and she brought us straight to the store. We spread our wares, and the owner chose several nice items and paid Sister Elisabeth. I was very proud that we had made so much money! We continued on to other stores, and each owner bought several items from us.

Evening descended. I was very tired. The suitcases were heavy, and I was famished. Apparently, the nuns were tired and hungry too, for they decided we had enough. We turned in the direction of the local convent where we were to spend the night, but it was far away. We walked on and on until I felt I couldn't take another step. All the great joy I had felt about this trip began to dissipate. Just then, a wagon driver passed by and offered to take us to our destination. With a sigh of relief, we climbed up on the wagon. The robust wagon driver lifted our heavy suitcases with ease, and placed them at our feet. We reached the convent in no time at all. I was very grateful to the wagon driver — had we walked the entire distance, it would have taken a very long time.

The convent was a small, miserable structure, without a yard or wall. We did not have to pass any guards — we just knocked on the door and walked straight in. The head nun, a very old woman, welcomed us. There were only a few nuns besides her. They offered us food and showed us to our room. After we prayed, I crawled into bed and fell asleep immediately. Without dreams, without nightmares and without crying. I was totally exhausted.

We traveled from town to town for five weeks, sleeping in nearby convents, meeting various people, and always being received with respect. Wherever we went, they spoke about the war. We heard that Germany had suffered one defeat after another on the Russian front, that the British were fighting like lions, and that the Americans had also been drafted to suppress the terrible evil in the world.

In just a short while, Belgium would be free. That's what people were whispering. Everyone told each other: Just hold on a little longer; don't give up.

Throughout that period, I didn't see one Jewish face. I searched. I fixed my eyes on every passerby. But they were all gentiles. The streets were full of German soldiers. We saw them stopping people on every street corner, brusquely digging through their packages. Our black nuns' habits protected us from them; they never stopped us.

At the end of the five weeks, we returned to the convent with empty suitcases, a full wallet, and exciting news to share with everyone. On one hand, the trip had filled me with hope, but on the other, it caused me much confusion and heartbreak. It had aroused in me a fierce desire to free myself from the convent — but I knew I had no choice. While I was outside the convent's foreboding walls, I had thoughts of escape, but they remained merely thoughts. How could I leave Irena behind?

# 39 Sirens!

HU-u-u-u-u-uuuuuuuuuu! A siren! I leaped out of my bed, crying from fear. The other girls also woke up and ran frightened to Sister Syril, who was watching us that night. Sister Syril wouldn't listen to us, though. She was very angry.

"Go back to bed immediately! What is happening here?" she demanded.

"A siren just sounded!" we explained to her.

"What are you talking about? I didn't hear a thing!"

Of course she didn't hear it; she was deaf. She understood what we were saying only because she could read lips. But she knew she was deaf, so why didn't she believe us? We wanted to run to the cellar, but she didn't let us. She forced us to return to our beds.

At breakfast the next morning, everyone berated us. "Where were you? Why didn't you go to the cellar?" Everyone in the convent, besides our group, had descended to the cellar. To our good fortune, nothing happened to us this time, but I was worried, as were many other girls. It was clearly dangerous to have Sister Syril supervising us at night. We didn't dare point this out — that would be considered brazen and would earn us an immediate punishment.

After several days, we heard the shrill siren again. We

immediately ran to the babies' room, as we had been told, and each girl picked up a baby and rushed down to the cellar. The nuns urged us to hurry and run quickly. The nun responsible for the baby room asked me to carry two babies, but I couldn't. They were heavy — I could barely run with one baby. She weighed almost as much as me, as I was so thin and undernourished.

Swarms of people ran through the large convent, rushing toward the cellars. There were several very large cellars in the convent, and each cellar had been assigned to a number of groups. We cried and shrieked hysterically as we ran to the cellar. The sounds of nearby explosions were deafening and we were very scared. The nuns, instead of calming us down, shrieked at us and with us.

The baby I was holding cried the entire time. I was holding her in my right hand, and when the all-clear signal was finally sounded, I had lost all sensation in my right hand. That evening, we went to sleep exhausted, but we were too nervous and scared to fall asleep easily.

There was a shelling every few nights, and the convent's strict order fell apart into chaos each time. Everyone ran, shrieked and cried. The babies continued to cry long after the explosions' echoes had faded away.

One night, when we were in the cellar, and the walls around us were shuddering because of the explosions, I felt I couldn't restrain myself anymore. "*Shema Yisrael!*" I called out hysterically. One of the older girls looked at me, aghast. She demonstratively kissed the cross connected to her belt, got up from her place and went to sit at the other side of the cellar, far away from me. I smiled to myself, and thought: Let her go — who needs her?

I put my hand on my eyes and I shouted again, "*Shema Yisrael*! *Hashem Hu HaElokim*!" From all corners of the cellar, many voices answered me fervently, "*Shema Yisrael*! *Hashem Hu HaElokim*!"

I couldn't remember any other prayers. I hoped that would be enough. All the Jewish girls had been ready to join me; they had bravely gathered around me. I may have been among the oldest girls, but since I looked so thin and short, I seemed younger than them. Nevertheless, they all listened to me.

When the all-clear signal was given, we brought the babies back to their room and returned to our beds. I felt remarkably content, even though this bombing had frightened me terribly. When we entered our bedroom, we saw glass shards from the shattered windows all over the floor. Nevertheless, I felt calm and confident, as I had never felt since my arrival at the convent.

In the morning we saw that all the convent's windows had been shattered, even though they had been covered with bullet-proof material. The nuns told us that the buildings on the street next to the convent had absorbed the bombing. They were completely demolished, and all the people who had taken shelter in its cellars were buried under the debris.

"The God of Israel watched over us." I didn't say this out loud, of course, but I whispered those words to all the girls who had gathered around me during the bombing.

On Sunday, Grandfather came as usual. "Aren't you afraid to go out during these days?" I asked him.

"I miss you," he answered serenely. "I also worry about you, and want to see that you are safe."

"Grandfather, you're taking a risk! I'm afraid that something will happen to you. You must remain strong and healthy, if only for our sake."

But Grandfather was not convinced. He was very worried about us and felt that he must come visit us, despite the bombings. He asked us exactly how we behaved when there was a siren. I told him what had happened during the most recent bombing — how I had called out "*Shema Yisrael.*" Grandfather was delighted. "You see, Chanah'le! Hashem won't punish you because they threw some water on you! You remained a pure Jewish girl, and the *Ribbono Shel Olam* is watching over you. Who knows? Maybe in the merit of the *Shema Yisrael* you and your friends called out, all the people in the convent were saved." I swelled with happiness.

Grandfather was also concerned about my sickly appearance, just like a real grandfather. When I saw how worried he was about me, I actually forgot that he really wasn't my grandfather, and I felt like his granddaughter. He went to speak to Sister Lucie and told her how worried he was about me because I was so pale, thin and sad. She told Grandfather that they had already tried everything for me, and nothing had helped. She had chosen me for the coveted honor of accompanying the nuns on their sales trip. She had hoped that this would cheer me up. It had helped for a while, but when the bombings began, my situation reverted to what it was.

"Anna Marie is simply unhappy in the convent," Sister Lucie said. "I really should not tell you this, but the truth is that I hope the war will be over soon. Then she'll be able to return to her family and people and be a happy, carefree child once again. If the convent would know that this is what I'm hoping for her, they would be very angry with me. But I see that she is suffering, and in my heart, I know that she belongs to the Jewish People."

When Grandfather repeated this conversation to us, he added sadly, "Don't have any fantasies, Chanah'le. You don't have a family anymore. But you will return to your people! How I hope that this will happen soon."

I didn't have any illusions. I had come to terms with the truth. I still dreamed of uniting with my parents and my brother, but I knew those were only dreams. When I had been out of the convent, on our sales trip, I had seen that there were absolutely no Jews in Belgium. I had heard many harrowing stories. In every city and village, people had told us all kinds of things that they had seen or heard.

I didn't believe all the stories; they had sounded too impossible to be true. But after traveling through numerous cities without seeing even one Jew, I was sorely troubled. The nuns also noted this sadly. They said that the Jews had been their best customers — they knew how to appreciate quality and had bought the most expensive pieces.

Grandfather promised me that the war would be over soon. The Germans were losing on all fronts, and soon we would see their final downfall. When? I wondered. When would that day finally arrive? How I wish I could leave the convent and these gentiles already. I've played the part of a gentile girl for so long — I want to be a Jew!

"Don't worry, Chanah'le," Grandfather reassured me. "I'll be back soon to take you out of here." But I didn't believe him.

# 40
# Dancing in the Streets

We were tidying our bedroom — part of our morning routine — when suddenly we heard music wafting in from the street. We looked at each other, puzzled. It wasn't a holiday — it was just a regular day in the middle of the year. None of us could remember ever hearing music from the street. It was queer and very surprising.

All the girls prodded me, the small, thin, wiry one, to climb up to the top of the tall window that faced the street and try to see what was happening. We dragged a night table to the window and placed a chair on top. I climbed up, but I couldn't see anything. I went down and we pushed another night table next to the first one. Breta climbed on the first night table and stood up on the chair, and I climbed on the second night table, and then clambered onto Breta's shoulders. Lisa also climbed up on the second night table and supported Breta so she wouldn't fall. Due to Breta's added height, I could see the scene down below.

It was an extraordinary scene. Crowds of people were dancing in the street, singing enthusiastically, and jumping and clapping. From my angle, I couldn't see the orchestra, but we all heard it well. I watched, and reported my observations to my curious roommates. As I was watching, rows and rows of soldiers paraded down our street. In straight rows, they marched in unison. People hurriedly moved aside to make way for the soldiers. Cheering exuberantly and waving, the people threw flowers and candies at the soldiers.

"My shoulders are numb!" Breta shouted. "If you stay there one more second, I'm going to fall!" I quickly slid off her shoulders, and other girls took our place on the night table.

We couldn't understand what we had seen. "Maybe the war is over?" one of the girls ventured. But there were so many soldiers there. If the war had finished, why is the street full of soldiers? Maybe the citizens received an order to appear on the street to sing and play music in honor of the soldiers?

It was a mystery. We quickly put the bedroom back in order so the nun responsible for us wouldn't realize that we had climbed up. We speculated together about what we had seen, but none of us could really figure it out.

And so, we headed to breakfast, hoping the nuns would tell us what had happened. Talking in the dining room was not allowed, but we were already experts in whispering short sentences without arousing the nuns' suspicions. It turned out that in every bedroom, girls had climbed up to look out the windows and had seen what I had seen. Many girls thought that these festivities were in celebration of the end of the war, but when we asked why soldiers were on parade, no one had an answer. We didn't want the nuns to know that we had defied the rules and climbed up, and besides, the custom in the convent was that girls who asked questions were punished. No one wanted to be whipped, so no one asked questions — and we remained in the dark.

On Sunday we took a trip to the library, where only nuns

worked, so we didn't meet any of the convent's workers. Although we met many "outsiders" at church, we couldn't speak during the prayers. There was no one we could ask. We were surrounded by a conspiracy of silence.

Two weeks later Grandfather came for a visit. I asked right away about the crowds of people I had seen singing and dancing in the street. "Grandfather, what was going on?" I asked.

Grandfather's voice cracked as he answered, "The war is over! Belgium is free!"

"But the soldiers, Grandfather! There were so many soldiers!"

Grandfather nodded. "Yes, Chanah'le, but those soldiers were not Nazis, *yimach shemam*. Those were American soldiers, who defeated the Nazis."

"The war is over," I said quietly, trying to digest the news. "Really? The war is finally over? I had thought that it would never finish... Now we can go home, Grandfather! Take us home!"

But Grandfather cooled off my enthusiasm. "Things don't go so fast. I'm afraid they won't let me take you out of here. Let's wait a little longer, and I'll try to find the right people who can help me take you out. It's not a good idea to try and force things, lest we lose everything. Please, girls, try to be patient. Right now, life is very chaotic. You see that I'm still wearing my blind man's disguise. I'm still afraid."

I was sorely disappointed. I had just glimpsed the shining light at the end of the deep, dark tunnel I was in, and now it became dim. Grandfather explained over and over again that it was best to wait. "We've waited so long, now we'll wait a little more and not take any risks. I know that now it seems harder, because you feel it's unnecessary; after all, the war already ended! But the very fact that the nuns didn't tell you this proves that matters are not so simple. In the meantime, don't tell anyone that you know that the war is over."

It was very difficult to keep this secret from our friends, but Irena and I controlled ourselves and listened to Grandfather. The nuns didn't mention the subject at all, even in a hint. They no longer covered the new glass windows with protective sheets, but when one of the girls asked about it, the nuns told her that the sheets had proved useless. Life in the convent continued as usual, as if nothing had happened. The strict daily regime hadn't softened even an iota — we were still punished for every trivial thing. My liberation from this place, which had seemed so close and real for a moment, was once again a far-off dream.

I lost all interest in my studies. I walked around the convent listlessly. I was in the middle of working on a number of craft projects; I didn't even want to complete any of them. I sat idly in the homework room as well. I was only required to fulfill my work shift. I refused to listen to the nuns and they punished me frequently. My face was always red from their stinging slaps, and my body was full of black-and-blue marks from being whipped with a belt. Despite that, I continued in my rebellion.

After a month, Grandfather returned again. He didn't have good news for us. He hadn't found people who could help rescue us. People had just begun to rehabilitate their own lives, and couldn't get involved with others.

"Grandfather, I don't want to be here anymore. Please take me with you!" I pleaded.

"I can't kidnap you by force," Grandfather explained patiently. "I can only take you if the convent's administration will agree to let you go."

"So speak with Mother Superior! Tell her that the war is over, and I don't want to remain here even one more day!"

Grandfather followed my advice. He approached the Mother Superior and told her how sad and bitter I was. He described how sickly I looked, and told her I would be better off if I would leave the convent. But the Mother Superior didn't agree. She claimed that she couldn't entrust two young girls to an old, blind man's care. She agreed that she couldn't prevent Grandfather from taking Marie Anaz (Irena), since he was her grandfather and had brought her to the convent. But she wouldn't give Anna Marie to him, after the convent had looked after her all these years. According to the convent's rules, I would have to remain there until my eighteenth birthday.

Grandfather told me the results of the conversation, and added, "I won't leave you here, Chanah'le. Don't worry! I'll take both of you out of here."

But I was desperate. Irena's grandfather had no permission to take me out! I would be forced to stay here, in this vile convent. I stopped studying completely, and was unable to eat. Sister Lucie noticed my deteriorating state and called me to her room. She promised that she would do everything in her power to give Irena's grandfather custody over me. "I know that he is concerned about you and will take good care of you," she said, "but he must bring evidence that he has a place for you to live and sufficient income to support you."

This was an unrealistic demand. Grandfather was dependent on the kind people in the nursing home for his own support. The senior citizens and the staff knew he was a Jew, and they had courageously decided to support him and protect his life, despite knowing that they were risking their own lives. They appreciated and loved Grandfather very much — he had worked in the nursing home for many years before the war with tremendous devotion. That's what prompted them to give him refuge during those turbulent years. I, however, couldn't expect them to declare in writing that they would support me and care for me as well!

A large barrier stood between me and my freedom. I felt helpless. I made a resolute decision: If Irena's grandfather would take her out without me, I would escape. Grandfather had promised me he would never do that, but I was still worried. I was afraid that if he found it was impossible to take me out, he would at least want to save his own granddaughter.

As part of my escape plans, I decided to start eating so I would have more energy. Lately, I had barely eaten. In my weakened state, I would be unable to escape and maintain myself outside. I decided to eat everything, without leaving a crumb on my plate. Once again, I began to behave properly and listen to the nuns, so they would stop hitting me. Their constant blows had weakened me very much.

For days I planned my escape. I checked all the convent's entrances — they were all locked, of course. I searched for a breach, no matter how small, through which I could slip. But at night, doubts and fears assailed me. I realized that escape was impossible. And anyway, even if I managed to leave the convent, where would I go?

Mademoiselle Vermeul thought she had a solution for me. She again tried persuading me to live in her house and be her adopted daughter. "You'll see, Anna Marie, Marie

Anaz's grandfather will take her in the end, and again you'll be here alone. It's in your best interest to come with me now!"

I was in a quandary. On the one hand, I thought there was truth in her words. Maybe it would be best to take up her offer and be free of this accursed convent. Afterwards, it would certainly be easier to escape from her home than from the convent. On the other hand, when she had wanted to adopt me in the past, I had claimed that I had to take care of Irena. In the end, I promised to give her an answer after Grandfather's next visit. I decided that if Irena's grandfather was planning to take her, I would go to the good Mademoiselle Vermeul.

The days passed with mounting anticipation for Grandfather's visit. Life in the convent continued as normal. No one spoke about the fact that the war had ended, and we didn't feel any change. The bombings had stopped, but they had only existed for a short time. The girls knew that the war had ended; the news had slowly spread among us. But no one dared to speak a word about it.

I couldn't understand it.

"Why are the nuns keeping such happy news a secret?" I asked Mademoiselle Vermeul.

"I also wonder about it," she replied. "We wanted to make a festive party to mark such an important event, but the Mother Superior refused. She forbade us to tell the girls that the war is over."

# 41
# A Jewish Woman

I was in the middle of cleaning the entrance lobby when suddenly an emaciated woman dressed in tattered clothes entered, accompanied by one of the nuns. Both of them went up toward the room of the Mother Superior. I dropped the cleaning brush in surprise and my eyes followed the woman until she had vanished from view. She was unquestionably a Jewish woman. Who was she? Where did she come from? What was she doing here?

A sudden trembling seized me, and I froze in place. I was afraid that one of the nuns would pass by and see me standing idly, so I forced myself to continue scrubbing the marble floor. After I had scraped the entire lobby, that woman still hadn't descended. I didn't want to leave the hall, so I recleaned the floor and wiped it dry again. I did this several times, until I finally saw the Jewish woman at the top of the staircase. She was holding one of "our" babies in her arms. To my joy, no nun accompanied her. I approached her and whispered, "*Ich bin a Yiddishe kind* — I am a Jewish child."

Shocked, she looked at my black clothes, my large cross necklace, and didn't say a word.

"Is that your baby?" I asked. She hugged the child tightly, and answered passionately, "Yes! This is my daughter! I entrusted her to the nuns during the war, and now I came to take her back."

"So maybe my mother will come to take me?" I couldn't hold back my hopes any longer. "Maybe you saw my mother? Sarah Zucker, that's my mother's name. She doesn't know that I'm here. She gave all her money to a gentile woman to hide me in her cellar, but the gentile brought me here."

"No, my precious girl, I didn't meet your mother. And I suspect that she will no longer return. Only a few Jews have remained alive."

"But I want my mother! And my father, and Meir…!" I cried, and she cried with me.

"They forced me to convert to Christianity," I told her. "They sprinkled their water on me and arranged my communion."

"You're a big girl," she reassured me. "You won't forget that you're a Jewish girl. You'll eventually leave this place and return to our people. But there are so many little children here. What will be their fate? I saw them in the nursery when I took my daughter. All of them appear Jewish, and they are all small and don't remember anything. If their mothers won't return, how will they know that they are Jews? This is also a result of this terrible war."

The woman sighed and turned to go. I grasped her hand before she could leave, and begged, "If you see my mother, Sarah Zucker, please tell her I am here in the Couvent Misericorde."

"I will," she promised and went on her way, leaving me behind, deeply troubled. The scene of the baby being lovingly embraced by her mother wouldn't leave me. Suddenly I felt with biting clarity how much my life in the convent was flawed. We had been saved from death and received all of our physical needs. But we desperately were lacking a parent's love and the warmth of family life.

At least Irena and I had Grandfather. The other Jewish girls were jealous of us because of that. I always asked him to bring a lot of candies so I could share them with my friends and also give them a little taste of home. I was unaware of how difficult it was for him to procure the candies for us, but he was happy that I had also asked for my friends. "Give the candies to those who have no one to visit them, Chanah'le, give it to them, so they should also feel a drop of sweetness," he used to say.

Although they felt the terrible void of not having parents and family, they weren't occupied with thoughts of the past as I was. They had become used to life in the convent, and didn't care about returning to the Jewish people. In the bomb shelter, in a moment of fright, they had called out "*Shema Yisrael*" together with me, but now I was the only one who cried, rebelled, and pined with all my heart to leave the convent and return to my people.

That night, before going to sleep, I snuck into the nursery. I went from bed to bed, looked at all the sweet little girls and whispered to each one, "You are a Jew." But I knew it wouldn't help. The nuns would take over these children's lives.

The month passed, and Grandfather again returned to visit. How much I had waited for him! He again approached the Mother Superior, and she again repeated her words, "You can take Marie Anaz, but Anna Marie remains with us. I cannot give her to you until you can prove you have a place for her and means of supporting her. Tell me the truth, how will you provide for her? How will you give her everything she needs? A nursing home is not a suitable place for a young girl. Here she has a refuge, food, clothes and even regular studies."

"But look how poorly she has fared! She is sad and depressed. It's difficult to believe that she's already fifteen years old; she looks like she's twelve and also acts like it. This proves that she is not doing well with you. If she truly had it good, she wouldn't be so sad," Grandfather claimed.

The Mother Superior was not impressed with his words. "I'm sorry. We cannot allow a girl out of the convent if her future is not assured. When Anna Marie turns eighteen years old, she can decide on her own if she wants to remain with us or leave."

Until the age of eighteen! I would have to remain in the convent for another three years. Three long, endless years. More than a thousand days. Every passing day felt like a year, and every night, an eternity.

I stopped learning again. I had been a diligent student; I enjoyed learning. Although most of the studies centered around theology and Christianity, we also studied history, geography, French and math. I enjoyed those subjects, but I had decided not to participate, or even listen. If the studies were the reason to keep me here, I thought defiantly, and because of that they wouldn't let me leave — I had no interest in them. I sat in class and daydreamed. "Maybe Maman will come and take me, like the Jewish mother I saw. She'll also hug me lovingly, just like that mother..." I blacked out everything during classes, and didn't respond when they rebuked and punished me.

I began to eat only bread and water. I wanted to be a Jew

again, and stop polluting myself with unkosher food. When they tried to force me to eat, I vomited. I stopped participating in the choir; there were no songs in my heart. I tried to remember the songs I had sung in my parents' house, but the memories were too far off.

In sewing class, the teacher tried to force me to work, but saw that I was just ruining good material, as if I had forgotten all the skills I had acquired. I couldn't even finish the slippers I had begun preparing. I held a slipper in one hand and a threaded needle in my other hand, and couldn't bring my two hands together. I ignored everything going on around me, and paid no attention when I was addressed. I became lethargic and unresponsive. So when Sister Germaine came to tell me that the Mother Superior had called for me, she had to grab me with her two hands to get my attention, and then she had to repeat herself several times until I understood what she was saying.

I apathetically went up to Mother Superior's room. Other times, I had trembled from fear when I had been called to her room. I would replay the day's events, trying to figure out what sin I had committed and what I was being punished for. This time, I knew for certain that she was very angry with me. I wasn't learning, praying, working, or eating. Let her be angry! What do I care? I thought. If she doesn't like my behavior, she doesn't have to keep me here anymore. She can't threaten me that she'll send me out of the convent and I'll be easy prey for the Germans. After all, I know the truth, even if she thinks that she can hide it from us. I hope she'll get so angry that she'll expel me...

# 42
# Free at Last!

I kneeled before the Mother Superior, as required and she asked me pleasantly, "What do you think about us letting you go?"

When I had entered, I hadn't bothered looking around me to see if someone else was there besides me, but suddenly I understood that I wasn't the only one in the room. This question couldn't possibly have been directed at me! I looked all around, but I didn't see anyone.

"Do you want to leave the convent?" the Mother Superior asked again.

"Are you speaking to me?"

"Yes, Anna Marie, to you. What do you think about leaving here?"

I couldn't answer. There was something stuck in my throat, and I felt like I was choking. The Mother Superior approached me, lifted me up from my kneeling position and embraced me. "What happened to you? You don't want to leave?" she asked gently.

Slowly my breathing returned. I kissed her and said, "This is the happiest day of my life."

"Why? Was it so bad here at the convent?"

"No, I didn't mean that," I answered in confusion. "I had it good here. You saved me and I am alive because of you.

But I must leave and travel to Brussels. If my father or mother are still alive, they will come home and won't find me! And what if my brother returns and finds no one at home? He is still a young boy. How will he be able to manage alone?"

The Mother Superior gazed at me at length, shook her head and didn't say anything.

"The war already ended, right?" I asked.

"Yes, you know that."

"Right. I have known about it for several months already. Grandfather told me. But why have you hidden this information from us?"

She didn't answer, and I didn't press the matter. My release was the only thing of importance for the moment.

"Why have you agreed to release me now? When my Grandfather asked for it, you didn't agree!" I said suspiciously.

"Anna Marie, you know that he is not your real grandfather. I was afraid that after he would take you out of the convent, he would abandon you and only take care of his granddaughter. But then I saw that he is resolute in his decision to take you, and is even prepared to leave Marie Anaz here as long as you're here. I understood that he is truly interested in taking care of both of you, even though I don't know how he will do this. We also saw that your well-being is plummeting, and decided to give him a chance. But Anna Marie," she added gravely, "you must promise me that if Grandfather can't take care of you properly, you will return here."

"I promise. If we can't manage outside, if life is hard — if we'll have no food or place to stay — we'll come back. We want to go out to live, not to die," I asserted. I didn't tell her that Irena's grandfather had told me that the Jewish community in Brussels would help us once we were outside. After all, she assumed that I would remain a faithful Christian.

"Can I tell my friends?" I asked hesitantly.

"Yes, why not? Run and tell them," she answered with a smile.

I ran as if I had sprouted wings. I impatiently searched for Irena. Lately she had kept a distance from me and kept company with other girls. It was too difficult for her to be around me in my depressed state. Perhaps she was angry at me inwardly. Were it not for me, her grandfather would have taken her a long time ago! When I found Irena, I grabbed her by the arms and, in a combination of sobs and laughter, I told her everything. My jumble of words, excited shouts and emotional tears were simply incomprehensible. She realized that I was trying to tell her something important, and was very patient with me. She hugged me and said serenely, "Anna Marie, calm down! Come, drink some water. You're so pale." She helped me drink and wash my face. Afterwards I managed to speak clearly. "We're leaving, Irena! We're both leaving! The Mother Superior agreed to release me!"

Irena looked at me doubtfully. She was afraid that I had lost my mind out of my misery. In light of my recent behavior her concern was understandable. I told her again and again exactly what the Mother Superior had told me, and slowly she began to believe me. We laughed and cried together, and the other girls gathered around in curiosity.

"We're leaving the convent!" we informed them. "We're leaving!"

The strict order fell apart as all the girls encircled us excitedly, asking questions and expressing opinions. Nuns quickly intervened and restored the order. After all the girls had been silenced and each class stood at attention in two straight lines, they inquired about the commotion. When the nuns heard that I had received permission to leave the convent, they were very happy for me. I was surprised; I didn't imagine that they would care. They had never seemed particularly interested in my welfare, but even so, they hugged and kissed me now, happy about the good news.

The next day I told Mademoiselle Vermeul. She was, of course, happy for me, but she was also sad that we would be leaving each other. "All the nuns were happy for me," I told her in amazement.

"I don't think you noticed, but they were very worried about you recently, when they saw you sinking into despair. Don't think that they are bad. They may treat the girls strictly, as they are expected to do, but after all, they took care of you all those years. They feel close to you. They all understood that the only solution for your miserable state was to take you out of the convent, and each nun had told Mother Superior her feelings."

I was stunned. Were these nuns, who punished me and hit me so often, really concerned about me in their hearts? It was astonishing, but I had no time now to think about it. I was completely involved with preparing to leave the convent, and was excitedly anticipating Grandfather's arrival. The Mother Superior told me that they had sent a notice to Grandfather. She said he would probably arrive the following week, as soon as he received the letter. I couldn't wait – just one more week!

If I thought that week would never pass, and every day would seem like an eternity — I quickly found out how wrong I was. The days passed in a blink of an eye, before I had managed to take my leave of every room and corner. I tried to make up for the time lost while I had been in my deep depression. I worked furiously to finish the slippers which I hadn't touched for so long. I wanted to finish all the studies I had missed, and to participate in the choir again, singing all the songs I had recently learned from Mademoiselle Shriver.

Our excited friends had decided to make a farewell party for us. They decorated the dining room festively on the day of our departure, and delicacies which had only been served on Christian holidays graced the tables. The girls prepared plays and speeches, and the choir sang all our favorite songs. They also composed a farewell song especially for us. The girls performed, recited, and sang as if they had prepared for this party over several months.

I was very embarrassed. After all the trouble I had caused, they had prepared such a beautiful good-bye party, and everyone took part in my joy... "I know I made you so angry," I said regretfully. "I kept you up at night with my sobbing."

"Even so, we liked you," my friends replied.

Grandfather arrived in the middle of the party. At first, he decided to sit in the lobby and wait for us. After a while, he agreed to sit in the seat of honor between Irena and me, and enjoyed the party made in our honor. Although the war was over, Grandfather still wore his dark glasses. He didn't dare tell everyone that he wasn't blind and had fooled them all these years.

At the end of the party, the nuns and the girls gave us gifts. The nuns gave us small icons and pictures depicting various scenes from Christian stories. The girls pooled together the few pennies they had received from relatives on visiting days and bought Irena and me a silver necklace with a cross at the end. I cried as I accepted the necklace. My friends thought I was crying from excitement, but truthfully I cried because of the cross. Even as I was leaving, a cross had to accompany me… I couldn't embarrass the girls, however. They had bought me the necklace with such self-sacrifice and love. I resolved to keep it always, despite the cross.

I hugged and kissed everyone, thanking them repeatedly for everything: for their friendship over three years, for the patience they showed me during my difficult times, and for the beautiful party. Afterwards, Irena and I went to take leave of the Mother Superior. She parted from us with a strong embrace, but first told us the following: "Remember, girls! I'm releasing you on condition that you say your evening prayers before you go to sleep, and that you attend church every Sunday! You were educated here in the Couvent Misericorde, and you must bring us honor. You must behave as we taught you here, and tell everyone you meet how our convent saved you and provided you with all your needs."

There was a large picture of the "founder" of their religion in the Mother Superior's room. She made us stand opposite that picture. Then she instructed us to hold the cross she wore on her belt and promise to do as she had told us. Afterwards, she added a threat. "Remember," she said sternly, "we will always know how you are behaving. We have agents everywhere and they will notify us."

This "swearing-in" ceremony dropped a veil of sadness on our pure joy. Before our talk with Mother Superior, we had been thrilled about our long-anticipated release, but now we were frightened and anxious. I was worried that she wouldn't release us because of her concern for the convent's good name. "We benefited greatly from our stay in the convent," I hurried to tell her. "You saved us. We know that you endangered yourselves to save many Jewish girls, and we will never forget this kindness. But we must go now to look for our families."

We left her room, our spirits dampened. We wanted to leave immediately, but we still had to say good-bye to Sister Lucie. She welcomed us happily, and hugged and kissed both of us again and again. "I love you so much," she said. "Please, write me letters because I know that I will long for you so much." She also gave us a gift — pictures of Christian scenes. On the back of each picture, she had written warm words of farewell. As we turned to leave, she said, "Dear girls, if you find you are not managing outside, you can always return. We will take you back happily. The main thing is that you should be content in life."

We thanked her for all her efforts on our behalf during our stay at the convent, and we left her room much happier than we had gone in.

I went to have one last look in the nursery. I had gone there the evening before, and had whispered "*Shema Yisrael*" to each of the little children sleeping there. Who knows? I thought. Maybe once, when they grow up, one of them will hear those holy words and they will remember me, and maybe they'll even remember that they are Jews.

We went downstairs. Our friends were waiting for us near the door. Again final hugs, kisses and good-byes. "Anna Marie, who will take care of you? Who will remind us that we're also Jews? When will we also be able to leave?" several girls whispered in my ears. Who knows if they will ever get to leave the convent... and even if they will, if they will ever return to Judaism? They were left without a relative or redeemer to take them.

I promised that I would try to write them letters and visit. We had grown up together for three long, difficult years like sisters. We had suffered together and shared happy occasions, too. I loved them. All of them.

It was also difficult for me to say good-bye to the nuns. Some of them had been very good to us. During those exciting moments of farewell, we forgot all the misery that the others had given us. We kissed them all tearfully.

On one hand, we wanted to go and be outside, beyond the high wall. On the other hand, it was so difficult to leave everyone. We continued giving our friends "just one more hug" and "just one more kiss." Grandfather saw that we would never finish, so he took Irena's hand and started moving to the door, where our packages of the clothes we had brought along with us years before awaited us. Our hands laden with packages, and hearts full of emotion, we called out our final good-bye. The gatekeeper swung the gate open, and replied politely to our greetings. The sound of the closing gate echoed dimly behind us. And with that, we proceeded to a new chapter in our lives.

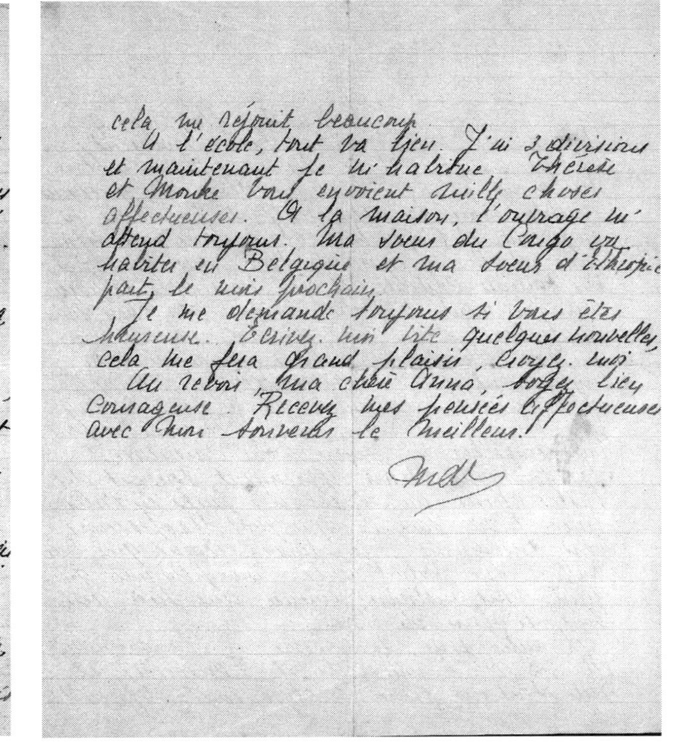

Ma chère Anna,

Il y a déjà longtemps que j'aurais dû vous répondre, mais vraiment j'ai été très occupée. Votre dernière lettre m'a fait très grand plaisir. Vous me demandez quelques conseils, mais les événements de Palestine, m'empêchent de voir bien clair dans votre situation actuelle. J'espère de tout cœur que vous êtes toujours chrétienne et que vous vous préparez courageusement à votre avenir. Ma chère Anna, suivez toujours la voie de votre conscience, qui est celle de Dieu. Vous connaissez votre engagement pris en 1944. Rien n'échappe à la divine Providence, qui a tout arrangé pour votre plus grand bien. Personne ne peut vous empêcher de suivre votre conscience. Les journaux nous apprennent souvent des tristes choses au sujet des Juifs en Palestine, je ne sais ce que vos professeurs vous enseignent. Je suis certaine que Dieu mettra sur votre route une personne qui peut vous instruire mieux que moi qui suis si loin de vous!

L'autre jour, j'ai revu M. Claude Dubois, elle va à l'université de Bruxelles, et reste toujours fidèle malgré mille difficultés cela me réjouit beaucoup.

A l'école, tout va bien. J'ai 2 divisions et maintenant je suis maîtresse. Thérèse et Monike vous envoient mille choses affectueuses. A la maison, l'ouvrage m'attend toujours. Ma soeur du Congo va habiter en Belgique et ma soeur d'Ethiopie part le mois prochain.

Je me demande toujours si vous êtes heureuse. Écrivez-moi vite quelques nouvelles, cela me fera grand plaisir, croyez-moi.

Au revoir, ma chère Anna, soyez bien courageuse. Recevez mes pensées affectueuses avec mon souvenir le meilleur.

[illegible]

***A letter from Madamoiselle Vermeul to Chana after she had moved to the children's home.***

# 43
# "But We Promised"

It was late, and Grandfather urged us to hurry toward the train station. I had been there a short while ago, when I had gone on the sales trip, and I thought I knew what it looked like. But I was completely taken by surprise.

The windows facing the street, which had been covered with heavy fabric to protect against shellings, were covered no more. Potted plants in a beautiful array of colors, decorated most of the windowsills — just like before the war. Sidewalks and roads were undergoing repairs Workers fixed broken water pipes and lay new stone sidewalks. Customers walked in and out of the many stores that dotted the streets. When I had traveled with the nuns, every store's display window had been boarded up. But now, the display windows were lit up and sported attractive displays of merchandise. The stores now carried an abundance of goods: toys, newspapers, clothes, and primarily food — the variety of food and candies was more noticeable than other products.

People also looked completely different. They looked like normal people, intent on carrying out their business at hand. Each person proceeded at his own pace — some slowly and others quickly. There were even some who pushed their way through the crowds. People spoke openly, shouted, and even laughed. They weren't sad and somber, quiet and withdrawn as they had been during the war.

I felt as if I was observing different people, a completely different city, and completely different houses and streets, even though we were going the exact same way that I had gone with the nuns. The entire scene had transformed into one of rebirth and happiness. Even the advancing train's toot seemed merrier.

Irena and I skipped and jumped and chattered boisterously. Grandfather removed his sunglasses and folded his cane, and joined in our merry mood, laughing and chuckling out loud.

The train station was full of people. Grandfather already had tickets. He had purchased them when he had alighted from the train on the way to the convent, so he would have proof to show us that we were really returning with him. When he told us this, I suddenly realized that waiting for our release had been difficult for him, too. He had also longed for this joyous day.

The train was packed. We crowded in with everyone. When I had traveled with the nuns, everyone had moved aside for us respectfully. We had received ample room to sit, but I had felt strange, as if I didn't belong. People kept a distance from us; we weren't part of the group.

This time, we sat crowded next to Grandfather, balancing our packages on our knees — just like everyone else. Outside it was getting dark. We weren't able to see a thing through the windows because of the descending twilight and because of the little children who were pressing against the windows. As the train sped along, I heard its wheels singing merrily, "I'm outside, free! I'm outside, free!"

When we reached Brussels, my home town, it was already night. Torrents of rain fell, but I still wanted to see the city a little. Irena asked to see her parents' house at least from the outside, but Grandfather wouldn't let. "Tomorrow, if it's not raining, we'll see whatever you want," he promised. "But now — we're taking the trolley straight to the nursing home."

All of Grandfather's friends were waiting for us in the nursing home's lobby. They looked very old. Grandfather appeared to me the strongest and sharpest of them all. Without his dark glasses, everyone saw his eyes shining from happiness at having brought us home.

The old people welcomed us by clapping their hands. "Oh, finally! The granddaughters have arrived!" It was apparent that they, too, had been awaiting our arrival. Grandfather had shared his disappointment and pain with his fellow residents when the Mother Superior had refused to release us. They had read and reread the letter Grandfather had received from the convent, that special letter informing him of our release. They could practically recite it verbatim. They were very happy for us — and I was astounded. I had thought that Grandfather, Irena, and I were the only ones happy about our release.

Grandfather brought us to the director's room, and announced proudly, "Mr. Morris, these are my granddaughters whom I traveled to visit every month, and for whom I hoped and waited for so long."

"Welcome!" the director greeted us with a heartfelt smile. Mr. Morris had white hair and bright blue, kind eyes which were wreathed with laugh lines. I was very moved to meet this noble man, who had kept Grandfather in his institution despite knowing he was a Jew. In his merit, Grandfa-

***Chanah at the entrance to the nursing home.***

ther hadn't been murdered like the rest of our families. Mr. Morris was a great man, both externally and internally, and I was happy that Grandfather had spent the war years with a person of his caliber.

"I will never be able to thank you enough," I told him. In response, he pointed upward and said, "You don't have to thank me, but the One Above. How I wish I was able to save more than a handful of Jews whom I managed to hide here. I'm ashamed that there are men like Nazis, and I'm happy that the fact that you and your grandfather was saved shows that not all men are evil." In Grandfather's room there were another two men, both of them Jews. In the privacy of their room, they were able to live like Jews during the war years. Grandfather told us that there were more Jews in the nursing home — they always had a *minyan* for prayers. The only thing they didn't have was a *sefer Torah*. The director had asked them not to bring one in, because a *sefer Torah* was a large object which might be seen by unwelcome eyes. Grandfather had a shelf full of French books. At least, that's what it looked like. But Grandfather showed us that, although the books' covers were from French books, the pages were *sifrei kodesh*.

The nursing home's management provided us with a

temporary room right near Grandfather's room. A nursing home was not a suitable place for young girls, and Grandfather was looking for a better solution. I don't know how they were able to prepare a room for us next to Grandfather's room. The elderly people who lived in that room must have vacated it and crowded into other rooms to make room for us.

During my stay at the convent, I hadn't gained any weight, and had barely grown. The clothing I had brought with me to the convent still fit me. Irena had grown and her old clothing were too small for her, so I shared my clothes with her. My clothes were outdated, but the colors — vibrant and cheerful. After years of wearing black, we were thrilled with these clothes. They represented freedom to us.

We were free! We could come and go as we pleased. Regardless of our freedom, we took very few walks. We didn't even visit our former homes. We decided that, actually, they didn't interest us. We stayed around the nursing home, playing in its yard and relaxing in its garden. We had no desire to "sight-see." It felt good to be in the nursing home's warm, protective environment.

We only went to one place to fulfill our promise: to the church. On the first Sunday morning, we were afraid. The Mother Superior had told us that she would know if we broke our promise. We couldn't throw off our fear of retribution as easily as we had our black convent clothes.

Grandfather came to our room on Sunday and didn't find us there. He searched for us in the garden, but we weren't there either. Since we hadn't told him that we were going anywhere, he was very frightened and waited anxiously for our return.

"Where were you?" he asked in alarm when we returned.

"We were right there," I said, motioning with my hand, "in the church across the road. We just went to pray," I explained simply.

Grandfather was shocked. He became very pale and a shadow of sorrow clouded his eyes. He spread out his arms beseechingly and entreated us, "Why? Why did you go to the church? You are Jewish girls!"

"But Grandfather, we promised," said Irena. It was quite simple to us — we *had* to keep our promise. "If we don't keep our promise, they'll catch us and bring us back to the convent."

Grandfather slumped heavily onto a chair and looked at us, deeply pained. We were frightened, confused and helpless. After a long moment of silence, Grandfather told us that he forbids us to ever enter a church again.

"Under no circumstances! Is that understood? You are Jewish girls! The Holy One blessed be He knows and is a witness that you are good, kosher Jewish girls. The accursed waters which they poured on you didn't change a thing. We don't care what the Christians think. We know the truth.

"Besides that, the convent will never know if you went to church or not. And even if they did, they can't force you to come back. They are not fools; they knew very well that when you left the convent you would return to Judaism. That's why they were so opposed to releasing you."

I was not so easily convinced. I was sure that we had to keep our promises, and I tried to explain that to Grandfather. "The Mother Superior made us swear that we would go to church every Sunday, and we did."

"Oh, girls, forget them!" Grandfather waved his hand.

"The people from the convent won't bother to check if you are keeping your promise. The nuns are sure that you already forgot everything."

He was right. When he spoke in his confident voice, we knew he was right, and we even told him so. But the moment he left the room, apprehension assailed us again. Our fear of the church never left us; it was rooted deep in our hearts.

The next day, when we returned to our room after breakfast, we were shocked! All our good-bye presents from our friends — the little icons and pictures — had been flung to the ground, and were broken and torn. While we were standing there, looking sadly at the shambles, Grandfather entered the room. "I did it," he said. "I broke and tore everything. You don't need those vile things! You are Jewish girls!"

"But these were our farewell gifts, mementos from the nuns and our dear friends!"

"Even so. These are Christian symbols, objects of idolatry. A Jew may not have such things."

Grandfather hadn't yet seen the crosses under our dresses. We still weren't able to part with those necklaces. Grandfather wouldn't have understood us. He didn't understand that such a change requires time and patience, and he didn't know how apprehensive we were. He also had difficulty believing that we liked the girls we had lived with during those trying years. We had shared difficult experiences, and had become attached to each other like sisters. We also still loved the nuns. I didn't know how to explain this to Grandfather, but it made no difference, because he wouldn't let us talk about the subject.

He didn't know that we continued to kneel next to our

beds every evening to whisper the Christian prayers. Afterwards, in bed, we would also say "*Shema Yisrael,*" just as we had done in the convent. The influence of years could not be erased with a few forceful words. It was a process that would take time.

Our fear of the convent's power may have been the true reason why we didn't like to stroll through the city. We were afraid of meeting nuns or priests. I was even afraid to walk around in the street next to the nursing home; I was scared of the many soldiers there. I knew they were British and American, but I was still wary. Maybe war would break out again? I thought. Maybe it just seems to us that they're on our side, but they're actually German soldiers?

# 44
# The Orphanage

Grandfather wasted no time or effort trying to arrange for permanent housing for us, somewhere more suitable for young girls. He also turned over every rock in search of our families. He visited the Jewish Committee every day. Refugees returning from the death camps would register their names in the Jewish Committee's ledgers. Grandfather would check the list daily, hoping that someone had come back... He searched for Irena's and my parents in vain. Their names did not appear.

He would return from these excursions sad and depressed, and he would sit with us and whisper, "What a miracle that at least you remained, a remnant and continuation of your families."

At the Committee, Grandfather met Jews who had returned from "that place," who told him shocking, terrifying stories. Afterwards, he would sit with the other elderly people in the nursing home's lobby and quietly tell them what he had heard. Everyone, including the gentiles, would listen and weep. But Irena and I didn't listen. We didn't want to hear those heartbreaking stories. We preferred going out to the garden and playing, enjoying our freedom and trying to forget all the suffering we had experienced. We still didn't have the mental strength to participate in the suffering of others. It wasn't narcissism on our part; it was simply that we weren't able to face the depth of agony in those stories.

Grandfather tried all the time to find a suitable residence for us, with other girls our age. A place where they would remove all the nonsense and fears which still pervaded our minds. We were happy with him in the nursing home, but we also understood that it was only a temporary arrangement. It wasn't a place where young girls could be kept permanently. Although a number of Jews lived there, it was a gentile institution, and Grandfather very much wanted to transfer us to a Jewish place.

Brussels had a number of institutions for Jewish children survivors, but Grandfather was not willing to compromise on certain matters. He was searching for a religious institution which would educate us to keep Torah and *mitzvos*. At the same time, he wanted a place which would provide us with a warm, homey atmosphere, to act as a replacement for the family life we had lost.

Not only that, Grandfather wasn't willing to hear about separating Irena and me. "They are like sisters, and must remain together," he passionately argued.

In the end, the Committee recommended an orphanage that was suitable in every way, but it was, of course, also full. Grandfather went to check it out, and he liked what he saw. He pleaded with the director to accept us despite the crowding. Grandfather told him our story and explained that he had to return the room that the nursing home had allocated for us. They had initially given him the room for only "a few days," which had since turned into several weeks. Grandfather tried everything — beginning with applying pressure, and heartfelt pleadings and finally, involving influential people in his quest. The orphanage agreed to accept us.

Grandfather was very satisfied, but I was afraid. Again, a new place. New people, new conditions I would have to get used to, and worst of all — we would be leaving Grandfather.

Grandfather patiently explained to us that moving to this new place was for our good. "Everyone there is Jewish," he said, "all the staff and the children. You won't have to worry about meeting nuns; the long arm of the church won't reach you in the orphanage."

We were still apprehensive, but Grandfather asked us to give it a month's trial. "If you don't like it, I'll take you back," he promised. "Don't worry, I'll come to visit you often. There are no visiting days there; visitors can come whenever they want. If I see you are unhappy, I can take you back immediately."

This promise calmed me down, and I slept soundly that last night in the nursing home. When we wished the elderly residents good-bye the following morning, they all blessed us and wished us success in our new home. The director assured us that if we were unhappy in the orphanage, we were welcome to return to his nursing home.

After a short trip, we arrived at a side street of downtown Brussels. A prominent sign was displayed on one of the buildings, welcoming us to "De la Patriot Orphanage." The building looked just like all the other buildings on that street. It didn't have a lobby; we walked through a simple corridor to the office of Mr. Tiffenbrunner, the director.

Mr. Tiffenbrunner welcomed us warmly. "Welcome, dear girls! We were waiting for you. We're very happy that you came to join all of our children," he said in a friendly, kindhearted way. Afterwards, he called the housemother, Mrs.

Bamberger, who hugged us affectionately, as if we were her beloved daughters who had returned from abroad. I took to her immediately.

We sat in the office and spoke together. Irena and I told Mr. Tiffenbrunner and Mrs. Bamberger in brief about how we had spent the war years. They told us about the institution's daily schedule. Afterwards, Mrs. Bamberger took us to the second floor where the girls' rooms were. Irena and I were to sleep in separate rooms — each of us with girls our ages. Grandfather said good-bye after he saw our rooms, completely satisfied with the staff and their warm welcome. He promised to come visit us within the next few days.

Mrs. Bamberger gave us a quick tour of the orphanage, her arms lovingly draped over our shoulders. It was such a pleasant, wonderful feeling! I didn't want her ever to take her arm off my shoulders. It brought back fond memories. When Maman and I would go out together, she would do the same.

"What's your Jewish name?" Mrs. Bamberger asked me.

"Chanah. Chanah Zucker. I was named after my mother's grandmother. Maman loved her very much, and always said I was born in the merit of Bubby Chanah's prayers. She passed away a short time before I was born."

Mrs. Bamberger hugged me tightly and said, "Chanah, Chanah'le. No more Arlette, Anna Marie doesn't exist, only our Chanah. You were born Chanah, and Chanah you will remain. *B'ezras Hashem*, you will build a true Jewish home, like your parents' home, as they yearned for you."

She introduced me to the girls in my room. "Girls, this is Chanah, your new friend. Please welcome her like a sister and help her adjust."

Then she turned to me. "Our girls are wonderful, Chanah, and you will find them good friends."

The girls introduced themselves, but in all the excitement, I didn't catch their names. The newness of this home suddenly blended with my last home — the convent — as images of my friends from the convent suddenly appeared in my mind and confused me. One of the girls had the same name as me — Chanah — hers was the only name I remembered. "Don't worry," one of the girls said. "Everything is new for you now. It will take time to get used to things and remember everyone's names."

They showed me my bed. There were two bunkbeds in the room and another single bed — which I received. I looked around me. Three girls sat at a writing table, while another arranged clothing in a closet. There was a pleasant atmosphere in the room, but it seemed to be missing something. "Where are the other girls in our room?" I asked.

"There aren't any other girls in this room. Only us."

"Really? There are only five older girls in this institution?"

They laughed. "Why do you think that? Of course there are more, but they sleep in other rooms. There are forty-five children here, and five or six sleep in each room.

"Oh... I'm used to a room where approximately forty girls sleep together."

They understood immediately. "You came from a convent? We have other girls here who came from convents, but they're younger." One of the girls asked hesitantly, "Tell us, are you really fifteen years old, as Mrs. Bamberger said?"

I nodded, answering both questions. "Yes, I came from a convent and I'm fifteen years old."

"Was there enough food in the convent? Is that why you're so small and thin?"

"There was enough food. But I didn't want to eat pork, and in general, I was feeling depressed and had no desire to eat with the gentiles."

"Look, Chanah," the other Chanah told me. "You have to forget about what was there. Here we are trying to forget and not remember, so we can proceed in life. If we keep thinking about our memories from the past — we'll fall apart."

I knew she was right. I must open a new page; I must forget all my troubles and be happy that I'm here among fellow Jews.

# 45
# "The Convent Protected You from That Horror"

Our room was a real homey bedroom, and not a large, aloof dormitory sleeping hall. It had a table, chairs, a closet, shelves filled with books and even scenic pictures on the wall. The beds were covered with pretty bedspreads, but the table was bare. "Don't you have a tablecloth for the table?" I asked.

"No. But we're happy with what we have, and don't think about what we don't have."

I decided to embroider a tablecloth and doilies for the shelves. At least they had taught us something useful at the convent! I was happy to be able to contribute something of my own good will. I didn't give of myself willingly in the convent; I only did what was demanded of me. I embroidered during our crafts class, I sewed during our sewing class, I scraped when I was told to scrape. I had just arrived at the orphanage — I hadn't even had a chance to remember my roomates' names, but I already felt an overwhelming desire to give. It was a lovely feeling. I felt that I belonged, and I wanted to contribute.

I arranged my few things in the closet, and noticed that the other shelves were almost empty. There weren't many belongings here, in the children's home, but it didn't make a difference. We were together and that was the main thing.

I sat down on my bed and looked at the girls and at the room. The row of books lined up neatly on the shelf reminded me of all the books we had had in my home, and of all the books I had read to Meir. I wanted to flip through those books, but I didn't know if it was permitted. In the convent, we were not allowed to just take a book and read it.

The other girls were all doing their homework at the table. I didn't dare ask them anything. In the convent, speaking in the homework room was strictly prohibited. If something wasn't clear, you had to raise your hand, approach the nun and ask her. Even if you had finished your homework, you had to sit with your hands folded and head down until homework hour was over. We may have whispered to each other, but we were careful not to get caught.

I still wasn't sure what was permitted or forbidden in the orphanage, and I preferred to sit quietly and not break any rules. I sat and looked at the girls — who were engrossed in their work. I was jealous of them. I also wanted to learn! There was a pleasant atmosphere in the room, an atmosphere of studying because you liked it and not because you were forced. Every so often one of the girls lifted her head and smiled at me. One of them even got up, came to me and said a few words. No one seemed to mind.

Finally, I asked in a whisper, "Am I allowed to leave the room? I want to see my cousin."

All four of them looked at me astonished. "Of course! Feel free to do whatever you want. You're in your own home," said one girl. Another asked, "Is the sweet girl who arrived with you and that old man your cousin?"

"Yes. The old man is her grandfather, who also adopted

me as his granddaughter."

"You're so lucky! You have a cousin who remained from your family!" I didn't tell them that in fact, she was a distant relative. For me, Irena had always been like a real cousin.

I found Irena in her room. Five girls had been living in that room and she was the sixth. The other girls sat around a table doing homework, and Irena stood near them, talking to a tall girl. When she saw me, she ran to me happily.

"Chanah'le! Look! These are my roommates and they're all Jews! This is my counselor, Annette." She introduced me to all the girls, calling each one by name. I couldn't remember the names of my roommates, maybe because when they introduced themselves to me I had been thinking of my friends from the convent. Irena was great — she lived in the present and enjoyed it. Why can't I be like her? I wondered.

I wanted so badly to leave the convent. I had dreamed about it day and night. And now, the miracle has finally happened — I have left — and I am still thinking about the girls there, remembering them and longing for them. I keep asking myself, what are they doing now? Now they're certainly in the homework room, with one of the nuns watching over them, and woe to the one who dares lift her head! Why am I thinking about them? Why are my thoughts still behind those tall walls? Had they performed some magic act that tied me so strongly to them? Why am I afraid that somehow they'll find out that I stopped going to church, and that Grandfather broke all the little icons and tore the pictures they gave me? They can't punish me any longer. I don't belong to them anymore. Even when I was in the convent, I didn't belong to them, and especially now that I left them, I certainly don't!

"Chanah'le, why are you sad?" Irena inspected me with surprise. "It's good here in the orphanage. Here everyone is Jewish."

Annette, Irena's counselor, came over and asked me gently, "Are you still 'there' in your memories?"

I was stunned. How did she know? Did she read my thoughts? Annette smiled understandingly and said, "Don't worry. It's impossible to erase everything all at once. Slowly you'll free yourself. I am the same way."

"You were also in a convent?" I asked.

Her answer was strange. "No, not in a convent. I was — 'there.'"

I didn't understand. "Where is 'there'?"

A pair of astonished eyes opened wide. "You really don't know?"

***Irena (at left) with friends from the children's home.***

"No, I don't know. Since I've left the convent, I've heard that word several times."

Annette placed her hand on my shoulder and told me quietly, "I understand that you didn't have it easy either." Then she raised her voice, "But you should know: 'there' was the worst place of all. The convent protected you from that horror. You were lucky! You may have difficult memories, but normal ones, memories that you can live with, memories that are bearable. 'There' wasn't normal. 'There' was beyond life. We, the remnants who returned to life, are trying to think as little as we can about what we went through. We are trying not to remember. Otherwise — we can't continue living. And we must live, because that is our revenge. We must continue despite everything. The sweetest revenge of all will be rebuilding a new Jewish people!" She spoke passionately, and her face had turned red. The bottomless sadness in her eyes sent a chill through my bones. I didn't understand what she was saying, but I understood that it was something far worse than I could imagine. Despite what she had experienced, however, even while she was speaking about revenge, she held her head proudly.

I was taken up with her enthusiasm, even though I didn't understand anything. I promised I would heed her advice.

"I know that it's hard to continue, but one must," concluded Annette.

Mrs. Bamberger asked me about my studies in the convent, and I told her that we had studied mostly theology — everything connected to Christian history, their Saints, and the Vatican. I knew how to repeat by heart every pope's name and his life history, and other related information. Besides this, we had studied Belgian history and geography, reading, writing, grammar and a little math. It turned out I was missing a good part of the studies for my age, and I was only at the level of the girls in Miriam Neuberger's class, who were younger than me. Mrs. Bamberger said I might be able to join the second age-level — Mrs. Perlman's group, but under no circumstances would I manage in Mr. Katzenellenbogen's class, where the older girls studied. In the end, it was decided that I would study privately, so that I wouldn't be embarrassed. If I'd progress rapidly, there was a chance that I'd be able to learn with my age group the following year.

A doctor gave me a thorough examination and he determined that I was suffering from malnutrition. He instructed the staff to give me food in abundance.

The children's home was a friendly, loving place, with a warm family atmosphere. Our counselor, Frieda, was a cheerful, happy girl. When the girls would talk about the daily regime in the institution, I used to laugh. What daily regime? I would ask them. Because you have to get up in the morning or eat meals at a certain time? Because you have a bedtime? The girls here didn't know what a real daily regime was. They didn't understand why I was so thrilled about going to the bathroom whenever I wanted, alone, and not in a long, straight line with everyone standing in pairs.

Since I knew how to sew a little, they arranged for me to work with a seamstress in town. I would learn the profession while apprenticing. Every morning I went to work, and did all the sewing and finishing manually. The seamstress cut, sewed on a machine, and did the fittings on clients. The atmosphere there was also pleasant. At noon I returned to the orphanage and ate lunch together with the rest of the girls.

In the afternoon I learned privately with the counselors to cover the study material I was missing, and in the evening, I attended classes in *Chumash*, *Tefillah*, and Hebrew language together with the other girls. Mr. Tiffenbrunner and Mr. Bamberger taught these classes.

There was a *shul* in the orphanage. The boys *davened* there daily, and the girls *davened* there only on Shabbos. Every morning, when we got up, everyone said *"Modeh Ani"* together. After straightening up our room, we sang the Shacharis prayers together in melodious tunes, and I burst with joy. In the dining room all the children washed their hands before eating, and recited *Birkas HaMazon* afterwards. During Shabbos meals, one of the adults gave a talk on *parashas hashavua*. Religion ruled our lives, but it was my religion, Judaism!

Several days after we had arrived, Mrs. Bamberger called me to her room and asked me to take off my cross necklace. "It's impossible to have a cross in our institution," she told me. "We suffered enough from this cross, and I never want to see it again!"

"It's just a memento from my friends in the convent," I answered hesitantly. "They saved their pennies to buy it for me as a good-bye present."

***On the way to sewing lessons.***

But Mrs. Bamberger wouldn't be swayed. "You want to remain here, Chanah? You want to live among Jews? Then no cross." She removed the necklace from my neck, tore it and broke the cross. "You'll have to manage with the good-bye letters your friends wrote you," she said. "I'm sure you'll remember them always in your heart, even without the necklace."

I did remember them well. When my longings for them overcame me, I read their letters again and again.

# 46
# Filling Maman's Place

I loved to learn, and did well in my studies in the orphanage. In the convent I had been considered a diligent student, aside from the times when I was withdrawn and refused to participate in the lessons. I had known much more than my friends there. But in the orphanage, I knew much less than the girls my age. I threw myself completely into my studies so I could make up what I lacked.

I also enjoyed my sewing work. The seamstress was a very good woman who treated me very kindly. When I received my first paycheck, I bought candies for all my new friends. We invited the girls from the adjoining rooms into our room, and held a merry party together. We ate and sang.

At one point, the other girls stopped singing. I didn't notice and I continued singing alone. The girls clapped their hands excitedly, What a beautiful voice you have!" they said." From now on, you must always sing for us." They taught me many lovely songs. ne of my favorites was about a bound calf:

| | |
|---|---|
| *Oifen firel ligt das kelbel* | A calf is lying on the wagon |
| *Ligt gebunden mit a shtrick* | And he is tied by a rope |
| *Hoich in himmel* | High in the sky |
| *Flit das shvelbel* | The sparrow soars |

| | |
|---|---|
| *Freit zich, dreit zich,* | This way and that |
| *Hin un krik* | He happily turns |
| *Lacht der vint* | The wind laughs |
| *In korn* | Through the corn field |
| *Lacht un lacht un lacht* | Laughs and laughs and laughs |
| *Lacht er up a* | Laughs and jumps |
| *Tag a gantzen* | The whole day |
| *Mit a holber nocht.* | Until the middle of the night. |
| *Dana, dana, dana* | Moo, moo, moo |
| *Dana, dana, dana, dana...* | Moo, moo, moo, moo |
| *Shreit dos kelbel.* | The calf moos. |
| *Zogt der foyer,* | The driver says, |
| *"Vershe heist dir zein a kalb?* | "Who told you to be a calf? |
| *Volst gekent doch zein a foigel* | You could have been a bird |
| *Volst gekent doch zein* | You could have been |
| *A shvalba."* | A sparrow." |
| *Lacht der vint* | The wind laughs |
| *In korn* | Through the corn field |
| *Bidne kelber tut men binden* | The poor calves are bound |
| *Un men shluft* | And taken |
| *Zei un menshecht* | To be slaughtered |
| *Ver s'hot fligel* | While whoever has wings |
| *Flit aroif tzu...* | Can fly away... |
| *Iz by keinem* | And to no one |
| *nit kein knecht.* | Is he beholden. |

This song expressed the difficult feelings I had felt when I was imprisoned behind the walls of the convent.

The room's appearance changed for the better after I arrived. Frieda got hold of a piece of cloth for me and I embroidered an attractive tablecloth for the table and small doilies for the shelves. I embroidered one larger doily for one of the shelves. One of the other girls had decorated a pitcher with a beautiful drawing, and I placed that on the shelf with the large doily. We made sure to always fill it with flowers.

When I finished my embroidery projects, I began to knit curtains for the windows. I finished them on the day the Tiffenbrunners, who had founded the orphanage, left us and moved to Antwerp. I gave them the curtains as a good-bye present from us all.

Mrs. Bamberger was so impressed with my work that she asked me to knit new curtains. I was happy to comply, but her next request filled my heart with tremendous pride. These were her words: "Could you first embroider a tablecloth for the *shul*'s *bimah*, so we can place the sefer Torah on it when it is being read? Do you think you could do that?" I can't describe to you my intense joy and satisfaction — I would be embroidering for the *shul*, for the Torah's honor! I embroidered the covering for the *bimah* working straight through several nights, humming while I stitched, singing in contentment.

In every Jewish home, Shabbos is the highlight of the week. Shabbos in the orphanage was always extraordinarily special. How eagerly we waited and prepared for Shabbos! On Friday, we threw ourselves wholeheartedly into the preparations: we cleaned, cooked, set up the dining room, and rushed to shower and dress in our Shabbos finery so we would be ready for the thrilling moment when Mrs. Bamberger lit the candles.

All of the children of the children's home stood around, together with the children of the Bamberger family. We all felt like brothers and sisters.

When Mrs. Bamberger covered her eyes with her hands after lighting the candles, I envisioned my mother doing the same. I "saw" Maman's special, white Shabbos scarf covering her head, and "watched" as she lowered her hands to reveal a glowing face. I "saw" her look at Papa, Meir, and me and say, "*Gut Shabbos*," in a calm and loving voice. Like Maman's, Mrs. Bamberger's face also shone when she uncovered her eyes and wished us "*Gut Shabbos*."

She looked at all of us: her caring eyes didn't pass over any of the forty-three children. Those were unforgettable moments.

***Chanah (first from the right) and a friend with the Bamberger children.***

The men went to *shul*, and some of the girls also went along to *daven* in the ladies' section. The rest of us sat around Mrs. Bamberger, relaxing and chatting together. Each girl would relate something — a story about *tzaddikim*, something from Jewish history, or something from her own personal history — whatever she could remember from before the terrible war.

I would sit close to Mrs. Bamberger, clutching her hand. Mrs. Bamberger filled my mother's place. I clung to her at every possible opportunity. I wasn't the only one who loved her so much; we were all orphans, and she treated all of us affectionately, with devotion and love. I loved sitting next to her on Shabbos night, quietly listening to the girls' stories. Sometimes they spoke about how the orphanage had managed during the war years, during the period when Mr. Tiffenbrunner had run it.

Mr. Tiffenbrunner had founded the institution when refugee children began pouring into Belgium from other countries. At first, the institution had been in Antwerp. The Tiffenbrunners had married on the day that Belgium was occupied and immediately moved with the children to Brussels. More and more children joined the original group, and then moved into the present building on the De La Patriot street. Over time, the institution was named after the street.

Incredibly, the children's home functioned under the "protection" of the Gestapo! They had lists of names — both of the children and the staff members, and Mr. Tiffenbrunner went to the Gestapo headquarters every month to receive ration books. Each time he knew he was entering the lions' den. One of the older boys always accompanied him and waited for him on a street corner. If, after an hour, Mr. Tiffenbrunner hadn't returned, the boy was to run back to the orphanage and tell the staff to disperse the children immediately.

But an open miracle occurred there: Mr. Tiffenbrunner left each time with the ration books in his hand. Sometimes he even left the place with a new child he had managed to save. No one knew how to explain how his orphanage, together with another six Jewish orphanages, managed to survive under the Gestapo's protection in Belgium.

Toward the end of the war, an emergency warning reached all of these children's homes: Flee immediately! The children of our institution fled to the church of Father Rubina, a righteous gentile, who cleared out a meeting hall for them. He took out benches and put in beds instead. Father Rubina also provided them with food for an entire week, until the Americans entered Brussels.

There were another six children's homes like "De La Patriot," and Jews had also been sheltered and saved in nursing homes and hospitals. The girls claimed that it was in the merit of the Queen Mother — Elisabeth, the grandmother of King Baudouin, and also in the merit of the righteous gentile Yvonne Nevejean. Nevejean, a rescue activist, worked ceaselessly on behalf of Jewish children and also influenced others to take part in saving Jewish children in Belgium. We felt profound appreciation for Yvonne Nevejean, and other people — unfortunately, too few — who showed true kindness to our people during some of the murkiest days in the history of mankind.

When the boys returned from shul, everyone sat around the large table like one family. Mr. Bamberger and the boys sang *Shalom Aleichem* to the same tune that Papa had sung it. Afterwards, all the boys lined up in front of Mr. Bamberger and he blessed them. Mrs. Bamberger blessed all the girls. During these moments, I felt as if we were one large family, and they were our real parents. After all, only parents blessed their children that way. We didn't call them "Papa" and "Maman" — those words would always be reserved for our real parents, may Hashem avenge their blood. But we felt toward them just like toward real parents.

"Purim will soon be here!" cheered the children one day.

I was stunned. I didn't remember the existence of this holiday at all. Who knows what else I had forgotten? What other important things had vanished from my memory?

We planned a large party and everyone was supposed to dress up. I didn't want to. I had lived enough of my life in disguise. I had been disguised as a gentile, first Arlette and then Anna Marie. I was finally Chanah, a Jewish girl. I wanted to be myself — I didn't want to dress up as anyone else. But my friends managed to convince me. "You have to wear a costume like everyone else," they persuaded me. "You'll see that you won't regret it."

***Purim party in the orphanage. Chanah is first from right, dressed up like a man. Second from the right, standing, is Mr. Tiffenbrunner. His wife, who is holding their daughter, is on his left.***

***Purim. Chanah, dressed up like a gypsy, is posing with her friends in the orphanage yard.***

In the end, I didn't regret it. Purim was such a nice holiday! All the boys dressed up like Mordechai the Jew or partisans. No one wanted to dress up like the wicked Haman or Achashverosh — we had had enough of evil. The girls were all Queen Esther or princesses. Many Jews who had come to the orphanage to hear the Megillah reading remained for the *seudah* and greatly enjoyed themselves. The happiness was overflowing.

I kept reviewing key phrases in my mind, repeating, "Purim, Megillas Esther, *mishloach manos, la-yehudim hoisah orah v'simchah v'sasson v'yekor...*" the whole day, but I absolutely couldn't recall what they meant. Could it be that my mother hadn't dressed Meir and me in costumes? How could it be? She had done everything for us!

When Grandfather came to visit, I asked him about it. "Of course you celebrated Purim," he said. "I still remember the *mishloach manos* your parents sent me." I was sorely disappointed that this beautiful holiday had been erased from my memory.

After Purim began the preparations for Pesach. The orphanage had a special oven for baking *matzos* in its cellar. Since I was among the older girls, I helped in the baking of *matzos*. Everything had to be done with exceptional cleanliness and amazing alacrity. In the beginning, I found it difficult to keep up, but after several training exercises, I learned how to work quickly as the mitzvah required. The *matzos* that we baked were also distributed to other Jews in Brussels.

I remembered Pesach. I remembered the Seder night in our house, the matzos, the elegant tableware, even a little bit of the *Mah Nishtanah*. However, I had no recollection of cleaning the house. Apparently, I hadn't taken part in the cleaning; Maman must have done it alone. I remembered only the things that had left an impression on me as a child. In the orphanage, everyone participated in the cleaning campaign. The convent had also done "spring cleaning" after the long, austere winter, but here it was completely different: the main effort was devoted to eliminating even the tiniest bit of *chametz*. I remembered the word "*chametz*," but I didn't remember the issue of "*bal yera'eh u'val yimatzeh*" — that it had to be entirely eliminated and not seen in our possession. That was new for me.

We cleaned the rooms, the shul, the coatroom and the

dining room, but the hardest work was done in the kitchen. Everyone participated in the cleaning, including the counselors and Mrs. Bamberger — not just the students. We all worked together, in contrast to the convent — where some gave the orders and others had to carry them out. We worked happily, sang and even acted a little mischievously. We went to sleep every night very tired, but very happy.

We completed the first Seder very quickly because everyone was exhausted. We had an entire day to rest before the next one, though, so we celebrated the second Seder in all its majesty. We were full of joy and energy, and the Seder was so special and poignant!

We sat around the table, dressed in our holiday clothes — orphan boys and girls, the Bamberger family and other staff members. We had been slaves — and now we were free! None of us found it difficult to fulfill our Sages' dictum: "In every generation, each individual is obligated to see himself as if he actually went out of Egypt."

During *Chol HaMoed*, we enjoyed trips to Belgium's public gardens. The lush gardens, in full bloom, filled our hearts with joy. Spring in Belgium is a wonderful period. Although it rained sporadically on *Chol HaMoed*, we still enjoyed our strolls through the beautiful gardens.

After Pesach, we returned to our pleasant routine: school, sewing, and chores. We also had Grandfather's regular visits to look forward to and various social events. In the evenings, we all sat together and sang. We learned new songs, songs about Eretz Yisrael. We sang them in Hebrew, a new and difficult language we were learning. The plan was that we would be taken to Eretz Yisrael when it would become possible, so we had to be prepared! We adopted the first song we learned in Hebrew as our personal "anthem," and we began our sessions with that song each evening.

| | |
|---|---|
| *Kahn b'eretz* | Here in the Land |
| *Chemdas avos,* | That our fathers desired, |
| *Titgashemna kol ha-tikvos.* | All hopes will be fulfilled. |
| *Poh nichye* | Here we will live |
| *U'poh nitzor,* | And here we'll create |
| *Chayei zohar,* | A life of radiance, |
| *Chayei dror.* | A life of freedom. |
| *Poh tiheye* | It will be here |
| *Ha-Shechinah shorah,* | That the *Shechinah* will dwell, |
| *Poh nilmad* | Here we'll learn |
| *Es s'fas ha-Torah.* | The Torah's language. |
| *Shiru shir, shir, shir;* | Sing a song, song, song; |
| *Niru nir, nir, nir;* | Plow a field, field, field; |
| *Od yinatzu nitzanim.* | Buds will yet blossom. |

I taught the girls some of the songs I had learned in the convent's choir. No one cared about their source; the main thing was that there was singing in our house. After an evening of singing, we immediately fell asleep — without nightmares.

# 47
# A Visit to the Convent

With time, my longings for my friends in the convent became overpowering. I had suffered so much in the convent, and all I had wanted then was to leave. But now, I was "homesick." Not for the way of life in the convent, not for the strict, harsh rules, but for the girls — my friends with whom I had spent the difficult war years.

I used the money I earned working for the seamstress to buy stamps. I wrote my friends many letters and had also received replies from them. Nevertheless, my yearnings for them intensified so much that I began to feel depressed. Once again, I was sad and nervous. I was also angry at myself: Why couldn't I detach myself from the past? Why couldn't I be happy and content in this wonderful Jewish orphanage? This anger only added to my gloom, and I couldn't break the cycle of feeling sad/upset/depressed.

One evening, Mrs. Bamberger approached me. She laid her hand on my shoulder and said, "Chanah, do you want to go and visit your friends in the convent?"

I was overjoyed! I hugged her tightly, and felt a glow of happiness wash over my troubled face. Mrs. Bamberger looked at me worriedly, though. "Chanah, you belong to us. You are a Jewish girl. Where do you want to be?" she asked.

"Of course I want to be here in the children's home," I assured her. "I am happy here. This is my place. I only want to visit the convent… because I miss my friends; I'll just stay there for a few hours and then I'll come home. I don't want to stay there, *chas v'shalom*."

"Well," said Mrs. Bamberger, "we are concerned about you and we see that you're suffering. We have decided to let you spend a day visiting your old friends."

I quickly wrote my friends in the convent to tell them the good news. I told them on which day I was coming, and made sure it was clear that I was just coming for a visit. During those days, there was no one in the entire orphanage happier than me. Every evening I sang our choir songs, and I sang merrily while I did my chores, too. All the children and staff members participated in my joy, wishing me to be as happy even after the visit. Only Irena didn't share in my joy.

"This is crazy. Why do you want to visit them? Who knows what they'll do to you? After all, you didn't keep your promise!" she reminded me. "I don't even want to go near the area of the convent!"

But I wasn't afraid anymore. "They can't do a thing to me. I'm a Jew. I don't mind telling them that straight out. What can they do? I don't belong to them, and I have a place to return to."

Irena didn't understand me. She didn't share my longings, and didn't understand them. Since we had come to the orphanage, a certain distance had formed between us. I no longer felt responsible for her; here, there were others who were responsible for her. Each one of us had integrated well with the girls our age, and we weren't dependent on each other.

The day of the trip finally arrived. I went on the way together with Helga. Mr. Bamberger wouldn't allow me to travel alone, and he sent Helga, who was older than me, to accompany me. She was told to watch over me — especially while we were with the nuns — and to make sure I returned in peace. I was very happy to have Helga's company on the long trip.

I was warmly received in the convent. My friends had received a special vacation in my honor, which of course only made them happier. No one asked me where the necklace was, no one asked whether I went to church. Even Sister Lucie, who left her private quarters especially to see me, didn't ask the questions I was so worried about. She only hugged and kissed me affectionately.

Mademoiselle Vermeul was thrilled. "Anna Marie, you look wonderful! It's obvious that you're happy now! I'm so pleased to see you like this... how lovely that you came to visit! I was very worried about you." I knew that she meant what she said — she really cared about me. She had loved me, and had even wanted to adopt me as her daughter.

We sat in the homework room and spoke. I told the girls about the Jewish orphanage which was now my home.

"What are you doing there among Jews?" Eva wondered.

I couldn't believe my ears. "Eva, you didn't know that I am a Jew?"

"You — Anna Marie — a Jew?!" Eva was stunned. Her eyes opened wide in disbelief, and she asked me over and over again, "You're really a Jew?"

I wondered what she thought Jews looked like. There are gentiles who think that Jews have horns and a tail hiding under their clothes. My friends in the convent knew I didn't have those things; we had all bathed and dressed together and I couldn't possibly hide horns and a tail from them... The girls probably had learned that Jews are cruel, swindlers, dirty and frightening... No wonder Eva was in shock! Everything she knew about Jews collapsed suddenly when she found out that I, her lovely and normal friend, was a Jew.

"Yes, I'm a Jew," I said proudly. "They brought me here to save me from the Nazis, and Sister Lucie knew the truth about my religion."

It turned out that many girls besides Eva also didn't know I was Jewish. They were very surprised, and one of them asked if Irena was also a Jew.

"Yes, of course, Irena is a Jew! Her grandfather who used to visit us every month and brought candies for everyone — he is also a Jew."

This was already too much. Also Grandfather?! Such a likeable man, whom all the girls were happy to see when he came to visit, even if only for the candies. Grandfather radiated honor and nobility. He always asked all the girls how they were, and always had a kind word for every girl. He treated everyone respectfully, unlike other visitors who fawned before the nuns and ignored the girls. And of course, besides Grandfather, no one brought candies for everyone. If the other visitors brought something, it was only for their relatives. And here, this precious man, who they esteemed so much — was a Jew!

"How I wish that all the Jewish girls who live in the convent could leave, like I did, and return to the Jewish people," I said. No one reacted. The girls who found it difficult to believe that I was a Jew certainly couldn't imagine that there were other Jewish girls among them, and the girls to whom I was referring kept silent. I don't know what was taking place in their hearts. After all, they didn't have an adoptive grandfather to take them out of the convent. They didn't have a single relative in the world who could demand their release. Everyone had been murdered.

When the girls went to the dining room for lunch, I didn't join them. I didn't even tell them why. Helga and I stayed behind in the homework room, and we ate the kosher food we had brought with us. Afterwards, I sat with my old friends the entire afternoon. I felt comfortable in their company as we reminisced, laughed together and even sang the song they had composed in honor of my good-bye party. I thoroughly enjoyed myself. In the evening I bade them farewell and traveled with Helga back to the Jewish orphanage — my true home.

My visit to the convent was a blessing. The distress my longings had caused me dissipated, and the last remnants of my fear of the church were completely erased. I was finally absolved of Christianity and everything it had represented for me, and now I was free to dedicate myself completely to my new life in the orphanage.

Other children also had to go through a process of freeing themselves. Slowly they began to open up and tell their horrific stories. It was a painful, but necessary, healing process, and everyone had stories to tell. The older children, who had spent the war years in the orphanage — sheltered from much of the horrors — had already received their immigration certificates and immigrated to Israel. The children who joined us instead had spent the war years in different places, and their stories made my hair stand on end. Each story was more dreadful than the previous one. How did they survive these horrors? How?

Every evening we sat together, and the children who had experienced the full horror of the Holocaust kept relating their stories, encouraged by the staff, some of whom had also experienced the same hell on earth. It was very difficult. The pain hovered around us in all its intensity.

"Are you sure that this is a good idea?" I asked Mrs. Bamberger one evening. "Maybe these stories are harmful. Maybe it's better for them to just push them out of their minds, and to live in the present?"

"It's impossible to forget them immediately," she replied. "When a child pushes aside his thoughts of past horrors, they remain hidden deep in his soul, rob him of happiness, and then resurface with greater intensity in the form of nightmares. The more they tell their stories and share them with everyone, the more it will release them from the past, *b'ezras Hashem*, so they can begin a new life."

I saw how true her words were. The children were suffering less and less from nightmares. The nights had become quieter, and the blood-curdling screams had become less frequent.

# 48
# Father Gabriel

When summer arrived, it was decided that all the children in the institution would go on vacation to further their emotional and physical convalescence. We spent long hours poring over maps of Belgium trying to plan the trip. In the end, we agreed upon a village which was located near a large forest. After spending some time in that village, we vacationed in another village, and then in yet another. Each was special in its own way.

In each village we lodged in a school building, sleeping on blankets we had spread on the floor. We explored the forests, rode bicycles, ran, and played outdoor games, reveling in nature's beauty and expanse. We also went on long hikes — with knapsacks on our backs and songs on our lips.

Wherever we camped, we rented boats and sailed down the river, even on rainy days. In Belgium we were used to rain falling all year round, and even occasional storms with lightning and thunder didn't cause us to change our plans.

We learned how to row with oars, climb trees, and do Omega rapelling. We drank milk straight from the cows and ate fresh eggs from the coop. The roosters' crows were our wake-up calls, and when we went out in the morning, we saw the cows on their way to pasture. Every farmer had a few cows, and one shepherd would gather them from all the cowsheds in the village and take them out to graze. In the evening, every cow returned straight to its cowshed; each one recognized its own place.

Our favorite of the many trips we went on were visits to ancient dilapidated castles. We explored the deserted buildings, discovered secret hideouts, the rooms which still remained whole or in part, and the huge dungeons. When we sat in some magical corner to eat the picnic lunch we had prepared, we let our imaginations run wild. We spun stories about the people who had lived in the castle... How they had lived, how they had fought and how they had been forced to flee. Since there were several castles like this near the three villages we visited, we had to invent new stories each time.

We lived like this for several weeks, without studies and feeling totally carefree. We tried to forget the past.

The staff spoke with us primarily about the future that would materialize in Eretz Yisrael. They told us stories about the Holy Land from long ago, stories from the time of the Bais HaMikdash. They told us stories about the *Churban* and the Exile from our Land, and stories about Eretz Yisrael of the present — which was in the process of being built up.

They explained to us that there were many *kibbutzim* and towns in Eretz Yisrael where the people didn't keep Torah and *mitzvos*, and warned us to be careful. When we would make *aliyah*, we would have to insist that the authorities place us only among religious Jews.

We returned to the orphanage tanned and healthy, happy and relaxed. During the vacation, we had a chance to interact closely with all the children in the orphanage — instead of just with our roommates. I became friendly with Chista, a girl my age whose personality was similar to mine.

She, like me, was mischievous, yet quiet at the same time. We began to go everywhere together, and I was thrilled to have found a friend after my heart.

***On a trip. Chanah is in the top row, first from left.***

"Chanah! Chanah Zucker!" a voice called from below. "Chanah, where are you? You have a visitor in the office."

How nice! Grandfather came for a visit! I raced down the stairs and happily hurried to the office. On the way, one of the counselors stopped me and said, "A priest is looking for you, Chanah."

What?! I grabbed hold of the counselor's hand, very shaken. "A priest? What does he want from me? I don't want to go. I'm afraid. Come with me," I pleaded.

"Don't worry. Mr. Bamberger is there with him. He'll watch over you."

I calmed down a little, but was still agitated. Why did he

come? I thought. Did he come to check if I'm going to church? After all, they know that I became Jewish again. What should I tell him? What should I do if he gives me the cross to kiss? In the convent, we kissed the cross reverently every time we approached a priest.

I had arrived at the office door. I quickly smoothed my clothes and my hair. I took a deep breath and knocked on the door timidly. It was unusual to knock before entering the office; the orphanage was our home, and Mr. Bamberger was like a father whose door was always open to his children. In a family, there is no need for formal etiquette. But the priest's arrival confused me and I had acted according to the convent's rules.

The door opened and I saw Father Gabriel. He stood up in joy when he saw me. "You look wonderful, Anna Marie! You grew taller and gained weight. You no longer look younger than your real age."

I was happy to see him. I had never been afraid of Father Gabriel; he was a good person. Seeing him again brought back memories. I remember clearly the day I had been kneeling, my back bent and head lowered, hard at work scraping the church stairs. Each marble step was decorated with a bronze runner at its edge to prevent people from slipping on the smooth marble. I was to clean the stairs thoroughly and shine each bronze strip, which, understandably, accumulated much dirt. My hands were red, swollen, and cracked, and dipping them into cold water with abrasive cleaning fluids was sheer torture. I cried while I worked. Suddenly I heard a voice behind me asking, "Why are you crying?"

It was Father Gabriel. I showed him my hands without

saying a word, and he was shocked. “Who sent you to clean with such chapped hands?” he asked.

“It’s my turn, and no one cares how my hands look. It’s more important to them how the stairs look,” I replied.

“Stop cleaning immediately. I’m going to tell Sister Lucie about this.”

“Oh, no! Please don’t do that!” I cried out, alarmed. I knew the nuns would not look favorably on that. They would force me to finish the work anyway, and in addition, they would punish me for involving a priest in the girls’ daily schedule, which was totally unacceptable.

But he didn’t listen to my entreaties, and in the evening, the nun responsible for me called me over and asked me why I hadn’t shown her how my hands looked. I didn’t reply. She knew, just as well as I did, that the girls’ “minor” aches and pains were unimportant and of no concern to anyone in the convent. But after that, I was never told to scrape the stairs, and Father Gabriel would summon me every so often to check my hands. The nuns had promised him they would give me ointment for my condition, and he would also make sure they had kept their word. He was interested in my well-being and treated me kindly.

I knew that he hadn’t come to the orphanage to inquire if I remained faithful to Christianity. He had come to visit me because he cared about me. He had made the effort to find out my address and to travel to the orphanage.

“Tell me about your life here,” he began.

I was only too happy to comply. “I feel here like I’m in my own home. The children here are my brothers and sisters, and the staff treats us like family. There is no daily regime here like there was in the convent. You can go around here normally, like in your own home, not in a straight line, or in pairs. There are rules here too; there's a schedule, but it's a normal schedule — like any family's routine — not at all like the convent."

I told him about our recent vacation — the joys of village life, and our refreshing nature hikes. I exuberantly told him how much this vacation had invigorated me.

Father Gabriel was very happy. "I can see that you're doing well. You were always pale and sad in the convent. Your friends asked me to give you their best wishes. I received your address from them and your new name." He thought that the orphanage had given me a new name, just as the convent had changed my name from Arlette to Anna Marie.

"It's not a new name," I told him. "Chanah Zucker is my real name, the name which my parents gave me at birth. When I arrived at the convent with such a Jewish name, they changed it to hide my origin. But now I can once again practice my religion openly, and that's why I'm so content. Despite all the suffering my people endured during this terrible war, I'm happy to belong to this nation — which is the most persecuted, but also the most exalted."

Father Gabriel didn't know that Mr. Bamberger was oft to repeat those words. While we were talking quietly at one end of the room, Mr. Bamberger was engrossed in his affairs, writing busily at his table at the other end. He seemed to be uninterested in our conversation. But at that point, I peeked at him and saw that he was smiling upon hearing my words.

I accompanied the priest to the outer gate and wished him good-bye, while many children stood on the porch above us, watching the scene, fascinated. Afterwards, Mr.

Bamberger called me to his room again.

"Tell me about Father Gabriel," he asked. I told him how the priest had been concerned about me and my swollen hands. He also visited me when I was in the infirmary, and was always friendly to me. Most of the priests in the convent didn't pay attention to the girls at all. We were required to bow when they passed by us, and they didn't even bother to look in our direction. Only Father Gabriel treated me so specially.

"This is the second time he came to look for you," Mr. Bamberger revealed. "The first time I told him you weren't here, and that you were attending classes outside of the orphanage. I'm sure you understand Chanah, that we don't want a priest coming to visit you. You left the convent. It's a miracle that you were there during the war, and because of that remained alive. But the war is over already, and you have no reason to keep in touch with them. We understood your longings for the girls you grew up with during the difficult years — and now that you have visited them, you have put your longings to rest. There is no reason to maintain contacts with the priests and nuns."

"You're right, Mr. Bamberger. I'm not interested in keeping up with them. I didn't invite Father Gabriel to visit. I didn't even dream that he would come. He came of his own accord. I don't care if you tell him the next time that I'm not on the premises."

In truth, what do I have to do with the nuns and priests? I knew that I would never even meet the girls again, whom I had longed for so much. I had wanted to visit them just once, to close a chapter in my life. I was finished with the convent for good.

That night, in the dark, my old fears resurfaced. Disturbing thoughts raced around my mind. Do the people in the convent want to bring me back? What do they want from me? Why did Father Gabriel come here? Maybe his visit wasn't so innocent? Maybe he hoped to beguile me back? I had tried to explain to him how wonderful it was here, and he saw that I was thriving and that I belonged to this place.

Maybe it's dangerous for me to remain here? Maybe I made a mistake by going to visit my friends in the convent, and by corresponding with them? Maybe, because of my letters and visit, the people in the convent think I'm still one of them? I had informed them of my new address, of my present name. That's how Father Gabriel had managed to find me.

I know that I can trust the Bambergers. They won't let anyone take me, but I am still afraid. I walk alone every morning to the seamstress, and return alone every afternoon. Maybe this is dangerous. They might lay an ambush on the way... I must ask for a companion... And if no one can accompany me, should I stop working?

In the morning I met Mrs. Bamberger and told her of my fears. She didn't laugh — she understood me and accompanied me to the seamstress. "Don't worry," she told me on the way. "The priests and nuns can't take you back. You don't belong to them. And even if they dare try abducting you, everyone will protect you. Every Jew who survived the war is an only child, precious and important, and no one will give him up. You have no reason to worry."

Nevertheless, when I left the seamstress's home at noon, I saw Claude, one of our older boys. He had come especially to walk me home. I was very touched by Mrs. Bamberger's

✠ PAX

ABBAYE DU MONT CÉSAR, LOUVAIN

le 31 déc 1944

Ma chère Anna,

Voilà déjà quelques jours depuis ma visite à Bruxelles. Je suis bien rentré le soir, un peu plus tard que je ne l'avais prévu cependant. Au lieu de prendre le tram vers 5 h je n'ai eu que celui de 7 h. qui m'a permis de me trouver à l'Abbaye vers 8.30 h. J'ai beaucoup regretté ne n'avoir pu voir Irène ce jour-là. Enfin ce sera pour une autre fois.

Tu vas toujours bien, ma petite fille? Et ta cousine aussi? Moi je me porte à merveille! Je viens vous souhaiter à toutes deux la même chose. Et mieux encore naturellement! Une année belle, grande, sainte, heureuse, pacifique. Ce sera sans doute la paix cette fois avec tous les retours et toutes les joies que cela comporte. Puissions-nous enfin être libérés des dernières entraves qui gênent nos mouvements. Je vous envoie à chacune de vous, une image qui sera l'avant-goût de la paix définitive et qui maintiendra, j'espère, le courage dans vos cœurs.

Au revoir, mes petites filles; croyez bien à toute l'affection de quelqu'un qui vous reste "bien uni." (Comme nous le chantions il y a quelques mois!).

F. Gabriel
O.S.B.

**A letter from Father Gabriel to Chana when she was staying in the orphanage.**

caring gesture. Although she had assured me that I had nothing to worry about, she still sent one of the older boys to accompany me and give me the feeling that I was protected. She showed me that I wasn't alone, that I had a real family who worried for me and watched over me.

# 49
# The Land of Our Dreams

The *Yomim Nora'im* arrived. On Rosh Hashanah, every member of the orphanage, from young to old, went to the large *shul* in Brussels. All the survivors gathered there – and yet, there were still empty seats, bereft of their former congregants. The synagogue had always been full to capacity before the Holocaust. There were many other *shuls* in Brussels that had been full too... When the sounds of the shofar were heard, all the congregants, a pitiful remnant, broke out in heartrending weeping.

And on Yom Kippur, one could have washed the synagogue building with our tears – which fell like water. For the first time in my short life, I participated in the *Yizkor* prayer, and prayed for my parents and my brother Meir. As the congregation recited this prayer, a terrible cry burst forth from each person's mouth, a cry that ascended heavenward to join our martyred families. Everyone joined in the orphan's *kaddish*, from young to old. All the refugees, together with the handful of individuals who had remained from Brussels' large community, mourned over the tragedy that had befallen our People.

My parents had come from large families and I wanted to pray for my grandparents and my uncles and aunts, but I couldn't remember all their names. I prayed for the elevation of their souls among all the six million Jewish martyrs, as Mr. Bamberger had taught us. *HaKadosh Baruch Hu* knows everyone's name.

The night after Yom Kippur, after we had broken our fast, the boys immediately began building the sukkah. They set up a large sukkah in the courtyard, and a smaller sukkah on a porch. The girls in the meantime sat in the dining room and prepared beautiful decorations from colored paper. The atmosphere was merry and cheerful.

On the first night of *Chol HaMoed,* I sat with my friends in the sukkah and we sang the song about the little sukkah, and the candles flickering in the wind which didn't go out, and which will continue to shine until the Merciful One will establish David's fallen sukkah.

A few other girls remembered the song. We taught the others and we sang it again and again, until the hour grew very late, and Mrs. Bamberger sent us to bed.

Throughout the holiday we tried to sit in the sukkah, even when it was raining lightly. Only when it was pouring rain did we return to the dining room. There were no tables and chairs — we had moved them all to the sukkah — so we sat on crates in a circle. Even the staff members who didn't live with us in the orphanage spent the holiday with us, like one large family.

Winter arrived, cold and snowy. On the very cold days, I would travel on a bus to the seamstress. But on pleasant days, I walked. I liked walking, because I could look around me and see life returning to normalcy. I watched people going about their daily routines, and I watched construction workers rapidly restoring the city from all the damage inflicted by the war. I liked to breathe the fresh, brisk air and feel life flowing through my veins.

In the early afternoon, I sat with one of the counselors or one of the older girls, and continued to make up the studies I was missing. Later on, in the afternoon, I studied Jewish studies with everyone, and in the evenings we sat around the heater basking in its pleasant warmth, while listening to stories about Eretz Yisrael — the land of our dreams.

Everyone longed to go there, to live among Jews in the Holy Land. Occasionally we received a few immigration certificates. Seven of the institution's children had already made aliyah. On those cold winter evenings, while we huddled around the heater, we read letters they had sent us from Eretz Yisrael.

They told us that the winter in Eretz Yisrael is milder and there was no snow in the winter. Only sometimes is there rain in the fall, and the rest of the days the sun shines. The summer is hotter, even too hot for their liking, they wrote. I would look at the windows covered with snow and wonder, how could it be too hot?

One day, toward the end of the winter, I was called to the office. "We received a new certificate," Mr. Bamberger told me, "and we decided that this time, you'll travel to Eretz Yisrael."

"I'll travel to Eretz Yisrael?! To the land of unreal heavenly dreams?" I was astounded.

Mr. Bamberger chuckled loudly. "Oh, Chanah! We've been talking to you all the time about Eretz Yisrael, and we've been showing you pictures and reading you letters from our students in Kibbutz Chofetz Chaim — and you still think it's in heaven? It's time to wake up, Chanah! Eretz Yisrael really exists. You'll travel there soon and you'll live in

Kibbutz Chofetz Chaim too."

I knew that Eretz Yisrael was a real land. I even knew, from the letters, that life there wasn't easy. You had to work even on very hot days, in heat which we're not even familiar with in Belgium. The living conditions in the kibbutz were not comfortable. They lived in tin huts which were very cold in the winter and scorching hot in the summer. Food and clothing were rationed. Nevertheless, our institution's students wouldn't exchange these difficulties for any comfort they could get in the Diaspora among gentiles.

And now they were telling me, "You're going!" They gave me an exact date and name of a ship! Despite knowing the facts, I found it difficult to actually believe the news. It all felt like a fairy tale that I had suddenly become a part of. My happiness was immense, but at the same time, I was worried. "Alone? How will I be able to travel alone?"

"You have to travel alone. Only one certificate arrived," Mr. Bamberger explained. "Over time, more of our children will make aliyah, until everyone has made it to Eretz Yisrael."

"But why did you especially choose me? There are older children than me here, who have lived in the institution for many years!"

"We decided to send you right away to help you free yourself completely from the convent. We didn't tell you, but that priest was here several other times. Last week, he came again, and to make sure he wouldn't come another time, we told him that you left the institution. The number of letters which you've been getting from your friends in the convent has been growing, instead of diminishing with time. It's healthier for you to leave, and to put as much distance between you and the people in the convent as you can."

At that point Mrs. Bamberger entered the office. She kissed me with great excitement and wished me *mazel tov*. "But what about Irena?" I was suddenly worried. "I can't leave her."

"Chanah'le, you're no longer responsible for her," Mrs. Bamberger said. "We're responsible for her. Besides that, she has a grandfather to worry about her, while you have no one in the world. The kibbutz in Eretz Yisrael will be your home, and *b'ezras Hashem*, you'll build your own home when the time comes."

I went upstairs to tell the news to everyone. They surrounded me excitedly, asking questions and taking an interest in the details. Suddenly everyone broke out in a spontaneous dance. What a wonderful feeling! Everyone, all my new brothers and sisters, were happy for me and thrilled at my happiness. Chista, my new friend, was also very happy. But she had a special request.

***Many years later, when Chanah was already a grandmother, next to the entrance of the children's home.***

"Chanah, promise me that you won't sing any more songs from your convent choir," she begged. "You are going to Eretz Yisrael, the holy land, and you need to be pure. You mustn't sing songs whose source is impure, even though you like them."

I knew that Chista was right. I loved the choir songs, and every night, after we lay down, I would sing them to my roommates. I knew it wasn't right. Just as I had freed myself from all my other ties to the convent, I had to give up the songs I had learned behind those walls. I promised Chista that I would fulfill her request.

I told Grandfather about my imminent trip, and he quickly came to visit the children's home. "I'm so happy to hear this," he said emotionally. "A heavy stone has rolled off my heart, Chanah'le. You see, I already submitted a request for a certificate for me and Irena, but I didn't tell you because I wasn't allowed to include you in my certificate. I was apprehensive about leaving you behind, but Mr. Bamberger encouraged me to submit the request anyway. He promised me that he would personally make sure that you would make aliyah to Eretz Yisrael. And now — you are traveling even before us! Only now I feel completely happy."

***Chanah and Irena with their friends in the children's home.***

Grandfather promised to come again to the orphanage on the day I was traveling to say good-bye. "You'll wait for us in Eretz Yisrael, and we'll come after you," he told me.

Mrs. Bamberger took me shopping in the city. She bought a coat and other essential clothes for me with the money the Joint had sent them on my behalf and at their request. They didn't make a good-bye party for me, because my farewell was only temporary. Soon, they would all come to Eretz Yisrael, and again we would be together.

But in the evening before the trip, we spent a long time together in the dining room, speaking and singing almost until the morning. In the morning, Grandfather came to say good-bye, and Irena remained with us instead of going to class. At noon, I said good-bye to all the children and counselors, to each person in our large family.

# 50
# More Hardships

I still hadn't gotten used to good-byes, despite having gone through so many in my life. I had said good-bye forever to Papa, Maman and Meir. I had taken my leave from my home, Mrs. Salsky and her dark cellar, from the convent which had saved me, from my friends with whom I had spent a very difficult period, and from Mademoiselle Vermeul who truly loved me. And now — good-bye to Irena and her precious Grandfather, due to whom, I had been saved from the convent. I had to say good-bye to all the people in the orphanage with whom I had built a new life, and discovered anew my Jewish identity. I had to bid farewell to Chista and my other friends, the counselors whom I loved so much, and Mr. and Mrs. Bamberger, who were like parents to me.

I was headed for the unknown, again alone. Again leaving everyone, and traveling alone to a new, different place. To a different land, to a new language, to a new culture.

Mr. Bamberger accompanied me to the central train station of Brussels, where we met a group of religious youths from a distant orphanage. Mr. Bamberger had written to them before and arranged that I join them. I was happy that at least I could travel to Eretz Yisrael with a group that spoke French.

We traveled by train to the French city of Marseille. On

the way, the children sang songs of Eretz Yisrael which I knew. In the beginning, I was too shy to sing, and besides that, I was thinking about all those whom I had left behind. But slowly, I became swept up in their music and gaiety, and I joined in their singing.

We were housed in a camp of shacks in Marseille, with another group of children. We received two shacks: one for boys and one for girls. The conditions there were terrible; it was filthy, and full of bedbugs. The beds — which had no mattresses — were crowded next to each other. The beds were lined with sacks which were supposed to serve us as both mattresses and blankets. When we arrived, we sat outside on the bare ground, and only entered the shacks when it was very late. I lay huddled in my bed, completely dressed in my clothes and holding my suitcase. I was carrying the money which I had received from the seamstress I had worked for, and I was afraid it would be stolen. That's why I couldn't fall asleep.

In the morning, we woke up full of bites and exhausted. We were miserable, and the counselor, who saw how nauseated we were by the place, decided to take us on a trip to Paris. During the trip from Marseille to Paris, we sang again, and slowly recovered from the unpleasant night we had endured. We alighted the train not far from the Eiffel Tower, and continued walking toward the tower. We climbed the tower, and under us stretched out all of Paris: an enormous city with the Seine River crossing through it. We also visited the Champs Elysee, passed under the large, beautiful gate, and from there continued to the Old City. We walked around its picturesque alleyways, ate in a large garden, and sat on the grass and played.

In the evening, we returned to Marseille, to the filthy shacks. I was very tired, and I knew I would collapse if I spent another night without sleep. I asked one of the girls what I should do, and she suggested that I hide my money in my socks. "I also hide my things in my socks," she told me.

When I awoke in the morning, I discovered in agitation that my socks were empty. I looked around me, looking for the girl who had given me the advice. Had she stolen the money? She wasn't on the bed next to mine — where she had slept the previous night. In the end, I found her sleeping on the other side of the shack. What could I do? There was no one to whom I could even complain. I was a girl alone in a group of foreigners, and now I was penniless. I only had my small suitcase — which contained my few clothes, letters and mementos. I hadn't taken off my new, beautiful coat the entire night, and maybe because of that it wasn't stolen.

I sat on my bed, feeling humiliated, not listening to the conversations being held around me. Only when I saw that everyone was going out, did I take my suitcase and go out after them. Outside, everyone arranged themselves in groups, each group with its counselor. I joined "my" group and we strode toward the port where the ship awaited us. It was a small ship called *Kaera Citi*. We were the only religious group that was traveling on the ship.

Each person received a bed in the ship, and a place to put his belongings. "Tonight is *bedikas chametz*," the counselor reminded us. "Everyone has to check the food he brought with him. You can keep fruits and vegetables. Everything else must be thrown into the sea."

I still had candies from the orphanage. I ate as many of them as I could, divided some of them among my new friends, and the rest I threw into the sea as the counselor had instructed us.

At noon, the ship set off, and I immediately began to feel seasick. I thought I felt this way because of all the candies I had gobbled down. I threw up non-stop. One of the sailors came to our room and promised me and the others that we would feel better the next day.

I slept that entire day, and in the evening woke up with my body aching all over. I tried to get up, and immediately began to throw up again. A terrible dizziness overcame me. With great effort, I stumbled back to my bed and crawled under the covers, all the while feeling terrible.

At night, they invited us to attend the Pesach Seder, but whenever I tried to stand up, I felt dizzy. The other girls urged me to join them anyway, and in the end, I stood up and went to the dining room where the Seder was being held. I sat there trembling, covered with cold sweat. "What happened to you?" asked the counselor, shocked.

"I am seasick. I feel awful. I think I better go back to bed."

"Maybe stay with us anyway? We're celebrating only one Seder night since we're already on the way to Eretz Yisrael. If you miss this Seder — you won't have a second Seder tomorrow. It's a shame to miss it."

I tried to remain with them a little more, but after a short time I felt I couldn't. I crawled back into bed.

We sailed an entire week, with me laying deathly ill the entire time. I couldn't eat a thing; I threw up everything I put in my mouth. One of the sailors came daily to bring me tea. On Sunday, he brought me a sandwich, but as soon as I saw the bread I shouted, "Throw it into the sea! It's *chametz*!"

The sailor didn't understand my language. I explained to

him what I meant with hand gestures, and he threw the bread out the window, feed for the fish. He left me tea, and after that only brought me drinks.

I was sure I was going to die. I felt terrible. When I tried to take a few steps, I almost collapsed. My roommates helped me reach the sink and return to my bed. My legs and arms were so heavy, and the dizziness never left me.

Just now, when I'm so close to Eretz Yisrael, I'm going to die, I thought. Why did I have to travel, and all by myself? I was happy in the orphanage. I had found my place there, among people whom I loved and admired. And now, I'm going to die alone, without one relative or friend around, on my way to the Holy Land! I didn't even have strength to cry; I was so weak.

On the eighth day of our trip, my friends came to tell me the news that we were almost in Eretz Yisrael. "We can already see the shore from afar. You must come see!"

"I can't," I answered weakly. They hurried to go up on the deck, not wanting to miss the special scene, and I remained lying in my bed, without a drop of strength.

When the ship anchored, I understood we had arrived. I tried to stand up, but I fell back in my bed. The girls returned to the room and said I must stand up because we are leaving the ship.

"Forget about me, I'm dying in this bed. I can't get up and pack my things, and there's no way I can walk up to the deck."

My devoted friends didn't leave me. They packed my few belongings for me and, supporting me on each side, helped me ascend to the deck where all the youth groups were standing with their suitcases, impatiently waiting for the moment when they could disembark from the ship.

My friends led me to the railing and showed me where to look. We were viewing the heavenly land! There was Mount Carmel! For the first time in my life, I saw a real mountain, and it was Mount Carmel of all mountains, the mountain I had heard so many stories about in the orphanage — and I hadn't the strength to get properly excited.

The counselor approached us and looked at me in surprise. "Are you Chanah Zucker? You're the girl from Mr. Bamberger's institution, the one who joined us in Brussels?"

The seasickness had left its mark on me. I looked completely withered, like a squeezed-out yellow lemon. My clothes hung limply on me, and I was barely able to stand. With great effort I managed to say, "Yes, I'm Chanah. I'm just very sick."

My friends helped me disembark from the ship and they carried my suitcase for me. Finally my feet stepped on the land of Eretz Yisrael.

# 51
# The Kibbutz

The platform. A regular port platform, just like in Marseille. Everything was black and filthy. Noise, crowding, and a large commotion. I was barely able to stand, but there was no place to sit. This is Eretz Yisrael? This is the promised Holy Land?

In one second, my Eretz Yisrael in the stars fell to the ground. There is nothing heavenly here. Everything is very physical, very earthly. I took it very hard. My great disappointment together with my feeble physical state, sunk me into despair.

People were running in all directions. Trucks arrived, and every children's group climbed aboard a truck and left. The group I was traveling with also was about to leave.

"Chanah, come with us. We're leaving," the counselor called to me.

"I'm not going with you. Mr. Bamberger told me that someone would come to take me to a religious place."

"We're also religious. Come with us, don't stay here by yourself."

"No," I insisted stubbornly. "Someone is supposed to take me to Kibbutz Chofetz Chaim, where a few of our former students are already living."

The group couldn't wait at the port until someone would

come pick me up. They left and I stayed behind. Slowly the place emptied out, and I remained alone with several other children. We stayed together, trying to soften our loneliness and fear. Suddenly I heard a call, "Chanah Zucker! Where is Chanah Zucker?"

I didn't have the strength to go see who was calling me. I asked one of the children to go to the person who was looking for me and explain that I could barely move. The child returned with an adult man who asked me, "Are you Chanah Zucker?"

"Yes, I am."

"You have to travel with him," he said, and pointed to a teenager who stood nearby. The boy was wearing shorts and had a head full of hair, but did not have a hat or a yarmulka.

"No! I'm not going with him! Mr. Bamberger warned me precisely about such a thing. I am religious and I'm only going to a religious place." Despite my weakened condition, I was adamant.

"But look, it's already evening. No religious person came to take you. You have no choice. You have to go with him."

"I'm not going with him! I'm remaining here, and I'm not going!" I protested. But I was no match for this strong, grown man.

He lifted my suitcase and told me sharply, "It's impossible to remain here. You must leave. It's late already. I also have to go home."

I tried to pull my suitcase away from him, but I had no strength. "If it's impossible to stay here, I'll return to the ship. I have my bed there."

"You can't go back on the ship! The ship is about to disembark."

"So I'll also return to Belgium," I said, fighting to restrain my tears. I felt so miserable. "No one wants me here. No one came to take me. No one will even mind that I'm not here."

But he wouldn't let go of my suitcase. "To travel back to Belgium you need to buy a ticket. Do you have money?"

I didn't have money. I showed him my empty hands helplessly.

"You see? You have no choice. This young man will take you with all the other children who are still here to a transit camp in Kiryat Shmuel. Tomorrow he will take you to your kibbutz."

I was immediately suspicious. "Which kibbutz?" The teenager, who had approached us in the meantime, told me the name of the kibbutz and verified my suspicions: It was a HaShomer HaTza'ir kibbutz.

I mustered my last bit of strength and declared, "I'm going back to Belgium, and I'm not going to your kibbutz. I'm not going somewhere where they don't keep Torah."

"Right now you don't have any choice," the young man said and smiled. "You're traveling with me to a transit camp in Kiryat Shmuel, and tomorrow we'll see what to do with you."

I didn't have a choice. I was alone in a new land, without a penny to my name and unable to speak the language. I traveled with him to Kiryat Shmuel, and he brought me to a room in a shack and showed me my bed. I slept well that night, without even throwing up once. The floor was stable under my feet, and when I awoke in the morning, I managed to stand up easily and walk straight. One woman brought me food and I was able to eat it. I felt much stronger and tried to plan what to do next, to think of someone to whom I could turn for help. Suddenly I heard my name being called on the loudspeaker.

Someone showed me the way to the office. I went there and tried to decide how to react if they would try to take me to another place besides Kibbutz Chofetz Chaim. But I didn't need to worry. Waiting for me in the office, next to the young man who had brought me to the camp just the day before, was a religious Jew with a white beard and kind, affectionate eyes. He looked just like an angel. An angel who had been sent by Heaven to save me. He asked me gently, "Are you Chanah Zucker?"

"Yes," I answered, greatly relieved. "Did you come to take me?"

"Yes, I came to take you to Kibbutz Chofetz Chaim."

It was Rav Shlomo Greenfeld, *zecher tzaddik livrachah.* He saved me from despair and spiritual destruction. Until my marriage, he took care of me like a good grandfather.

"I'm so sorry I didn't come yesterday. They told me about your arrival only late last night," he apologized. I wanted to tell him that he needn't apologize, that I was happy he had come now. But instead of words, I broke out in heavy sobbing.

I cried for my lost years, for my parents and my little brother. I cried for the Jewish girls who had remained in the convent — for everything I had undergone in the past seven years. Rav Greenfeld sat next to me, waiting for me patiently. He didn't try to stop my sobbing; apparently, he understood it was an emotional need. After a while, he got up and brought me a cup of water. I drank and calmed down.

Then I pointed to the youth and said, "He wanted to take me to a HaShomer HaTza'ir kibbutz. I was prepared to return to Belgium instead of going to that kibbutz. I have already lived without Torah for three years in a convent as a Christian. They even baptized me."

"That baptism was nonsense," Rav Greenfeld calmed me down. "*Baruch Hashem*, your body and soul were saved, and now you will live in the Holy Land. *HaKadosh Baruch Hu* will preserve you and watch over you. You are now a pure Jewish girl living in the Holy Land."

Oh, what dew of revival he had injected into my heart! He took me from the transit camp in an old, creaking car to Kibbutz Chofetz Chaim. Rav Greenfeld, my angel of deliverance.

***Chanah on her wedding day, in Kibbutz Chofetz Chaim. Her wedding gown was a simple white dress which every bride in the kibbutz wore on her wedding day. Her veil was a white curtain which had been taken down from a window for the day.***

Kibbutz Chofetz Chaim became my home. My husband and I were married on the kibbutz and lived there for many years. We eventually moved to Yerushalayim, where we raised our children. My husband was also the sole survivor of his family. My children and grandchildren viewed Mrs. Bamberger as their grandmother in every way. May Hashem grant her days and years, and may she see complete *nachas* from her biological and adopted children.

A number of years ago, I traveled to Belgium. I walked down the street I had lived on, but didn't enter the home which had belonged to my parents. Why should I? To see the gentiles who are living there? I did travel to the Couvent Misericorde convent, however, and paid the convent one last visit. I was sad to hear that Mademoiselle Vermeul was no longer alive, and I couldn't thank her for everything she had done for me.

Most of my friends weren't there either. I don't know what happened to the other Jewish girls. Only the head nun and one other nun had been students in my time and had remained in the convent their entire lives. They didn't remember me.

The convent has undergone substantial changes. Today it doesn't have a dormitory, but only a day school. The strict regime has softened somewhat, and black is no longer the dominating color. The girls dress in gray and white, and even the black habit has been replaced with a simple scarf.

My last visit to the convent came to an end. I went behind the walls for the last time.

***Chanah at the entrance of the house where her family lived before the war. She went up to the entrance, but didn't dare go inside.***

When I look at the picture of myself together with my husband, our children, and most of our grandchildren, I think: This is our revenge. We merited to build a Jewish home. On my wedding day, Rav Greenfeld gave me this wonderful blessing, quoting the verse in *Iyov* (8:7): *Ve'haya reshis'cha mitzar, ve'acharis'cha yisgeh me'od* – "Your beginning was small, but your end shall greatly increase." *Baruch Hashem*, his blessing was fulfilled.

***Chanah with her husband, children and grandchildren.***

My oldest daughter returned from her first day in highschool, very excited. "Ima, do you know who one of our teachers is? It's Rav Greenfeld."

"Really? Are you sure it's my Rav Greenfeld?" I was very excited. Since my wedding, I hadn't seen him. "Sarah, you must tell him you're my daughter."

But Sarah was too shy. The opportunity arose only four years later, when she was about to complete her studies. One day, they had a free period, and Rav Greenfeld didn't want the girls to spend the time idly. He entered the class and asked the girls to recite *Tehillim*. He also took a *Sefer Tehillim* from his pocket, and Sarah knew that the time had arrived. She approached his desk.

"Rav, I am Chanah Zucker's daughter," she said hesitantly. "The one that the Rav took from an immigrant camp and brought to Kibbutz Chofetz Chaim."

Rav Greenfeld didn't say a word, but tears appeared in his eyes.

"My brothers, sisters and I are what we are today because of the Rav," Sarah added. "If the Rav hadn't taken my mother from the transit camp, they would have taken her to a HaShomer HaTza'ir Kibbutz. Who knows how she would have appeared today, or how we would have appeared today, if not for your intervention."

Rav Greenfeld continued sitting in class another few minutes with tears rolling down his face. When he left, Sarah's classmates surrounded her and asked, "What did you tell the Rav that made him cry?"

So Sarah told them my story.

# Epilogue

When Israel became a State 1948, all the children in the De La Patriot orphanage, besides Irena, made aliyah.

At that time, Irena's grandfather was very ill, and Irena couldn't leave him. She remained with him and cared for him until his last day. Those were difficult days for the young girl; her grandfather suffered greatly and she spent the entire day at his side, doing whatever she could to alleviate his suffering. She took comfort that he wasn't alone and forsaken during this period.

Grandfather kept repeating to her, "You are my only comfort. You are the only one left from my entire family. You will continue on, build your home and a remnant will remain of our family."

After Grandfather passed away in 1949, Irena made aliyah with *Aliyat HaNaor*, and eventually married and had two daughters.

As the years passed, the children from the orphanage all established their homes and became parents, raising beautiful religious families. Today they are grandparents and great-grandparents, blessed with beautiful families.

For many years, Chanah wrote to her teacher, Mademoiselle Vermeul, whose letters she holds dear until today.

Chanah never found out about her parents' and brother's

specific fate, although it was generally known that Brussels' Jews were sent to Auschwitz. She observes the tenth of Teves as their *yartzheit* and the *yartzheit* of her extended family, according to the *p'sak* she, and many others, were given.

She always prays — and doesn't take for granted — that her children, grandchildren and great-grandchildren live blessed, happy lives. She constantly asks Hashem that they only experience tranquility and contentment — together with the entire Jewish nation.

# Appendix A
# Jewish Children in Monasteries: A Story of Courage, Heroism and Grief

CHANAH'LE, THE HEROINE of our story *Behind the Walls* has exposed one of the most dramatic stories that occurred in Belgium during the Holocaust — that the Jewish underground managed to hide 4,000 (!) Jewish children in monasteries and non-Jewish homes throughout Belgium. These 4,000 Jewish children were taken from their mothers' laps during this period of tribulation and secretly transferred into the hands of devout Catholic nuns or to the homes of gentiles who agreed to hide them — either out of compassion or in exchange for money. Their heroism put them at risk even to the point of endangering their own lives.

This article researches the fate of these children. How were they saved? Did their life among gentiles during their formative years affect them? Did they all return to Judaism after the war? Or did they remain among gentiles until this very day? Let us follow the story from its beginning.

### *C.D.J.*

A Jewish underground called the *Cime De Des Juifs*, The Committee for the Defense of Jews (C.D.J.), was active in

Belgium during the Nazi regime. This small group of fearless Jews ignored the danger to their lives and courageously undertook the holy task of at least saving Jewish children who were threatened with liquidation together with their parents. They risked their lives, and with great daring and indefatigable strength carried out one of the greatest and most dangerous rescue missions. Their rescue work allowed thousands of Jewish children to return to their heritage, found Jewish homes and proudly continue the chain of their fathers.

The organization was founded by members of the FL underground — the Independent Front. This underground was founded on March 14, 1941 by a group of Jewish and non-Jewish underground fighters, whose common denominator was their Communist ideology. Under their auspices, Christian priests, and Jewish and non-Jewish senior journalists, who were members of the Communist party, worked hand-in-hand.

Of all their underground activities, which we cannot detail here, the one that stood out the most was their "Children's Department," whose goal was to hide as many Jewish children as possible in safe places. This activist group, unique throughout Europe, will be recorded for eternity in the "Golden Book" of those who rescued Jews.

How was the connection made between the organization's activists and the mothers who sought to hide their children? The Jewish Belgian journalist Mr. Silvain Brachfeld, who was one of the hidden children, described the organization's novel and daring work methods in his fascinating documentary book *He Verleefdze Hee* (The Life in Camp) published by Yediot Achronot Sifrei Chemed 2000:

> The organization's agents were "planted" in every place where Jewish mothers were likely to turn for assistance and aid. In those days, the Nazi's tightening choke had not reached its zenith. The organization's activists, who already smelled what was being planned for the Jews, demanded and received exact details about the children, as well as exact addresses. They then referred the mothers to addresses of other social organizations which dealt with their problems.
>
> This last action was intended to cover up and mislead them, for then the mothers wouldn't know that the social worker who arrived several days later to take the child to a hideout was actually an activist of the underground. They thought that she was connected to one of the various social organizations they had turned to. In this way, the organization maintained its secrecy.

At the same time, the organization's activists combed the length and breadth of the country to locate as many potential hideouts as they could. Even when a hideout was arranged, there still remained the problem of providing forged papers and successfully transferring the children to their hideouts — located hours away by train — without arousing suspicion.

The secrecy and the compartmentalization were necessary conditions for the mission's success. Any leak could put an end to their activities and endanger the lives of thousands of other children who were hiding under fictitious identities throughout the country.

On the other hand, to successfully organize and run such a complex and complicated mission, they had to keep precise books recording where each child was and who his parents were. Reality demanded it. They managed to overcome this problem too with the assistance of a solution that was both simple and brilliant — instead of registering all the details in one book which might one day fall into the hands of the enemy, they "stored" the information in several separate books. One book held the name, a second held the parents' address, and a third, the forged identity. Each book was hidden away in a separate place. The information in all the books was connected by an identical serial number which was given to each child.

Even after a child had arrived at his hideout successfully, the activists didn't rest on their laurels. They insured that the foster parents were caring for their charges properly. It happened more than once that a child was immediately transferred to another place after it was discovered they weren't being treated properly. Most of the children were hidden in government institutions and shelters and even in Jewish orphanages which were maintained under the auspices of the Germans! (God willing, we will discuss this absurdity at greater length on another occasion.) Many individuals also hid Jewish children in their homes. In various diaries, hundreds of astounding stories were documented of the self-sacrifice demonstrated by compassionate gentiles.

### *The Danger Involved*

The danger these gentiles placed themselves in by sheltering Jewish children was unimaginably great. There was no lack of neighbors who were willing to inform on the "new faces" which suddenly appeared in the neighborhood. In many cases, people who had hidden Jews were caught. They were dragged to court, sent into exile, and a number of them never returned. One of them was Mr. Konier the principal of a school in the Bassin castle in the Belgian village of Mian-an-Condro. During Belgium's occupation, the castle was a hideout for labor crew refuseniks and underground activists. It held caches of ammunition and had a secret radio transmitter. The group in the castle began most of its rescue work on July 29, when the first orders were sent to the homes of Jewish youths to appear for forced labor. The following day, a Jew sought refuge with Mr. Konier, and Mr. Konier welcomed him into the castle. Very quickly, the castle became a hideout for Jewish youth.

But one day, the farmers living nearby informed on them. The Germans came and arrested everyone on the castle grounds. Konier was sent to Germany and never returned. Konier's secretary, who at the time had gone to the train station to receive a new "shipment" of three Jewish youths, was warned that Konier had been arrested. She immediately realized that the castle had been uncovered and she quickly escaped from Belgium on the next train.

A similar fate befell Attorney Albert von Don Berg of Liége, who, together with the local church leader Bishop Monsenior Louis Josef Kraukhoffs, ran a complete industry of hiding Jewish children. The bishop put his monastery and institutions at the attorney's disposal, and von Dan Berg issued the forged documents and official papers. He was shipped off to Germany in an order signed by the Gestapo. Von Dan Berg survived the war but hadn't managed to return to his homeland before he met his death in Germany.

In a raid carried out in his office, two of the office workers were also arrested. During the search of the office, they found files of forged documents. One of the workers, Mr. Kona, received eighteen months of prison "for displaying patriotism on behalf of forced labor refuseniks and Jews." He was shipped off to Germany, and returned with a fatal illness from which he never recovered. Both of them were recognized as righteous gentiles.

The punishment for hiding Jews was not as severe in Belgium as it was in Poland, where those who hid Jews and assisted them were sentenced to death without a trial. However, Belgians still faced severe punishments for hiding Jews, and those who undertook the mission feared for their lives. One woman who hid a Jewish toddler related that when she received the child, he only spoke Yiddish, and she was afraid to travel with him on public transportation lest he open his mouth. She had no choice but to "close" his mouth with candies.

The difficult economic situation also added to the hardship in hiding Jews. Every family was suffering from hunger. Food and clothes were doled out according to government ration books — which were apportioned according to the official number of family members. Families who hid children had to take from this minuscule amount of food to provide for the "unofficial" boarders.

Nevertheless, despite the danger and the difficulty, requests for Jewish children arrived from all over the country. "They arrived from all sectors of the population — blue-collar workers, simple people, wealthy bourgeoisie, notaries, lawyers, industrialists and others," noted Morris Heiber, one of the C.D.J. heads.

### *In Hiding: Suffering Mixed with the Good Life*

A small peek into the world of the children in hiding reveals a heartrending picture of deep emotional suffering. The parents, and all the more so, the children themselves, never imagined that in most cases, they would be saying good-bye for the last time. "We thought in our innocence that our parents were being exiled to labor camps," Brachfeld told *Mishpacha* magazine. "We, and like us, other children, never imagined in our worst dreams what was the fate of most of our parents...

"In 1991, forty years after the War, I attended the World Conference of Children Hidden in the Holocaust in New York. I will never forget that elderly woman from Holland who related how her mother brought her to a Christian family for protection. Her mother confidently assured her daughter that she would return within an hour or two – and both of them were sure the mother would return. Suddenly, in the middle of retelling her story, the woman began sobbing hysterically, and said that she never forgave her mother for leaving her behind and not returning. 'I would have preferred to be expelled with her rather then remain behind... She lied to me; she never returned to take me!' sobbed the now elderly woman."

The children, particularly the older ones, suffered from longings for their parents. They never gave up hoping for their parents' return. As they could not express their hopes openly, they would silently spin a web of fantasy, and secretly dream of the great day when they would reunite with their relatives. These melancholy thoughts disturbed their peace of mind throughout their hiding, and they were desperate to share them with any ear that would listen. Sometimes, in their desperation to express their feelings, children even risked revealing their identity. The following story, which happened to Brachfeld when he was in the La Providence orphanage, is one example out of many:

> One day, the boy who slept in the bed next to mine opened his heart to me. We were about ten years old. I knew he was a Jew, as were several other boys, but he thought I was a non-Jewish Flemish boy. We were on the way to school, chatting about this and the other, when suddenly he whispered to me in confidence, "In our house, we spoke a different language than French. I called my mother 'Mama' and my parents were imprisoned by the Germans."
>
> I listened quietly to his words and asked him a few other questions about his parents. It was obvious to me that if he wouldn't give expression to the misery he felt, he would turn to other boys in our group and tell them what was in his heart. If he would have done that, he might have put himself in danger. I asked him not to speak with anyone besides me, and told him to come back any time he felt a need to speak about his parents. I felt awful to see his distress and suffering.
>
> Several weeks later, the youth "by accident" stood next to me. When the nun teaching us put down her guard for a moment, he asked me, "Do you also learn the Book of Daniel?" This comment was enough for my friend to understand that I was also a Jew. We were able to continue talking together in complete confidence.

From a physical point of view, the hidden children fared better than the rest of their families. They had regular meals, and in most cases, were treated decently. However, primarily when children were taken into hiding for financial remuneration, they were treated poorly and sometimes — even cruelly.

Mr. David Inovloky, the vice president of the "Hidden Child" organization in Brussels, was one of those children. "The C.D.J. hid my brother and me with a woman who had six children of her own," he related in an interview with *Mishpacha*. "With the money she received for our care, she was able to provide for her six children. She treated us cruelly and cynically. More than once we felt the brunt of her blows, and sometimes, she even beat us with sticks. We had to roam the streets and collect food for her. After the war, I met her son, who told me that when the war broke out, his father left home and never returned. His mother, who remained alone, made her 'living' from hiding Jewish children."

Inovloky and his brother were later taken to a fortress in southern Belgium, which served as a government shelter for Belgian children whose parents were serving on the front. "We were about eighty-seven Jewish children. The difference between us and the non-Jewish children was that they, the Belgians, only stayed in the shelter for a few months, and were replaced by different children, while the Jews remained throughout — maintaining a fictitious identity, of course. We were the old-timers who taught the newcomers the rules of the place."

Here he already enjoyed a life which was "content and devoid of all worry." Those who were responsible for him were very caring, and they provided for all his needs. The Jewish children's tranquility was, on occasion, disturbed when German soldiers came to inspect the area. Someone notified them that enemy paratroopers were hiding in the area of the camp. "We were deathly afraid. The gentile citizens who were also hiding there to avoid being shipped off to forced labor outside of the country were also in danger."

"The housemother didn't lose her wits. She took control of the situation with the help of her fluent German. The Germans would carry out roll calls early in the morning immediately after wake-up, inspecting all those present. The beds were still "warm" and they compared the number of "warm" beds to the name list in their possession. During one inspection, this cunning search method revealed that one person was staying in the camp illegally. It was a Jewish soldier who had fled from captivity. The Germans carried out an extensive search until they found him in the attic. To our good fortune, the storm troopers were satisfied with this easy prey, and they left. We breathed in relief.

"Before the soldier left with the storm troopers, he came to take leave of the gentile housemother. She asked him, 'Please do not try to run away from them again, for they will always come here to search for you, and then the lives of the Jewish children will be in danger.'

"After the war," Inovloky completed the second half of the story, "I met that soldier. He told me something which moved me greatly. 'On the way from the camp to the train station, an elderly German soldier accompanied me. I could have easily dodged him and escaped to freedom. But the housemother's warning rung in my ears. I knew if I would escape, I would endanger you...'"

Brachfeld's personal story also demonstrates the housemother's profound concern for the Jewish children: "One day the housemother, Sister Marie, heard the older students spreading a rumor that there were several Jews in thc institution. I must point out that this was no simple "rumor" — some of the children had faces which were the perfect Jewish prototype.

"On that same day, Sister Marie assembled all the older students and told them that she could not understand how such rumors could be going around. 'In such a distinct Christian religious institution as La Providence, there aren't and could never be Jews!' she said decisively. The rumors stopped immediately.

"In another case, when we received word that the Germans were planning a raid on the place, she immediately took all the children of the institution on a trip."

### *Christianity: Jewish Souls in Captivity*

The long stay in monasteries and Catholic institutions sharply exacerbated the problem of assimilation and conversion to Christianity — one of the greatest tragedies of the children who spent the war years in monasteries. This tragedy came about because of various reasons.

First, because of the circumstances. The Jewish children were forced to adjust and assimilate as much as possible among the students of the institutions. Every deviance from or evasion of religious expression could arouse suspicions. The religious ceremonies they were forced to participate in also forced them to push their Jewish identity into the dark recesses of their minds. The Catholic music and stories with which they were constantly indoctrinated, even without ill intentions, automatically and subconsciously drew the children's hearts to Christianity.

It was no wonder that in the Beaux monastery, thirteen girls converted to Christianity of their own free will. At the dramatic and unexpected return of the girls to their families, this difficulty added to all the other difficulties.

Despite the difficulties, many, particularly the older ones who had received a solid Jewish upbringing, continued to cleave to uncompromised Jewish faith.

"In the orphanage where I stayed," related Brachfeld, who came from a devoutly religious family, "we had to kneel down before a statue in the dormitory before we went to sleep. But as soon as I was in bed, I covered my head with my blanket and fervently whispered the *Kerias Shema*. When I recited the words "Shema Yisrael..." I nullified everything I had done in the church during the previous day. With this act, I declared my faith in Hashem and Judaism. I was aware that I was a Jew, and a Jew I wanted to remain! On Shabbos nights I would quietly hum *zemiros* that I used to sing with my father at the Shabbos table. I knew them by heart. I sang and cried together, but it gave me tremendous strength to maintain my Jewish identity.

"I was upset at another event," he describes in his book. "One Sunday in the summer, during the priest's sermon in church, he said that Jews would never enter Paradise. His words angered me greatly, because every Shabbos, in my own home, my father and I had learned *Pirkei Avos* together, and we had always begun with the verse, 'Every Jew has a portion in the World to Come...'"

However, for many, the borrowed identity nearly became permanent. Solomon Aibshitz, in his testimony, tells about his life in a monastery: "I adapted myself to the life in the monastery. They knew that my parents had been taken away, and their goal was to turn me into a devout Catholic. I participated in mass every day. I also sang in the choir. They told me that they were preparing me to become a Christian and I really wanted to become one of them...

"Before I left the monastery, the Mother Superior called me to her room. I promised her that I would remain a good Christian. She stuck a strand of Christian rosary beads in my bag, and told me that I must take it with me everywhere. When I lived in my aunt's house, I stole away to attend church every Sunday. I felt an emotional need to do so. One day, my aunt found the rosary beads, and threw it into the garbage. Slowly I returned to Judaism."

Chanah'le went through a similar transition during the first weeks after her release from the convent...

Ari Livnah, who had also been hidden in a Catholic monastery, also describes in his testimony the strong attraction to Christianity, and his great difficulty to free himself from it: "The interior of the church was beautiful: the choir boys, the songs, the music. This all had an immense pull on a young child."

About the days after the war he relates, "It was very difficult in the beginning... I didn't want to return and begin everything anew. When I crossed myself before the meal, my aunt almost fainted. I told her that I want to visit the local priest and be baptized. I also said that I planned to become a missionary. My aunt didn't know what to do with me." In the end, Livnah's uncle helped him detach himself from Christianity. His uncle began taking Ari to shul often, even though the uncle usually didn't go.

Inovloky also relates of his hardships in forging a new life as a Jew: "For a few weeks after I was liberated, I used to sneak secretly to the church near our home every Sunday..."

These were not isolated episodes. At the end of the war, there were many similar cases. Parents had to battle with their own children who couldn't free themselves from the Christian education they had received. Many of them continued to secretly visit a church and hold onto Christian symbols for many weeks. But after a short time, most of the children returned to the faith of their fathers.

Tragically, a small number of children did leave Judaism forever, an almost unavoidable result of not receiving a Jewish education. Not everyone had the courage to cross over to the other side again. Imagine giving up a tranquil life, free of worry, to live the life of a victim of persecution and hate. This was the case with Yisrael Karsutzky and his brother. Their story is particularly painful because of its sorrowful ending. They had relatives in Israel, and when they were liberated, they were offered the opportunity to make aliyah. They rejected the offer and remained in a nearby village, maintaining their Catholic lifestyle. Five years later, in 1949, the two chose to be baptized.

The reasons for their actions were more emotional than ideological. Apparently, they suffered from the "monastery children syndrome" and couldn't release themselves from it. "Then, I had this feeling that since I had left Judaism, it would be difficult to return to it. I wanted to continue with the lifestyle I had adopted... the lifestyle of people who had risked their lives to save me..." Karsutzky wrote in his testimony.

His brother died at the end of the 1990s. He lived in the Belgian city of Charleroi, married and had children. He lived most of his life as a devout Christian, although his children knew of their father's "former" Jewish identity. Yisrael considers himself a Christian until today.

### *The Home: The Hardships in Returning*

The war was over and Belgium was liberated from the occupation, but the children discovered that their tribulations hadn't ended. A small minority were reclaimed from their hiding places by their parents, or at least by one who had survived the war. However, in some cases, the children couldn't remember them. After years of suppressing their memories, they found it difficult to get used to a new custodian and all the more so, to the different life.

Inovloky relates: "After the war, when Father came to claim us, we didn't recognize him. In fact, we had almost forgotten that we had once belonged to a different family. If I would have met him in the street, I doubt I would have said hello to him... In the first meeting between us, I told him politely, 'Bonjour Monsieur — Good morning, sir.' We felt strange and alienated from him. Only on the way home did several fragments of memory resurface. His Yiddish accent and manner of speaking awakened dormant emotions. '*Yoh, dos is der Tatta* — Yes, it's Father,' I whispered to my brother quietly, who nodded to me in return..."

The majority of the children lost their parents and remained dependent on the kindness of their adoptive parents, who were in no rush to return their "prey." To justify their actions, they resorted to all kinds of legal ruses which sometimes had to be resolved in court. At this point, the massive work of many Jewish organizations and individuals began, and they labored to take the children out of the jurisdiction of those who had adopted them and help them become independent. In several cases, the children's saviors demanded sums of money to "cover" their expenses. In this aspect the fate of children who had been hidden by the C.D.J. was better. The precise records which the organization maintained gave them an advantage.

Although in many cases the refusal to return the child emanated from humanitarian reasons which applied equally to adoptive parents and the child itself, sometimes the refusal emanated from the desire to "save a Jewish soul" and to prevent the child from finding his way back to Judaism. This is what happened to children who were placed with Fernand Anrar. This woman worked in joint cooperation with Father Antoine de Broker and set up a hostel for Jewish children in her home. After the war, she refused to give the children back. In one case where she refused, the courts were called upon to decide the case.

At the focus of the lawsuit was a child, Henri Elias, who was born in Antwerp in 1941 and handed over to Anrar's care. After the war, when Henri's uncle found out of his existence, he took action to remove his nephew from the monastery's jurisdiction. Letters which he sent were not replied to. When he involved the legal authorities, he discovered that his nephew, who had survived throughout the war under his true name, had just received a new identity. For Henri, life in disguise began only at the end of the war.

Eighteen children had found asylum with Fernand Anrar. She gathered them from various institutions in 1945 and became their guardian. She transferred them from one institution to another, and abusing her rights as "guardian," she punished or rewarded them for their behavior. Worst of all was the confinement she imposed on them. During vacations, she would take them to an isolated home near the beach. She would close the shutters tightly, and wouldn't permit "her" children to join in other children's games.

Whenever she was interrogated about Henri, she ardently claimed that she didn't know who Henri was. When she could no longer deny his existence, and she knew people would be coming for him, she revealed to Henri his true name. However, she explained to him that people were searching for him and she had to hide him to save him. She did not tell him that his uncle was looking for him — she told him that the man searching for him was a "man conscripting youths to fight in Israel..."

It was only in 1955 that Henri met his uncle for the first time — in court. This was after he had been suffering from severe emotional problems, phobias, and nightmares about being caught by the "Israeli army recruiter." In court, Henri refused to look at pictures of his parents who had perished. The court ruled that the youth must be returned to his family. However, Anrar and her lawyers urged Henri to flee, which he did. He was gone for three days, and spent that time in a psychiatric facility. When the doctors came to treat him, he told them, "Watch out for the Jews who want to kidnap me..."

Henri's fate had its ups and downs, but ended on a good note. He recovered. In Geneva, he married a Jewish girl and they had two children. Fernand Anrar was absurdly awarded "righteous gentile" status in 1979.

As we said, each story had a different ending. Brachfeld estimates the number of children who never returned to Judaism at about two hundred. The parents of most of these children had surreptitiously given them to Christians for safekeeping — without telling anyone else what they had done. When their parents perished in the war, there was no one who even knew that the children were still alive. Most of them continued their lives as Christians. Several of them discovered the truth of their identity later in life: sometimes their adoptive parents confessed it to them in their final dying days; other "hidden children" would recall distant childhood memories when they came in contact with Jews.

### *The Children: Emotional Bonds to Gentiles*

Even among those who were freed and even returned to the bosom of their families, emotional ties to their adoptive families frequently continued. Some even maintained warm connections with their second and third generations. Inovloky describes his visits to the Mother Superior: "She was already ninety-eight, sick and partially blind, but completely lucid. She remembered everything. She gave me her picture album as a gift — I still have it."

Brachfeld, who presently serves as the chairman of Belgian Expatriates in Israel, also maintained ties with Sister Marie until her death. He visited her every year — at whichever convent she had been transferred to. He talks about the nun's great respect toward Judaism, which she expressed her whole life. On more than one visit, she affectionately recalled her "little Jews," and mentioned how worried she had been for their welfare.

In 1970, Sister Marie visited Israel. She was welcomed in Yad Vashem and in the presence of one of her proteges, and several nuns from her Order, she planted a tree in the Avenue of Righteous Gentiles.

At the same time, many preferred to close this chapter of their lives, choosing rather to focus on opening a new, blank page. Any involvement in their past, even today, arouses difficult and oppressive associations.

The following event, which Mr. Inovloky personally experienced, serves as a classic example of the trend to ignore the past which was common among survivor children. At the first reunion held with all those who had hidden together with him, he had a shocking surprise. Among the participants was one of his closest friends! "I rubbed my eyes and didn't want to believe it was him," he said. "We are soul friends. We have never hidden a thing from each other. Nevertheless, he had never revealed this part of his past to me..."

### *The Documentation: The Hidden Child Organization in Brussels*

In 1999, the L.F.C. (an acronym for the French of "The Hidden Child Organization") was established in Brussels. The primary goal of this organization was to trace the whereabouts of thousands of hidden children. It also sought to find those who had provided shelter for these children, in order to properly thank them — on behalf of the children and the Jewish people — and to award them certificates of honor.

The organization was established by a group of "children" who had spent the war years in monasteries. Mr. David Inovloky from Brussels, who served as vice president, told *Mishpacha* magazine how the organization was founded: "We were a group of sixty 'graduates' who had hidden in the same shelter during the Holocaust. We became acquainted with each other because of an ad which I publicized in newspapers, and since 1986 we have been meeting regularly." This group formed the nucleus of the organization.

The organization assigns great importance to creating ties with other "children," and documenting their personal stories. "We frequently serve as a listening ear to these people who experienced difficult trauma, whose repercussions are still having an impact today, sixty years later," he said.

They also provide a listening ear to telephone calls of a different kind, which reach the organization's offices. In one of them, the speaker identified herself as someone who had been in hiding during the Holocaust. At a certain stage, she had converted to Christianity. Now that she was ill and felt that her end was near, she begged the secretary, R' Yisrael Dahan, to say *Kaddish* for her tormented soul.

Close to fifteen hundred men and women are registered with the organization. The vast majority lives in Belgium, mostly in the suburbs of Brussels and the Wallonia region.

The organization also organizes a range of various activities in an effort to commemorate the private Holocaust of the "hidden children," and to commemorate, for generations to come, the massive rescue enterprises that took place during, and after the war.

### The Saviors

There were many participants in the extensive, widespread activities to rescue children, both Jewish and non-Jewish. But it appears that the most outstanding among them was Mrs. Yvonne Nevejean. This gentile woman, refined and noble in spirit, headed a government institution called ONE (Oeuvre Nationale de l'Enfance —National Children's Society), an organization whose goal was to care for needy children. Most shelters and children's institutions were under her direct supervision.

She took advantage of her position to save numerous Jewish children. She was also a member of the C.D.J. underground and was the driving force behind the "Children's Department." She didn't hesitate to activate her personal connections with senior government officials, to provide additional hideouts for more Jewish children. When she found out that the expulsion of the handful of remaining Jews in Brussels was imminent, she turned to Queen Elisabeth, and asked her to use her influence to cancel the decree.

Yvonne was particularly active in amassing the financial sources required to run the C.D.J.'s extensive operations. At one point, she secretly appealed to the administrators of the Suisseta General Bank, who cooperated by giving her a fixed monthly stipend. When she realized that she needed more financing, she appealed to the Belgian government-in-exile in London through the assistance of the "Services and Messengers" underground group of which she was a member. They sent her money through messengers who parachuted into occupied Belgium.

Yad Vashem recognized her noble deeds and bestowed the Righteous Gentile award on her. Yvonne passed away in 1987, leaving behind her good name and thousands of people who owe their lives to her.

The silent defiance of the Belgian Cardinal Van Roey also contributed to the cooperation between the activists and the Catholic monasteries. Many staff members of Catholic organizations in the country testified that they drew inspiration for their deeds from how the Cardinal, the highest Catholic authority in the country, ignored Nazi orders. It should be noted that he instructed his priests concerning Jewish children: "Do not baptize children whose parents were exiled, besides those whose parents expressed their agreement..."

When the war broke out, the Jews in Belgium numbered more than sixty thousand. About thirty-two thousand Jews — more than fifty-three percent — were saved by their Belgian neighbors (according to other sources, twenty-five thousand — about forty-two percent). By way of comparison, there were one hundred and forty thousand Jews in Holland before the war, of which only thirty-three thousand survived —twenty-three percent.

The following is a quote from a letter by Alfred Schuldhan, a senior Nazi official:

> We couldn't do much. In Belgium, many of the Jews succeeded in evading detection due to the sympathy which the Belgians felt for the Jews. They took care of them completely. The Underground actively helped them. Even the Belgian Nazis didn't oppose them properly. The Belgian monarchy was involved in helping them...
>
> We must painfully say that in Nazi Europe, the Jews found a safe corner in Belgium. I am obliged to report that the three large parties in Belgium — the Catholic, Socialist and Liberal parties — financially support defense organizations which assist Jews."
>
> — From *Der Sonei in di Moiren* by
> Yeshaya Zondberg, Israel, 1963

The motivations of the rescue organizations ranged between feelings of revenge for the German occupier, and Catholic compassion in the face of the brutal expulsion of innocent women and children. (However, do not forget that in the name of that same "compassionate and kindly" religion, many tens of thousands of Jews were slaughtered throughout history.) There were many whose deeds were motivated by their sincere empathy for their Jewish neighbors, and from a powerful desire to alleviate their suffering. Many of them were awarded the Righteous Gentile award, an award which they rightly and justly deserved.

# Appendix B
# Memories from the Nursery

*A reporter's interview with Chanah, the heroine of this story, and Miriam Cohen, the author, following the story's publication in the Mishpacha magazine under the name "The Jaws."*

After many months in which the story "The Jaws" received feedback from *Mishpacha*'s readers, we met for a discussion with the heroine of the story, Mrs. Chanah Kaufman, her oldest daughter Sarah, and the talented author, Mrs. Miriam Cohen.

The walls of the Shaare Zedek hospital café had seen plenty of tears. Every Wednesday at 10:15 A.M., they would be witness to a scene that repeated itself, and usually raised the level of tears to new peaks.

Two women would sit at a small side table. One of them would speak, tears streaming from her eyes, while the other would be taking copious notes, sometimes finding it impossible to read the page in front of her because of her own teary eyes.

Later, they would stand up, gather up the papers and blow their noses. To an onlooker, they seemed to be returning to their daily routines. But in truth, the impressions from the dark, frightening cellar in Brussels and the intimidating cross hanging above the bed in the convent remained ingrained firmly within them.

Mrs. Chanah Kaufman had once again become Chanah'le Zucker, or, if you prefer, Arlette or Anna Marie.

That's how "The Jaws" was written by Mrs. Miriam Cohen, Chanah's friend.

"When Chanah became my co-worker in Telzstone's post-partum mother and baby convalescent center, she told me that she was a Holocaust child," Miriam recalls. "I asked her where she was from, and when I heard she was from Belgium, I tried to draw her into conversation, to hear about her war experiences. Chanah waved me off. 'I have nothing special to tell,' she said. She didn't want to tell her story."

Only later did Miriam find out that Chanah had a story to tell! Her unique story, which *Mishpacha*'s readers awaited every week, testifies to itself.

"How did you squeeze the story out of her?"

"Squeeze — that's the right word," Miriam admits. "It was difficult to ask Chanah to tell, but I didn't give up. She had aroused my curiosity while we worked together in the sweet commotion of the nursery. We would pick up the sweet, pure newborns to bathe them — and while holding a new Jewish infant in her hands, Chanah would suddenly say, 'Oh, do you know how they washed us in the convent?'

"I loved brushing the few hairs on the babies' heads — and for Chanah, this too brought back memories. 'They cut off my two long braids...' she would tell me. Almost everything she did brought her back there, to those days. I told her on several occasions that she must write about what she suffered, to pass on the story for coming generations. 'You must!' I would tell her emphatically."

Chanah's husband thought it was worthwhile to document her stories for the sake of their children. Later, when the material was already written, they made five copies with spiral bindings for each of their children. A book, a home product, to serve as a memento.

"In the beginning, we weren't planning on publishing the book for the public," Miriam says. "I thought that to write a story for Chanah's children one doesn't have to be a great writer." Miriam does not profess to be a writer, even though she wrote the story with amazing skill. She worked for her living as a kindergarten teacher, and she also spent five years working in Telzstone's post-partum mother and baby convalescent center. Four years ago she decided to begin writing Chanah's story.

"They met once a week for two years," Sarah, Chanah's oldest daughter, relates. "My mother is a very busy woman — even though she is retired. Every Monday she volunteers in Yad Sarah, an all-volunteer medical-support organization. On Tuesday, in Neveh Simcha, a religious nursing home in Yerushalayim. On Wednesday, in the Shaare Zedek hospital's nursery. She would finish volunteering at 10:00 a.m. and fifteen minutes later, would meet with Miriam in the hospital cafeteria."

"Sometimes," Miriam adds, "I would tell Chanah, "It's time to stop! No more listening and writing! You already filled your own Lake Kinneret with tears. I don't want to cause you to cry so much." The Wednesday meetings stopped until they had the emotional strength to meet again, talk and write.

"I showed the chapters which we had completed to the

author Yehudit Golan," Miriam says. "She encouraged me and was adamant that 'a story like this must be continued and written down.' So after every break, despite the tears, we pulled ourselves together and continued."

### *I Couldn't Talk*

When Sarah, Chanah's daughter, told us how she lapped up everything written in the spiral book and afterwards, the newspaper, we were amazed.

"But didn't you know about everything already?"

"When I was in seventh and eighth grade," Sarah said, "they mentioned the Holocaust in school, and I began to ask my mother where she was and what she had gone through. That's when I began to hear things – a story here, an episode there. When my friends would come visit, Maman would tell them in a disjointed fashion – a little from the beginning, then something from the end – about her life in the convent. But when we read the entire story from start to finish, our whole family was stunned.

"Not without good reason did Miriam once tell my sister, 'I know your mother better than you....'"

Chanah, the heroine of our story, says, "When my friends read the story in the newspaper, they were shocked. Those who had known me from Kibbutz Chofetz Chaim and Netiva called me and asked, 'How were you able to maintain your silence all these years?'"

"Why didn't you tell?"

For a moment, silence prevails. "I couldn't bring myself to get it all out," Chanah finally admits. "It was emotionally draining to return and recall my experiences. Telling the story in minute detail to Miriam wrenched my emotions. Suddenly, old fears were rekindled. I am afraid today when I see a nun in the street. All the difficult memories return." Even as she says these words, Chanah is trembling.

"As was mentioned in the story, when we were released from the convent, my cousin Irena and I promised the nuns that we would continue going to church every Sunday. I kept the cross necklace they gave me as a good-bye present only to have a memento from my beloved friends. I cried when I had to give up the necklace, because I felt so bad for my friends who had scrimped and saved their pennies and made a great effort to buy me something for a memento.

"It was difficult to free myself from the shackles of the convent, especially in my thoughts," she sighs. "I always missed my friends — only my friends — and Mademoiselle Vermeul, my beloved teacher. No, of course I didn't miss everything I experienced in the convent...

"Women approach me in the street and ask: 'How were you able to get through such a long, difficult period?' Strangers call me and ask the same question."

"And what do you answer?"

"I had *siyatta di'Shemaya*, Heavenly assistance. I survived in the merit of my faith. *HaKadosh Baruch Hu* wanted me to live — so I lived. My parents made every effort so I would remain alive. They sold the entire contents of their house in Brussels. If they could have sold the walls, they would have sold them. They knew what awaited them, and they wanted to save me. In those difficult nights in the gentile woman's cellar, while delirious from high fever, I envisioned my father promising me that I would live."

## *Like the First Man, Adam*

Chanah still has dreams about her experiences — both day-dreams and nightmares. More recently, the memories have become even more acute.

We won't leave it up to the psychologists to provide an answer to the question of why Holocaust survivors begin to experience their childhood anew particularly in their later years. "She was busy her whole life," is Miriam's and Sarah's explanation for it.

"She was occupied with revenge," Miriam says. "With building a life, raising children, day-to-day existence, and other concerns. Now, when day-to-day life has become quieter, she has more time for reflection."

"Our house was a happy house," Sarah, Chanah's oldest daughter, is quick to note. "We didn't feel like the 'second generation after the Holocaust.' My father had survived the camps. He didn't tell us what he went through. Nevertheless, our parents weren't sad or bitter. We had a home full of energy and *simchas ha-chaim*, joy. My friends loved coming to play in our house. We laughed a lot together. Our parents always gave us much warmth and love, and they showered us with whatever good they could. I remember that Papa would buy us candies for Shabbos even during periods when other children didn't even know what a candy was. The only thing we were missing were relatives," Sarah admits.

"I remember that our neighbors would go out every *Motza'ei Shabbos* to visit their grandparents or uncles and aunts. For us, our father and mother were also grandfather, grandmother, uncles, aunts, cousins, and all other relatives which others had. R' Moshe Grylak's father, another Holocaust survivor, used to tell his son, 'We're like Adam HaRishon for you...' So that we wouldn't be envious of others, used to take the entire family out on *Motza'ei Shabbos*, spend time with us and buy us something."

"When I gave birth," Chanah adds, "there was no one to help us besides neighbors. My oldest daughter was a preemie, and I didn't know how to take care of her. Only Hashem helped me raise her and my five other children..." Over the years, in order to survive emotionally, Chanah pushed aside her memories. They erupted and mushroomed when she told Mrs. Miriam Cohen the whole story.

"When I wrote it down," Miriam says, "I felt, without exaggeration, it was a mission... It was important to me that the public would read this story."

"Why?"

Miriam doesn't hesitate. "For my sake, for the sake of my children and grandchildren, for everyone. So they should know what people went through and should realize the tremendous self-sacrifice of Jews who had strong faith in Hashem. So they would read about the ordeals that young children passed successfully. It is a great service to our children, an asset for all generations.

"The further away we are from the Holocaust," Miriam notes, "the harder it is for us to grasp and understand the depth of the tragedy conveyed in the number of six million Jews. The number six million is beyond the grasp of the human mind. For people to get just a slight inkling of what the Holocaust was, they need to read the fine details of personal stories.

"I was in the Holocaust Memorial Museum in Washington, D.C.," Miriam continues, "and I saw Dr. Yaffa Eliach's reconstruction of the town of Eishishok. She built the city's bridge and placed pictures of people around it – pictures of living, active people. There was a child laughing, a man working... the faces were so real. This is the only way a person can begin to grasp the immensity of our tragedy. It is only once you enter the precise details of people who lived and breathed — and whose lives were cruelly shattered — can you begin to comprehend it.

"Chanah's story is another small piece in the mosaic of the tragedy of the Holocaust. To begin to understand what happened then, one should see other small pieces as well — in the Yad Vashem museum, for instance."

"Oy — Yad Vashem," Chanah sighs at the mention of the museum. "I can't go there."

### *Suddenly I Became Arlette Again*

She isn't able to visit Yad Vashem, but she has visited her hometown — Brussels. Five years ago, Chanah took a trip to Denmark. When she was there, she felt a need to visit the Jewish orphanage in Brussels that had welcomed her in as part of "the family" after the war, after she had left the convent. "I called Mrs. Bamberger and told her that I wanted to come visit for three days with my husband. Mrs. Bamberger was happy, and said 'I'll treat you like a prince and princess — just come!' Those were her words."

The Kaufmans traveled from Denmark to Brussels to see Mrs. Bamberger. Afterwards, Chanah went to see the convent. She stood opposite the familiar building with conflicting emotions. She had last seen the building fifty years before — it had aged considerably. As Chanah walked along its dark corridors and rooms with high windows that reached the ceiling, memories flooded her mind. She imagined seeing her friends whom she had longed for all these years.

"Suddenly I felt like twelve-year-old Arlette again, whom everyone thought was deaf since she didn't answer when she was told, 'Come here, Arlette!' I hadn't yet realized that Arlette was me, Chanah. The enormous cross hanging at the entrance again terrified me. Memories of scraping the steps until the point of exhaustion, the punishments I received, everything returned all at once.

"They don't use black so much anymore," she says. "Today the building serves as a regional school, and the uniform is gray and white."

Chanah discovered on the walls of the convent a picture of herself among her friends in the convent. "The first question I asked myself was, 'Where are my friends, those girls who were all wearing black?' They of course were no longer there. I was told that they work as nuns in other convents. Some of my friends left and some even married. Only two of the nuns, the head nun and another nun, had been with me in the convent. I told them who I was, but they didn't remember me. I told them that the convent had saved me and in its merit I remained alive..."

"Didn't you visit your parents' home?"

"No!" Chanah says surprisingly." I had nothing to return to. To me, the house was Papa, Maman, and Meir. They wouldn't be there. From my point of view, the house could still be around, but from the moment they took my family to Auschwitz — I no longer had a house in Brussels. The truth is," she adds, "my husband asked me not to go and visit the house. It's a good thing that he told me not to go. I don't know if I would have been able to step inside it..."

"Did you visit the cellar where you had been hidden?" Miriam asks.

"No," Chanah replies. "There was no point. The lady had already died."

Miriam doesn't give up. "Why didn't you go see the cellar, just for memories' sake?"

"I'm afraid," Chanah replies. "I feel that I wouldn't be able to endure my fears returning. The long months I was forced to be there were enough for me."

Whoever read just one chapter of Chanah's life in the convent will realize how miserable she was there. The wellspring of tears is still abundant as she recalls her experiences. The tears didn't dry up after telling the story to Miriam Cohen. And every Thursday, when she read a chapter of her story in the *Mishpacha* magazine, her vision would become blurred again.

"Sometimes my entire body would tremble while I read the magazine," she testifies, and adds another stream to the never-ending river of tears she has cried since her childhood until today.

### *Crying to Communion*

"What happened to all the Jewish girls in the convent?"

"I don't know," Chanah admits sorrowfully. "Several years ago there was a meeting of "convent children" in Kibbutz Lochamei HaGeta'ot. We sat around tables according to the countries we came from. The woman sitting next to me was holding the same picture I was holding." Chanah hands me a picture of a priest surrounded by a group of girls wearing black convent uniforms. "I excitedly told the same woman, 'Oh, I'm also in this picture! What's your name?' It turned out that she was one of the younger Jewish girls in the convent, and *Baruch Hashem*, she had been released. What happened to the others? I wish I knew."

Miriam Cohen, the author of this book, also took part in the meeting of "convent children." "In the beginning," Miriam says, "Chanah didn't want to travel to the meeting. I convinced her that she should go, and I promised her that I would come along as her companion. The kibbutz had built a 'Children's Museum' — which displayed pictures of children who had survived the Holocaust. We saw the pictures and heard the children tell their stories in their own voices as adults today."

"It was unbearable," Chanah recalls. "I couldn't bear the cries of 'Mama! Mama!' Everything around us was dark. I'm still afraid of the dark from the days I was in the cellar, when I was hiding with the gentile woman..."

"At that meeting of 'convent children,'" Miriam continues, "It was interesting to hear all those former convent children describe how they waited impatiently for their communion ceremony. The communion — the ceremony in which they converted out of their faith — was seen as a lovely birthday party. The child didn't have to wear his black clothes; instead, he wore a beautiful suit or dress. The children also looked forward to eating a delicious meal and being the center of attention. Chanah was the only one who cried the entire night before her communion, afraid that she would be cutting herself off from Judaism."

"But after all that," Chanah adds, "I still felt excited during the actual ceremony, because of the many nice things they gave to us."

"In the meeting, one of the survivors said that they didn't celebrate her communion," Chanah and Miriam both point out. "She was a very young child and her mother had dressed her up to save her. They trekked through the forest for many days until they reached a convent. The mother left the daughter on the stairs and warned her not to say that she was a Jew. The guard opened the gate and called the head nun. 'Please accept my daughter into your convent and save her,' the mother begged. 'But do not make her a communion ceremony.' The girl, now a woman, said that she still remembers that she was the only girl in the entire convent who didn't receive a beautiful white dress in honor of her communion."

Hundreds of convent children came to the meeting. A priest and nun from Poland spoke to the former children and told them how the church had saved many lives. "Who knows," Chanah says, partly to herself and partly to us, "how many hundreds of boys and girls remained there, removed from their parents' heritage, not even knowing that they were Jews. They saved their bodies, but their *neshamos* were lost..."

## *An Entire Generation Grew Up Alone*

"How do you feel about telling others your story?"

"I felt a certain release when I opened up and told everything," answered Chanah.

"Were you afraid of publicity?"

"Yes. I was very afraid," she admits. "I cried each time I read the chapters," she recalls. "When I saw it published in the newspaper — I cried even more."

"Were you afraid of how the public would react to your story?"

"Sometimes I ask myself if it was a good idea to let my personal story become public. I was afraid, and I'm still afraid," Chanah admits, but her daughter and Miriam, the author, encourage her efforts. "You don't know what your story did for the young generation," they say. "It strengthened their Judaism! It made many feel stronger about their convictions."

"I have an eight-year-old granddaughter," Chanah says after a long moment of silence. "She once asked me in astonishment, 'Savta, how did you grow up alone, without a father or mother?' I answered her, 'An entire generation grew up alone without a father or mother.'

"Not long ago I met a friend from Mrs. Bamberger's orphanage," Chanah continues. "When we had said good-bye to each other then, I signed her autograph book and never saw her since. When we met again, fifty years later, she looked at me and said, 'Are you Chanah Zucker? You haven't changed! Your eyes have the same sad look I knew then..."

Her eyes are still sorrowful when she mentions Rav Shlomo Greenfeld, *zt"l*, who saved her from the HaShomer HaTza'ir kibbutz. "He showed me how to live a Torah life. In his merit, my children and I appear as we do today."

Chanah keeps a picture of all her children on her pillow. When she sees the picture, she cries. This time, they are tears of a different sort.

"Today, my father and mother spend a lot of time with their children and grandchildren — visiting, and going on trips," Sarah says. "It's a kind of compensation for the years when they sat at home, lonely survivors without relatives, when they had nowhere to go and no one to visit. They shower us with love and buy the grandchildren whatever they can — in place of all the things they never received..."